Praise for Philippa East

'Written with subtle intellige
DAILY M

'Smart, fresh, beautifully wri
JANE SHEM

'Cleverly written, with many layers – a compelling read.'
CATHERINE COOPER

'An engrossing, twisty tale.'
NELL PATTISON

'Taut, tantalizing suspense . . . *Safe and Sound* is
gripping, spellbinding, and completely addictive.'
SAMANTHA M. BAILEY

'A thought-provoking thriller.'
HEAT

'Breathtaking suspense. A phenomenal talent.'
HOLLY SEDDON

'An addictive and gripping read which kept me obsessively
turning the pages; it is heart-breaking in its conclusion and
packed with complex characters who stayed with me for days.'
LOUISE MUMFORD

'Terrifically engaging.'
JO SPAIN

'Tense.'
ARAMINTA HALL

'Heart-breakingly realistic.'
GYTHA LODGE

Philippa East grew up in Scotland and originally studied Psychology and Philosophy at the University of Oxford. After graduating, she moved to London to train as a Clinical Psychologist and worked in NHS mental health services for over ten years.

Her debut novel *Little White Lies* was shortlisted for the CWA John Creasey New Blood Dagger for best debut of 2020, and this was followed by two further psychological thrillers, *Safe and Sound* and *I'll Never Tell*. *A Guilty Secret* is her fourth novel.

Philippa now lives in the Lincolnshire countryside with her spouse and cat, and alongside her writing, she continues to work as a psychologist and therapist.

Author's Note: Please be aware that this book deals directly with the issue of suicide.

A GUILTY SECRET

PHILIPPA EAST

ONE PLACE. MANY STORIES

HQ
An imprint of HarperCollins*Publishers* Ltd
1 London Bridge Street
London SE1 9GF

www.harpercollins.co.uk

HarperCollins*Publishers*
Macken House, 39/40 Mayor Street Upper,
Dublin 1, D01 C9W8, Ireland

This edition 2024

1
First published in Great Britain by
HQ, an imprint of HarperCollins*Publishers* Ltd 2024

Copyright © Philippa East 2024

Philippa East asserts the moral right to be
identified as the author of this work.
A catalogue record for this book is
available from the British Library.

ISBN: 9780008455798

For my parents,
Brian and Claire East

PROLOGUE

Carrie

2003

The plastic cigarette lighter clicks. The orange flame jumps high, illuminating our features: pale, drawn, serious, exhausted. My friends' faces are warped by the weird radiance, but each one still looks as familiar to me as my own.

Mae holds the lighter; she's in charge, the rest of us circling around her. Our breaths rise and fall together in the darkness of the dormitory; it's like we're breathing as one.

'Hold your hand out,' she says.

Serena goes first. She's tough and loyal, and always the person next in line to Mae. Still, Mae makes sure to hold her wrist while Serena says the words Mae has given her.

Victor is next. He tries to duck out of it but no one's going to let him. We've started this now, and we all need to make the pact.

Swear on the pain . . .

Next is Alex, stepping up quickly. He wants it over and done with. In the darkness afterwards, I want to take his hand in mine and kiss it where it hurts.

Now it's my turn, and I'm totally ready. Of course I know it's going to hurt, but I don't care; I want it. Mae clicks the lighter and the fire flares up again. I hold out my hand, balancing it right over the flame. Mae doesn't need to hold me. I do it willingly, hungrily.

I feel a bit like I'm going to cry again, even though I've been crying all day. It's so awful what's happened, but right here, right now, I want to capture and preserve this moment forever: all five of us huddled together in the dorm room, transgressing all of St Michael's rules in the middle of the night, taking it in turns to hold our hands above the scorching heat. I feel drunk, completely high, even though I'm neither. I'm one hundred per cent sober, but this feels more intense than any of the games we've played or things we've done before. They're doing this for me and we're all in this together. Never have I ever known friendship like this.

There's darkness at the edge of the circle; all that's happened beats its wings at the boundary of my mind. When the lighter flame goes out again, it will all rush in on me and I can't bear to think about what will happen after this. I want to stay here for eternity, in this circle with my friends, making this promise to each other again and again.

The pain is agonizing, overwhelming – beautiful in a way I can barely describe. It's excruciating and totally pure, and I want to hold my hand in it forever.

CHAPTER 1

Finn

2019

I was already up the stepladder when my phone went off. My face was close to the harsh strip light that ran down the middle of the garage ceiling like a spine, and I could hear the light's buzz and feel its pale heat on my scalp where my hair had started to thin. The garage was dim, musty, full of dust, cobwebs and dead spiders. Beneath me, the empty concrete floor was cracked and gritty.

The phone's ring was like a scream in that empty space, and my body lurched with the shock. How had I missed something as simple as not switching off my phone despite having so carefully prepared everything else? Why had I even brought my mobile into the garage? Because, like everyone these days, I was used to carrying it everywhere with me? Of course, there was a more obvious explanation: the same reason I had 'forgotten' to turn it off. I knew what it really meant.

After a wrenching moment of hesitation, I let go of the canvas strap that I'd been so carefully arranging in place and left it swinging softly, innocuously, while I climbed down, legs loose and hollow, to answer the shrill ring.

It could have been anyone calling. It could have been work or my dentist or someone about an insurance renewal quote, even spam, but I still answered it. Later, I would wonder whether this wasn't a strange twist of fate. A perfectly timed, preternatural message.

I climbed down and took hold of the shiny ringing handset, that little gossamer lifeline. I swiped the green icon and answered, 'Hello?'

*

It took me a couple of seconds to recognize her voice, especially as she said simply, the way she always used to: '*It's me.*' Everyone knows that it takes a very particular kind of relationship for someone to greet you on the phone like that. Plus, I was disorientated, shaking, even feeling a little nauseous by then, which further slowed my reaction times.

Still, my voice was surprisingly steady when – a few heartbeats later – I said: 'Mhairi?'

I should have recognized that voice immediately. Once upon a time, it had been my whole world. My ex-wife spoke in a rush, her words tumbling over each other. I had to ask her to slow down.

'What?' I said. 'What?'

Mhairi took a breath and the line went silent for a while. I waited, bracing myself. I imagined her standing in her kitchen with Tom and the girls – or perhaps they would be through in the living room, or upstairs – standing with the phone pressed to her chest, eyes closed while she battled to compose herself. In that moment, any anger I might have felt towards her was pushed aside by concern.

'I'm sorry,' she said, finally, 'for calling you out of the blue like this. It's about Kate.'

Our friend's face swam into my mind: the fine bones of her jaw, the frame of blonde hair, the laughter lines scoring the corners of her eyes. And the lines of concern that replaced them when she brought me to stay with her, took care of me and did her very best to fix things.

'What's happened? Is everything all right?'

'No. No, she . . . Finn, Kate hurt herself.'

'What?' I pictured an accident: our friend slipping down a flight of stairs or mishandling a chopping knife or wrenching a steering wheel to try to avoid a crash. That thought was terrible enough, but already I feared that wasn't what Mhairi meant. 'When you say she hurt herself . . . ?'

'They said it was deliberate.'

My chest went tight. 'Well,' I managed after a moment, 'is she okay?'

'No . . . No, she's . . .'

'Oh, Mhairi, what are you—?'

'She didn't make it, Finn.'

A silence like a vacuum stretched between us. I tried to scramble across it, my tongue catching against the sharp edges of my teeth. I was struggling. 'My God,' I said. 'This is such a shock. This is terrible. Mhairi, I'm so sorry.'

'It is. It's awful.' I could hear the tears pushing their way in with her words. Kate *hurt* herself? This time I imagined a car screeching to a stop too late to avoid the tumbling figure in the road; I imagined plumes of pinkish blood in a bath. I pictured a figure stepping off a building or a bridge. And at the same time, I really struggled to imagine Kate doing any of that.

'They found her at home,' said Mhairi. 'In her clinic room. She'd . . .' She broke off. 'But it's more typical for women to use pills, isn't it?'

I could hardly believe we were having this conversation. I had never expected Mhairi to call me for this. Pills. Not slashed wrists or a hurtling jump. Of course Kate wouldn't have done something as violent as that. She would have tried to cause as little disruption as possible. Even so, the details released a black flash of horror through my mind. There was a rushing in my ears: a wave of grief, shame, sickness. I needed to sit down, get blood to my head. I lowered myself to my knees on the gritty concrete floor.

'I'm glad you . . . Thank you for calling.'

'Of course. I had to. But I don't understand, Finn. How could she do it? It's *Kate*.'

I knew what she meant: *Kate wasn't like that*. She wasn't haunted or damaged. She helped people and made them better. She was never the crazy one. She had the answers. She was supposed to be the one who made everything all right.

'It happens,' I said. 'It can happen to anyone.' I wasn't sure that I really believed that. There were people who seemed to be luckier than that.

I could sense Mhairi vehemently shaking her head. She repeated: 'Not Kate.'

No, she was right: not Kate. But it had been. And there was no way I could tell Mhairi now what I had been doing when she rang. Not that I had ever planned on telling her. Or anyone.

'I'm so sorry,' I repeated, the conversation unfolding between us with so much else left unsaid. 'But I'm grateful for you calling. For telling me. I might not have known otherwise. Listen, Mhairi.' I tried to pull myself up a bit. 'How are you managing? How are you and Tom and the girls?'

She didn't answer that. 'There's a funeral,' she said instead. 'Next Wednesday. You could get a train, take time off work . . .'

The request was implicit and I never meant to hesitate. Of course I wanted to be there; never in a million years would I not go to Kate's funeral. The idea was unimaginable – more shocking almost than the news of her death. It was just that a few minutes ago, the future had been nothing to me. A nothingness. A blank. It was completely bewildering trying to recreate it for myself now and the confusion of it blocked up my words.

'I . . . I don't . . .'

'I need you to come,' Mhairi said, into the silence I was leaving.

It was like shaking myself, violently pulling myself away from the place I'd been about to step into just moments before: that black chasm. I drew a breath, like the first breath of a newborn.

'Mhairi,' I told her. 'Kate was my best friend too. Of course I'll come.'

And that was when she really did break down crying, a sound that carved fractures across my heart. From then on, all I could hear were her sobs on the line, and then Tom's voice appeared in the background, coming closer, saying, *'It's okay. It's okay.'*

The line cut off. She must have hung up. I pictured her rolling herself into Tom's strong arms, in a way that – by the end – she had become too frightened to do with me.

I clicked my own phone back to black and knelt on the cold concrete floor, panting. Devils, hellfire, the haunting of souls.

A vast shudder ran through me as I pushed myself to my feet. I'd been pulled back just in time from the lip of an abyss. By some ironic, tragic coincidence, Mhairi's phone call about our friend had saved me just in time.

From: mhairi_1981@gmail.com
To: katefallon@hotmail.com
Sent: 15.05pm, 05/09/2009
Subject: Moving to Cambridge!

Hello Kate!

How are things with you? I hope life is good.

I wanted to let you know that I'm moving to Cambridge next month! I thought it was time to get out of London and a job came up in the East Anglian branch. I saw in the college newsletter that you're still working (and living?) there, so I wondered if at some point you'd like to meet up? It would be handy to have someone to show me around the city a bit!

Anyway, I hope everything is good with you and looking forward to hearing from you.

Love,

Mhairi x

From: katefallon@hotmail.com
To: mhairi_1981@gmail.com
Sent: 14.17pm, 08/09/2009
Subject: Moving to Cambridge!

Hi Mhairi,

Lovely to hear from you and congrats on the new job. Yes, I'm still living in Cambridge and it would be lovely to meet up. When are you actually arriving? Cambridge is lovely and a really nice place to live.

Very happy to show you around. Let me know what dates might be good for you.

I hope all goes smoothly with the move and see you soon!

Kate

CHAPTER 2

Finn

2019

The last funeral I attended had been my father's, three decades ago, when I was fourteen. I remember scattering his ashes at the end of a long, arid summer, in the pinewoods where the three of us used to take walks together, the ones that sloped down to the rugged beach behind our house.

My mother had lost weight since his death. I'd tried over the weeks to look after her, making her small plates of food, preparing endless cups of tea, and she'd said it helped, but it was hard to tell. Standing on the ridge that overlooked the beach, unscrewing the chunky plastic urn, she looked almost skeletal. She tipped a pile of chalky grey ash into my cupped palms and immediately, I wanted to wipe my hands on my jeans. I tried not to think about how this was his flesh, his blood, his bones . . .

My mother was muttering something as she cast handfuls of ash into the wind, breathing fast, hands shaking. It wasn't a prayer; they weren't words you'd hear in any church service, and on this occasion, in this setting, they really got to me. It sounded as though she was talking to herself – or to my dead father – the way a crazy person might do. I knew it was just one of the mantras she used to calm the anxieties that had been escalating in her those last few weeks. But I didn't like it; I told her to stop.

I recited the Lord's Prayer, loudly and defiantly, instead.

*

These memories flooded my mind as I travelled from Grantham by train and then by taxi to the funeral in Cambridge, where Kate had lived and worked, and Mhairi still lived too. I had been painfully wired since Mhairi's phone call as though waking up from general anaesthetic, skin raw, nerves stinging.

It was a church funeral, not a cremation. I had never known Kate to be religious, but perhaps she was – or her family were at least. When I arrived at the church, a handful of mourners were gathered outside. The wind whipped at my coat, tangling it around my legs, and there was a drizzle of rain. I scanned the group for Mhairi, the features of her face always so fresh in my mind, even though it was over four years now since we'd last seen each other in the flesh.

She was hovering on the outskirts of the group, coat pulled tight around her. As I stepped over the sodden grass and cracked flagstones, a blackbird skittered in front of me; the sound caught Mhairi's attention and she looked up.

That moment when our eyes caught hung in time longer than it could ever have been, as all our history seemed to pass between us: surges of joy and terror and pain. We knew each other so well – or perhaps, so badly. She had seen me at my very worst. There hadn't been much we could hide from each other.

The blackbird swooped up to the top of the nearby shrubbery and Mhairi excused herself and came over. Her hair was greyer than I'd expected and she'd cut it much shorter, right up to her jaw.

'Finn,' she said, the syllable of my name like an exhalation. 'You came.'

'Of course I did.'

'I'm so glad you could get here, with work and everything.'

'It was fine. I had some leave to take.'

Our exchange was painfully stilted. We stood like enemy soldiers for a moment, and then I tentatively opened my arms. Even if it was wrong of me, it still felt natural and after a moment of hesitation, Mhairi stepped forwards. *You're here,* our bodies said to each other. *I'm here,* as though what had happened to us before didn't matter or had vanished just for now. Her hair was damp; she had been caught in the rain too. She let go of me and stepped back.

'You're looking well,' she said kindly, squinting against a shard of sunlight.

'Am I?' Perhaps it was because I'd recently lost weight. 'But how are you?'

'Fine. Sort of . . . Can't stop crying!' I saw the tears welling up in her eyes.

'I'm sorry,' I said. These two pathetic little words. 'Here.' I handed her the packet of tissues I'd brought with me but hadn't used. My own eyes were dry; they had been for weeks. Perhaps I'd gone beyond tears.

'Thank you for coming,' she repeated. 'It helps to have someone who understands what she meant to me.'

For a moment her words jarred, then settled. It was true; I knew how close we'd all been, back when Mhairi and I had been together, and before everything in our marriage blew up. Kate had been there for both of us, consistently, unfailingly, even after Mhairi and I broke up. And, I thought now, what had I ever done to repay that?

I swallowed, cleared my throat. People were beginning to trickle inside. 'Should we go in?'

Mhairi wiped her nose with the tissue and we made our way into the damp, stone-smelling chapel, sliding into a pew to the mournful notes of the organ.

I scanned the benches to see if there was anyone else I recognized, but of the faces I could make out, none were familiar. Kate had been so loyal to me and Mhairi, and the three of us had been so tightly bonded, we'd never seemed to need other friends. I'd always thought I'd been doing Kate a favour when I'd walked away, but now the possibility crept up on me that maybe – to her – it hadn't felt like that at all.

There were embroidered cushions at our feet, and Bibles and orders of service on the shelf in front of us. Kate's picture stared up at me. Laughter lines. The frizz of hair. That smile. *Kate Fallon, 1978–2019.* I calculated the dates; she was forty-one. Nothing. Half a life. She should have been at her peak, in her prime, looking ahead to everything she still wanted to achieve: the research she was so passionate about launching, all the places in the world she wanted to visit, all the journal articles she was planning to write.

Not lying there, dead.

Something in her life had made her so desperate and I had no idea what it was. A huge marble of guilt pressed its way into my gut. *Because where were you, Finn? Where were you?*

The organ stopped and started again, louder. The minister gestured for us to rise to our feet. They were carrying the coffin in, five men in black, the casket draped in a cascade of white flowers. I realized then that she wasn't being cremated. She would be buried, no doubt right here, in the churchyard outside.

The minister prayed; we sang a hymn. I strained to hear Mhairi's voice next to me, but when I glanced over, she had a tissue pressed to her mouth, trying again not to cry. I looked back down at the order of service, this time adding up just how long it had been since I'd last had contact with Kate. Five years, six. . . and she was once supposed to be one of my closest friends? It made me feel sick. Suddenly, I felt I shouldn't even be here. What right did I have to mourn her so publicly, when for half a decade I hadn't even been in her life?

The hymn faded and we took our seats again, and now a man stepped up from the front pews. He was elderly and hunched, but I could see the resemblance right away: the high forehead, the Grecian nose, the blue eyes. Kate's father. He unfolded a pale sheet of paper onto the pulpit, the plinth almost as tall as he was.

'Thank you all for coming,' he said. His voice was paper-thin, his eyes watery and rimmed with red. 'Kate would have been touched to know she was so loved.'

The marble in my stomach grew heavier, sharper. Beside me, Mhairi was gripping the order of service so tightly her knuckles shone white.

'We loved Kate so much, Marybelle and I. She was our only daughter and a late surprise. From the moment she was born, we knew that God had truly blessed us. She arrived like a shining miracle in our lives.'

He broke off, tears catching in his throat, faced with the stark reality of how that miracle had ended.

'It didn't surprise us at all,' he continued, 'that she chose a career as a therapist. Even as a child, Kate was the kindest little soul we knew. *You* all knew her. You knew what she was like. She made it her mission, in her work and life, to help people.' He lifted his head a fraction, so that his rheumy eyes met ours, as though challenging us: *why did no one help her?* 'Well now,' he said, lowering his head again, his voice cracking. 'Well, now that's over. All we can hope is that she's now at peace.'

His words sent quivers of new anxiety through my chest. The Kate he described was the exact one I knew. Warm, kind, generous, steady. Someone whom – at one time – I had leaned my entire weight on, never once thinking she could stumble or break, never considering that one day she could need something from me. And so what had happened? What atrocious thing had I missed?

The eulogy ended, we stood for the final hymn and the minister intoned for the last time: '*Let us pray.*' I clasped my hands together and pressed my forehead to them, willing the blood to swim back to my brain. I did my best to pray properly this time. For Kate's soul. For Kate's parents, her friends and her patients. For Mhairi. For everyone who had lost someone. As the minister invited us to stand for the last time, at the very last moment I prayed for myself.

*

Afterwards, we emerged blinking into the daylight.

Mhairi and I stood to one side near a row of moss-stained gravestones as the graveyard slowly filled up with mourners. I watched as Kate's parents shook the hand of the minister, nodding at whatever small words of consolation he could offer.

Over Mhairi's shoulder, I could see bright green Astroturf laid out where they had dug the hole to lower Kate into the ground.

'Are we supposed to go over there?' I said.

'I don't know,' Mhairi said, and impulsively I thought, *I don't want to.*

Mhairi shook her head. 'I think that's just for family. Anyway, I don't think I want to see that part. I didn't realize it was a burial.'

My shakiness was relief this time. 'That's okay. I feel the same.' Neither of us moved; we just stood there. Her tears were still coming, even as she caught them in another one of my tissues. A drop of rain fell on my neck from the tree above me: a yew tree, a species that always grows near death.

'Listen,' she said. 'There's the wake afterwards – or whatever you call it. At Mr and Mrs Fallon's house. I was planning to go for maybe fifteen, twenty minutes but then maybe you and I could go into town, just get a drink and . . . talk?'

I looked down at her, taken aback. I'd prepared myself as best I could for coming here, but I had not expected this. It struck me suddenly that Tom wasn't here with her. Perhaps he couldn't come or perhaps they'd needed someone to take care of the girls, but all the same, it was strange, wasn't it? Surely

Tom would have known Kate, his wife's closest friend? Surely he would have wanted to pay his respects? But instead I was here, as though it were me Mhairi was still married to.

'Will you?' she repeated.

Part of me wanted to stay out of this, tell her I had to leave soon for my train and that she should go home to her husband instead. But the stubborn part of me said, *Why shouldn't you?* Mhairi and I had both just lost a dear friend. Wouldn't we both want – need, long – to talk about that?

'Yes, absolutely,' I said. 'The wake for twenty minutes then, you and me, a drink.'

For the first time that day, I saw Mhairi smile. Then she reached out and took my hand. Hers was small, cold, the skin chapped over the knuckles. And it fitted perfectly in mine.

Text from: Mhairi
Sent to: Kate
21.09pm, 25/10/2009

Oh my gosh, Kate. Thank you for all your help today!
You were a godsend. I can't believe how many boxes
we moved! I hope your back is okay. Mine is killing me!
You didn't need to give up your Saturday like that, but I
want you to know how hugely I appreciate it. Once I get
all unpacked, I'll have you round for dinner or something
to say a proper thank you. Anyway, thank you SO MUCH
and see you soon!
Mhairi xx

Text from: Kate
Sent to: Mhairi
21.26pm, 25/10/2009

No worries! Glad I could help and I hope you'll be
nicely settled in soon. It was lovely to see your new
place too (definitely a good plan to paint over that
weird green in the living room!). Good luck for starting
work on Monday too. I'm sure you'll be great.
Kx

CHAPTER 3

Finn

2019

Turned out there weren't any pubs nearby, so we found a basic café instead.

'What can I get you?' I asked, automatically reaching for my wallet as we approached the counter.

Mhairi shook her head. 'It's all right. I'll pay. I'm the one who asked you here.'

As though she needed to bargain for my time.

'Okay . . . Just a tea, then. I'll find us a table, shall I?'

The café wasn't busy: a couple of young mums with babies, an elderly man leaning over a newspaper. I chose a corner table, instinctively wanting privacy for us both. It wobbled as I swept loose crumbs from its surface and I banged my kneecap on its iron leg as I sat down.

I tried not to look at the mothers and babies in my sightline, scrolling through my phone apps to distract myself instead. I was on edge with Mhairi, fumbling to know what to say, what to avoid saying, how to get my head round any of what had happened. It had been over four years since we had last met in person, and now we were thrown together under circumstances that I couldn't even begin to grasp.

Mhairi approached carrying two tall white mugs and instinctively I got to my feet.

'Careful,' I said, solicitous, fussing. 'This table's a bit wobbly.' I held it steady for her while she set down the drinks.

'Milk and one sugar, right?' she said as we sat down.

I smiled. 'Yes. And I see you still like yours black.'

The exchange danced again on the edge of our old intimacy. Mhairi twisted round to hang her coat on the chair, revealing the plain black dress she wore underneath. Just like I'd just done, she caught the leg of the table so it wobbled again. Miraculously, our teas didn't spill.

I reached out and took the warm mug in my hands. 'It's good to see you,' I said, in case I hadn't told her that already.

'And you, too. I'm just so sorry it has to be like this.'

Mascara had smudged under her left eye. In our previous life, I would have leaned over and dabbed it away for her.

'Tom couldn't come? I thought he'd be here with you.'

'He couldn't get the time off work. He did try but . . .'

'That's a shame.'

'It's okay. It would have been . . . different if he'd come. He only knew Kate much more recently. He wasn't friends with her before.'

Before what? Before Mhairi and I got married? Before our marriage imploded? Before I moved away and stopped keeping in touch?

Mhairi smiled shakily. 'Do you remember,' she said, 'the night I first introduced you? Kate was so nervous, Finn, you've no idea.'

'*She* was nervous?'

'Yes. She was funny like that, for a long time as I got to know her. She was so lovely but it was like she was always expecting someone to catch her out. See through her or something.'

I thought about that. How the three of us had been so tight, and how Kate hadn't seemed to much need – or want? – other friends.

'But she was lovely,' I said. 'She was wonderful.' I paused. 'Do you think that's why she burned the paella?'

Mhairi gave a wobbly laugh. 'Probably!'

I smiled. 'She saved the day with the takeaway pizzas. She was so kind and welcoming to me, Mhairi. She could have served cardboard and I still would have had a good time that night.'

I turned my eyes away as my mind slipped on to other memories, the ones that we were skirting around, that also said so much about Kate's nature, but were far more complicated and painful to recall. It was Kate who had insisted Mhairi visit me in hospital, and afterwards had brought us together at her house. *Listen, Mhairi,* I'd overheard her saying when perhaps she thought I couldn't hear. *Right now, he needs all the help he can get.* She'd pushed Mhairi to keep seeing me even weeks after my wife had said those agonizing words: *I'm so sorry, Finn. I've met someone else . . .*

I stared down at my tea, and forced myself to say it. Like Kate's photo in the order of service, my failure was staring me right in the face. 'I should never have let things between me and Kate drift. It was stupid of me. I should have done better.'

Was I saying it before Mhairi could get in there with the

accusation herself? Because I already felt so bad about it and couldn't face the idea of someone else beating me up? She lifted a shoulder then let it drop, taking a sip of her scalding tea – *asbestos mouth*, I used to call her. She always drank things so hot.

'I understand,' she said. 'It's not like we could all just carry on being best friends.'

I winced, her words like a jab to the stomach. She was right, brutally, painfully right, but it was still hard to hear her say it. All right, so Mhairi and I had separated, divorced. We could hardly have gone on as we were. But if Mhairi had been the lucky one to keep the friendship that I'd had to walk away from then—

'Didn't you notice *anything*?' I blurted out. I didn't mean to but the words had been in my gullet from the moment I'd spotted Mhairi at the church.

She flinched, like I'd returned her own blow, then she pressed the heels of her hands to her eyes. I waited for her to speak, my skin prickling under my damp jumper. One of the babies across the café started wailing, a desolate cry that tore at my nerves. I wanted to yank those hands away from Mhairi's face, shake her, demand an answer. I wanted to turn my anger with myself onto her.

'It's not – it wasn't like that. The last time I saw her she was fine. She *said* she was fine.' Mhairi dropped her hands, exposing her eyes again, red raw. 'We went for a walk, like we've done a million times together. That was two, three weeks before and don't you think I've already gone over and over it? That last time was the same as any other. She wasn't any different, Finn. She was *Kate*.'

The antagonism in me deflated. I squashed it down; I wasn't being fair. Now I didn't know whether to lean forwards to comfort her or lean back to try to give her some space. 'I'm sorry. I didn't mean to come at you like that. It's just . . . still such a shock.' I clenched my hands, the steel ball of my own guilt squatting again in my stomach.

You're going to be a crap friend to Mhairi now as well?

'It's okay. I get why you asked. She was busy . . . we hadn't been texting as much . . . But, Finn – this is why I want to talk to you. I've tried with Tom, but he doesn't—' She broke off, changed tack. 'What I mean is, I couldn't say on the phone.'

'Say what?'

'I was the person who . . . Finn, I found her.'

'You *found* her?' Despite everything, I wanted to reach out then and take her hand, hold it again the way she'd let me hold it earlier.

'I hadn't heard from her in days even though I'd been texting. When I tried calling her, all day, she never picked up or rang back. I went to her house, because she'd never, ever done that before. When she didn't answer the door, I used the key she'd given me . . .'

Fuck it. I reached out and took her fingers in mine, pressing our hands together. Her palm was hot and damp from the mug, but she let me do it.

'The door of her study – you know, her therapy room – was locked. She'd left a sign on the outside.'

The baby shrieked in short, sharp yelps.

'I couldn't go in,' she went on. 'I couldn't get to her. When the police came, they made me wait downstairs in the kitchen.

They wouldn't let me see her, but I saw the officer's face, after they broke the door down and he came back out.'

Just let her talk, Kate had once advised me. *Don't keep jumping in and trying to fix things. She doesn't need that. She just needs you to listen.* Communication skills 101. I bit my tongue against the words rising up.

'The officer looked *terrible*. He wouldn't let me see her. His face was . . . I can't even describe it.'

She shook her head. She had seen something that horrified her and her descriptions set my own heart thudding too. But for her sake, I had to stay steady. 'He was shocked probably. Finding her dead like that. Even with pills, it isn't always peaceful.'

'What?'

I squeezed her hand tight. 'People don't always just fall gently asleep. They might . . . Sometimes they might vomit, for example.'

'What? She didn't vomit, Finn. She didn't overdose.'

'But you said—' I stopped, my hand going loose as I replayed that first phone call back in my head. No, Mhairi *hadn't* said, had she? She'd only commented that, for women, pills were more typical.

She slid her hand from mine and pointed upwards, some-where above us. 'I saw the rope, Finn. They had to cut her down.'

My body jerked in an involuntary spasm. The baby wailed again, a moan of anguish. 'Kate *hanged* herself?'

'Yes.'

I felt as though the blood in my veins was leaving me. Not an accident then, and I realized part of me had been quietly clinging to that idea right up till now. What if it had just been a pounding headache, losing count of the painkillers? A week of insomnia and an attempt to finally get a decent night's sleep?

But hanging yourself in your own home, with the door of the room locked so that no one could get in. That wasn't a mistake. That suggested you knew exactly what you were doing.

A crushing heaviness settled in my heart as Mhairi went on speaking. This was real now. This was the truth.

'I've been trying to explain it to Tom. When I saw her in person, she still seemed the same. But something changed, I'm sure of it, when she began working with this new patient. From then on, I saw less of her. She didn't text me as much. She kept cancelling plans.'

'A new patient?'

'It's so little, Finn, but it's the only thing I can think of. She'd started working with a client who went to this boarding school in Scotland. St Michael's?'

'Kate talked to you about her clients?'

Mhairi reddened. 'Not really. I was just round at her house one time and saw she was looking up this school on her laptop. When I asked, she said one of her patients had gone there. She shut the screen down and that's all she said. But after . . .'

It was nothing, hardly anything. Kate doing some research to better understand a client. Kate being busier than usual, Kate cancelling some plans. Did any of that explain her *hanging* herself?

I pulled out my phone and typed in *St Michael's school,*

Scotland. A short Wikipedia article popped up and I read it aloud.

'Independent boarding school in the Highlands of Scotland. Established 1963, for children aged eleven to eighteen.'

'I know,' said Mhairi. 'I already googled it.'

I flicked down the Wikipedia page, but there was only a short paragraph about the history of the estate.

I flicked back to the main list of search results and clicked something else. 'This one's a recent article, from a few months back. Says the owners of the estate are selling off the land.' I held my phone out to her, and she took it from me and glanced at the page.

'Oh. Yes. I saw that too.'

'So wait – the school's closed down?'

Mhairi rubbed a hand over her face. 'Yes. It shut in 2010.'

I went silent for a moment, then said gently. 'It's just a school, Mhairi. An old school.'

'Then why was Kate *researching* it?'

'You can't even be sure that she was. Maybe she was just . . . curious to see the place her client grew up in.'

A woman from the café approached. 'Can I get you folks anything else?'

We both shook our heads. 'No. No, thank you.'

As the woman stepped away, Mhairi set my phone down hard on the table. 'Is that it, then? That's all there is to it?'

Immediately, I felt again that I'd failed. In my mind's eye, I saw Kate's face looking up at me from that order of service. I could almost believe her mouth moved and she spoke to me. Asking something, wanting something. But it felt impossible to understand what she was saying.

I shook my head, so much guilt and frustration rising up in me again, spilling over everything. 'I'm so sorry, Mhairi. I wish so badly that I had an explanation.'

She ground her teacup round and round in its saucer. For a moment I pictured her throwing it at me. I sensed the hot anger she must still harbour, for every other failure and everything I did to her back then. The other voice butted in now. *See? You shouldn't have come here, thinking the two of you could just cosily reminisce together. This was a bad idea. You've made things worse.* I glanced at the café's clock. Twenty to five. I was suddenly desperate to get going.

'Come with me, then,' said Mhairi.

I went still, caught in the middle of pushing back my chair. 'Come where?'

'To Kate's flat. I still have the key.' She held my gaze and, despite everything, I found my old tenderness, my old deep love for her holding me back.

I closed my eyes for a second. 'Tell me what you're thinking we'll find there.'

'I don't know. Something.'

Something. Anything. I opened my eyes again and I took in the dark circles under her eyes and the pallor of her skin. I read the jitteriness in her movements and how frequently she blinked. She wasn't sleeping properly. She was deeply shaken and upset, and she needed me to help her. She was literally asking for my help. Deep down, the good part of me – the best part – felt how much I owed her. She had undeniably hurt me back then, but I had broken her heart too.

I hadn't left my seat yet. 'How far is it?'

'Not far. You remember: Glisson Lane. It would only take maybe ten minutes to drive.'

I had an open ticket and the trains ran until eleven.

I looked at the café clock again as though consulting the numbers for my decision. I didn't need them. I'd already made up my mind.

I couldn't walk away this time.

'Let's go.'

Text from: Mhairi
Sent to: Kate
00.06am, 01/01/2011

Happy New Year!
It's been great hanging out this last year and so nice to
get to you know you better than we ever did at college.
Wishing you all the best for 2011!!
Mhairi xxxxx

Text from: Kate
Sent to: Mhairi
08.45am, 01/01/2011

Happy New Year to you too! ☺ Did you have a good
night?

Text from: Mhairi
Sent to: Kate
08.58am, 01/01/2011

Actually . . . I went to bed before the bells. (Lame, right?
But I hate having nobody to kiss at midnight!) Hope you
had a great evening at your psychology bash in London.
Any New Year's resolutions for you?

Text from: Kate
Sent to: Mhairi
09.02am, 01/01/2011

I did, thanks. It was nice to see old colleagues. I left fairly early too. Not sure about my resolution. Maybe if I could time-travel, there'd be things I would fix.

But that's more a wish than a resolution. Probably focus on setting up my own practice?

Text from: Mhairi
Sent to: Kate
09.08am, 01/01/2011

Well, at least neither of us is horribly hung over! My resolution is to get myself a sexy man!

BTW I'm not back at work till next Monday. Fancy a coffee sometime this week? We could chat about your private practice plans.

Text from: Mhairi
Sent to: Kate
09.16am, 01/01/2011

BTW what do you mean about the time travel? Fix things like what?

Text from: Kate
Sent to: Mhairi
09.17am, 01/01/2011

Nothing – ignore me! Definitely coffee. Clearly I'm
more hung over than I thought!

CHAPTER 4

Finn

2019

We hardly spoke on the drive to Kate's house. Mhairi and I had already said so much that I felt winded, struggling to regain my breath. I let her concentrate on the traffic ahead of us and tried to keep up with the thoughts in my head.

I had missed Kate. Perhaps until now – now that she was utterly gone – I hadn't even realized how much. I had packed up my things and moved out of her house without even telling her, and shut down our history, thinking it was for the best. I'd told myself she and Mhairi would be better off without me; I'd told myself it was the best means of protecting myself and never allowed myself to see it as a loss. But it was, wasn't it? It always had been.

Before Mhairi introduced us, I had never met anyone like Kate: stable, generous, always knowing what to say. Deep down, I must have craved that kind of optimism and confidence: I'd lost my father when I was only fourteen and lived with a mother crippled by anxiety and inhibition for years afterwards.

I never thought Mhairi would marry someone like me,

unsure of myself, of my broken background, but Kate had believed in me right from the start. We had both loved her for that; Mhairi and I had let her champion the two of us for years. We'd had our relationship, and Kate had her true passion – her work – plus our friendship. The arrangement worked; all three of us were happy. Never once had I questioned it. Never once had I stopped to wonder how Kate might have felt when I left.

I jerked back to the present as Mhairi pulled in beside a row of smart Victorian houses, the yellow door of Kate's flat instantly recognizable to me. Yellow was a good colour, one my mother had always trusted.

Mhairi dug a set of keys out of her bag. 'I suppose I should give these back,' she said. 'I probably should have mentioned it to her parents . . .'

The rain was coming down more heavily as we climbed out of the car. It had been raining for weeks, non-stop, it seemed. Even on days when the sun made it out, the pavements and railings stayed spotted with wet.

I walked up to Kate's front door behind Mhairi. The key was stiff when she inserted it in the lock, but with a shove she popped the front door open. And then we were there, inside.

Without Kate.

*

Her ghost was everywhere. I felt it as soon as we stepped inside. It felt impossible that she wouldn't materialize from the kitchen, glass of wine in hand, arms wide to welcome us. Her absence hit me again like a physical pain, a bitter taste on my tongue, someone's fist in my gut. My reaction to her death was coming in waves, a reminder here, a trigger there.

Now they weren't just thoughts but vivid recollections. Here was where I first met Kate, over the dinner she cooked that Mhairi invited me to. In the warm bright space of the kitchen ahead of me now, she had taken my hand, then hugged me, then said: *I feel as if I already know you.* A week later, we'd sat in the lounge I could see to the left of me and she'd told me how good she thought I would be for Mhairi. *Because you've experienced things. Because you've felt them deeply.* I was a bit tipsy when she said that, the two of us sitting up late-late, so I just laughed and clinked my glass against hers. Cheers. I didn't ask what she meant, just took it. *You're good for her.* I was delighted to believe that.

And even after all the terrible destruction I caused, Kate had refused ever to think anything else.

'We're not doing anything wrong, being here,' said Mhairi. 'Are we?'

She was prising off her wet shoes. I stooped down to unlace mine as well.

'No. No, I don't think so.'

There was post in the hallway: letters for Dr Fallon. Mail would still keep coming for a good while yet, until whoever was in charge of contacting the utilities had ticked off every name on the list. And even then, there was the spam, the junk. The clothing catalogue no one ever wanted, the charity appeals, the circulars.

I picked up the letters and stacked them on the hallway table. Mhairi steadied herself on the clean white wall of the hallway.

'Are you okay?' I asked. 'Do you need a minute?'

This wasn't just coming to Kate's house, I realized. For her, it was stepping back into a place of hideous shock.

'Have you been back here,' I asked, 'since they found her?'

'No. I couldn't.'

I could hear the unspoken words: *not on my own.*

We made our way through into Kate's living room. So neat. Sofa, armchair, coffee table, TV. Art on the walls, by artists Kate had loved to tell me about. The Kate I remembered had always been a little messy. Someone – her parents? – had tidied up.

'Don't touch anything,' said Mhairi. As though it were a crime scene.

And what were we looking for? What exactly was Mhairi expecting to find?

'I don't know what I'm looking for,' she said, reading my thoughts. 'I'll just know when I see it.'

She was heading through into the kitchen now. Again, the surfaces were clear and clean, everything put away. No dirty dishes in the sink or cereal left out. Mhairi ran a hand along the smooth worktop. 'She loved this kitchen,' she said. 'Even though she was a bloody awful cook.'

I allowed myself to laugh a little then. 'Yeah. She never improved, did she?'

A cork noticeboard hung above the sink. I peered to look at what Kate had stuck on it. A journal abstract about a new treatment for depression. A postcard from what looked like Fiji. And – my heart lurched in surprise – a photograph of Mhairi and me.

'I suppose,' Mhairi was saying, 'she would have had to keep things tidy for when she had clients here. She moved to working from home these last couple of years.'

Of course – Mhairi had mentioned that, hadn't she? Her study, her home therapy room. When I'd last heard from Kate, she'd been seeing clients at a rented clinic room in town. And where were they all now, I wondered? What had happened to all of Kate's clients now she was gone?

'There's nothing here,' said Mhairi. 'Let's go upstairs.'

I left Mhairi to look in the bedroom, the space too intimate for me. In the bathroom, I opened the medicine cabinet. In movies, this was where there were always clues. Something that revealed the state of mind of the victim. Antidepressants. Dementia medication. Antipsychotics, even. In Kate's cabinet there were only plasters, cotton buds, ear plugs and soap. But now that journal article on the corkboard downstairs came back to me. Had she cut it out for her client work – or herself?

'Finn?' Mhairi was calling me. I closed the cabinet door, catching my reflection as the mirror swung round, gaunt cheeks and eyes that still didn't look right.

Back on the landing, Mhairi had climbed the little flight of stairs to Kate's study.

'You find anything?' I asked.

She shook her head. 'Nothing. But, Finn . . . this is the room where she was.'

She meant where they found her body. Kate's study. I couldn't recall ever going in there in all of my visits to her home over the years, but I sensed it was my turn to take the lead now. I climbed the stairs and stepped through the doorway. As soon as I did so, instinctively, my eyes were drawn upwards.

'Jesus,' I said, jerking back. 'What is that?'

'It was always there. An old feature of the house. Kate said the hooks would have supported slats of wood – making a shelf to hang baskets, lamps on, that kind of thing.'

My heart was pushing up into my throat. 'Jesus,' I repeated. 'Well, didn't her patients mind? Such a morbid thing hanging over them like that?'

Mhairi shrugged. 'She used to hang dried flowers from it. She made it a nice feature.'

A dark brown wood beam ran across the high ceiling: characterful, you might say. Except that screwed into the wood was a black iron hook.

And Kate went and hanged herself from it. Nobody needed to tell me that. The hairs on my neck stood up again. *Devils, hellfire, the haunting of souls.*

Mhairi was crouching down beside a grey filing cabinet, tugging at the drawers. 'Look in the desk, Finn. There must be a key.'

'Mhairi.' I stepped forwards and took hold of her arm. 'Leave that.'

'But we've looked everywhere else!'

'Mhairi, we can't go breaking into her things. These are private possessions, confidential files.'

'But I haven't *found* anything.'

I let my hand rest on her shoulder, risking another gesture of intimacy. 'But you knew we might not. There are other ways we can try to get answers.'

She went on resisting me, crouching there as I tried to draw her back up to her feet. In the end I crouched down beside her.

'It doesn't mean it wasn't a good idea to come here. Maybe there'll be other ways it will have helped?' I meant

38

helping Mhairi get over the shock of the discovery, a chance to return to Kate's space without a body and police and paramedics.

'I don't know. It doesn't feel that way.'

I understood her urge for answers, I really did. If we could discover some shocking news Kate had recently received – a sudden terminal diagnosis, some terrible financial blow – then we wouldn't have to face the awful reality that Kate had been struggling with hideous black demons, and Mhairi and I, supposedly her closest friends, *hadn't known*.

A thought struck me. 'Didn't she leave a note?' Because that was what you did, wasn't it? You left something to soften the blow, even if just a tiny bit, for those you left behind. You took the time to compose a message for your loved ones, saying that you were sorry, letting them hear what they needed to know. You wrote that kind of thing if you were doing it properly.

Mhairi shook her head. 'They didn't find anything. The police said there was nothing. Only the instructions that she left on her office door.'

A small shudder ran up my back. 'Instructions?'

'"Do not come in here. Leave this door closed. Call 999".'

I closed my eyes for a moment. 'She wrote that?'

'Yes.' When I opened my eyes again, Mhairi's cheeks were wet with fresh tears. 'Her parents didn't know anything either. I tried to ask them in the days after. It was awful, Finn. They were so distraught—'

'Oh, Mhairi . . .'

'She could have called me, Finn! Why didn't she call? Or email or WhatsApp or anything? I was her friend – I thought she was my best friend. But she never said she was feeling like that.'

My knees were aching from being crouched on the floor. Outside the window, the rain was still falling and the light was fading, the damp afternoon smoking out. Time to stand up, turn around and go. There was nothing here that could give us the answers we wanted; that much was obvious.

'Come on, Mhairi,' I said gently, tugging her arm again. This time, finally, she let me pull her upwards.

Once on her feet, she smacked the secured filing cabinet with her fist.

'Mhairi!'

'But it's so *stupid*!'

There was such pained anger in her voice. Anger with Kate this time – and why not? I could imagine Mhairi wanting to shake her friend, slap her and yell at her: *How dare you do this, how dare you not let me try to help?!*

I thought again of what had happened between us. How, in that situation, Mhairi had also failed to notice. Did that make it worse now? Or was I the one selfishly wanting her to feel bad?

Mhairi went still. 'Finn – look.'

She pointed.

A sheet of paper had fallen out from behind the cabinet, released from where it must have slipped down and got stuck. We stared at it, neither of us moving, as it landed face-up on the wooden floorboards at our feet.

Then we both reached down, simultaneously, to grasp it. Mhairi got there first. The creamy paper was marked with handwriting, looping gracefully in blue fountain pen ink.

Dear Carrie,

*Forgive me for writing instead of seeing you face to face.
I don't know what you want or if there's anything I can
give you. Just please know I'm sorry and*

The note ended there. I went shivery. Chilled. 'Is it Kate's
writing?'

'Yes,' Mhairi stuttered. 'Or – I'm not sure, but I think it
is, yes.'

'Do you understand this, then? Do you know who Carrie is?'
She shook her head. 'A client? A friend? A relative?'

But Kate didn't have a relative called Carrie. And Mhairi
would know if Kate had a friend by that name. So, a client,
then? 'Didn't police find this before, when they were looking?'

'How could they? We only dislodged it just now.' She pressed
her fingers into the lettering as though she might feel Kate's
intention through the page. 'Finn, this has to mean something.'
She was pointing to the date in the top right-hand corner.
'Look: she wrote it three days before her death.'

I shivered again. She was right about the date, the handwriting, everything. I had wanted a note and look what we'd
found, but this didn't feel like an answer; it felt like a gaping
new question.

'We can't know that . . .'

She turned it over again in her hands, ignoring me. 'Kate was
trying to help this woman. She wanted to apologize. She men-
tions meeting face to face – does that mean for an appointment?'

'I don't know, Mhairi. How are we supposed to tell?'

'It sounds formal, doesn't it, the way it's written? *Dear*

Carrie. It's not a casual letter to a friend or something – and who writes *letters* to friends these days?'

I didn't say anything else. Mhairi clearly wasn't listening.

'This Carrie came to her for something,' she went on, 'but then why did Kate not arrange to meet her? Why write to her instead . . . ?'

She trailed off, and for a moment I thought she might actually turn away and leave it; I should have known better.

'Dr Hart. Sebastian.'

'What?' The name meant nothing.

'Her supervisor. Kate spoke to him every single month. He'll know if this Carrie was one of her clients.'

'Mhairi.' My tone said *stop, come on, what are you doing?* 'All of this – it's private. Her therapy work.'

She lifted up her sharp little chin. 'Well, like you just said, we can't know that. We don't know *who* this Carrie person is. But Sebastian knew Kate. He was her supervisor. Maybe she opened up about . . . about whatever this was.'

'We can't—'

She faced me square on. 'Can you really just leave it, Finn – just go on with things with absolutely no explanation? Our best friend dies, and you don't care why?'

That wasn't fair. That was really a low blow. I crossed my arms defensively. 'Of course I care, Mhairi.'

'Well then, listen to me. Sebastian knew her. He would have discussed all her patients and he was there to help her. Maybe you're right and he won't be able to explain anything. But can you really walk away without giving him a try?'

CHAPTER 5

Carrie

2003

We were driving through woodland, basically through a forest, all these pine trees for miles and miles. Ferns and moss and mud, and the sky overhead was grey and lumpy, like cold porridge. Sure, I'd eaten porridge. I'd been preparing.

The road we were on was shitty, gravelly, the edges laced with crushed brown ferns. I sat hunched in the passenger seat of the hire car, watching all that dreary scenery blurring past. My stepmother Valerie tapped her fingers on the steering wheel to a pop song playing on the radio. We were on the last leg of our journey after being squashed in this cramped car for the last hour and forty-five minutes, just as we had been in the taxi that took us to the train station, and then on the train ride all the way from King's Cross to Dundee. My eyes were gritty, and in the pull-down mirror my teenage make-up was flaky and smudged.

'I do think it's a good choice,' Valerie was saying. 'Of all the schools we looked at, St Michael's was my favourite too.' Her American twang seemed to have got stronger since we'd crossed the border, like her 'Scottish' heritage was poking through. Valerie was American, my dad's new wife of one year, and I'd been living with them both in the States until a few months ago. 'This scenery reminds me a bit of where I grew up. All these trees, and no houses for miles. Except it was warmer back home.' She laughed. 'It's freezing up here.'

'Yup.' My jaw cracked in a yawn and I felt the throb of a new spot on my chin as I pictured my dad back in the house in London. Maybe he'd be sipping a whisky in the drawing room or flicking through important documents in his study. I wondered if he'd given in to the temptation to call my mother while Valerie was away, and whether my mother would have responded when she was sober or drunk. I pressed my cheek against the glass of the window, trying for the hundredth time not to care. So what if he had chosen not to come with me? He had too many other commitments to travel all this way.

'You never went to boarding school, did you?' I asked Valerie, mainly just to get out of my own head. I knew the answer already, but I wanted her to tell me again. I didn't mind talking to my stepmum really, even if she was only twelve years older than me and my dad was forty-seven: contravening that rule of half-your-age-plus-seven. It was such a cliché, his new wife young, pretty, blonde, like he wanted to rub my mother's nose in it, payback for all the money he'd had to sign over in their divorce. But despite the age gap – her twenty-eight and me, his daughter, sixteen – I'd come to admit that Valerie wasn't so bad. At least she took an interest in me, in an older-sister kind of way. At least she had offered to drive me all this way.

She shook her head, bright hair bouncing. 'No – but I did

44

read all those Mallory Towers novels as a kid. You'll have to let me know if it really is like that.'

'Ugh,' I said, way more flippantly than I felt. 'It better not be.'

We were pulling out of the forest now, onto hillocky, bouncy moorland that flipped my stomach about. 'Shit!' Valerie swerved to avoid a pothole, righting the car by slamming on the brakes. I pitched forwards, the seatbelt tearing at my neck.

'Whoa!' said Valerie. 'Sorry!'

I dragged the belt away from my jaw. 'It's fine. These crap roads.'

After that, I did feel a bit nauseous. Valerie sang along with another song on the radio: Whitney Houston's 'I Wanna Dance with Somebody'. Properly cheesy. She had an okay voice though.

'How long do you want me to stay with you once we get there?' she asked as we drove on. 'I don't have to rush back.'

I hesitated, the lonely part of me and the survivor doing war inside. 'To be honest, it's probably better if you just drop me off. It's usually easier when I just go right in.'

This would be the sixth school I'd attended, and we'd had to go over all the details with the headmistress by phone, because I'd missed the open days and usual arrangements for new pupil visits, yet my dad had been insistent that I start straight away, not next term, so now I was going into this kind of blind. What I knew was that St Michael's was in the Highlands in the middle of nowhere. There were plenty of private schools back in London or in England generally, but I'd liked the idea of *Scotland*. It had sounded exotic to my friends back in Illinois. Most of all I'd liked the idea of being far away from my mother with her needy, drunk phone calls to Dad's apartment; and away from my father who would always make me answer the phone. My mother had friends now – apparently these days she even had a therapist. And my father had Valerie to make him feel better.

*

When we reached the school, it was after five o'clock. In the falling dark, the school loomed over us, appearing even more Gothic than it had in the prospectus: all grey Scottish stone and jagged-looking turrets. It was halfway between a fairy-tale castle and a small fortress, and it wouldn't have surprised me one bit if a swarm of bats had come flying out of there.

Valerie parked the car on the gravelled drive in front of the school's big entrance, like we were pulling up at a country manor in one of those period dramas that British people loved. When she switched off the engine, everything around us was silent.

'Is someone coming out to meet us?' she asked.

'Ms Rowlins, I think. That's what it said in the email.'

'Oh right.'

We waited.

'Let's get the luggage out of the trunk at least,' Valerie said. Most of my belongings had been sent on ahead, so I just had a couple of bags with me. I opened the car door onto the chilly air and got my numb limbs to lift me out of the seat. I helped Valerie heave my suitcase and rucksack out of the back. She slammed the boot then blipped the car locked.

'Let's head in,' she said. 'Maybe we've just arrived a bit

early.' Even though it was twenty past and we'd said we'd aim to arrive at five. I tried not to see it as a bad sign.

I let Valerie go ahead of me, trailing behind as she tugged open one of the wide glass doors that spanned the entrance. It was kind of chilly on the other side as well, and there were all these plaques and old paintings on the walls – proper Hogwarts stuff.

'Hello?' called Valerie.

No answer. I wrapped my arms around me. 'Now what?'

Valerie pulled out her flip phone. 'I'll call the school office.'

It seemed ridiculous. I mean, we were standing right here. I looked around though; the place was dead.

Just as Valerie keyed in the number, a woman came bustling out through a door at the back. I recognized her face from the school website – Ms Rowlins, deputy headmistress. In the photo she'd looked a lot younger and slimmer; actually, she was one of those people who had skinny heads even when they had big bodies, so probably even in a recent headshot, you wouldn't tell.

'So sorry, Mrs Greaves . . . and Caroline! I didn't hear the car – the photocopier was going!'

My stepmum smiled. 'Please. Call me Valerie. And my stepdaughter goes by Carrie.'

'*Carrie*. Of course. Well, welcome to St Michael's! Have you got everything? Do follow me this way.'

She led us along a dark-panelled corridor, explaining that the pupils would soon be going into an evening assembly and probably it would make sense for me to join them there.

'But you can put your luggage in here for now,' she said, opening a door onto a bright administration office with five latest Macs on clean pine desks. 'I'll introduce you to Mae and

Serena in a second. They'll show you to the dormitories, and then of course we'll all be having tea.'

'Sure,' I said, even though I had no clue who Serena or Mae were, or whether tea meant the drink or a meal. I smiled at her. 'Sounds great.'

I pushed down every bit of me that was feeling anxious, because what good were those parts of me right now? You couldn't show weakness on your first day; you had to be fearless. Standing there in that bright reception area, I could literally feel the autopilot mode switch on. It was stupid but it was a matter of survival: *Like me, accept me, don't you dare mess with me.* Honestly, I was so used to it now.

I smiled again at Ms Rowlins, encouraging her to smile back. *Be confident, be charming, be sweet.* But as I tugged my coat off in the eventual heat of indoors, her smile faltered and she gaped at my neck.

'Goodness!' she said. 'Are you all right?'

Valerie craned to look too, taking me by the shoulders to turn me towards her. It was only as I put my fingers up to the skin under my jaw that I realized it had been stinging and throbbing all this time, where the seatbelt had cut into me, and much later, in the dormitory bathroom, when I finally saw it for myself in the mirror, I was shocked to see it looked like I'd done something crazy, like try to hang myself.

Text from: Mhairi
Sent to: Kate
12.59pm, 05/02/2011

Okay! I'm off to meet him. Wish me luck!

Text from: Kate
Sent to: Mhairi
13.01pm, 05/02/2011

Good luck!
xx

Text from: Kate
Sent to: Mhairi
17.51pm, 05/02/2011

So . . . ? How did it go??
Kx

Text from: Mhairi
Sent to: Kate
19.45pm, 05/02/2011

Good. He's so nice, Kate!
Only just got home ;)
Will ring with all the details tomorrow!!

xxx

CHAPTER 6

Finn

2019

Mhairi called again the very next day.

'I did it, Finn. I've arranged an appointment.'

I was sleeping, at one o'clock in the afternoon. I sat up from the sofa, eyes stinging and my chin rough with stubble.

'Sorry, Mhairi . . . what?'

A pause. 'You sound weird, Finn. Did I wake you?'

'No . . . Yes, I was just having a nap.' The air in my one-bed flat was chilly; the heating never worked that well, but under normal circumstances I wouldn't have noticed. Under normal circumstances, I would be at work in the IT offices nine hours a day, five days a week.

'Hmm, well, lucky for some!'

I barked out a laugh. 'Yeah . . .'

I wished now that I'd explained the situation properly to her, but on the day of Kate's funeral I hadn't wanted to upset her any further. It wasn't annual leave; last week, my GP had written out a further sick note. I'd thought I was ready to go back, but my GP had insisted not.

'Well, anyway, I got his details.'

I rubbed my eyes. 'Hang on – whose?'

'*Sebastian's*, Finn. Kate's supervisor.'

It took me another moment to hook the name onto something, my mind still stuck on another train of thought. After leaving Mhairi in Cambridge yesterday, I'd googled St Michael's again and dug deeper. I found other articles and announcements: for open days and fundraising drives. One of those articles about pupils on exam results day, a happy group of students snapped leaping in the air. More coverage of the recent sale of the estate, including a group of campaigners who were vehemently opposed. A news alert from 2003 for a local man who'd gone missing, listing his age, colouring, height and distinguishing marks. An old news article headlined: *Unknown illness affects girls at local school*, and a follow-up piece that downgraded the 'illness' to anxiety attacks.

I sat up properly now, focusing. 'You made an appointment with Kate's supervisor?'

'Honestly, Finn, he was so nice on the phone. He completely understood why I wanted to talk. I think he's really shaken up by Kate's death too.'

I walked stiffly through to my small kitchen to run a glass of water, the cold liquid stinging my dry throat as it went down. I felt shaky, my mind disconcertingly fragile, even though my doctor had increased the dose of my medication. I hadn't wanted to hear it, but last week he had said it: *Finn, stop. Listen, you aren't well.* And since that appointment, a great friend of mine had died suddenly by suicide, and on top of that, I was floundering in the resurrected relationship with my ex – a relationship cut through with anxiety and loss.

51

I should step away; I shouldn't involve myself. I should simply tell Mhairi, as gently as I could, that I wasn't in any position to help. That was what my conscientious doctor would advise me.

But there was absolutely no way I could do that. I couldn't walk away again. I did that before, and look what had happened. It wasn't about self-protection this time. It was about helping Mhairi find out what had happened to Kate.

'When is it?' I said. 'The appointment.'

At the end of the line, Mhairi drew a breath. 'It's Monday. Four o'clock.'

My next words came tumbling in a rush, as though I had to get them out now or I might never say them. 'I'm sorry, Mhairi, for everything. I know I hurt you and I hate that I did—'

'What? Finn, stop . . . It doesn't—'

'It *does* matter. I am *sorry*,' I repeated stubbornly. 'You need to let me say that.'

She was silent. She didn't say anything.

I let out a sigh. 'Listen. I'll book a train ticket now. I'll come.'

CHAPTER 7

Carrie

2003

Before long, I was saying my goodbyes to Valerie. Hugs and pats on my back and a kiss on the cheek and *call us anytime* and *be sure to let us know that you're settling in*. I ignored the hollow pit in my stomach and the dangerous stinging at the backs of my eyes as I hugged her back and cheerily waved her goodbye. Then Ms Rowlins was whisking me down another gloomy corridor, up two flights of stairs and along yet another hallway to what I took to be a common room. On the bright yellow walls hung amateur artwork and posters, and there were beanbags and sofas in garish primary colours, a kettle and microwave, and a flat-screen TV.

Two girls about my age were flopped on a yellow sofa, but got to their feet simultaneously as soon as Ms Rowlins and I came in. With their matching uniforms the synchronized movement was kind of unnerving, but then one of them smoothed down her green kilt and took a half step forwards, breaking the illusion.

'Now,' said Ms Rowlins. 'This is Mae and Serena, our fifth years. They're both prefects, and Mae here—' she gestured to the prettier, bright-blonde-haired one '—is our head girl.'

I took them in. Mae was slim and pretty, her skin near flawless. Serena was taller, with thick ash-blonde hair and that British ruddiness that I'd never developed. They were pretty girls. Confident girls. I knew the exact type.

'Welcome to St Michael's,' Mae said. She had a cut-glass accent, some kind of posh Scottish. 'It's brilliant to meet you.'

It was obvious they'd been trained well, but even so, the immediate friendliness was disorientating, like someone snapping on a bright light at midnight. Flustered I let Mae's cool hand take mine.

'You too. Thank you.' My American accent shrilled; I'd picked it up and now couldn't seem to lose it. This close, I smelled the tang of Mae's mint chewing gum; I'd been travelling for nine hours solid and was terrified I stank of B.O.

'You're welcome,' said Mae, and for a moment I was convinced she was mocking me: my awkwardness, my weird accent, my smudged make-up and the spot on my chin . . .

'All right, then,' said Ms Rowlins, checking her watch then literally clapping her hands. 'Assembly in five minutes. Serena, Carrie's luggage is in reception – do fetch it up to the dorm straight after, all right?'

Serena made a gesture that was so like a curtsey I was sure she was taking the piss. But Ms Rowlins didn't notice, already sweeping out of the common room, the wood-and-glass door banging shut behind her.

Now it was just the three of us: head girl, prefect and new girl. I already knew I'd do almost anything to make them accept me. In these first days, honesty, integrity – none of that mattered as much as fitting in. For a new girl, that was make or break.

*

The assembly hall was actually the chapel. Back at my last school, our assembly hall had doubled as a gym, with bleachers on three sides and room for fifteen hundred people. The chapel where we assembled was way, way smaller, but joining two hundred other pupils who were total strangers was pretty daunting.

The three of us – me, Mae and Serena – made our way to a tall pew at the back and sat down. Someone up front was rapping on the lectern: the headmistress, Ms Dunham. I just about recognized her from the prospectus too . . . so now that was a total of four people I knew.

For the next fifteen minutes, I tried to concentrate on what Ms Dunham was saying, not least since I needed to absorb as much knowledge and information as I could. But pretty much the whole lot went right over my head. The headmistress referred to so many people and places and rules I didn't understand and that hadn't been explained in the prospectus that in the end I just zoned out: gave up. The pew was hard and uncomfortable: the worst after nine hours in trains and a car. I longed to be curled up somewhere. All I wanted to do was to eat, wash and crawl into bed – any bed. I could feel my eyelids drooping and snapped the elastic hair bobble on my wrist, hard, to stop myself passing out. The day had another five hours to go at least.

The headmistress was saying something about a shower in the junior bathroom that had broken, implying that it had been somebody's fault. Her eyes swept the congregation, settling momentarily on me, and I found myself reddening, pulling the hair bobble on and off my wrist, even though I'd only just got here and I'd had nothing to do with it.

The bench in front was also filled with girls, but they looked younger, and I thought I heard one of them whisper '*the ghost?*' It seemed someone laughed, a high-pitched giggle, but at the same time none of their heads seemed to move.

The headmistress moved on. Sports fixtures, prep rotas, and a prayer that everyone but me knew the words to. I knelt on the hard cushion beneath me, vaguely aware of the younger girls in front of us fiddling with something – the Bibles on the little shelf in the pew-back, beige-coloured things with a dark brown Christian cross on the front. I looked away again, but I could still hear them: the rustling, scrabbling sounds they were making.

Then maybe I actually fell asleep for a moment, because it seemed like someone whispered into my ear: *He's coming!*

My eyes snapped open: the assembly was over and the rows of pupils were getting to their feet. I stumbled to mine too, my left leg fizzing with a wave of pins and needles.

'This way,' Serena was saying, stepping over the floor cushions to clamber out of the row. I followed her, holding on to the wooden pew-back to steady myself. It was only as I darted back to snatch up the frayed hair bobble I'd dropped that I noticed something on one of the Bibles on the row in front.

One of those whispering, scrabbling girls had stuck a little paper cut-out on the front of it. A pretty thing, like those folded-up paper snowflakes you made in elementary school. But it wasn't a snowflake, it was more like a star. Only when we'd left the arched space of the chapel did I realize the specific shape of it.

A star in a circle: a pentagram.

CHAPTER 8

Finn

2019

That Thursday, rain was falling again. Mhairi was bundled up in a scarf when she met me at the train station, and she was holding a cup of takeaway coffee for me, thick with sugar, the way I always took it. She'd remembered that, as well as the tea. I could feel the warmth of the liquid through the cardboard.

'Thank you.'

'We can walk from here,' she said. 'It isn't far. Honestly, thanks again for coming. I think it will help to talk to him together.'

She didn't say anything about what I'd blurted out on the phone: my barefaced apology for everything I did. I was glad that I'd said it, but couldn't help the frustration that Mhairi had said nothing in response. We'd never properly talked about it, even at the time. We'd had blazing rows instead, thrashing round in exhausting, bruising circles.

One conversation, Mhairi? We can't have one proper conversation about it?

Because it doesn't help! It doesn't change anything.

Because you don't want it to! There are so many ways we can pick things up and move forwards, but you aren't trying one bit to do that.

We had the same argument over and over in those weeks after I was discharged, when I was officially sane again but things between us were clearly not the same. We went round those circles until I thought I would go mad again; until she finally came out with it.

The truth is, I don't want this marriage anymore. I'm sorry, Finn. I've met someone else.

Mhairi tapped my elbow, jerking me from my thoughts. 'Cross the road. Number twenty-three. We're here.'

For some reason I had thought we'd be going to a clinic; it hadn't occurred to me that, like Kate, Dr Hart might work straight out of his own home: a Georgian house, beautifully maintained. I followed Mhairi across the street, empty coffee cup in hand, and together we climbed the bright white front steps.

When the heavy front door swung open, there was a teenager standing there. Mussed blonde hair, black T-shirt and big lavender-coloured socks. At first glance, I couldn't tell whether I was looking at a boy or a girl. In my head, I heard Kate's voice: *Maybe that's exactly the point* – and just like that a new avalanche of memories unspooled.

I remembered celebrating when Kate got her own practice, booking a once-in-a-lifetime restaurant that none of us could really afford. I remembered toasting with Kate when Mhairi and I moved in to our flat together, sitting on the floor, sharing the cheap wine straight from the bottle – a perfect cliché, because we hadn't any furniture and hadn't yet unpacked the meagre belongings we did own. I remembered telling Kate we were planning a family, and her emailing me that same night with her 'top ten psych tips' on how to be a good dad . . .

I went dizzy again with the loss and had to grip the railing of the steps to steady myself.

'Hi,' the kid said. 'Are you here to see my dad?'

Mhairi nodded.

The teenager swung the door open wider. 'Okay. He's still with a patient right now, but he said I should let you wait in the living room.'

We followed them inside, into the hallway that smelled of fresh paint.

'In there,' the teenager said, pointing to a high-ceilinged front room with a huge bay window and marble fireplace. 'You guys want, like, a drink or anything?'

Mhairi smiled as she stepped through and unwound her scarf. 'No, we're fine. We've just had coffee,' she said, shaking her cardboard cup.

'Cool. Hang on, let me take those. Well, anyway, my dad won't be long. Just make yourselves comfortable or whatever.'

We sat down as the kid disappeared along with our empty paper cups, socks whispering on the polished wood of the hallway. There were magazines on the coffee table, copies of *The Psychologist*. I felt as though we were clients coming for a session ourselves – for the couples therapy that Mhairi had refused even to try. I'd had therapy in hospital and saw how it had helped me; our best friend was a *clinical psychologist*, for heaven's sake. And still Mhairi had insisted there wasn't any point.

The clock on the mantelpiece read two minutes past four, then three. The fifty-minute hour should have finished at ten to. A car swished by on the wet road outside. I looked down at my hands in my lap.

'You okay?'

Mhairi had lifted a hand and for a moment I thought she was going to lay it on my knee, my heart jumping in surprise, my mind suddenly unable to distinguish *back then* and *now*. She didn't, of course, just reached up to tuck a loose strand of hair behind her ear.

I turned to her. 'Listen,' I said. 'What I said on the phone – I'm not trying to dredge everything up, I promise. I just had to say that one thing. If I'm going to be . . . seeing you, I needed you to know.'

Mhairi shook her head, fussing at something on her jeans, some invisible piece of lint or leaf or memory. 'Honestly, Finn, it's fine. You don't have to—'

'I *know* I don't, Mhairi, but that's not the—'

A clatter from behind interrupted us, a creak of stairs. Instinctively, I got to my feet, turning to face the doorway, and Mhairi got up hurriedly too. I saw them then: Sebastian and his patient, the one that had overrun by almost fifteen minutes, leaving us waiting, spilling over the end-of-session time. She was a tiny, birdlike thing. She couldn't have been more than five foot with tangled grey hair that made it hard to judge her age. Her eyes sent a judder through me in the swift moment they met mine, as though communicating something malevolent. *Like a witch,* I found myself thinking, the thought coming unbidden into my mind. *An eldritch witch.*

She passed by the doorway of the living room and made

her way down the hall, Sebastian following. I heard the jangle of the door as he let her out, his muffled voice murmuring something and a sound that might or might not have been her reply.

The door clashed shut and Sebastian appeared again, alone this time, framed in the doorway of the living room. He was tall – at least six foot – but slim in a way that made him seem elegant. His hair was dark, his skin Mediterranean.

'Mhairi? Finn?' He was smiling at us, seeming quite unruffled. 'Sorry to keep you. Would you like to come up?'

*

Sebastian's therapy room was nice too: dove grey, with tasteful artwork. He directed each of us to a plush armchair, and sat himself down in a leather swivel chair.

'Thank you for making time for us,' said Mhairi. 'We just . . . We were such good friends of Kate.'

Sebastian nodded. 'It's no problem. I'm happy to help in any way I can, although . . .'

I waited. 'Although?'

Sebastian cleared his throat. 'I mean to say, there are of course certain things I won't be able to discuss. About particular patients, I mean.'

Mhairi was nodding, fumbling in her handbag. 'No, of course, we completely understand. Sorry, I wrote down a list of questions. Do you mind . . .' On her lap, she smoothed out a crumpled sheet of paper. 'I can read them out?'

Sebastian adjusted his position in his chair as though preparing himself. 'Please. Go ahead. I'll do my best.'

Mhairi held out the paper in front of her, hands shaky.

'First thing . . . Did Kate seem unusually down or depressed?'

Sebastian hesitated and looked down at his hands. 'With Kate . . . it would have been hard to tell. She liked to be seen as very capable. I know she was working hard; her private clinics were full. She had a number of very difficult patients. She was carrying a fair amount of risk.'

'And you helped her with that?' I said.

'I did my best to. That was my role: to discuss those cases with her, help her identify how best to treat the clients' difficulties . . . As well as giving her a chance to offload.'

'But you didn't know she was struggling,' said Mhairi. 'She never told you she was going to hurt herself.'

A pained look crossed Sebastian's face. His chest rose and fell as he drew a deep breath. 'No. Of course not. I knew she was finding her work stressful, but this is an inherently stressful job. But she never mentioned wider troubles. In fact, when she . . . when it happened, she was taking her Easter break from the practice. She never even hinted . . . But the thing is . . .' he knotted his fingers together in a way that looked almost painful '. . . often suicidal people don't.'

Mhairi pressed her lips together. 'But you never asked her?'

Sebastian rubbed one hand against the other. 'She never gave me a reason to. Perhaps that was remiss of me . . . not to have asked anyway. But you knew Kate, so you know what she was like. Never keen to talk about herself. Supervision is a space to raise personal problems; she chose not to. She only ever talked about her clients. I challenged her on that, sometimes. At the same time she was incredibly competent. Having come to know

Kate over the years, I realize she wouldn't have wanted me to view her like that.'

A pause. 'Like what?' said Mhairi.

Sebastian caught my eye, seemingly only accidentally. He lifted his palms. 'Flawed? Weak?'

I swallowed.

Mhairi looked back at her questions, catching me off guard with a sudden change of tack.

'She had a patient, didn't she, who attended St Michael's? A boarding school in Scotland.'

'St Michael's . . . ? I don't . . . Wait.' He broke off and frowned as though racking his brains, then snapped his fingers. 'Carrie G.'

Mhairi's head jerked up; mine too. A shuddering wave of anxiety sluiced through me.

'"*Carrie G*"?' I said.

Sebastian pressed a hand to his mouth. 'I'm sorry. I shouldn't have said that. I absolutely should not have mentioned her name.'

'But you know her? You know about this patient?'

Sebastian's jaw clenched. 'I'm sorry . . . I shouldn't . . .'

'Sebastian,' said Mhairi. 'Please.'

He let out a breath then shook his head. 'Only as a name on Kate's caseload. She emailed her patient list to me, once a month. She'd jotted down something about St Michael's.'

'What happened to her, then?' I broke in.

'You mean . . . ?'

'I mean, this woman, Carrie. Kate was her therapist so who's helping her now?'

'As her supervisor, I contacted Kate's clients to explain what had happened and make alternative arrangements.'

64

'Alternative arrangements?' I asked.

'Help them access another therapist. A number of them I took on myself.'

'Including Carrie?' said Mhairi.

Sebastian clasped his hands firmly together, a barrier. 'I can't tell you that. I'm sorry, Mhairi. I can't discuss specific details of Kate's clients. I've already said more than I should.'

Mhairi leaned forwards in the grey armchair. *Including Carrie?*

Sebastian tilted his head. 'Why are you so interested in her?' It was defensive, clever therapy-speak. *Tell me, how do you feel about that?*

Mhairi caught my eye and held my gaze. I found myself giving her the tiniest of nods.

'We found a letter in Kate's home,' she said. 'Or – more like a note. Something she'd started writing, or drafting, then abandoned.'

'A note?'

'Addressed to this . . . Carrie.'

Sebastian went still. 'Do you still have it?'

'No,' said Mhairi, just as I said: 'Yes.'

Sebastian looked back and forth between the two of us.

I reached out a hand towards Mhairi. 'Show him.'

She ignored me for a beat, then she reached down and pulled the sheet of cream paper from her bag.

He scanned it, flipping it over and back again; read it again. Suddenly, I found myself desperate for him to decipher Kate's words and – like a magician – reveal the dazzling explanation of her death.

Instead, he folded the paper in half, creasing it right down the middle. 'I'd best keep this,' he said. 'I'll add it to Carrie's file.'

'But – it isn't Carrie's,' said Mhairi. 'It's Kate's.'

'Everything related,' said Sebastian, 'should be kept together. Next week I'll be going through all Kate's case files myself.'

He set the letter on his desk and tapped it with his fingertips, psychologically taking possession of the thing.

'But don't you think this is something important?' said Mhairi. 'I think Kate changed, Sebastian, after she took on this client. And now, in her house, we discover this note?'

The look Sebastian gave her seemed to me almost pitying. He leaned forwards, and for a moment I thought he was going to take her hands in his.

'Listen, Mhairi. As far as I know, Kate only saw this woman once: a new assessment. She would have updated me more at our next meeting, and if there was a problem, we would have discussed it.'

'But she never came to you,' I said, challenging him. 'She never came for that next meeting.'

'No. The supervision was scheduled for after her holiday. And by then—' He broke off.

I answered for him.

'By then, she was dead.'

CHAPTER 9

Finn

2019

We left Sebastian's house at close to five p.m. I was shaky, realizing I'd had no lunch that day and no breakfast either. The thought of the train ride home, back to my apartment where I already knew the fridge was mostly empty, set off a further wave of fatigue.

Mhairi was quiet as we headed back towards the train station. She held her coat bundled tightly round her, even though it wasn't all that cold.

'What now?' I asked as we walked. What were we looking at and what did she want from me?

She lifted one shoulder in a shrug. 'Don't know. I'm not sure.'

'You still think there's something to it, don't you? That letter.'

'Well? Don't you?'

I didn't reply. I felt like pulling my own coat around me too.

'Listen, why don't you come back with me?' she said suddenly.

'Come back where?'

'To ours. For dinner. I can call Tom, pick up some extra bread on the way.'

My reaction was immediate. I stopped short. 'I can't do that.'

'Why not? I think maybe it would help, for Tom to see you.'

Help who? I thought. *Help how?*

'Given that – like you said,' she rushed on, 'we're spending some time together. And you're here anyway, and you must be tired. Hungry.'

I *was* tired. I *was* hungry. But the idea still seemed like a crazy leap. Instead of the olive branch I would have been grateful for, Mhairi was suddenly dragging over a whole tree. I had only ever met Tom once, and so briefly, when he had come to pick Mhairi up and I was staying at Kate's house. He'd appeared like a thick dark shadow in the hallway; I had looked up from the couch in Kate's living room and caught his eye. He had looked – stared? glared? – at me, then turned away, practically dragging Mhairi out of the house. Now Mhairi suddenly wanted to bring us together?

There was a cloud of starlings above us, a murmuration. I tried to picture being in the same room as Tom. I thought about us sitting down to dinner together, breaking bread. Tom must know what I had done, surely? So why would he let me anywhere near his wife?

But then . . . he had, hadn't he, these last few days?

'Mhairi?' I asked carefully. 'Where *is* Tom in all this?'

'What do you mean?' She set off walking again and I hurried to keep up, not sure now whether we were still headed to the train station or her house.

'I mean—' I broke off, fumbling for the right words. 'Tom

could have come with you to Sebastian's, couldn't he? Of course I loved Kate and I'd do anything for her – especially now. But you *also* know—' it was as painful as ever to say it and I swallowed at the spiky lump in my throat '—that I hadn't spoken to Kate in years. Of late, Tom would know far more about her life than I do.'

She shook her head, still walking, not looking at me. 'It's not that simple. I told you before, I *have* tried to talk to him.'

'Okay . . . So then—'

'But . . . Tom's Tom.'

'And?'

She stopped and finally looked at me then. 'And because it was always me, Kate and *you*.'

*

Her house was warm – almost too warm. Tom must have had the heating on full blast. I took off my coat as soon as we were in the door, but I wanted to take my sweater and shirt off too.

The girls pummelled into their mother as soon as she stepped inside. I'd seen photos of her daughters on Facebook, but never met them in the flesh. The children she'd had with Tom. They were adorable; of course they were. Kitty and Imrie, aged four and three.

'Hi!' Tom shouted through from the kitchen. His voice sounded natural and normal. Relaxed.

'This is Finlay,' Mhairi murmured to her daughters as they looked up at me askance. 'He's a special friend of mine.'

Her phrasing caught me by surprise. She could have said old friend, or even just friend, but she chose to say *special*. Maybe she was laying the groundwork for when they were older, when they would learn that their mother had been married once before, to a man named Finlay, a man who— But I snapped that thought off.

'Hello,' I said to the two of them. 'Lovely to meet you.'

They just giggled, of course, and ran away, back to their father in the kitchen, and then I glimpsed them briefly again, scampering upstairs.

'Come on through,' Mhairi said.

I followed her into the kitchen, and there Tom was.

He looked almost as though he was standing to attention, ramrod straight. 'Hello, Finlay,' he said.

I swallowed. 'Hello, Tom. Thank you so much for having me.'

'Of course.' He stepped forwards and for a split second I wasn't sure what he was about to do until I realized he was holding out an open palm. We shook hands, his grip so much stronger than mine.

'Want a drink?' said Mhairi. 'A beer or anything?'

'Yes . . . Thank you. A beer would be nice.'

I didn't normally drink, because of the medication, but I didn't want to seem difficult or odd.

'No problem.' She hadn't kissed Tom, I noted, but then she probably wouldn't with me there.

'I was so sorry to hear about Kate,' said Tom smoothly. 'I didn't know her well, but she seemed a lovely person.'

'She was.' I hesitated. '. . . You didn't?'

'Not really.' Tom turned to the stove, giving the simmering pan a stir. 'Of course, she and Mhairi have always been very close. And she's told me how close all three of you were, back then.'

His words were disorientating, flipping over my whole framework. I had assumed that Tom had pretty much replaced me in Kate's orbit. I had pictured them falling into just as tight a threesome as we had been. But apparently Kate and Tom had never been like that.

Mhairi was pouring me a glass of Leffe – a beer she knew I'd always liked. She set it down next to me on the shiny countertop.

'Wine for you?' she said to Tom.

'Yes. Let's have that Sauvignon Blanc.'

I took a sip of the beer, refreshing and frothy, and cleared my throat. 'I'm sorry you didn't have a chance to get to know Kate better.'

'She never took to me, I don't think.'

Before I could reply to that, or even react, Mhairi banged open the fridge door and made a clatter pulling out an already-open bottle of white wine. 'Are the girls eating with us,' she said, 'or have they already eaten?'

'With us,' said Tom. 'It's nearly ready. Why don't you call them back down?'

'Sure.' Mhairi stepped outside of the kitchen and I heard her footsteps on the stairs and her voice calling out: *Kitty, Imrie!*

It was just me and Tom in the kitchen now. I wondered if he could hear my heart bumping from across the room. This was our chance to spend some proper time together, put the past behind us and effect a reconciliation of sorts, but I was questioning all over again what he'd meant about Kate. Kate knew people; it was part of her job to read people and make assessments of their character. But she hadn't 'taken' to Tom. Why not?

'That smells great,' I said, squashing the thoughts down.

Tom looked up, and yet again it hit me: he must have known everything – or almost everything. My illness, the breakdown, what happened in that flat . . .

'Hope it will be.' He gave a quick smile. 'Want to sit? Why don't you take that one.' He gestured to a seat at the head of the table that spanned the length of the bi-fold sliding doors to outside. The table was set already, a bit messily; perhaps the girls had done it. It was nice. Homely, though I'd never pictured Mhairi in a home like this. When I'd been with her, she'd dreamed about living in a cottage by the sea; sometimes we'd laughed about buying a campervan together and taking to the road. But she was happy here now with Tom and her daughters.

'Sure you don't want me to help you?' I asked him.

'I've got it. Almost ready . . .' He was charming, cordial, coming across with the big bowl of pasta and another bowl of salad, then returning with a stack of plates.

He sat down with me at the table, and a moment later, here were Mhairi and the girls: five of us in the warm, bright dining room. Tom reached out his arms and we linked hands around the table to say a grace. As Imrie and Kitty slipped their little fingers into mine, I bowed my head and sent good thoughts up to heaven, picturing Kate looking down on us, wondering if she was glad that things had worked out for one of us at least.

*

Afterwards, I helped Mhairi clear the dishes while Tom took the girls upstairs for bath and bed. Dinner had been fine, without a word of anger or blame. I realized this was Mhairi's crude way of smoothing things over and making right both her past and her future. If things were fine now, well then – the past could be left alone and forgotten.

It left me with a burden of guilt still inside. But I knew this was Mhairi's way; the best she could do right now. I could reject it or accept it; that was the choice. And maybe I would have left things there; set the past to one side, where it wouldn't interfere.

Except that, once we'd stacked the dishwasher and I was readying myself to catch the train home, Mhairi whispered that she had something to show me.

She led me back into the narrow front hallway, where our coats were hanging up. For a crazy moment, I thought she was going to push me against the wall and kiss me. Instead, she leaned past me and reached into the inside pocket of her coat.

I stared down at what she held out to me.

'Mhairi, what are you doing with that?'

'I took it back from him. When we were leaving, and the two of you went out ahead of me, I picked it up off his desk.'

She held the folded piece of notepaper out to me and reflexively I took it off her.

'This is supposed to be in Carrie's file,' I said mechanically.

'Kate never finished writing it, Finn. It doesn't belong in Carrie's notes when she never sent it. And what was Sebastian planning to do with it anyway? He doesn't seem that interested in finding out the truth. This is a clue, Finn – a clue to *something*. And it was us who found it; Sebastian's the one who took it off *us*.'

She was sort of right. But it still seemed bonkers.

'Okay, so what are *you* going to do with it?'

She hesitated. 'I think we should find this Carrie. Talk to her. Find out if there's anything relevant she knows.'

'Mhairi. Come on . . . That's a ridiculous idea.' But even as I said it, something came back to me, and an uncomfortable rush of adrenaline weakened my legs.

Mhairi scanned my face; she could read me like a book. 'Tell me, Finn – what is it?'

I could hear Tom back downstairs now, opening and closing cupboards in the kitchen. I shook my head. 'It's nothing, Mhairi. Forget it.'

She shook my arm. I felt like she wanted to kick me. 'Don't say that. I can tell when you're lying.'

'Mhairi, it doesn't . . .'

'Finn – *what?*'

I didn't want to say anything to encourage her. The truth was, we might never find the answers to Kate's death. Most likely, Mhairi would have to find a way just to accept her death, but if we kept on going in this direction – hunting, digging, searching for resolution – wouldn't we be stuck in all the wrong stages of grief?

I tried to speak carefully. 'I know you think there's some big mystery here, Mhairi. And I wish as much as you do there was a clear and simple reason. But maybe the truth is that Kate was just . . . unhappy. Maybe she'd always struggled and was just brilliant at pretending—'

She cut me off. 'I don't believe that.'

I gazed down at her. 'Don't believe it? Or don't want to?'

'I don't want to believe she was *just unhappy* and *pretend-ing*—'

'Mhairi—'

74

'—because the truth is, Finn, it was me. *My fault*.'

I flinched away in the cramped space of the hallway. 'Mhairi. Come on. What are you saying?'

Mhairi pressed her face into her hands in the gloom. 'Kate pulled away. She cancelled our meet-ups. And you know what? I didn't call her back. I didn't bother to chase her or take the time to check.' Her words were all coming out in a rush. 'I just carried on with my own stuff. *I* was fine, so what did it matter? I was happy, busy with Tom and the girls, so I left it – like always – for her to come to me.'

I didn't know what to say or think as I pulled Mhairi's hands away from her face. How easy, how clichéd it would be for me to say: *It isn't your fault, Mhairi; you can't blame yourself*. But it doesn't work like that, does it? You can't just magic away someone else's guilt.

'Ah shit, Mhairi.'

'Yeah. Exactly.' She sniffed and wiped her eye. 'So whatever it is, Finn, that you've just remembered, do me a favour and say what it is.'

CHAPTER 10

Carrie

2003

'Our dormitories are in a whole other wing from the boys',' said Serena as I followed her along a maze of corridors, Head Girl Mae bringing up the rear. 'You know the whole school used to be boys-only? They only took in female boarders last year.'

She was talking *at* not to me, like a tour guide. I already knew those facts about St Michael's, but I let her carry on. She was being friendly enough and I wasn't going to disrupt that.

'Huh!' I said. 'That's so random!'

'They needed the money; that's the only reason they did it . . .' She pushed through a set of heavy swing doors, holding them open for me with her heel. I swapped hands on my suitcase to hold them open for Mae in turn. 'But boys still outnumber us girls three to one.'

I got it. Despite the claims in the glossy prospectus of *impressive exam results*, *first-rate facilities* and *a wealth of extra-curricular (many outdoor!) activities*, how many kids would actually want to come here? To a spooky-looking castle surrounded by moorland, fifteen miles away from the nearest tiny town?

'So . . .' I cleared my throat and hitched up my suitcase. 'Are you the oldest girls here, then?'

'Mmm-hmm. Next oldest is Bryony and she's only fourteen. There are no girls in the sixth year, but that's fine. It's pretty good, right, Mae?'

'Sure. We like it like that.'

It felt like they were saying, *We're fine without you. We're not looking for a new friend.*

Before I'd arrived, it had literally been just the two of them. It hit me worse than ever; if these girls chose not to be my friends, I'd have to hang out with girls two years younger – or just boys, which would be a nightmare – or I'd be on my own.

We started up another flights of stairs.

'So when did you start here?' I asked Serena. *Always ask people questions about themselves.*

'End of last year,' she answered. 'I decided to move because they've got all this sports stuff. Up here, I can do competitive sailing and kayaking on the loch.'

I'd seen St Michael's famous loch through the staircase window: an expanse of dull grey water that I hoped I'd never actually have to go in. I lumped my suitcase up another steep flight as a horde of younger girls scuttled past us, kilts swinging. I was sure they were the same ones who had mucked about with those Bibles.

Serena paused just before the last flight, like she'd only just thought about it. 'Sure you're okay with that? Like – I dunno – did you want me to help?'

I smiled at her, heart thudding. Clearly she had no clue what it meant to look after the new kid. It was up to me, then, to be the easy, helpful friend. 'Not at all, it's fine. Thanks, Serena. I already appreciate you showing me up to the dorms.'

'That's okay,' she said. 'Anyway, we're here now.'

Through a final set of doors, thicker and heavier than the previous ones, the landing opened out into a wide corridor, doors hanging open all along it.

'We're in this one,' Mae said quietly. Since the assembly, she'd hardly said anything. She was pointing through a doorway halfway along the corridor, and I followed her inside. There were four beds, but only two occupied. Okay. Just the three of us then.

'That's yours.' Mae pointed to the one under the window. I spotted the rest of my belongings that had been sent on in advance tucked in at the foot.

A scream ricocheted down the corridor outside. The sound of laughter, running footsteps, someone wailing, '*Give it back!*', then another burst of laughter and a door slamming.

Mae disappeared out into the corridor. 'Faye! Polly! What the hell?'

I set my suitcase down and turned to Serena, who had sat down on her bed, bouncing like she was testing the springs. She lifted a hand to study her nails. Short and stubby, I noticed. Her sleeve fell back as she examined them. I took a breath. Next move.

'I like your bracelet,' I said, pointing to the macramé braid on her wrist. 'I have one just like it.'

'Mmm. Do you?'

I stepped forwards and sat down next to Serena. The mattress dipped, rolling me against her. In contrast to Mae, Serena smelled of coffee and shower gel.

'Yeah! Look.' I held up my arm to show off three matching bracelets: one purplish, one yellowish and one blue. Just like I'd seen girls on the St Michael's website wearing. 'My friends back in Illinois made them for me when I said I was leaving.'

I heard Mae outside. *'I don't give a crap who started it – give it back or I'll snap yours in half.'*

I flinched, glancing at Serena to gauge her reaction; she looked back at me blank-faced.

'She's joking, right?' I said.

Serena wrinkled her nose. 'Some of the younger girls are absolute delinquents. You have to be brutal with them or they never learn.'

I swallowed, digesting this new aspect of head girl and prefect. Maybe not all sweetness and light after all.

Serena touched a finger to my blue bracelet then the purple one. 'Huh. I like them. They're nice.'

The butterflies in my stomach slowed their wing beats. 'Thanks, Serena.' I smiled widely. 'Yours is too.'

Mae did a double take when she came back in and found us like that. But – to her credit – she didn't let it break her stride.

'Little shits,' she said, shoving the door closed. 'Sometimes I feel this close—' she held up a pinch of thumb and forefinger '—to wringing their necks. Anyway . . .' She looked back and forth between the two of us. 'What are you two up to?'

'Nothing,' Serena said. 'Carrie was just showing me her bracelets. She got them from some friends back home.'

'How cute,' said Mae with what sounded like sarcasm.

I got up from where I was tucked in beside Serena and sat down on the bed they had allocated me.

'Yeah,' said Serena. 'Well, I thought they were nice.'

Another few stretched beats of silence followed as Mae lowered herself carefully into a chair at one of the four desks that kitted out the room and I felt something pass between her and Serena, a communication I wasn't meant to read.

'From your accent,' said Mae directly to me now, 'I'm guessing you're American?' She said it like it wasn't a very cool thing to be.

'No,' I said, pulling my sleeve back down. 'I mean, I was living there with my dad and stepmum until recently. But I'm British originally.' Like that would win me points. 'I went to primary and high school before in England.'

Before the divorce and – much later – before my dad got full custody. Before Valerie, and before my dad uprooted me yet again for his work.

'Problems at your old school, then?' said Serena, tossing a scrunched-up scrap of paper at her friend. 'That's how our darling Mae ended up here. Though best not to mention that, huh, Ms Head Girl?'

Mae batted the ball of paper away – more aggressively than I'd expected. So this was how St Michael's girls were behind closed doors. My heart rate yanked up a notch, as I smoothed my expression and tried to answer the question.

'No. Not really. My dad thought we should move back closer to my mum. My real mum, I mean. She lives in London and has a few issues.'

Mae raised an eyebrow. 'And your stepmum agreed to that?'

I opened my mouth, closed it. I hadn't actually thought about it that way. I pictured Valerie: her generosity, her kindness. I looked down at my bracelets. 'Guess she did.'

'Huh,' said Mae. 'Well, that's interesting.'

But she didn't sound especially interested. I realized they hadn't even suggested I unpack. On her bed, Serena lay back and rocked herself into a shoulder stand, her muscular legs like a wall so I could no longer see her face.

'Brothers or sisters?' she said blandly. 'Pets?'

'Um . . . Only child. No pets. My dad . . . doesn't like animals.'

'Right. Hey – how long till teatime?'

I checked my watch, like I even had the answer.

'Six minutes,' Mae answered. She went into the en suite attached to our dorm room. Under the yellow glow of the light in the bathroom, Mae fiddled with a run in her tights.

'Dammit. Serena, have you got any clean ones?'

'My grey ones. Top drawer of my dresser.' She was cycling her legs in slow, controlled circles.

My heart banged. Despite my efforts, I could feel their interest in me waning, like colourful threads unravelling. It could happen like that. I'd had that before. Initial friendliness, initial interest, then all of that burning up, fizzling out.

But it's all right, I told myself over the squeezing of my heart. There was still time. I had only been here a few hours. I wasn't done, and even from the little I'd seen, I already knew so much more than I did before.

Little shits . . .

We have to be brutal with them . . .

I knew now which would be my strongest card to play.

*

The opportunity came quickly, during that first teatime – a stodgy meal of fish and boiled potatoes, it turned out.

Serena asked the question, through a mouthful of food, and I set down my knife and fork before answering, determined not to squander the opportunity – what, in that moment, felt close to my last chance to impress.

'Where'd you actually go to school before, then?'

I cleared my throat. 'Jackson Ridge, Illinois.' I waited a beat, then said, 'Maybe you've heard of it.'

Serena went on chewing and looking at me. Mae peeled the skin off her portion of fish. 'Jackson Ridge?'

I left a pause before I said the next part. 'The school itself was Kelviston High.'

I waited again, fingers tightly crossed, for the name to sink in.

'Wait.' It was Mae's eyes that widened first. 'Kelviston?'

Serena frowned without looking up, her knife scoring through the chunks of white flesh on her plate. 'I've never heard of it.'

Mae turned to her friend. 'You have. Kelviston High, Jackson Ridge? It was on the news.'

Now the penny dropped. 'Oh,' Serena said. 'No way.'

Her eyebrows lifted as she turned her cool gaze onto me. Her eyes were slate grey, I noticed. 'You were there? Like, when it happened?'

I met her gaze. 'Mmm-hmm.'

Mae stared at me, her pupils widened, black pools spilling open. Fear or excitement? By now, I knew which I'd guess.

So I gave them all the details they wanted. I told them about the boy my age who'd never seemed to have friends or any normal kind of hobbies, but whose white Christian family had had a whole house full of guns. Then I told them about the blood and the screaming, and the bodies in the hallways; and finally about the bullet that had lodged in our class teacher's head.

As I described it, tendrils of relief exploded inside me. I'd done it. I hadn't disappointed them.

In this new country, at this new school, with these two unknown girls, I had read the signs and played it just right.

Mae and Serena were the allies I needed, and my hook had landed. In the tight cat's cradle of their friendship, for now at least, I'd fashioned my in.

CHAPTER 11

Finn

2019

'It's her, right?' Mhairi said as soon as I picked up her call. I was getting used to her phone calls by now. '*Caroline Greaves*,' Mhairi said. 'Kate's Carrie.'

'I really don't think it's anything,' I said tentatively. 'I particularly don't know how it helps.'

Fuck it, I had said to myself last night at her house. *It's for Mhairi.* And I'd gone on to explain how a few days ago I'd searched for more info on St Michael's and come across a 2004 article about Highers results day. After getting home last night, I'd emailed her a copy of the newspaper article, with the picture of five pupils leaping in the air, two boys and three girls.

Five Firm Friends and their Fantastic Results!

One of the girls had her name listed as Caroline Greaves.

On the phone, Mhairi's voice was excited. 'Caroline Greaves. *Carrie G.* We've got her real name now.'

'We still can't be sure of that, Mhairi. *Carrie* could be short for a completely different name. Carla or . . . Carina, or something. And the "G" could just be a coincidence. There might have been a dozen Carrie Gs who went to that school.'

'Yes, but I checked that already. I spent a good two hours last night on LinkedIn, Facebook, pages of Google searches – the lot. I searched for every C-A-R name I could think of, along with St Michael's. There was a Carla, but her surname was Thomas. The only "Car G" alumna that ever shows up is this one. The girl in the picture. Caroline Greaves.'

I pinched the bridge of my nose. 'I don't know, Mhairi . . .'

It was all too easy to join the wrong dots. I should know. I remembered those days and weeks, when my vision was so blurred I was struggling to see, when I was cooking and cleaning and shopping relentlessly, and didn't want to let Mhairi out of my sight. When I built the furniture we would need single-handedly, Mhairi so nauseous she could barely get out of bed. But the cot's bars were terrifyingly low; the altar of the changing table terrifyingly high, even though when I called, the manufacturers insisted the measurements were safe and correct. I lost track of the hours I spent in the little room next to our bedroom, decorating, trialling yellow swatch after yellow swatch, terrified that I would never get the colour right. Then came the charms I hung from the window and doorframes: more and more of them as the weeks went on . . . It had taken Kate to finally realize what was going on.

'Really, Finn?' Mhairi's voice pulled me back. 'Surely it's obvious. Kate was working with a client named Carrie – *Carrie G*. Sebastian told us that much. We know this Carrie attended St Michael's: Kate was researching the school, and she wrote the name St Michael's in her caseload notes. And there's the article featuring Caroline Greaves.'

It wasn't watertight. Not by a long shot. But I couldn't keep pretending it wasn't plausible.

'You agree, don't you?' Mhairi said. 'All of this – it has to be relevant. There's something in here, I'm sure of it.'

'Then where are you going with it, Mhairi? So, Kate's client's name was Caroline Greaves. How does that help? What difference does it make?'

'I told you. We'll find this Carrie and speak to her,' she said.

'How? Has she posted her address and phone number on her Facebook page?'

Mhairi went stone silent. My stomach sank. That was harsh of me. Cruel.

'I'm sorry, Mhairi. I didn't mean it to come out like that.'

The silence stretched. I closed my eyes, kicking myself for my stupidity. Our relationship was only just re-finding its footing and I was jeopardizing it all over again.

After what felt like an eternity, Mhairi's voice came back on the line.

'I miss her, Finn. I just miss her so much.'

My heart beat a sharp ache. This. It all came back to this. 'I know. I'm sorry . . . I feel exactly the same. I can't stop thinking of how much I owe her. Everything she did for me . . .'

'I keep having this dream, Finn. Over and over. Kate and I are in the kitchen of the old flat – *our* old flat, and I'm talking to her, just the way I always used to, moaning about something inane like how I can't get some stupid packet of sultanas to open, and then I look up and there's nothing. One moment, she's there and then she's just gone.'

I swallowed, my words all gone too.

'I hear you calling out,' she went on. 'You're calling my name from somewhere: maybe upstairs, maybe through in the study, I can't tell. I start walking, running, through the apartment trying to find you. But I *can't* find you, Finn . . . It's just me, alone, and I'm running and running . . .'

'It's okay,' I said, heart pounding, terrified of wrecking this. 'I'm here now; I'm listening.' This was the lowest Mhairi had let her guard down so far, the most vulnerable she'd let herself be with me since then. I couldn't squander it.

'Tell me what you want me to do. We don't have contact details or know where Carrie lives but okay, tell me: what's your plan?'

Mhairi drew a long breath. 'You're right. We haven't got those details. But we already know someone who almost certainly does.'

CHAPTER 12

Carrie

2003

After my disclosure about Kelviston High, Mae and Serena seemed much more willing to give me a chance. During the rest of dinner that first night, I learned where I should always sit, what food was good, what food was gross.

'But don't be weird about what and how you eat,' said Serena. 'St Michael's hasn't got time for that stuff.'

They'd both been at boarding school before, they told me: Mae in Edinburgh and Serena in an English county called Rutland.

Later they gave me a run-down on all of the teachers: who was a ball-ache (Ms Jefferson) and who was a pushover (Mr Graham); who was dreamy (Mr Witham); who was a stickler for rules like skirt length (Ms Myers). Mae had been here less than two terms and Serena three months, but they had the staff all worked out and I admired them for that.

'Knowledge is power,' Mae said, and she was right.

*

Still, even with the help of Mae and Serena, it was knackering to smile and copy and read other people to make sure I didn't miss a single remark or cue. It only takes one slip to lose your footing, and by Friday night, I was exhausted. I'd crashed out early in the dormitory and was dreaming a sweaty dream about my mother holding one of my hands and my father the other, each of them pulling me in opposite directions so that my arms stretched out like chewing gum. *I'll use her,* my mother was yelling; *no,* I'll *use her,* my father yelled back, and all the while I was coming apart at the seams . . .

I was in it thick but I woke up fast enough when I needed to, screeching into consciousness.

When I opened my eyes the dormitory was dark, but there was enough moonlight seeping in through the tacky curtains that I could make out some details in the gloom.

Serena was standing between our beds, her tall shadow spilling over me. She was wearing jeans and tugging on a jumper.

Very softly, making sure not to let her know I was awake, I turned my head to look towards Mae's bed. There was a mound under the duvet, but I knew it wasn't Mae. It had only been a week, but by now I knew exactly how Mae slept: spread-eagled, with the covers pushed back, and snoring. Plus, the pillows were missing. Such an old trick, I thought, stuffing your bed like that.

So, Mae wasn't in bed, and Serena was up and getting dressed. I reached out through the darkness and grabbed the wrist that dangled in front of me, almost knocking my Point Horror book off my nightstand. Serena let out a little scream. Mae appeared, a dark silhouette in the doorway of the dormitory. She was dressed in a light cagoule zipped up at the front.

'Shush, Serena!' she whispered. 'What is it?'

Serena yanked her wrist free. 'Carrie's awake.'

I drew a quick breath and took the initiative, sitting up and snapping on my lamp. 'What's going on?'

Mae squinted against the glare, blinking. 'Jesus, Carrie,' she hissed. 'Turn that off. You want Ms Rowlins to come storming in here?'

I quickly clicked us back into darkness. 'What are you doing, though?' I repeated, quietly. Clearly they hadn't just got up to go to the loo; Serena was holding a pair of hiking boots.

It was another of those moments, like on that very first day. *Kelviston High.* An opportunity; or a test. No wonder they hadn't been keen to open up their dorm to a new girl if they were sneaking out like this at night. I could be a tattle-tale, go running to Ms Rowlins and spill the beans.

I weighed my choices. I could roll back over in my bed, pull the blankets over my eyes and ears and pretend I'd heard and seen nothing. *Ignore me.*

But there was also another option. 'Serena?' I directed my voice specifically to her, letting her name, my appeal, hang between us. I slid my fingers down to touch the pretty bands on my wrist – the ones I'd woven for myself before coming here.

Through the darkness, I could sense them eyeing each other.

Please, I thought. *Let me in on it. Say yes.*

Serena shifted, transferring her weight from one foot to the other. It was such a tiny physical adjustment, but to me it spoke volumes; I read these dynamics through my nerves clear as day and a bubble of hope expanded in my chest.

Serena shrugged, palms held up. 'Why don't we let her come with us?'

Mae's silhouette was still framed in the doorway. She probably couldn't see my eyes, but she must have known I was watching her. I didn't even care where the two of them were going: to raid the canteen, turn cartwheels on the hockey pitch, vandalize the pavilion, drown themselves in the loch. All I cared about was being included.

At last, Mae let out a soft sigh, and I knew I had it.

'Sure. Whatever,' she said. 'Fine.'

By the time she answered, I'd already started getting dressed.

*

I tugged on the jeans I'd been wearing the previous evening, as well as a bra and my school hoodie. I knew it was cold out, but I didn't want to keep them waiting while I searched for a T-shirt.

I followed them along the dark corridor outside the dormitory, and then down the staircases to the lower floor, everything silent and still and cool. We carried our outdoor shoes in our hands, and padded the route in our bare feet or socks, so as not to make a sound.

I still didn't ask where exactly we were going. I had earned the right to join them, but not to ask questions. Mae was in the lead, I was in the middle, and Serena followed behind.

On the ground floor, we passed by a bunch of classrooms, Mae lighting the way with a torch. The full layout of the school was still fuzzy to me only a week in, and all the corridors tended to blur into one.

Eventually we reached a small door, leading out from a back room in the school gymnasium. I tried to picture whether I had seen it from outside but, like I said, my sense of the school's geography wasn't great, and the door was small, narrow – probably quite unobtrusive from the other side. It wasn't locked, even though it should have been secured, surely? If not to stop students getting out, then to stop dangerous strangers getting in.

'The key went missing,' Serena whispered over my shoulder, making me jump. Her breath smelled of the vanilla ice-cream we'd been given for pudding that night; she hadn't brushed her teeth. 'Long story,' she added.

The latch of the door snicked easily, and the door swung open silently as a ghost.

'We put WD-40 on the hinges,' Serena whispered again. 'It used to make the worst racket.'

It was obvious by now that they had done this – whatever this was – dozens of times before I'd arrived on the scene and I was impressed that they'd managed it repeatedly without getting caught. And also, like the unlocked door, it gave me a funny sense of unease to think the boundaries of this school were so permeable that anyone could get out. And pretty much anyone could get in.

The cold was sharper than I'd expected when we stepped outside and I wished I'd put more layers on under my hoodie, but it was too late now. I wrapped my arms around myself and opened my mouth to let the cold burn my tongue. We hopped about pulling on our shoes under the stars. It was a crisp night, and up here in the wilds of nowhere there wasn't any light pollution to speak of. It looked like someone had chucked a handful of silver glitter across the sky. Pretty.

We'd stepped out into a small back alcove of the school lined with a couple of steel bins and a long wooden shed, which Serena said housed the fibreglass kayaks they used on the loch in the spring and autumn months.

'Ready?' said Mae, and I nodded though I still didn't know for what. I could feel Serena shivering beside me.

We set off walking, Mae's torch making a bright puddle and catching strange shapes at the edges of the beam. I was in the middle again, sandwiched between them. You would have expected me to be more like the third wheel, dragging behind a little, orbiting the twosome of the girls who had been best friends long before I came. Instead, I felt weirdly like a divider, or a buffer. For a moment, my mind skipped back to those weeks and months before my parents split for good, when the two of them couldn't be left alone together in a room. When they'd tried to use me to stop their entire marriage falling apart.

'We're heading up there,' Serena said, pointing to the sloping bank behind the school that led up to woods at the top where Serena had told me they sometimes had to do orienteering in the summer, running around between trees and gullies looking for bits of laminated plastic tied to bushes. 'It's just a place we go to hang out. School's so boring. It's good to mix it up sometimes.'

I didn't question or challenge her, just followed them up the rise. The ground was dry despite the cold, and little twigs cracked under our feet like tiny bones. At one point as we climbed, I looked back over my shoulder to where the school squatted below us. There was just enough light from the moon and the stars to make out its bulk, plus there were specks of light showing from some of the windows, lamps that I supposed were left on all night, outside the housemistress's bedroom, for example.

It felt a bit like the school was watching us. Stupid thoughts: it was only a building after all, with a bit of history. And despite the kind of books I liked to read, I didn't really believe in ghosts or vampires or demons – not like those third-year girls with their pentagrams in chapel. Still I kept looking back as I climbed, until I caught the toe of my sneaker painfully on a tree root and stumbled forwards, Mae catching me under the arm.

'Careful,' she said. 'You have to watch your step.'

At the top, they led me down into a hollow in the woods over the other side of the ridge. It was sheltered there, and it looked like the girls had previously dragged together logs and big stones to make a sort of encampment. I brushed away the dead leaves and specks of dirt and sat down on one the rocks.

It didn't much surprise me when Mae produced a joint. I'd guessed they were up to something like that.

'You've smoked before?' she asked me.

I swallowed. 'Sure.' At least that was true and I wasn't going to make a fool of myself like I had my first time, coughing my lungs out and turning sickly white.

'That's cool.'

Mae produced a plain plastic lighter and my eyes tingled as she sparked the light. As the familiar smell washed over me, I breathed in deep, tension leaving me. This was good. This was what I'd hoped for, a recognizable breach of rules that I could handle.

Mae took a drag and passed the joint to Serena, then

I watched as she exhaled the smoke upwards, towards the sprinkle of stars and bright button of the moon.

The roach was damp when it came to my turn, soggy from both Mae and Serena's lips. I didn't care. I took the hot twist of paper into my mouth, sucking in my own deep lungful, feeling high already just from being with them here.

I took another small draw and passed the joint back to Mae, then sat silently, respectfully, just listening to them talk. They talked about the falling-out Mona and Felicity in third year had had, and how Mona was being scapegoated as the one to snub and blame. About how one of the third-year girls had wet the bed the other night, an act so bizarre and shameful that no one had even ribbed her about it yet. About how Mr Witham had put his hand on Mae's knee when he'd squatted at her desk to help with a line in *As You Like It*, and how Serena thought that was gross not 'sexy', like Mae called it, and how if he'd done it to her she'd have gone straight to the head.

They talked like that and my thoughts drifted along with them as the little joint circled round between us. Eventually, it was all burned down and Mae dug a hole with her heel to bury the tiny butt. Serena yawned and I rubbed my eyes, eyelids gritty.

On the way back, the school seemed smaller, as if all of its watching had only been a sort of envy. I felt tired but also high, giddy – energized more than sedated, and it seemed Mae and Serena did too. Maybe it was just the effects of the weed, but I felt like something profound had just happened, like I'd gone through an initiation of some kind. It all felt symbolic, the ritual of smoking, the shared drug connecting us.

We let ourselves half-run, half-skid back down the bank, and I bit my tongue to keep from letting out my shrieks. *Knowledge is power.* Well, I had power now. They'd let me in on their secret and so I could finally relax, stop worrying. I was still the new girl, and they were still Mae and Serena. But now I'd made it. After tonight, I was on the inside.

Text from: Kate
Sent to: Mhairi
10.17am, 04/04/2011

Hey Mhairi!
I finally did it. I handed my notice in this morning.
 Eeek!
xxx

Text from: Mhairi
Sent to: Kate
11.26am, 04/04/2011

Hooray, I'm so proud of you! I know the NHS was driving
you mad and I know you're going to do brilliantly with
your own practice. We need to celebrate!

Text from: Kate
Sent to: Mhairi
11.29am, 04/04/2011

Thanks, Mhairi. I know. There are so many ways
we've been letting patients down. So many of
them have histories of trauma. They never got the
protection or help they needed back then, and
they still aren't now. Now the overstretched NHS
just offers them six sessions of bloody anxiety
management and pretends that'll get to the root of
their wounds. It terrifies me what we let slip through

the cracks, and I swore right back at the start of my training I'd never let myself work like that, not again.

Anyway. So glad I'm finally taking charge.

Text from: Mhairi
Sent to: Kate
11.30am, 04/04/2011

Terrifies is a strong word! Deep breaths . . . ;) Anyway, I'm just glad you're getting out of there.

Text from: Kate
Sent to: Mhairi
11.30am, 04/04/2011

Yes. You're right. And yes – we should celebrate. Fancy dinner at mine on Saturday?

Text from: Mhairi
Sent to: Kate
11.31am, 04/04/2011

Sounds lovely, so long as you don't mind cooking?

11.31am, 04/04/2011
Oh! And can I bring Finn?? 0:

Text from: Kate
Sent to: Mhairi
11.32am, 04/04/2011

You mean I *finally* get to meet him?!

Text from: Mhairi
Sent to: Kate
10.58am, 10/04/2011

Thank you for the "dinner" + wine last night 😂
What did you think????

Text from: Kate
Sent to: Mhairi
11.14am, 10/04/2011

Oh my God, I'm never cooking again!
    Can't believe you both stayed after the inferno.
    But I'm so glad you did. I really liked him, Mhairi.
He seems thoughtful. And kind. Complex, but in a
good way. Not superficial. Like he cares about the
things that matter.
    I think he'll be really good for you, Mhairi.
    Lots of love

Kate xx

CHAPTER 13

Victor

2019

My flat on the outskirts of Madrid was stifling and I'd been sitting in my box of a living room with the curtains drawn for over forty-eight hours, inhaling yet more coke or soaking myself in yet more beer every time I felt the last hit begin to wear off. I had holed up here to figure out a plan but instead I'd shoved a mountain of coke up my nose – a mountain I was seriously in debt for.

I knew it would only be a matter of time before the knock came at my door and I knew it probably wouldn't just be Jose this time. Inevitably he would bring some friends of his, guys a foot taller and a foot wider than my kindly, friendly neighbourhood dealer. Sitting on the plush sofa, empty beer bottles scattered round me, just the thought of it made me hate myself a little more. I was weak and always had been.

When I'd moved out here five months ago to head up the European arm of one of my father's many companies, I'd thought things might be different this time. But once I'd got out here, it quickly became clear that my 'executive' role was nominal only. The people here didn't need me and when I called my father to point that out, it became clear he didn't want me back in London either. For a while, I'd tried to swallow my pride and make the best of it, taking a back seat to the other execs, listening in each board meeting rather than speaking. Even that turned out to be more than anyone wanted.

When I stopped going in on time, no one seemed to care. So, eventually, I stopped going in at all. Instead I spent my time haunting the late-night bars and clubs of the city, indulging all my worst habits, finding the people who weren't afraid to break a few rules, waking up in one unfamiliar bed after another, ending up with a drug dealer's number on my phone.

Now in my sweltering, minimalist apartment, I wiped another line of sweat from my forehead. I'd switched off my mobile a few days ago, to avoid any messages or calls. Stupid for me to be waiting here at home, in this stark city apartment where they knew I lived, but where else was I supposed to go? I couldn't wander the streets all day, every day. They would find me eventually anyway, wherever I went. I wasn't far gone enough not to realize that.

I looked down at the lines I had laid out in front of me, steeling myself to take another hit. Through the open window of the bright white room, I could hear the shouts of kids outside and the jangle of someone's radio playing classic Eighties hits. I could smell someone's cooking, the ubiquitous tomato-onion-garlic aroma of *sofrito*, and right then, Jesus, how I wished that was me: out with friends, enjoying music, settling down to a home-cooked meal. It *had* been me not even that long ago, before I managed to fuck it all up.

All I could pray was that I was reaching my rock bottom now.

I leaned down over the white powder, telling myself this would be my last hit.

*

By sundown, they still hadn't come and I had used up all of my stash. I was exhausted, hungry, thirsty, and knew I should go out to get food or at least try to tidy up the place. Instead I just sat there on my expensive suede couch, holding a crumpled wad of tissues to my nose, thinking about the four hundred euros stuffed in a drawer at the side of my bed. All the ready cash I had left and absolutely nowhere near enough to pay what I owed.

The kids outside had stopped playing and the cheerful radio had been switched off. I hated silence; I would do anything to fill it. I picked up my phone from the white-speckled floor and held down the button to turn it back on. I pressed it against my chest while I waited for any new messages or voicemails to download. My heart was automatically juddering, dreading what might be on there, but what harm could Jose and his crew – or anyone – do to me through my mobile?

When I finally peered at the screen, there were only a couple of texts anyway: one from a senior exec at the office and one from some guy I'd met last week at a bar. I deleted them both. There weren't any from acquaintances at the clubs checking up on me. I'd been telling them I might be away for a bit, getting out of the city. It's funny, isn't it, when people take you at your word?

The only other thing that showed was a red dot on my email app. These days I had most things directed to junk; my father's team would have had little reason to contact me on my personal address; and I was pretty sure Jose and his crew didn't collect debts via email. So I had no clue what this was.

I clicked the app open, the new email appearing in bold at the top of the page.

I didn't recognize the sender's address. At least, I didn't know who the sender was but the actual email handle sent a chill through me.

backwoods03@protonmail.com

What the fuck? With a sweaty thumbprint I opened the message, still with no idea what I expected it to say. In the end it was just two lines of text.

Plus an attachment.

The email had been auto-forwarded from an old account of mine that I hadn't used in years and which should have become obsolete, but as soon as I clicked open the attachment it was clear the message was real, not spam or a virus or anything.

I pressed my thumbs into my eyes, trying to stop the burning sensation that had taken over my head.

It was a screen shot of a newspaper report, dated four months ago. The headline told me everything I needed to know.

'*Shit,*' I whispered, biting my knuckle hard enough to leave teeth marks, as if the pain might cut through my stupor. I forced myself to read the paragraphs below, half-hoping the whole thing might be a prank, but scanning the details only made it more real.

My head burned; my lungs burned. I was sobering up fast now.

'Shit,' I said to myself again. 'Shit, shit, shit!'

In that moment, I could almost have welcomed Jose's knock at the door. I could almost willingly have allowed myself to be dragged from my apartment, taken to some waste ground, bashed in the head and dumped in some shallow grave.

Anything to escape *this* reality.

I read the email again, my brain twitching and jerking to figure out who had sent this.

One of the girls? Alex? *No, not Alex.*

Whoever it was, I couldn't believe they'd dare send such a message, after everything we had done, everything we had promised each other.

If the anonymous sender had been standing in front of me, I probably would have slapped them right across the face.

Instead, it was *their* words that were like a punch to my head.

Are you feeling how I'm feeling, Victor? Don't you think it's time to speak up?

CHAPTER 14

Finn

2019

Mhairi made me switch to a Zoom call, so she could show me exactly what she was doing. I knew we were in it now; both of us together. I'd agreed – tacitly and explicitly – to help her. We'd crossed lines and kept on going. What was one more line after that?

She had her home landline handset in her hand, and I watched as she dialled Sebastian's number. I could hear it ringing and I jerked a little when his voice came on the line.

'*Hello, you've reached Dr Sebastian Hart. I'm sorry I'm unable to answer your call . . .*'

'Voicemail,' Mhairi mouthed. 'That's good.' She waited until we both heard the beep. 'Dr Hart? I'm calling from the council . . . the coroner's office. We're putting together a final report on Dr Fallon, and we're keen to speak briefly to one of her patients. If you have any contact details for – one second . . . yes, a Ms Greaves, we'd be very grateful for your assistance. Alternatively, do ask her to get in touch with us directly. We have it on file that she's given permission but somehow her contact details weren't logged. Anyway, if you can be of any assistance, we can be reached on . . .'

I stared at Mhairi as she left her own home number. She stared back at me, lips pursed, daring me to challenge her. I didn't. If I had been going to stop her, I would have done it by now.

She pressed the button to hang up. 'Now we need to record a new answering message.'

She tapped through the menu on the handset, and when she got to the right option she altered her voice slightly. '*This is the Cambridgeshire Coroner's Office. Please leave a message after the tone.*'

Mhairi listened back, then pressed '1' to save the fake answering message to her own landline. 'Perfect,' she said. 'Now we just have to wait.'

*

Four minutes later her landline rang, but Mhairi made no move to answer it; she had this strategy all worked out. After what felt like an eternity, the ringing stopped and I counted the ensuing seconds of silence. Twenty-nine, thirty . . . I pictured again that image of the happy, leaping pupils, each of their names inscribed underneath. *Margaret Forsythe, Serena Whittingham, Caroline Greaves. Victor Dupont, Alexander Fontaine.*

Who *was* this Carrie? What had Kate been writing to apologize for?

Now it came: the bleep of a new voicemail message. Mhairi

pressed a button on the handset for playback. This time she kept the phone pressed to her ear, listening.

'What did he say?' I asked. 'Has he left a message?'

She held up a staying finger, still listening. A moment later, she looked up at me through the computer screen.

'You got it?'

'Bingo,' she said.

CHAPTER 15

Carrie

2003

One chemistry lesson in my third week at St Michael's, I got paired with a boy in my year called Victor. He was skinny, dark-haired and tall, and I'd seen him around with a blond-haired boy called Alex. Like me and Mae and Serena, the two of them kept to themselves, didn't mix that much with the others. When Victor and I got paired for the experiment that was pretty much the first time we'd talked.

That week in chemistry we were learning how to produce salts – specifically copper sulphate salt crystals – and that involved lighting the Bunsen burners. Our teacher Mr Graham was explaining about *real-world applicability* as ours purred like a ferocious candle on the workbench. Mr Graham's voice was low and monotonous, with a mildly hypnotizing effect. I rested my sleepy head on my hand and pulled a curtain of hair down so I could close my eyes while pretending to listen.

Beside me, I could sense Victor moving. I opened my eyes and saw him passing the palm of his hand back and forth in front of the Bunsen flame. Not above it – Mr Graham would have spotted him if he'd done that – but back and forth in front of the pillar of heat, like a fish swimming round a column of seaweed, a little bit closer each time.

He wasn't doing it to show off; I could tell that. He was in his own world, so absorbed that I wondered whether he was even feeling the pain. Mr Graham droned on; I watched Victor's hand swaying, like a form of hypnosis. Until I saw the bright red of his palm and saw how close to the flare he really was.

I could have turned away and ignored him, left him to scorch himself if he liked. I hardly knew him. What did I care? Instead, without saying a word, I reached out and wrapped my fingers around his, my knuckles taking their own sear from the flame.

I drew his hand away and set it down on the workbench. Like coming out of a daydream, he turned to look at me. We stayed like that for a moment, eyes locked, red-hot hands clasped.

He gave a small nod, a form of thank you.

Silently, I mouthed, *You're welcome.*

Then someone across the classroom knocked over a glass beaker and I gently slipped my hand out of his grasp.

*

That lunchtime, Serena had another kayaking lesson and Mae was having a one-to-one about her English essay (the one she'd already gotten an A on). Before, when my timetable didn't line up with Serena or Mae's, I'd eat my food quickly in my usual seat in the dining hall, then hole up in the school library with the latest Point Horror book.

This time as I crossed the room with my tray, I heard some-body calling my name. I turned to see Victor gesturing to me. He and Alex always sat at the back right of the hall but it was only Victor at that table now.

I stopped walking, swallowing. I already had my seat, my table, the one I shared with Mae and Serena. If I didn't guard it while they weren't here, a group of girls from the first year might try to take it.

'Carrie,' Victor called again. 'Are you on your own? Why don't you sit here?'

His face was flushed. He wasn't confident. If I ignored him, I had the power to cause hurt. But it was stupid, anyway, wasn't it? All these random rules about *seating*. Why shouldn't I sit wherever I liked?

I turned and headed in his direction, just as a memory came sliding into my head. Telling my mother I wanted to live with my father, and later choosing to move to the States with my dad. *Because you were a nightmare: a drunk and a train wreck. I'm not stupid enough to think Dad is perfect but at least he isn't as fucked up as you!*

Victor almost got to his feet as I approached his table, like he was Mr Darcy or something.

'Hi,' he said, trying to be calm, casual. We sat down. It was weird seeing the dining hall from this angle: a different table in a different part of the room. Disorientating.

'Thought you might like to join me.'

'Thanks.' I set down my tray and school bag. 'How's your hand?'

'Oh fine. Forget about it. It's just . . . Mr Graham's lessons make me want to stick pins in my eyes.'

I snorted a laugh that mostly came out through my nose. 'Yeah.' I nodded. 'Got you.'

I could feel other pupils in the dining hall looking at us. I wonder if someone would start up a rumour that we were kissing, dating, fucking. I wondered what Serena and Mae would say when they heard.

'So, you've moved from America?' said Victor.

'Yep,' I said. 'Illinois'

'But England before, right?'

I glanced up at him. Seemed he'd been paying attention. 'That's right. What about you? Where did you grow up?'

He pushed his dark hair out of his eyes. If he hadn't been so skinny, the gesture would have been cute. 'I was born in Edinburgh, grew up in Singapore. Lived in Columbia for a bit.'

'Oh,' I said. 'Huh.' I wasn't sure if he was just stating the facts or trying to impress me. Did he think I liked him? Was that what this was? I unwrapped an egg-mayo sandwich, wondering how to eat it without making a mess. This was starting to feel like a mistake. I shouldn't have sat down here; I should have gone to the library.

'Hey, Victor. Hey . . . Carrie.'

I glanced up, and my whole face fired red. Alex was standing there.

'Sorry,' I said. 'I was just about to head to the library . . .' I shoved my tray aside, grabbed my bag.

He shrugged. 'Stay if you want. Be my guest.'

'If you're sure . . . ?' He slid in beside me. 'Thanks.' I wished my cheeks would stop burning.

'Where are Sporty and Posh Spice?' he said.

It took me a second. 'Oh,' I said. 'You mean Serena and Mae.'

I didn't call him out on the nicknames. One night in the dorm after lights out Serena had asked me which of the St Michael's boys I'd hook up with, and I'd said, *Oh man, none of them*, then, *probably Alex Fontaine, he looks cleanest*, and both of them had laughed.

'At training. And a one-to-one for English.'

'Right. So today it's just you, then.'

I smiled at him then at Victor. 'Just me!'

He set down his bag, elbows and tray taking up plenty of room. A moment later, he pulled something out of his shoulder case.

'Ah, put it away, Alex,' said Victor. 'We're eating.'

'So what? That's best sometimes – candid shots.' He held the thing up, lens gleaming. A video camera. Immediately, I covered my face.

'Come on . . .' said Alex. 'I want to get all your new-girl impressions.'

I kept my hands up. I could hear the thing whirring so I knew he was recording. I kept grinning, shaking my head. It really had been a dumb idea to join them.

Alex set the camera down and up held his hands. 'All right,' he said. 'Truce.' He was still looking at me though and my cheeks were still flaming. Would there be rumours about me and Alex now instead? 'I'll film you another time . . . If you like.'

I tried to think of something witty and flirty to say, but all I managed was, 'Maybe. Sure!'

'Alex got that camera for his birthday,' said Victor. 'Now he won't put the stupid thing down.'

Alex leaned back in his seat. 'I want to be a filmmaker. Documentaries, film journalism, all that kind of thing.'

His tone was serious, and now that I didn't have that lens in my face I was able to relax a little. I adjusted tack. 'Oh! You mean like Nick Broomfield?' I'd seen his films about loopy serial killer Aileen Wuornos earlier that year. 'I think that would be great. Really cool.'

'Yeah. *Would* be cool, wouldn't it?' He grinned at me and I smiled back. 'Maybe I'll do a film about your old school, Kelviston. Did you see *Bowling for Columbine*? That was great.'

'Yeah . . .' Except I needed to steer the conversation away from that. Hard.

Victor spoke up through a mouthful of macaroni. 'He'll probably cast you in some zombie horror movie.'

Alex put his chin in his palm, sizing me up like he was seriously considering it. I *did* fancy him; it was stupid to deny it. I made myself catch and hold his eye. 'Oh yeah . . . As what?'

'The monster,' said Victor. 'Scary Spice.'

But Alex was still looking at me. 'Nah. I'd have you as Sexy Final Girl, don't you think?'

*

After lunch, I hurried along one of the back corridors to my history lesson, heart still jittering from my conversation with the boys. Someone would say something – it wasn't going to stay a secret after everyone saw us together – so shouldn't I just tell Mae and Serena up front? But then it would be like confessing to something that was honestly nothing and, like, what was I supposed to have done wrong?

I turned another corner and to my surprise I spotted Mae

slipping out of one of the small back offices – spaces that were more like box rooms than classrooms, usually used for pupils who needed to sit exams under special conditions.

'Hey!' I said, coming to a halt. 'What are you doing here?'

She was surprised to see me as well. 'Nothing. I had a one-to-one on my English paper, like I said.'

'In there?' I pointed into the poky room behind her, light barely leaking in from the dirty skylight in the ceiling.

'Yeah. It's quiet. And no one usually needs it.'

'Oh, okay. Did it go well? Hey – oops, you've got chalk on your arm.' I pulled at the sleeve of her school shirt, so she could see the deep pink smudge on her shoulder.

'Shit,' she said. 'Must have bumped the blackboard. Will you tell Ms Myers that I'm literally just coming? I'll need to get to the dorm and sponge it off. Say I had a meeting and I'm going to be late.'

'Sure,' I said. 'No problem.' Seeing Mae had set me off thinking about my lunch break with Alex and Victor again. It felt like it did when we broke the school rules and snuck out, but honestly, what had I actually done? Had lunch with two boys who had taken an interest, instead of spending the whole lunch break on my own? Still, I couldn't help feeling weirdly shitty about it.

'I'll make sure you don't get into trouble,' I told her.

We both ran off in different directions, guilt squeezing up in my stomach, thinking I could do her this small favour at least, and if she found out about me not sticking to the rules of our usual seating arrangements, I'd explain *they* had invited *me*, and what was I supposed to have done – just say no?

These thoughts were whirring through my head like the

machinery in Alex's camera, when I turned a final corner and ran slap-bang into Mr Witham.

The stack of workbooks he was carrying went flying.

'Shit!' I exclaimed, and then immediately, 'Sorry!' – both for crashing into him and for swearing in his face.

'That's okay.' He was smiling. I crouched down next to him to help scoop up the scattered books. 'Accidents happen,' he said. 'What were you running for?'

The class bell went, answering for me. I could feel the heat across my chest from where our bodies had collided. 'Because,' I panted, 'I didn't want to be late. But now I guess I'm going to be anyway.'

'Need me to write you a note?' he said, smiling. And the craziest thought flew through my head: *Is he flirting?*

I looked up at his handsome face, my cheeks as hot as that Bunsen burner. *Don't be ridiculous*. He must have been nearly twice my age. But he *was* cute. I handed him the last jotter.

'There we go,' he said, standing up again, the stack of workbooks reformed. 'Thank you, Carrie.'

I mumbled stupidly, 'You're welcome,' surprised for some reason that he'd remembered my name. Then I went on standing there, like I was waiting for him to kiss me or declare undying love or propose.

He raised an eyebrow and laughed. 'Well, run along then!'

As I slipped around him and scuttled away again, I thought the only thing that would have made it more humiliating would have been if Mae had witnessed the whole thing.

CHAPTER 16

Victor

2019

Twenty-two hours later, I found myself on a street in Monaco, staring up at a luxurious pink building. It was a gorgeous thing, set a few streets back from the waterfront, but towering high enough that guests would enjoy glorious views of the sea.

The glass doors of the entranceway swished open promptly, and inside it was blessedly cool, the sheen of sweat on my forehead and back quickly turning cold. The withdrawals had kicked in on the plane over: the cravings, the jumpiness, the sickly exhaustion, and I hadn't even been able to fly first class. I didn't have enough money left for that, so I'd just moaned away in cattle class. Never had I been more glad to get off a plane in my life.

'I'm here to visit a friend,' I told the concierge at the hotel's reception, after introducing myself by name. 'I believe she's staying here?' I gave him her full name, the one she hated: *Margaret*.

Carrie, I had tried a million times before I'd left, dialling the only number I had for her. As I pressed the call button over and over, the memories had come spooling: talking to her for the very first time, her American accent sharp in my ears; pulling her up the hill in the dark, both of us giggling as our feet slipped and slithered in the mud. Then other, darker memories: sneaking into her dorm room that second night, my hand over her mouth, trying to stifle her sobs . . .

But the number never connected, a total dead end. And then through my beer and coke haze I had stopped myself. What was I doing? I didn't know who had sent the email, but I knew one thing. Someone was fucking with me, and I needed to tread carefully. Not go throwing myself right into their trap.

I'd made myself stop again, and think. It had to be one of them: Serena, Alex, Carrie, Mae. No one else knew about it. Who then? It absolutely, definitely could be Carrie, even if right now she seemed to have dropped off the face of the earth. Alex was a no-go, but on the other hand, what about Serena? At school, she hadn't shied away from kicking a few hornets' nests and I'd never exactly trusted her to keep to her word. But Serena was famous now, a sporting celebrity; she had more to lose by coming clean than any of us.

Which had left Mae.

My old friend Mae.

Now in the glossy reception of the hotel, the concierge smiled warmly at me and said, with a charming French accent, 'Yes, of course, sir.' Clearly my name – or rather, my family's name – still had sufficient influence in the world. 'Right now, I believe she is out by the pool.'

Of course she was. Almost every one of her recent Instagram posts had included that pop of blue water. The concierge gestured, showing me the way, and now I could see a wide, beautifully tiled corridor leading outside, with the sparkle of clean blue water beyond.

'I can just go through?' I asked, like some peasant. These withdrawals were really messing with my head.

The concierge smiled again, as if thoroughly amused. 'Of course.'

I was desperate for a shower and change of clothes, a respite. I hated myself and I hated the world, and I would far have preferred not to meet Mae like this. But at least I had made it this far.

'Thank you.' I slipped a five-euro note across the marble desk. I may have been a sweaty, brain-addled mess, but I still knew how to diplomatically tip.

*

The heat blasted me all over again when I stepped outside and for a while the sunlight was too bright for me to see anything properly, let alone any*one*. Finding my sunglasses would require more energy than I currently possessed, so I stood on the hot tiles, letting droplets splash me as someone dived in, and scanned the area.

When I saw her, supine on a sun lounger, it was obvious. No one else could have been her and you couldn't mistake her for anyone else.

She was wearing a brilliant turquoise bikini, her skin bronzed to perfection, sunglasses covering her eyes, showing off the perfect arc of her cheekbones.

We'd kept in touch since school, two privileged lost souls,

both as bad as each other. Alex and Serena had always had their ambitions: Alex for film school and Serena for sailing. And Carrie had never moved in quite the same circles, but Mae and I had attached ourselves to each other as we drifted uselessly about the world.

My shadow passed across her as I came up and she immediately stirred and raised herself onto her elbow to stare at me over the rim of her sunglasses. Blue-green eyes and a mouth waxed red with lipstick that had barely smudged.

'What the fuck are *you* doing here?'

All at once, the adrenaline of the last two hours, two days, two weeks drained out of me, pummelled by all the bleak thoughts in my head. I felt weak as a kitten; I was desperate to sit down. It took everything in me to crank up a smile.

'Hello, stranger,' I quipped. 'Long time, no see.'

She rolled onto her side and snorted. 'Hardly.'

I tried to get an opening read on her, but my head was swimming and my eyes were still half-blinded by all this light.

Her bare shoulders glistened and the skin of her thighs glowed, reflecting shimmers from the pool. She was right: it was only a month or so since she'd last visited me in Madrid – a flying visit, one indulgent night out at the city's top restaurant, me trying and failing not to let my coke problem show.

She'd never mentioned anything about *speaking up* then.

'I was passing through,' I answered. 'Thought it would be nice to drop in on you in return.'

The heat was intense, sweat dripped off me, but – as always – she seemed utterly cool. She was good at that. As I remembered it, she always had been. I lowered myself onto an empty sun lounger, the pale wood burning the underside of my thighs.

A wrinkled towel was draped over the end, no doubt the property of one of the other guests.

'Missing me, huh? But how exactly did you know I was here?'

I held her eye, trying to make her feel like I was testing her even though in the end all I said was, 'You share ridiculous levels of information on the 'Gram.'

'Ugh. Whatever.' My lame challenge didn't seem to have fazed her one bit. '*I* was trying to get away for a bit. If you wanted to see me, Victor, you could have just called.'

Nearby, someone splash-dived into the pool again, spraying us with icy water. A couple of drops landed on the tanned skin of her forearm but she made no move to brush them away. Instead she pushed her sunglasses back up over her eyes and lay back under the sun.

If she was rattled by my surprise appearance, she was doing a damn good job of not showing it. Meaning what?

Meaning I didn't fucking know.

Just ask her, I hollered at myself internally. *You've come all this way, man, for God's sake, cut to the chase.*

But I didn't. Instead, I just sat there with this beautiful woman in this beautiful hotel, letting my suspicion and paranoia bloom.

A waiter drifted round the edge of the pool. Mae cocked her head to me. 'You want a drink? Let's go inside, shall we? Get out of this heat.'

She pushed herself up and shook out her hair. It was almost impossible not to look at her: she was like something out of a fashion magazine, in her bikini and sarong, the Prada sunglasses, those perfect lips. I noticed the other men and women round the pool watching her as I stood up too, aching muscles protesting, following her into the shade of the indoor bar.

She slipped up onto one of the barstools and I climbed up beside her, shoving my dusty travel bag out of sight at my feet.

'What's your poison this month,' she asked, pushing up her sunglasses. 'Beer? Spirits?' Maybe she was planning to get me drunk, film me, force me to confess . . .

'I'll have whatever you're having.'

The bartender came over. 'Two Pink Ladies,' she told him. His eyes flickered over me, assessing. *Touché*. Whatever.

'Certainly,' he said. 'Anything else, ma'am?'

'No. Thank you, Emile. That's all for now.'

'*Prego*.' He faded away, leaving the two of us alone again. My tongue felt like a wet sandbag in my mouth.

'So, where are you headed to?'

'Headed to?'

'You said you were passing through.'

My head throbbed. Did she really not know anything? 'Oh yeah. Right.' I gave a nervous laugh. 'Not sure yet. I just wanted to get out of town for a bit. Like you.'

She stared at me, eyes piercing. 'Really? How come?'

I looked back at her. 'Why d'you think?'

Emile approached, interrupting us, to deliver our drinks. 'Thanks, darling,' Mae said, smiling up at him. She lifted her shiny glass and clashed it against mine. 'Cheers, then,' she declared as the waiter slipped away. 'To old friends.'

The cocktail was pink and sticky and sickly with pomegranate seeds that caught in my teeth. But at least it was cold; at least it was liquid. Hair of the dog; maybe just what I needed. I drank down half of it in one go.

'It's divine here, isn't it,' she said. 'Just the right place to get away from it all. That is, until your washed-up friend decides he'll gatecrash.' She was grinning at me with a bite in her smile.

Fuck this. I was tired of this dance. If she wasn't going to come out with something, I would.

'You're right,' I told her, setting down my glass again. 'I wasn't just passing. I came here specifically to find out if it was you.'

She pulled back – and it did seem genuine. 'If *what* was me, Victor?'

I made myself fix my eyes on hers – both easier and harder since she'd lifted those damn sunglasses off. 'You know.'

She almost glared at me. 'Do I?'

I waited a beat, but I was no good at this. Never mind that I could hardly trust a single thought in my head right now, every staring contest we'd ever had at school – or since – she'd won.

'Fine.' I wiped the sweat from my palms and pulled my phone from the pocket of my shorts. I clicked the email app open and slid the phone across the bar to her, the fucked-up message displayed vividly on the screen.

Very slowly, Mae picked it up, blotting the screen with her sun-creamed fingers. She read it. My heart galloped miles before she set my phone down again.

'And – what? You think *I* sent this?'

'Well . . . Didn't you?'

'Really, Victor?' She fished in her bag and pulled out her own phone, clicking it open, just as I'd done, and slid it across the counter to me. 'I did not send that email . . . But maybe you did.'

I stared down. Her screen showed the exact same message, only with the name *Victor* swapped out for *Mae*.

'I didn't,' I said immediately, an instinctive response of self-preservation.

'You sure?'

'*Of course* I am. That would be ridiculous. Why would I send the same message to myself?'

'I don't know. Perhaps you've got a guilty conscience. Perhaps you did it in a . . .' she side-eyed me '. . . drug-addled haze.'

I shook my head and pushed her phone back to her. 'No,' I said. 'I definitely didn't.'

'Well, neither did I.'

I shifted on my seat. 'So who did, then?'

For all her seeming transparency, I still wasn't completely sure it hadn't been Mae, and that she wasn't enjoying having me here, watching me wriggle.

'Carrie? Serena?' Mae rested her fingers on the elegant stem of her cocktail glass, spinning it round and round. 'If it wasn't you then my money's on Carrie.'

My breath eased. We were on the same page. 'Mine too.'

I waited.

She took another long drink of her cocktail, then set it down and delicately wiped the smudge of pink foam from her lip.

'Uh . . . *Mae?*'

'. . . Yes?'

I shook my head in disbelief. 'Well, what are we going to do about it?'

'About what?'

I threw up my hands, almost knocking over my drink. 'About *this*! Forget about whether or not it's even Carrie. Didn't you see the article she attached? For heaven's sake, Mae, they're *digging up the land*.'

123

She didn't react in the face of my hysteria, just went on swirling her sickly pink drink.

'Mae?'

'Listen, Victor. You're spinning out right now, in your comedown. Chill out. Who would ever make the connection? Anyway, it was just a silly game.'

I stared at her again, in disbelief this time. Withdrawals aside, no way was this *nothing*. How could she remain so unruffled and so beautifully composed? She even yawned, her fingers pressing against her drink-stained lips.

'You've got to be joking,' I said.

She turned to look at me again now, fixing me with that dark turquoise gaze. I was aware of Emile, the bartender, hovering somewhere in the gloom behind my shoulder.

'Come *on*, Mae,' I hissed, 'we can't just do nothing . . .'

'I told you to chill *out*. You think I haven't considered all these eventualities over the years? One random email? It's our word against Carrie's. And the land? It was years ago. By now there'll barely be anything to find.'

I did my best to hold firm for one beat, two beats, even though by now my eyes were stinging and I was desperate to blink . . . Three beats. I gave up.

She took my arm and leaned against me, gesturing to the sun, to our surroundings.

'Look around you, Victor. Once you're over this . . . *blip*, you'll get it. You're telling me that we can't just "*do nothing*". And I am saying, trust me, Victor, that's exactly what we'll do. Absolutely nothing to jeopardize this.'

From: gifts@riddlingtonspa.com
To: katefallon@hotmail.com
Sent: 10.00am, 18/03/2012
Subject: Your Gift Card

We are delighted to welcome you to Riddlington Spa
Click <u>here</u> to download your gift card

Experience: Full pamper day
Expiry date: 17/03/2013

Message:
Happy Birthday, Kate!
I think you need some pampering! You've been working
super hard.
Hope you'll enjoy this birthday treat on me!
Xxx Mhairi

From: katefallon@hotmail.com
To: mhairi_1981@gmail.com
Sent: 11.34am, 18/03/2012
Subject: Your Gift Card

Aw, Mhairi,
Thank you so much for the lovely gift card! Probably
exactly what I need. It's been crazy (no pun intended!).
I never expected the practice to get so busy so quickly.
There's so much to keep on top of and even with
Sebastian's help, I lie awake at night thinking *did I miss*

something? I never want that to happen again; I couldn't bear it.

But it's knackering!

So I will absolutely enjoy this treat. Let me know if you – or Finn! – want to come along too!

Speak soon

Kxxxx

CHAPTER 17

Victor

2019

All right, maybe I was being a coward, but after a couple of hours in Mae's presence I also no longer seemed to care. The panic that had propelled me here floated somewhere in the distance, magicked away by Mae's charm and composure, and I was lying flat out on the huge white bed in her room.

I had my own room reserved in a more modest hotel downtown, but it was seven p.m. now and I still hadn't checked in. Mae had winced when I'd told her where I was staying – *why are you acting like a pauper, Victor?* – and the thought of going there was hardly appealing now. There was an unspoken agreement that I would spend the night here, maybe even a few days, giving myself some more time to dry out. Spreading my arms across the wide bed, my haze thickened: lethargy, indolence, dissolution.

'I need to start getting ready.' Mae was nudging my shoulder, shaking me awake.

I rubbed my gritty eyes and sat up. 'Ready for what?' I must have fallen asleep, since my Patek Philippe now read eight thirty p.m.

Mae told me she was going to a party, on the yacht of some guy she'd met, an investor in tech start-ups, kind of old but filthy rich.

'You should totally come with me.'

'Yeah . . . I didn't exactly bring clothes for that.' I plucked at my crumpled Gucci shorts and sticky T-shirt.

'Hmm.' Mae looked me up and down. She was wearing a thin blue robe – not one of the hotel dressing gowns, naturally, but something unique and elegant of her own. 'I'm pretty sure we can find you something.'

I'd seen clothes boutiques nearby; perhaps they opened late. I groaned, rolling myself up from the bed. 'I'll need to take a shower, at least.'

'Of course.' She gestured behind her. 'Be my guest.'

Mae stood aside to let me slip past her into the bathroom, and as I closed the door and locked it behind me, I could still hear her out there in the bedroom, clattering about. I had to laugh. Despite her own immaculate appearance, Mae's hotel room was a mess. She had left the *Do Not Disturb* sign on while she was out by the pool so housekeeping hadn't been in and the bed was a muddle of kicked off sheets and three-quarters of the room's surfaces were littered with dirty crockery. The room was huge – she'd secured a whole suite. Even for Mae, that was extravagant, and I reckoned there had to be someone else in the picture contributing to the cost.

I stripped off, catching sight of myself in the gilded bathroom mirror. Tall, broad, still well-toned despite my recent punishing behaviour. So different to how I'd looked as a teenager when

I was thin as a rake and people had described me as 'lanky' instead of 'slim'.

When I came out again, wrapped in a white terrycloth robe and steam-broiled, Mae was laying a set of clothes out on the bed.

'Where'd you get these?'

'The wardrobe,' said Mae. 'I have a . . . friend who sometimes keeps a change of clothes here. He's built like you. Tall and slim. I think these will fit.'

I looked at her appraisingly. 'A friend, huh?' Perhaps that explained the suite.

'He won't mind. I'll tell him that you needed to borrow something. Just put them on while I fix myself up.'

She was already shrugging herself out of her robe, revealing that tanned skin and the bikini again. Up close, she stank of sunscreen and bright girl-sweat, and for a moment I saw her as a teenager again, impulsive and mysterious and intense, then she slipped away and that moment passed.

I flopped on the sofa, not ready to get dressed yet. In my comedown, everything took twice as long as it should. Under the crockery on the coffee table, I found a magazine, folded open at an article featuring Serena Whittingham, our friend, who we'd just been talking about. The page had a wine stain on it, a ring of red cutting across her bronzed cheeks. Serena was a famous yachtswoman these days, garnering hundreds of thousands of pounds in sponsorship and featuring in lifestyle magazines like these. In the shot, she leaned from her craft at an impossible angle, abs like fists. She'd been ridiculously strong, even as a sixteen-year-old. They probably hadn't Photoshopped those muscles one bit.

I slid the magazine away again and gathered up the outfit Mae had offered me. In the bedroom, I pulled on the trousers and the shirt. She was right: these clothes fitted perfectly despite my long frame. Her friend and I must have matched inch for inch.

Once I'd done up the buttons and the fly I looked at myself again in the mirror. The shirt was an excellent colour on me: deep wine red against my tanned skin. I adjusted the cuffs and slicked my wet hair back with my palms. It had grown long over the last few months because getting it cut had been the last thing on my mind and now it framed my jaw like a mane.

'Not bad.'

In the bedroom mirror, Mae was outlined over my shoulder, in her blue robe again, blonde hair glistening wet.

I turned to face her. 'He has pretty good taste, your friend.'

She took a couple of steps towards me, coming right up close. She cocked her head, coyly. 'He does, doesn't he?'

Standing this close to her, my heart jittered, the remains of the coke oozing out of my pores. I still wasn't sure I entirely trusted her. Now that the shower had woken me up a bit, there was something about how she'd reacted when I showed her my message. Genuinely caught off guard; she hadn't sent it, I was almost sure of that. It was something else. It was this studied play of casualness. Too perfect. Too extreme, as if she was fighting tooth and nail not to let even a sliver of concern show. As if there was something sickly shifting underneath. Something she knew but wasn't saying.

Something she'd rather obscure and drown in a night of drunkenness and partying than tell me about.

Mae and I walked to the yacht from her hotel room, Mae dressed in a shimmering black jumpsuit, her eyes blackened with kohl to within an inch of their life. She truly was a sight to behold as she held my arm and teetered across cobbles on the way down to the dock.

The yacht, too, was almost grotesque in its opulence, moored at the far end of the marina. The other boats that cluttered the bay shrank in comparison. This craft was something else. A super-yacht.

'Who shall we say you are this time?' Mae asked as I escorted her down the curved harbour steps and onto the wooden pier that ran almost the whole length of the boat. It was close to ten p.m. and cooler now, but there was still light in the sky and the smell of salt and seaweed from the slapping waters below us caught in my nostrils: pungent and sexual.

I glanced at her. 'This again? Why not just say I'm your friend? And old school friend.'

She slapped my arm. 'Come on. That's boring. We never do that.'

She was right. I'd lost count of the number of lies we'd told when we went out together. There was that time at Le Gavroche when she'd taken the sommelier to one side to explain I was her gigolo. The episode in Montreal when I'd posed as a therapist eloping with his patient. That time at Hay-on-Wye Literary Festival when the two of us pretended to be brainwashed survivors of a cult.

'Come on.' She pouted, shaking my arm. 'Choose something, or I will.'

There was a steward in a bright white naval uniform to welcome us aboard. Mae fished in her clutch bag as we approached, pulling out the invitation card she'd been given. She handed it to the steward, her smile wide and red as she swayed on my arm. She'd had a drink before we came out; we both had. The Champagne bottle back in the hotel room was empty now, but I could still taste the sweetness on my tongue. I told myself I'd be fine without the cocaine.

'Welcome aboard, Ms O'Hara.'

O'Hara? I glanced at Mae; she was grinning and not meeting my eye.

'Sir.' The steward was nodding at me too. I was her plus-one, then. As a friend? As a lover? 'Enjoy your evening.'

'Oh, we will,' said Mae.

She was already dragging me towards another steward who was waiting to usher us up the flight of steps onto the deck. The shoes I was wearing – also from Mae's 'friend' – were beginning to pinch as I followed her up, groping at the handrail. There was music, lights, dozens of faces and I could feel eyes looking down upon us as we boarded, sizing us up.

'I'm Ms O'Hara tonight,' said Mae, 'and you can be my long-lost stepbrother: a fugitive, running from the law. We came across each other yesterday in the *piazza* and somehow recognized each other after all these years you've been in hiding.'

The fantasy cut a little close to the bone and I wanted to tell her to stop it, forget the silly games we used to play. But she was already dragging me onto the boat.

Waiters in penguin suits proffered trays of Champagne and platters of food. We each took a glass and wandered across the deck. There were old, white men with sinewy wives, young models dancing, and a Black contortionist surrounded by a circle of onlookers. I spotted a hot tub, adorned with women in bikinis. The whole thing felt kind of gauche and dated, but it was a decent enough setting to let your petty sorrows fly away.

'Let's get a real drink,' Mae said, her Champagne glass already half empty. The bar – one of them, anyway – was below deck, down a steep metal stairway in which the heel of Mae's stiletto shoe caught. She laughed and swayed as I helped her to free it, the tendons of her ankle hot under my grasp.

In the low-ceilinged cabin bar she made me do three shots of tequila.

The night began to grow blurry after that.

'Isn't this brilliant?' she squealed. 'Isn't this fun!'

And sure it was, or sure it was supposed to be, but I just couldn't get into it. Part of me just wouldn't cut loose. Usually, this would be exactly my scene. Music, alcohol, whatever party drugs you wanted. But I didn't have any drugs, and my thoughts were flapping like smothering, dark bats. *You're fucked. They're digging up St Michael's. Mae's got no answers. Look at her, hanging herself off some rich old guy's craggy neck. She doesn't know how to handle this. What are you doing here?*

Over the thumping music, I yelled to her that I was going up on deck, and made my way back up into the open where the air felt cooler.

From the deck, I could make out the lights of the harbour. We'd left the marina and were at sea. I breathed in and out, trying to slow down my hyper breaths and convince myself of what Mae had said to me: *Who would ever make*

*the connection? It was just a silly game . . . Trust me, Victor,
that's exactly what we'll do. Absolutely nothing.* And I wanted
to. Fuck, how I wanted to. We had got away with it back then
and for all these years, and I'd reconciled myself to taking that
shit to my grave. But now . . .

I pushed myself back from the railing, banging into a couple
behind me, staggering drunk. He was holding her up, half-
dragging her, laughing. They were both laughing, weren't they?
I scanned the deck for Mae. I'd told her exactly where I was
headed, but fifteen minutes had passed and she hadn't come
looking for me, so now we were separated on this hulking
yacht, with no rendezvous point and – I'd bet my last hundred
euros on it – if I called her she wouldn't answer her phone.

'Everything okay, sir?'

I turned to find one of the waiters at my shoulder, a look of
solicitousness on his face.

'Sure. Absolutely. Just drank a bit much.' The nausea was
building up as I said it. Jesus. My head reeled even though
I really hadn't drunk all that much, and my legs felt disconnected from my body. Fucking withdrawals. If I'd known they'd
be this bad I would have kept using.

'Perhaps you should sit down, sir.' He was probably right.

This waiter was handsome. Young, slim and blond. He
reminded me of – someone. I lowered myself onto one of the
deck chairs that scattered the deck, letting my head hang
between my knees.

'Can I get you anything – paracetamol? Water?'

I managed to smile up at him. 'Thank you. I think both . . .
would be good.'

'I'll be back shortly,' the waiter said.

'Thanks.'

While he was away I was violently sick over the ship's rail. Thank God, I felt a little better after that.

The waiter returned with two chalky tablets and a pint glass of water, and crouched beside me as, gratefully, I swallowed them down.

'What's your name?' he asked.

I wiped my mouth. 'Victor. I came here with a girl but now I can't find her.'

The waiter grinned. 'It happens.' He rose to his feet and dug in his pocket. 'I'm on my break,' he told me, pulling out a packet of cigarettes. 'Want one?'

I shook my head. 'Not right now. Maybe later.'

'Sure,' said the waiter, smiling at me. 'That would be nice.'

I smiled back, sitting upright in the seat now and turning my face to the inky sky. My heartbeat was slowing, flickers of calm washing over me. The waiter leaned on the rail beside me and blew a spiral of smoke into the dark. There were stars out, crystal shards on velvet, and I was fine; all was well.

Mae found us like that, stumbling up the deck in her stilettos. Her eyeliner was smudged and she was wearing someone's blazer over her shoulders.

'There you are!' she exclaimed. 'We should go.'

The waiter stubbed out the end of his cigarette. 'This your girl?'

'This is my—'

Mae grinned up at him. There was a feverishness in her manner, an instantly recognizable chemical high. Lucky her. '*This* is my missing stepbrother, Victor. He's been on the run for years, and yesterday, we ran *into each other*!'

'Oh,' said the waiter, grinning privately at me as I rolled my eyes. 'Well, nice to meet you both.'

'Victor. *Victor.*' Mae was dragging on my arm, heavier than ever. 'Victor, we should go.'

'See you again, maybe?' The waiter touched my arm.

'Sure. Thanks for the painkillers, and the water. And the company.'

Mae tugged at me. The waiter mock-saluted. 'Any time.'

I followed Mae back along the deck, down the steps and back towards the gangway. The boat was docking now in another marina, further along the coast. We'd have to find a taxi to get us back home. Looking at her properly I could see that Mae was pretty dishevelled. There was a red scratch down the side of her cheek.

'What happened?'

She grinned up at me, her pupils outsized. 'I did some dancing. I chatted to our host.' Her smile was lopsided as she looked down in surprise. 'I think I've still got his blazer.'

The yacht's huge gears churned as she slid into the port. 'Come on,' I said to Mae. 'Let's get your sorry ass home.'

*

Thirty-five minutes later, we were back in her hotel room. I pulled the covers over her where she had collapsed into bed. I'd managed to get her shoes off but that was all I could accomplish so she would just have to sleep in her jumpsuit, make-up still on, teeth unbrushed. I set a glass of water at the bedside and wished I had some more paracetamol to give her. I knew I'd need another dose for myself soon too. I clicked off the lamp, leaving her to sleep, taking a pillow to set myself up next door on the suite's sofa, but she caught me by the wrist as I turned from the bed.

'Victor?' she whispered.

'Yes, Mae?'

'You know . . . all that about St Michael's?'

It was like she was nicking my heart with a knife. *Now* she'd decided to bring this up?

'What about it?' I had to bend down to hear her properly. In the gloom, I could see that she had closed her eyes again.

'I never wanted to leave him. I didn't. When we realized . . . and then, we just kept going. It was terrible, Victor, that second night. You weren't there, and I never wanted to do that to our friend. I didn't want to. Please tell me you get that, Victor, right?'

Now I was the one who tried to shift away, mind racing. What did she mean about the second night?

She squeezed my wrist, pressing hard on the veins. 'Please, Victor. Tell me you understand that I didn't have a choice.'

What could I do? I was already complicit. Heart racing, stomach sickened, I smoothed her tangled hair back from her forehead.

Half of me wanted to yank it out from her scalp. Instead I placed a kiss there.

'Yes. Of course, Mae. I understand. Sleep tight.'

CHAPTER 18

Carrie

2003

It was late October when the girls started fainting.

One Thursday a week or so before Halloween, I was standing with Serena in the lunch queue, bouncing my tray against my leg, impatient. Mae was having a meeting with Ms Rowlins about head girl duties and I'd promised to try to save her some pudding. I was hungry and hot. We'd had PE that morning, burning off a load more calories. It was an unusually mild day for late October and the heating in the school was on full blast.

We were near the back of the line; at St Michael's the younger pupils were always fed first. At the front of the queue, Bryony Matthews was taking ages, peering through the glass counter, sizing up the lunch options – sausage, chips and beans. She was a skinny, red-headed kid, a third year with a weird flair for the dramatic, sometimes telling stories that bordered on outright lies.

The queue finally shuffled forwards as Bryony carried her loaded tray towards one of the tables. I watched with interest, wondering where she would sit. She'd fallen out with a couple of friends lately; God only knew what it was about this time. It was often her that friendship dramas centred around: fallings-out, arguments, someone bursting into tears. Her group were the ones I'd overheard on that very first day in the chapel, whispering something about a ghost, sticking pentagrams on Bibles, a strange, insecure, immature bunch, their reactions to things always silly and intense.

Bryony took a few steps across the dining room, towards the pack of her friends huddled down the far end. One of the girls who sometimes hovered on the fringes of that group got up and began to come towards her: maybe to welcome her, or maybe to tell her to go away. Bryony came to a halt, and stood there stock-still, a tight, blank expression on her face.

Two seconds passed . . . five, six . . .

Then she just keeled over.

Knees, hips, elbows hit the floor in hard succession. Sausage, chips and beans flew everywhere. The nearby girls shrieked; a boy yelled, 'Shit!'

Ms Kennedy, the art teacher, was the first one to get to her, descending with a handful of napkins to wipe her down. I set my still-empty tray aside on a nearby table and stepped forwards, drawn to the scene. Ms Kennedy saw me and briskly beckoned me closer.

'She's fainted. Listen, will you take her to the sick bay? You and Serena. I need to stay and supervise things here.'

I looked down at Bryony, slowly coming to, eyelids flickering dramatically, skin deathly pale.

'I'll make sure you still get lunch,' said Ms Kennedy, like that was the reason for my hesitation.

'Yes, of course.' Serena was next to me as well now.

'All right then, Bryony,' said Ms Kennedy. 'Can you stand?'

Between the three of us, we got Bryony on her feet. A janitor came along with a mop and Ms Kennedy shouted to the rest of the school to stop gawping. Once she was upright, Serena and I took Bryony by the elbows, one on either side of her. Her legs were still floppy, her feet tangling with themselves as we walked her along, out of the canteen and off to the sick bay.

'That was a wild one,' Serena said to Bryony as we navigated the corridors. 'Those baked beans went everywhere.'

'Sorry,' mumbled Bryony. 'I was . . . I was . . .'

'Doesn't matter,' Serena said, magnanimously – or bored already. 'We'll get you to the nurse.'

'What happened anyway?' I asked. 'Did you faint?'

Bryony shook her head adamantly. 'No . . . No, I didn't. I rose up in the light . . .' She tugged her arm free from my grasp and gestured upwards. 'I was lifted up by it, out of my body.'

Looking at me over Bryony's garish-orange hair, Serena rolled her eyes and mouthed at me: *drama queen*.

'There were hands on me,' Bryony continued. 'Hard, powerful hands . . .'

'Okaay,' said Serena.

We were at the nurse's office now. I gave the whorled glass of the door a sharp rap. When Nurse Lewis opened it we handed Bryony over. Then we waited in the corridor while Bryony was inside. The walls were thin and we knew we could probably hear some of what was being said.

'Have you eaten this morning?'

'Mm-hmm.'

'Are you on your period, perhaps? Is that it?'

'Uh-uh.'

'Let's check your blood pressure then and your pulse.' There came the rustling noise of the cuff and the pump. 'Well, that all seems normal. Did you bump your head or anything?'

'Don't think so. It just felt . . . very strange . . .'

When Bryony came out again, she was eating a Mars bar. Not anorexic then, I surmised. A fair bit of colour had come back to her cheeks.

'Are you all right now?' said Serena. 'Allowed to go back to class?'

'I think so,' mumbled Bryony. 'Nurse Lewis said I just fainted.'

'Yeah,' I said as we set off back to the classrooms, 'but what was all that stuff about *hands*?'

Serena caught my eye and shook her head. *Don't encourage her,* she mouthed.

'That was . . . That was just . . .' Bryony stuttered.

'Never mind,' I said. Serena was right. What did we care? Bryony was always making things up for attention and the whole thing was dumb anyway. 'You're fine now. Clearly you just needed to get your blood sugar up.'

So did I; thanks to Bryony, I was properly starving now. We walked her as far as her maths form, then left her there, looking forlorn, to join her classmates.

'Ugh,' said Serena as we headed back to get the lunch we'd missed out on. *'Lifted up by a light . . .'*

'I know,' I agreed, feeling the familiar thrill that came from siding with your friends. 'Like – give me a break.'

Later, Bryony told other people the same story. Insisted on it, although no one actually believed her. Given that she had been sent to the nurse, and enough people had seen her faint, they were willing to humour her for a bit at least. But behind her back, *attention-seeker* were the words that they whispered.

By suppertime, people were fast losing interest. Like, maybe it was supposed to sound mystical or spooky or something, or maybe Bryony *was* just trying to explain what she'd felt, but obviously it had just been low blood pressure or weird hormones or – more likely – a skipped breakfast.

Big deal.

Except that the next day another girl collapsed, and claimed exactly the same thing.

Text from: Kate
Sent to: Mhairi
11.29am, 27/04/2013

Oh my gosh, Mhairi! Does that picture show what I think it does?

Are you at home now?? I'm coming right over.

Text from: Mhairi
Sent to: Kate
16.09pm, 27/04/2013

Hey Kate,
Thank you *so much* again for the flowers. They are so gorgeous (Finn loves them too). Sorry for being a bit of a blubbery mess when you were over earlier. Guess the hormones are already kicking in. It feels overwhelming at times – in a good way – just so huge.

finn and i are going to have a baby.

!!!!!!!!

I'm so glad to have you as my friend. You always talk such wisdom and sense! Seriously. What would I do without you???

xxxx

From: sender@e-cards.com
To: katefallon@hotmail.com
Sent: 14.17pm, 30/04/2013
Subject: Mhairi sent you an e-card!

Mhairi sent you an e-card!
Click <u>here</u> to open.

Message:
Hi Kate!
Just want to send a HUGE CONGRATULATIONS on
securing your place on the US training programme. Can't
believe you get to go to Florida! It's super fantastic news.
(And also can't believe you'll be
away for two whole months!)

Xxxxx Mhairi
PS: Sorry this e-card is so naff!

CHAPTER 19

Victor

2019

After the yacht party, Mae took a whole day to recover. I left her to it, making the most of the pool, room service and the hotel bar on her tab.

When she finally pulled herself together, rolling onto the couch next to me in a thick fresh white robe, neither of us said a word about what she'd said the night before, as I'd tucked her into bed. I had no idea if she even remembered.

Instead, she told me that her friend – the one whose clothes were in her hotel-suite wardrobe – wouldn't be back for another two weeks and I was perfectly welcome to stay with her until then. I didn't know what else to do so I agreed.

Aware of my temporarily dire finances, Mae wouldn't let me pay for anything. She never seemed to pay for anything herself either; she had tabs everywhere.

One day became two, became three, became four. By now, I was pretty certain Mae hadn't sent the email, and we'd both agreed it couldn't be Serena; she'd just won silver in the Barcolana, for heaven's sake.

Carrie, then. Which meant Mae was right: it was only Carrie's word against ours. And who would believe *Carrie*? Last I'd heard from her, her life had been a wash out, moving from one poky flat-share in London to another and through a succession of menial jobs.

While Mae lay indolently by the pool, every so often I checked online for more news about the land, but there was nothing. *Chill out,* I told myself. *Forget it.* These things always moved ridiculously slowly, mired in red tape and bureaucratic delays. It'd probably be years before work even started and, even if they did eventually dig up the land and found something . . . well – so what?

Who would make the connection?

I rolled onto my back on the sun lounger and let the sun's rays sink through my itching body like a balm.

Because there was absolutely nothing to connect a single one of us to that.

Because other than memories and accusations and hearsay, there was *absolutely no proof.*

*

On the fourth night, Mae said she had a headache. 'Can you go out and amuse yourself tonight? I'm going to lie down.'

'Want me to get you anything? Food, drink, painkillers? I can call room service.'

'No, darling. I'm not hungry. I'm just going to sleep.'

'If you're sure. Want me to stay here with you?'

She waved a hand. 'No, no. Don't be silly. You go and have fun. I'd actually prefer to be alone.' Both of us knew the whole thing was a cover, but I let it slide and went out by myself, borrowing more of those handsome clothes from the wardrobe. Mae kept up the charade for me while I got ready, lying in the bedroom with the curtains closed and a sleep mask on.

She didn't stir as I took the spare room key and left, but as I walked along the corridor towards the elevators, I spotted the waiter I'd met that first day – Emile – quietly, surreptitiously making his way to her room.

Outside the hotel, I set off with no destination in mind at all. Free as a bird. This place was ridiculous, everything hyper-real, stacks of buildings like Lego towers, restaurant parasols like white sails, the foliage such a bright green it looked fake. I wandered down towards the waterfront, the air cooling now as the day moved into dusk. I was dressed in the same dark trousers I'd worn the first night, with a sapphire blue shirt that I left unbuttoned down to the middle of my chest. I felt light, buzzed, elated, even without the coke.

I stepped into a bar on the waterfront and used what little cash I had on me to buy a beer that was eye-wateringly over-priced. I sipped it slowly, watching the boats in the marina and the stars pushing their way out of the darkening blue sky. A slow wave of melancholy seeped over me. Mae and I were here in one of the world's most glamorous locations, but the state of both our lives was laughable. We'd gone out into the world as *alumni of St Michael's*, upper-class privilege, top-flight schooling to open all the doors. Now here Mae was, hawking herself out in one exotic location after another and me battling a coke habit that would utterly appal my dad.

I would fly home tomorrow, I decided abruptly. Back to Madrid and the realities of my life, with all of its problems. I'd got the coke cravings pretty much out of my system now; I'd get back to work and find some way to pay off my debts. I would get myself straightened out and throw myself into the family business. And I would figure out any St Michael's stuff with Mae from there.

My beer was finished now, and I wasn't going to waste my limited means on another one. I nodded my thanks to the barman and left my empty bottle on the bar. As I made my way out, another man got up to leave as well. I had vaguely clocked him coming in earlier and taking a seat near the back, keeping his expensive sunglasses on, even inside. I'd noticed him because we were both drinking alone. He was well-dressed enough: tanned skin, silk cravat, silver hair. But he was clearly almost twice my age. Ultimately, definitely not my type.

It was growing dark now, the city lights in full force. I headed away from the waterfront, and as I walked I sensed the same man behind me. I walked faster, keen to lose him; I didn't want him catching up with me, exchanging words, offering a cigarette, asking what was good around here . . . No thanks.

A few yards up, I spotted the entrance to a nightclub, seeped in bright pink light. I glanced over my shoulder where the man was still labouring up the street in my wake. Fuck it. I handed over the entrance fee for the club, emptying my wallet down to its last twenty-odd euros, and ducked inside.

Descending the stairs was like descending into a cavern. It was heaving, the ceilings low, the pink light more intense than ever. I pushed my way through the crush and found myself on the dance floor, packed in between twitching bodies, surrounded by body heat, sweat, sharp elbows. I wanted a drink, ideally a tall, icy glass of water, but it was so hard to get anywhere through this crowd. My body knew how to move in these kinds of places, but tonight my feet seemed gummed to the floor. Right behind me, someone shrieked and I felt a slosh of liquid down my back. The lights pulsed, strobing in time with the music. I began shoving at the bodies around me, jutting my elbows to carve a path.

The crowd squeezed more tightly and I shoved again, only for a hand to fall on my shoulder, gripping at my neck. I spun around, ready to lash out or kick or bite if I had to but when I clocked who was behind me, it was *him*.

'Hello, stranger.' He was grinning at me.

It was the waiter who had looked after me the other night on the yacht and as soon as I realized it, I leaned into him in a rush of relief and pleasure.

He put an arm round me. 'How are you doing?' He had to half-shout above the music. 'Did the paracetamol do the trick?'

I nodded, my cheekbone brushing his, breathing in the woody tang of his aftershave. 'Yeah, thank you. I'm feeling much better.'

'And your stepsister? She got home all right as well?'

'She's fine. It's hardly the first time I've had to escort her home,' I told him, letting my hand rest on his arm. 'But she's not with me tonight. She has a headache and had to lie down.'

The crowd surged, pushing us right up against each other; desire flickered all over my skin.

'Are you drinking?'

I shook my head. 'I just came in here to . . . get in off the street.'

'Right. Got you. But it's packed in here, isn't it? Too hot, too loud, too expensive . . .'

I smiled, then nodded, my heart pumping.

He put both hands on my shoulders, sending a delicious shiver through me as he leaned in to speak right in my ear. 'Shall we get out of here?'

*

We went back to his, me hastily texting Mae to say I was staying out. *Hope you feel better,* I wrote. *Sorry about your 'headache'.*

The waiter was called Matthias and he lived in a modern block on the Rue Bellevue. His apartment was tiny but cute; bijou. Far more homely than my place back in Madrid. I paced his living room, fiddling with books and knick-knacks from his shelves, while he fussed with spirits and mixers in the kitchen. I always got like this: flush with anticipation, while at the same time always trying to play it so cool.

Matthias fixed us a couple of pretty strong cocktails, then put a record on an actual vinyl player. I had no idea what music it was, just that it was something bassy and slow. *That* kind of music. I sipped my drink, stomach taut with nervy excitement, as I busied myself asking questions about his work and interests, though his answers barely penetrated my head. Eventually he made his way over to me and slipped his arms around my waist. I set my drink down and kissed him, blood racing.

I let myself stop pretending. He was gorgeous, beautiful: everything I needed that night.

CHAPTER 20

Carrie

2003

'Here! Look what I found,' said Serena. 'Honestly, it's proper weird.'

The three of us were in our dorm room, lights out because it was well after ten, but Serena and I both had our torches, even if they made us look like ghouls.

Serena was sitting cross-legged in pyjamas on her desk chair, a big fat textbook balanced in her lap. 'Look,' she said, stabbing her finger at a page. 'There's a whole section about it, right here.' She'd found this hardback in the school library: a fat old tome entitled *Psychological Phenomena and their Psychosocial Sequelae*, which was a god-awful title if I ever heard one. The front matter said it had been published in 1987, and the cover design was a sickly mixture of purple and coral pink.

She tilted the book towards Mae to show her, but Mae was busy brushing her hair, dragging a plastic hairbrush through a bird's nest of knots. She always had tangles because she went to sleep with it wet. Serena held out the book to me instead and I scooted over next to her to take it.

I scanned the close-printed text, turning the page over to read the paragraphs there as well. 'Huh,' I said. 'Spooky.'

'Not really,' Serena said. 'It's just psychology. My question is, do they know they're doing it? Not the girls in this book, I mean our girls: Bryony, Anna, Ava, all of them.' It was three days after Bryony, and three more girls had collapsed now. 'They could just be acting out, messing around. Or are they really sick?'

'I don't know . . .'

We had both been there when Bryony collapsed and I honestly didn't think she'd been faking. She had covered herself in baked beans. Who would humiliate themselves like that? The others though . . .

I looked back down at the old-fashioned text. Maybe it was just the others who were pretending. Anything to get some attention or special treatment or avoid lessons in this place.

Little shits . . .

So, maybe some of them were mucking about, but what if Bryony was . . . Was what?

I passed the book back to Serena and she hunched over it again, fascinated. Normally she was all kayak paddle angles and squat thrusts. 'You know, the girls in the second year are convinced it's poison. They've got a whole theory about the ink in those gel pens Bryony and her friends use. And then I overheard Ms Kennedy banging on about how indoor mould can make people sick and that there's black stuff in her art room, so maybe it's that. And then the third year boys are all saying they're just faking, and that only girls like Bryony could get away with stuff like that. Like – imagine if it was boys throwing themselves on the floor! But *anyway*, I think it's definitely this.' She tapped the page again. 'Don't you? Although you'd think this sort of stuff would have died out in the Fifties. Back when girls were repressed and uneducated.'

'Yeah,' I said. 'Go figure.'

Across the room, Mae went on with her brushing. *Sccritch, sccritch, sccritch*. I lay back on Serena's bed, one hand on my stomach and one on my heart. I could feel it beating in there: ba-doom, ba-doom. I ran through the text of the article again in my head. There were pictures too, grainy black-and-white photographs of schoolgirls at some nineteenth-century educational institute that once upon a time could have been our school. *Mass hysteria*. The book said someone's physical symptoms or behaviour could 'psychologically infect' those around them, spreading like a contagion through a tight-knit social group. According to the book, that was what was going on here: a *psychosocial event*. The dizziness and fainting was *psychosomatic* – physical, yes, but caused by the mind.

Unless, like the boys said, those Fainting Girls down the corridor were just playing a prank, perpetrating some hoax for the fun of it.

There was no reason to imagine something paranormal or freaky. Victor and Alex had dismissed the idea when I'd let the thought slip to them, and now I was glad I hadn't voiced anything like that to Mae or Serena … and yet I still couldn't stop thinking about what the first girl, Bryony, had said.

It was like I floated right up out of my body . . .

Mae stopped brushing and the room suddenly fell silent. 'You know what it reminds me of,' she said.

I rolled on my side to look at her. 'What?' I was glad she'd finally joined in our conversation; she'd been weirdly preoccupied and aloof all night.

'That game,' she said. '"*Light as a feather, stiff as a board*".'

As soon as she said the words, the memory was there: a strange mix of hazy and visceral, like it had always happened outside our daylight awareness. That universal game that ten-, eleven-, twelve-year-old girls played at slumber parties or in a hidden corner of the playground. Making your best friend lie on the ground, school skirt rising up her thighs, hands crossed over a budding chest. You all tried to lift her up, clumsy hands grappling under her thighs and shoulders only reinforcing how heavy she was and how impossible she would be to lift. And yet, lo and behold, after you said those power-infused words, with just a skinny forefinger from each of you, you could pick her up.

Light as a feather, stiff as a board.

'Yeah,' I exclaimed. 'I remember.'

'You had that in America too?' said Serena.

I nodded. 'It was weird . . . Boys could never do it.'

'Yeah, it was just us girls . . . And Ouija boards – did you ever use them?' Serena was off now. 'I swear, it would move when none of us even touched it. And then there was, like, *Candyman*. From that film. Where you repeat that line in the mirror five times. I never, *ever* did it.'

I knelt up on Serena's bed, holding the torch right under my chin. 'What about summoning the devil by saying the Lord's prayer backwards?' I made my voice growly. '*Nema reve rof dna won sruoy era yrolg eht dna rewop eht modgnik eht rof.*'

Serena shrieked and scooted away, giggling. We were on a roll now. I tickled her feet and she shrieked again.

'The game *I* remember . . .' said Mae, jolting me as she

tossed her brush down and it clunked against Serena's torch, '. . . was where you stand against the wall and someone presses on your chest.'

'Huh?' said Serena. 'Which one was that?'

But I knew. 'You hyperventilate then get your friend to press on you.' I rubbed the heel of my hand against my sternum, feeling the ladder of bones there. 'It makes you black out.'

'Oh yeah!' said Serena. 'They banned it at my old school. It was wild. One moment, you'd be standing against the wall with them pressing on you, then you'd feel dizzy, see that black curtain and then you'd just—' she snapped her fingers '—go. Next thing you know, you're coming to on the floor with everyone gawping at you.'

'I remember one friend,' Mae said slowly, 'who was out for, like, ten whole minutes. We honestly thought we'd have to call an ambulance. Tell her mum.'

'Shit,' Serena said. 'She was okay in the end, though, wasn't she?'

''Course she was. She was fine. When she woke up, she said it had been like falling into a beautiful sleep.'

*

The teachers were trying to stop us talking about it. So of course we talked about practically nothing else. Especially after another girl, Polly, fainted – or collapsed, levitated, whatever. So now there were five of them, and the *psychosocial contagion* was threatening to take down the whole school.

That night, Mae, Serena and I snuck out again, back to the hollow up and over the rise. I found myself imagining bringing

Alex and Victor here (I still only hung out with them in the break times when I would otherwise have been alone). Or maybe I'd arrange it so it was just me and Alex coming here in secret, at night . . .

We were talking about the Fainting Girls and *light as a feather* again. We'd get onto another topic – whether Serena should take the Pill to fix her erratic periods; the fact that a boy in third year had called a first year girl a cunt – but the conversation always seemed to veer back again. We were smoking weed, as usual. A joint each this time; we were high.

'That was the thing,' said Mae. 'It was like a total blankness.'

I was lying on my back, not really following what she was saying, watching the branches above write words. *Loves you, loves you not, loves you* . . . I blew my smoke up to add a full stop.

'Sometimes,' I heard Mae say, 'sometimes, I wonder what it would be like to black out like that, whenever you wanted. Just step out of everything. No thoughts, no feelings.'

'Uh . . .' Serena said – or was that a leaf speaking? 'I guess.'

Like we'd been telecommunicating, we all fell silent. Then, maybe it was only a sprinkle of paranoia, but I got this weird feeling we were tiptoeing round something. I didn't know what it was – my mind kept picturing a blue, Dumbo-style elephant – but it was like hovering in the moment just before someone says: *I dare you.*

I pulled myself to a sitting position, slid over and put my head down in Mae's lap.

'It would be kind of . . . peaceful, don't you think?' she murmured.

She patted my head and I mumbled, 'Maybe.' *This* was

peaceful. This was really nice. But even as I thought that, images of my stupid parents came swimming up. I sat up and shook my head, trying to get rid of them; but that only seemed to make them worse.

I could see them, bright as day, right in front of me – a zoetrope of all those incidents I tried so hard not to think about. The parts of their marriage they never showed anyone, the memories I'd tried to bury down deep. They weren't just yelling in those memories, they were fighting. In those times, they were like animals, beasts. Physically tearing at each other, and I'd run to my bed and pretend I was dreaming, just having a nightmare, but experiencing the true horror all over again when my dad showed up the next morning with thick scratches down his face, my mother with finger marks on her neck . . .

I could feel Mae's hands on my shoulders. 'It's all right, Carrie. Go easy.' Like she was talking to a wild bird or a horse or a cat.

'I don't feel so good, Mae.'

'I know, Carrie. I know. But I know a way to make us feel so much better. Better than this crappy stuff we smoke. Something that makes it so nothing hurts, anywhere. And everything horrible just goes away.'

'Like . . . you mean . . .' said Serena, slurring, dumbly stoned, 'the fainting game?'

Mae's laugh bubbled up like a silver stream into the sky. 'No. Not that. That's for kids.'

'All right,' Serena said. 'Then . . . what?'

Mae just smiled. 'You'll see.'

*

The three of us were still kind of high the next morning. I could tell from the size of my pupils in the mirror and the floaty feeling that made my hands seem big and far away. No one noticed though, they were too preoccupied with the Fainting Girls.

That evening my stepmother Valerie called and suggested she visit. She said my father might be able to get away for a few days, too. 'We miss you!' she said. 'It would be lovely to see you! Even if it's just me, and your dad can't get away.'

She sounded bright and enthusiastic on the phone, but I hesitated. 'Are you sure? It's a really long way.'

'Well, we'd both love to see you. We've been thinking of you lots.'

'Aw, thanks,' I said brightly. 'I've really settled in here. I'm doing well in my classes, getting fresh air and exercise, sleeping fine.'

'Well, sweetie . . . that's great.'

The distance was working for me, I realized. It *had* been a good choice to pick a school all the way up here. I liked it. I liked being away from everything back home. I liked leaving the rest of my life far away.

'I've made friends too,' I went on. 'Two girls, called Mae and Serena. And there are a couple of nice boys in my year, Alex and Victor, who I've got to know too.'

Suddenly I knew I didn't want her and my dad to come. I didn't want to deal with the clash of my two worlds. I wanted to preserve the bubble around me, where I didn't have to think about my mum or dad, all of that. I wanted to be the girl who had friends like Mae and Serena, who regularly hung out with the boy she had a crush on, and who snuck out at night and smoked weed in the woods.

'Listen,' I told Valerie. 'It would be lovely to see you, but the Christmas holidays aren't that far away. Why don't I just see you and Dad then?'

'I mean, of course . . . If you'd prefer that, that's fine. But honestly, Carrie? I mean – are you sure?'

I did hesitate again, just for a moment. Out of all the adults who'd been in and out my life, Valerie had always been the nicest. And at the end of the day, I was still just sixteen. Someone who still – sometimes – should have had parents around.

But then I heard my dad yelling in the background. '*Valerie? I need a hand, darling; what are you up to? Can you come here?*'

'It's fine,' I repeated cheerfully, letting the conversation wind up. 'Don't worry about me. I'll see you at Christmas. Honestly, Valerie, I'm having the best time.'

From: katefallon@hotmail.com
To: finn_strachan@me.com
Sent: 09.12am, 04/05/2013
Re: HAPPY BIRTHDAY!

Hey Finn,
Happy 38th birthday!

I hope you're having a lovely day and I'm really looking forward to seeing you and Mhairi for drinks tonight.

I know I tell you this all the time, but I want you to know how much it means to have you as my friend.

I wasn't sure what to expect when Mhairi first introduced us, but you were so thoughtful and I could see you adored her. I knew right away you'd be great together – and I got a new friend out of it too!

Please know that I'll always be there for you (and for Mhairi). You mean the world to me and here it is in writing so that you know when I say it after a few drinks it's TRUE ☺

Here's to many, many more birthday celebrations!

All my love
Kate xxx

CHAPTER 21

Carrie

2003

'He says they're a bit like Ecstasy,' Mae said. We were watching *Hollyoaks* in the upper common room, just the three of us. 'Except these pills are better. Clean, and totally legit.'

I shuffled down on my beanbag, focusing on Ali getting all suspicious about a bruise on Liz's face.

Mae was explaining about *legal highs*. She said that's what she'd been talking about the other night, and she could get some from the same guy she got the weed from. I hadn't done anything like that before, but it couldn't be wrong if it was legal? No worse than weed, anyway.

'And,' said Serena, 'unlike weed, it doesn't get stuck in your hair.' She fiddled with an ash-blonde strand. 'What if I had to get tested for a competition?'

Mae rearranged her slim legs on the sofa. 'Exactly.' She turned to me. 'Carrie? You're very quiet.'

'Am I?' Before Mae mentioned the drugs I'd been thinking about how weird things had been at St Michael's lately.

How distracted and flustered all our teachers seemed. How everyone's behaviour generally seemed more out of control.

Mae leaned down from the sofa and slid her hands jokingly around my neck to give my head a shake. 'You're not going to blab on us, are you?'

I righted myself on my slippery seating, wriggling out from under her hands. 'No. Of course not. It sounds fun. Count me in.'

*

It *would* be fun. An experiment. And I liked what Mae had said: *It makes it so nothing hurts and everything horrible just goes away.* She said it would be easy to get hold of; she just had to arrange to meet up with the weed guy, in town. It wasn't as if we were locked up in the school. There were trips and excursions and we were allowed to go into town at the weekends. The school minibus would drop us off and pick us up a few hours later. It was about a twenty-minute ride.

The town was tiny and the shops were rubbish. Mostly you'd end up just walking up and down the depressing high street, eating a packet of soggy chips and then getting cold while you waited for the minibus to take you back home. Still it was better than being cooped up in the dorm or the common room with nothing much to do but watch another rom-com on DVD.

That was how Mae had met Luke and got talking to him, hanging around town one Saturday. Now we'd just have to wait till the next weekend for her to hook up with him. The three of us would have to be patient until then.

On the Wednesday, Ms Rowlins caught me looking 'peaky'

– Jesus, what a word – and I told her I was worried about the Fainting Girls; that was all. It wasn't a total lie. It *was* on my mind . . . I kept thinking about that very first time we'd snuck out, and Serena and Mae had shown me the door that was always unlocked, with no key.

Like anyone could get out. And pretty much anything could get in.

Something had snuck into the bodies and minds of those girls, and nobody seemed to know what it was. Now I couldn't help feeling like all the St Michael's rules and regulations that were meant to protect us had had holes in them all along . . .

Ms Rowlins patted me on the shoulder with her tubby hand. 'You just come see me if you ever need a chat.'

I didn't, obviously. We never told the teachers anything. But the truth was, the girls' behaviour *was* disturbing. Especially when, two days later, it happened during prep – when I was the oldest pupil there and Ms Jefferson had been called out of the class, leaving me temporarily in charge.

I had a headache and maths homework, and the numbers were swimming about on the page. To be honest, I was probably just knackered. I still wasn't used to the school's crazy timetable, and the late nights with Mae and Serena meant I wasn't really getting enough sleep. I pressed my pen to the paper to help me focus.

'Carrie?'

A girl's voice. Looking over my shoulder from where I was sitting at the front, all I could see were rows of pale faces. Almost all of the pupils in this prep class were boys; pimply, obnoxious boys, and only two girls, and I was struggling to pick the female speaker out.

'Carrie?' the question came again.

'Yes?' I twisted around properly and could finally make out who was asking. A girl called Frances with shiny black hair. 'What is it?'

'It's so stuffy in here. Can we—'

But before she could say anything else, another girl – Ava – got to her feet. I thought she was coming to the front to ask me something as well.

Instead she got to her feet and just stood there.

A cold wave came over me. 'Oh no.' I got to my feet too, my legs tangling in the legs of my desk. 'Ava, not again – oh no!'

Too late. Her legs crumpled; ring binders and coloured pens went tumbling off her desk. I wasn't fast enough to get to her before she hit the floor. Unlike the other girls – Anna, Cynthia or Polly, for example, who by all accounts sank to the floor in theatrical swoons, cautiously enough that there never seemed to be any real danger of them hurting themselves – Ava had gone down like the felled stag I'd once seen in a documentary about deer culling.

I crouched down beside her and shook her gently. 'It's fine,' I said to the rest of the class, even though I was freaking out inside. 'She'll be fine.'

There was a scraping of chairs as the whole class crowded round, peering down, gawping. I fumbled to pull down Ava's kilt to cover her; it had ridden up almost to the tops of her thighs, where – for a moment – I thought I glimpsed purplish bruises.

'Get water!' someone shouted, dramatically.

'A wet paper towel!'

'Open the window!'

They were jostling each other, giddy on the drama; giddy at seeing one of their own in such a state. It was comic almost. A *St Trinian's* scene.

The door of the classroom clicked open and our supervising teacher, Ms Jefferson, was back. 'What going on here?'

'It's happened again, Miss! Ava's had another fainting fit!'

I could have sworn Ms Jefferson let out an actual sigh. 'Everyone back to your desks. Let me see, now. Are you all right, Ava?' The impatience in her tone was clear.

'Come on,' I said to the shaky girl at my feet, suddenly so aware of how vulnerable she was, half unconscious, sprawled out on the floor like that. 'Come on, Ava, can you get up?'

She managed to tilt her head to look at me. With a shock I saw the size of her pupils: freakishly, morbidly large. I jerked back. Her mouth was moving; she was trying to say something. I was suddenly so aware of the sweaty, pimply boys crowding around her. I thought of the kinds of comments St Michael's boys shouted in the corridors, the gestures they made behind the younger girls' backs, the crude graffiti I sometimes glimpsed in their notebooks . . .

'What is it?' I whispered to Ava, shielding her with the bend of my body, leaning down to her until her lips were almost touching my ear. 'What do you need?'

But all I could make out was: *'Please may . . . please may . . . please may . . .'*

*

One week later, Mae got the pills for us, heading off to meet the guy who'd supply them while we distracted Ms Myers with stupid questions about an upcoming test.

One day later, we snuck out again at night.

We went up the rise and to the woods, like always. It was a dank, cold night; we were midway into November by now.

We arrived in the hollow with the rocks and upturned logs, and our joint butts on the ground. We'd got lazy with burying them, assuming no one else would come up here, but before we started that night, Mae made Serena and me join her in scraping up the earth with the toes of our shoes to cover over any incriminating evidence. We stamped the earth down hard on top of them, extinguishing any last sign.

'Good,' Mae said, like she was able to breathe a little more easily.

There was a pause then, like none of us was quite sure how to move the thing forward. Eventually, Mae plumped herself down on her usual rock and dug in the pocket of her thick puffer coat – because she had been sensible enough to dress warmly. I shivered in my thin Topshop jacket. Above us, in the treetops, something crashed about. A crow, probably. We were used to the night-time noises by now; they didn't bother us. I imagined bringing one of the younger girls up here with us. Jesus, we would be able to scare the living daylights out of her. I almost laughed out loud at the thought of it. Tempting, but it would probably only exacerbate the fainting fits.

Mae was holding out a crumpled see-through plastic bag.

'That's it?' I couldn't help blurting out. She could at least have found a nice box to put the pills in or something. Seeing the white tablets bunched up in a crumpled plastic wrapper made me feel like we were just junkies. When it was supposed to be cool and exciting.

'It's fine. Luke said we should only take half to begin with,' Mae said, misunderstanding my exclamation. She tugged open the bag. There were two pills inside. Two pills to split between the three of us. Plus half extra . . . for another time.

I noticed then that her hands were shaking. Her voice was tight, too, and I realized she was nervous in a way I'd never seen her before.

Carefully, I took the bag of pills from her. Someone needed to take control here, and of the three of us, I was the best at science, chemistry, all that stuff. I tipped the two pills out of their wrapper. The tablets were chalky white and plain. Nothing like the smiley faces you saw in textbooks, accompanied by the warning to 'Say no to drugs'. You could have easily passed them off as paracetamol. A good cover story, should Ms Rowlins ever confront us.

I studied them for a moment, wondering if these plain little tablets really could do everything Mae had said. I hadn't realized how much I wanted it until we were here. The weed was fine, but sometimes when we were high, bad memories would come back. I didn't want that. I wanted to feel blank and happy. This is what Luke had promised us with these.

'Here.' I broke one of the pills in half – it split easily, neatly – and I held out the semi-circular fragment to Serena, who was sitting leaning against her favourite rock. I handed the second half to Mae, then split the other pill and slipped the remaining half into the shallow pocket of my jacket. 'For another time,' I said, to reassure Mae. There would be no cheating each other here.

I curled my clammy hand round my dose.

'Ready?' said Mae.

The fragment of tablet had an acidic, bitter burn as I swallowed it down dry. Stupidly, none of us had thought to bring any water. For a moment, I wondered if they were paracetamol after all, and that all I'd get out of this wild experiment was a little respite from the period cramps I was having. For two minutes, three, there was nothing. Just us, and the woods and the dank cold and my tiredness and the bird – or whatever it was – still crashing around the treetops above.

It could have been any one of us, but it was Serena who went first. One moment she was sitting propped against her rock, hunched over, hands tucked in her armpits to keep warm, scuffing the ground with her toe where the joint butts were buried, in danger of unearthing them all over again.

And the next, she had slipped sideways and onto her back on the ground, head lolled to the side, cheek against the cold earth, arms flung out like a rag doll that anyone could pick up and play with.

Floppy as a Fainting Girl.

I locked eyes with Mae, but before I could move towards our friend, it happened to her, and then me too. One moment I was there and the next, I was gone. The world rose up and enveloped me, melting like caramel. The edges of everything became lace, crepe paper, sea mist. I inhaled and everything fell apart, like candy floss dissolving. Everything was soft and slipping, sliding apart from itself, and everything was beautiful and boundless and there was no cold, no weight, no pain, just everything spilling open in an exquisite, syrupy haze.

From: katefallon@hotmail.com
To: mhairi_1981@gmail.com
Sent: 04.03am, 29/05/2013
Subject: I've arrived!

Hi Mhairi!
I've arrived in Florida! The flight was a nightmare
(big delays at Heathrow), but we made it in the end.
Our Airbnb is lovely and training starts in earnest
tomorrow. Wish me luck!
　　How are you getting on? How was the scan?

Xx Kate

From: mhairi_1981@gmail.com
To: katefallon@hotmail.com
Sent: 09.25am, 29/05/2013
Re: I've arrived!

Hey Kate!
So glad you got there safely (and sorry about the
delays). Send pictures, please!! Is it hot there? Hope
you're not too jet-lagged. (I thought you'd been up
stupid-early from your email, until I realized – duh – the
time difference!)
　　I hope the training is good and not too intensive.
You're going to be so cutting-edge!!
　　Yep, we had the 18-week scan yesterday! Everything
was fine with the little 'un (phew!). I'm still feeling pretty

weak and queasy, but fingers crossed it'll settle down soon. Finn has been great, sorting everything out and cooking for me. He makes me lie in front of the TV when I get back from work (which I am more than happy with!) and gets on with everything. He's so excited (excitable?!). Spends hours looking at buggies and cots on the Internet and making 'favourites' lists of all the accessories we'll need.

Bless.

Good luck for tomorrow, and send those pictures!
Xxx Mhairi

CHAPTER 22

Carrie

2003

Mae and I were crossing the lawns from the side of the school, coming back from hockey practice, when the psychologist arrived.

It was late afternoon by then, the low sun sharp and bright. We'd been tasked with packing up the nets, so we were last to leave the pitch. We were muddy and chilly, and Mae was sporting a bruise where one of the boys had bashed her thigh with his stick. We had to play with the boys because there weren't enough girls our age to make even half a side. Later in the practice, I'd snuck up and bashed him back – a little bit higher than his thigh.

I figured out who she was as soon as we saw her; the school had been expecting her for days. Since the episode I'd witnessed with Ava, things with the Fainting Girls had only got worse. The school hadn't informed our parents or guardians yet, and we were being cautioned not to *spread rumours* when we didn't *have all the facts*. But we knew there was a total of seven girls affected now: Bryony, Anna, Ava, Cynthia, Polly, Stephanie and Faye. Most of them were from the same loose friendship group, plus two of them – Stephanie and Faye – from the year below.

A few days might go by without any incidents and we'd think that maybe, finally, it was over, burning out as mysteriously as it had caught alight. Then, for no reason, it would happen again. By now, all of them had fainted at least once. Bryony – the ringleader, as we had started to think of her – had had four attacks.

And still she was talking about how *there were hands on me, I'm out of my body, I'm floating up towards the light*.

Alex tried to film a collapse – to *aid with diagnosis*, he tried to convince me, even though it was obvious he just wanted something dramatic to record – but he never found himself in the right place at the right time. The one time he did manage to capture an attack – one of Ava's on the outdoor netball court one evening – the footage came out so blurred and grainy it was like some obstructive spirit had got behind the lens: Alex had got the wrong settings for the light conditions and you could hardly tell what was going on at all.

But maybe this psychologist would get to the bottom of it.

The psychologist looked thin and nervous – and *young*; she couldn't have been more than ten years older than we were. Still, she'd dressed the part: all professional with her black briefcase and dark grey trouser suit (from Next, I reckoned).

'Come on,' I said to Mae, pulling her in the side door as the psychologist disappeared in through the main entrance.

'What?'

'Come *on*.' I tugged her after me and we slid along to the offices as quietly as we could in our cleats, to listen at the headmistress's door. If one of the teachers came along, we would tell them we were looking for Ms Rowlins or Mr Witham because there was a timetabling error on the prefect rota. (That was true: Serena had complained about it.)

We pressed our ears to the door.

'. . . talk to them,' our headmistress Ms Dunham was saying. 'Individually, or if you see fit, in a group.'

'Yes. Of course. May I just ask . . . have any of the girls so far offered any insights?'

'No. At least . . . No. When we've asked them, they say they feel "dizzy" and "light-headed" and then "everything goes black".'

A rustling of papers. 'In the referral letter, the school's doctor suggests it might be primarily anxiety.'

'That's right.'

'Which can of course sometimes result in dizzy spells.'

'Indeed.'

'Well . . .' A pause. More rustling. 'Do they have exams coming up? Might that be something that's causing them stress?'

'No, not this year. Though, naturally—' here I could picture Ms Dunham pertly smiling '—they still do work very hard.'

'Yes. Of course.' Another pause. 'And you've done the physical monitoring. The doctor said that was all okay?'

'Yes. Dr Sanderson has checked all the girls very thoroughly. Bloods, blood pressure, weight, iron levels . . .'

'And there were no anomalies there? Nothing that would explain their symptoms?'

'Dr Sanderson assured me the girls' measurements were all within the normal range. As his referral says, he didn't find anything physically wrong with them. He suggested we consider psychological input instead.'

'Yes, absolutely.' The psychologist's voice was unnaturally high. 'I'm glad you contacted us and glad to see how we can help. It's good that you've screened for any physical factors; that's always important to rule out before considering psychological causes, but then you know the connections between mind and body are much stronger than you'd think.' She was rambling now. 'Even when there are emotional causes, it doesn't mean the physical symptoms aren't real . . .'

I turned to Mae, pleased to hear our number-one theory confirmed. *Psychosomatic,* I mouthed to her, smugly enjoying the technical word. Then I whispered, 'Serena and her textbook were right.'

Mae nodded, but my words didn't seem to register.

'I'd like to talk to other pupils and staff too. It all helps me put a proper understanding together.'

Mae was chewing at her fingernails. I pulled a silly face and gave her a nudge so that her hand fell from her mouth. She frowned back.

In the office, Ms Dunham and the psychologist were still talking. 'Of course . . . I know you'll need to meet the girls, but what are your initial thoughts about . . . treatment?'

A rustle of papers again, like the psychologist was trying to find the answer in her notes. 'I was thinking perhaps some anxiety management skills? We can do that in a group. Plus ideally some individual sessions, to discuss anything that's particularly troubling them.'

'Probably in a group would be better,' Ms Dunham said briskly. 'With a teacher present too, of course. Not least as . . . I do wonder whether it isn't all just a game? After all, it's very disruptive. The girls must realize that. Perhaps it's entertainment to them. A way of . . . oh, you know . . . being provocative. Some of these girls have a . . . flair for the dramatic.'

When the psychologist next spoke again her voice was less steady. 'Collapses carry a risk of significant injury, Ms Dunham. Bruising, joint sprains, head injury at worst. So, even if it is just to gain attention, I'd be concerned they're choosing such a dangerous way to do that.'

'Come on,' said Mae.

'What?' She was pulling at me, trying to tug me away. 'Why?'

'We've heard enough. They'll be coming out any second.'

To me it seemed they were right in the middle of it. But Mae's face was unusually pinched and I had never seen her looking like that, so I didn't argue.

'What?' I said again, wriggling away from her.

'That psychologist—' said Mae. 'She wants to stick her nose into everything. All that about anxiety management, group therapy. Instead of giving them even more attention, that psychologist should be calling their bluff.'

'She's just doing her job. It's not like she's going to find out about—'

Mae turned on me. 'Isn't she?'

I stopped, catching sight of my white shirtsleeve, blotched with bright red where Mae had touched me.

The mark bloomed there, like a little red warning sign. Mae had been chewing her thumb hard enough to draw blood.

CHAPTER 23

Finn

2019

To my amazement, Sebastian actually left a voicemail on Mhairi's landline, the fake answering message she'd recorded convincing him it was the Coroner's Office he'd reached. In his voicemail, he explained who he was, said he had struggled to reach Caroline Greaves himself, but that he was happy to help in any way he could.

'*I called the landline number she'd given,*' he said. '*Her flatmate said she'd gone to stay with a relative. Here are all the further contact details I have.*'

Then he listed Carrie's mobile number, her email, her vacant residential address and the details of her emergency contact: a stepmother named Valerie Greaves. Sebastian gave us all of it.

I couldn't believe we had all this information in our hands. It was as though we didn't need to make a choice anymore, just follow the path that was spooling out for us. A Yellow Brick Road leading to – what?

Actually, leading nowhere, it seemed. The phone number

he'd provided rang and rang then disconnected. Her flatmate said the same thing – '*she's staying with a relative*' – and when we pressed her for specifics, she didn't know, or wouldn't say. The email we tried to send immediately bounced back. Just like for Sebastian, our efforts to reach Carrie came to a dead end. It was as though she had deliberately dropped off the map, chosen to remove herself from the world.

Those obstacles could have been a reason for us to stop and pull back. Instead, Mhairi and I pored over the final piece of information Sebastian had unwittingly given us: Carrie's emergency contact. There was no phone number for this woman – Valerie Greaves. No email either. But there was an address.

'She lives in Edinburgh,' said Mhairi.

Well that was hardly just down the road. 'We don't even know that Carrie's there,' I said. 'She could be anywhere. She might not even be in the UK.'

'True. But her flatmate said she's staying with a relative, and this Valerie Greaves is her stepmum.'

And wasn't an emergency contact someone you would go to in a crisis – a crisis like your therapist winding up dead? The evidence here was all circumstantial, but in the absence of anything else, maybe this was the best lead we had.

Through the Zoom screen, Mhairi and I stared at each other. The name and address from Sebastian's voicemail played over in my head. *Valerie Greaves, Newbattle Terrace, Edinburgh.*

If we followed this lead, this would be a turning point. This wasn't going to Kate's flat or speaking to friends or family that she knew. This was pushing ourselves into other people's lives, demanding answers from those who barely knew her, on the off chance that they could help two strangers resolve their grief.

But my debt to Kate lay heavy on my shoulders, compounded by the debt I still felt to Mhairi as well. And now I knew about Mhairi's guilt also, driving her compulsive need for answers. Mhairi hadn't fought for us back then, hadn't tried to. Letting down Kate, though. That was something we had to put right.

*

I only took one night to sleep on it. First thing the next morning, I rang Mhairi and said yes. We would travel to Scotland, to Edinburgh, where we hoped to find Carrie.

Mhairi would be leaving Tom and the girls for two days. There was no one in my life who would miss me, but in Mhairi's situation – so unlike mine – she would be leaving a major gap. She had never done that before, she told me that afternoon as we boarded the train at Peterborough. 'I think it will be good for me though . . . to get away for a few days. My life at home with the girls . . . It gets so all-consuming. Sometimes I just need to take a breath by myself.'

Except she wasn't by herself, was she? She was here, with me. Her ex-husband.

'I can imagine it gets hard,' I said, heaving our overnight bags onto the rack. I smiled. 'Two little ones.' I ignored the tearing feeling in my heart. Mhairi had always wanted children. It hadn't surprised me that she'd got pregnant so soon after getting together with Tom.

I let her slide into the seat by the window.

'Kitty and Imrie are amazing. But . . . it wasn't always easy. Especially after Imrie. I think I had . . . you know! *The baby blues*.'

'Depression?' Was this Mhairi lowering her guard even further?

Mhairi winced. 'I don't know if I would call it *that*. I didn't see the GP or anything.'

Now we were on centimetre-thin ice. Holding our fingers millimetres from a flame.

'You didn't?'

'. . . No.'

You didn't get help, and neither did I – until it was too late.

'How did you manage then?'

'Oh . . . you know. My mum stayed and helped a lot. And the girls got older; we got past the worst.'

There was a lump in my throat. I was struggling to decipher what Mhairi was telling me. *Why* she was telling me, with all those undercurrents to everything she'd said. Surely she must understand the cuts her words would cause? To admit she'd struggled – but only half admit it. To admit she didn't seek help, but that help came anyway – for her.

For maybe the first time since it all went wrong between us, I got a real sense of ambivalence from her. Before, everything had been so certain in her mind, and in her words. *The truth is, I don't want this marriage. I'm sorry, Finn. I've met someone else.*

Now it felt as though she was provoking me to say something, while at the same time playing it down to make it so hard for me to speak.

'Anyway,' she said lightly, confirming my thoughts exactly. 'It's fine now. Kitty and Imrie are both doing great.'

That was Mhairi's way of closing down a discussion: a swerve of topic, a claim *all was fine*.

Recklessly, I wanted to push her but she had already turned away, pressing her lips together in the way that meant she was done talking, fiddling with her phone and earphones, humming to herself, busy taking off her coat.

'Shall I get us some food?' I said, letting it go, forcing myself to stay patient. The journey to York was over an hour, then a further two and a half hours on to Edinburgh from there. I hadn't thought to bring anything and there hadn't been much on offer at the station. 'I can get us sandwiches or something from the buffet car.'

'Sure. That would be good.' Mhairi dug down at her feet to rummage in her handbag, and I held up a hand to signal that I'd pay. She smiled at me. 'Thanks.'

As I set off along the narrow aisle, the train moved off from Peterborough, me walking one way, the train moving the other, swaying and clattering over the tracks. When I returned, Mhairi was on her smartphone, texting. She lowered it when she saw me.

'Everything okay?' I slid into my seat, scattering the feast onto the little tray tables in front of us.

'Just messaging Tom.'

'Don't mind me. Go ahead.' I wanted her to know that of course I didn't mind her contacting him – why would I? They should absolutely be keeping in touch.

She had the window seat and I settled down beside her. The carriage was busy, a little bit noisy; tourists still fumbling with their seat reservations, a little kid shrieking, an elderly couple fussing with a thermos flask across the way. I closed my eyes for a moment.

The train had been late leaving the station – only by a few

minutes, but it had set up an itchy sense of impatience within me. Mhairi fell asleep before we even got out of Cambridgeshire, head leaning against the thick glass of the window. I pulled my coat down from the rack above and carefully placed it over her so she wouldn't get cold.

I pulled out my phone and tried to read the news headlines and then a chapter of my e-book. But the words were slippery; my eyes, or my mind, refused to grasp them.

Instead my mind slid to Mhairi in that year after we were married, when I don't think I'd ever felt so much elation in my life. Or so much dread. I was so happy when Mhairi first gave me the news she was pregnant. Then I began to feel anxious. Understandably, at first. We'd have to re-budget. Would the apartment be big enough? Then other things, other worries. Which were the best buggy and changing table and feeding bowls? I found online forums where there were warnings about everything: chemicals, design flaws, product recalls. I spent hours researching, trying to hide from Mhairi the frenetic extent of my concerns. I went to bed later and later, saying I'd been watching a film and accidentally dozed off if Mhairi asked, not telling her I'd spent five hours on parenting forums instead.

But the more steps I tried to take to protect my child, the more the terrors multiplied in my head. In the end I stopped going to bed at all, letting Mhairi sleep in our double room peacefully instead, taking to the couch for real when my exhaustion finally set in.

Now, as the train rattled us away together and into the unknown, the worst memory loomed over me, digging its claws in, refusing to shake loose. Behind my eyelids, I saw myself telling Mhairi, *I can't protect her.* Saying, *I can't do it, nothing's safe.* I heard myself telling her, *I'm so frightened, Mhairi, nothing's working.* Pleading, *I'm sorry, Mhairi, please, I don't want this. I can't do it, I just want all this to stop.* I saw myself opening the door to our bedroom to find the blue and white bed sheets stained red. Darkest red.

I jerked awake.

Mhairi was shaking me. 'You were whimpering,' she said. 'Were you having a dream or something?'

I sat up, my neck painfully cricked. 'No . . . I was just— It's nothing.'

A nightmare. Only half real – but real enough.

'Here,' Mhairi said. She was holding out the tea I'd bought earlier – barely lukewarm now. I wondered just how long I'd been sleeping.

'How much longer to York, do you think?' she said.

I rubbed my eyes and checked my watch. 'Twenty-five minutes, maybe?' My heart was still racing from the terror of the dream, and my limbs and neck were painfully stiff.

Beside me, Mhairi stretched, and I did the same, shaking myself to chase away the horror. Now wasn't the time – maybe there'd never be a time, and I'd just have to live with it. Maybe there were some things in life that would never end with answers or redemption, but at least I could try to get answers about Kate.

I took a sip of tea and smiled over at Mhairi. She smiled back as she set her phone down on the tray table, leaning her head against the window again, closing her eyes. The phone screen was face up and I didn't mean to look, but as I sat there, more messages from Tom flashed up silently on the screen.

For heaven's sake, you need to be straight with him.

You're as bad as Kate used to be, going on about how it wasn't his fault.

My stomach dropped. Was this what Tom thought of me? Was this how he talked after letting me come for dinner and being so polite? And what did he mean: Mhairi saying it wasn't my fault – when all her actions towards me had done nothing but assert that? I tore my eyes away and bit into my sandwich, tacky cheese clogging up my mouth and throat. I pushed the packaging to the side so that it blocked Mhairi's phone screen from my eyeline. The words felt too much, too at odds with my sense of things, my mind stumbling and spinning over what on earth they might mean.

CHAPTER 24

Victor

2019

It was early when I woke up the next morning – far earlier than Mae would ever wake me up – and when I first opened my eyes I couldn't make sense of where I was: in Mae's hotel room or Madrid or St Michael's . . . ? It fell into place when I made out Matthias's form beside me.

He was sitting up in the bed and scrolling through his phone.

'What time is it?' I mumbled, burying my face back into the pillow.

'Six a.m. Don't worry. We don't have to get up for hours yet.'

'Thank fuck.' Still, I didn't plan on staying here very long. I had a flight to book and a travel bag to pack.

'You want coffee?'

'Sure. Thank you.'

The bed bounced as Matthias got up. I could hear my heart beat thudding in my ears as I lay there, my body floppy, doing my best not to fall back asleep.

'Here.' What seemed like only a second later, Matthias was

leaning over me, a mug of coffee outstretched. I shuffled myself up the bed to sit leaning against the headboard and took it from him. He got back in beside me, balancing a steaming mug of his own.

'Thanks,' I said, feeling my eyes close again.

'You're welcome.'

He started flicking through his phone again. Whatever he was doing, he seemed pretty engrossed. Typical millennial. Not very romantic for the morning after, I thought.

'What are you looking at?'

'Ah, nothing.' But he went on flicking.

I opened my eyes properly and purposefully nudged him. 'No, seriously. What?'

'Just . . . silly things. Creepy videos, that kind of shit.'

'Like what?'

'You know, urban legends, apparent footage of the para-normal and stuff.'

'You mean like that creepypasta site.'

He grinned. 'Yep. Exactly.'

My eyes were open now. 'You know it's all bollocks, though?'

'I still love it. I'm, like, addicted.' He shifted, sitting up higher in the bed. 'Look at this one. Like – what's going on here?' He tilted the phone screen towards me.

I sat myself up too now in the wrinkled sheets and looked at the image he was holding out on his phone.

It was a video, the thumbnail just a greyish blur. 'What's that, then?'

'It says in the description: *If you watch all the way to the end, you'll die.*'

'Oh, come on . . .'

'I've watched it five times already. Everyone's talking about it, trying to figure out what they're doing. Here – look.'

He thrust the phone in front of me and as soon as he pressed play, something jolted in my brain.

'What the fuck?' I said.

The video showed a group of teenagers on the dark fringes of a wood. A blond boy was lying on the ground, his face tilted away and in shadow. In the background a second boy, tall, dark, holding a torch, and then the girls, three of them, kneeling round the blond boy, murmuring in a sort of rhythmic chanting.

'It's just some scene these kids staged, obviously,' said Matthias. 'You can't even really tell what they're doing. But people love this kind of weirdness – and that death warning is a total hook, after that film, *The Ring*, you know?'

'How did you get this?' I sat bolt upright in the bed, trying to keep my voice steady. The images I was seeing were hideously familiar.

'It says it came from some school in Scotland. It's going viral. The video is all over TikTok too.'

On the video, someone shouts something like *stop!* or *up!*

'Stop it,' I said. 'Matthias, stop playing it.' I grabbed for the phone, but he swooped it out of reach.

'What's wrong with you? No one's *actually* going to die. What do you think's going to happen – this?' He stuck his tongue out sideways and closed one eye, a parody of death.

On screen, the tall, thin boy runs forward, laughing – or crying? The kneeling girls clamber to their feet. The blond boy sits up and turns towards the camera.

I felt like crying. I almost *was* crying. 'Don't! Please, Matthias. Just stop it.'

The camera skews sideways, lens raking the tree trunks, flinching away . . .

'Ah, come on. It's just some kids messing about. You said you didn't even believe in this stuff.'

I had no choice. I couldn't let him look at this.

I grabbed the phone and threw it across the room. It hit the wardrobe with a crack and I knew at once that the screen had shattered.

Matthias froze. 'What the fuck, Victor.'

'S-sorry.' My voice was hoarse, gasping. I got out of his bed and scrambled for my clothes. 'I couldn't let you.' I pulled on my trousers, creased and reeking of sweat and cigarette smoke. 'I'm sorry. Please, if there's any way you can – please get that taken down.'

Matthias ignored me. 'Get out,' he said. His voice was stony. He was on his feet as well, his face pale. It was as if I had assaulted him. I might as well have. 'Just get out.'

'I am . . . I am, believe me, I'm going.' I was dressed now and sick to my stomach. He came after me as I left, slamming the door of the apartment behind me, like closing a portcullis against a monster.

Seconds later I was back outside in the blinding daylight. I only had one shoe on and my shirt was open. I steadied myself against the rough stone wall of the building as I tugged on the other and buttoned myself up. I was shaking, horrified by what I had done. What I had *seen*.

I recognized every one of those five figures in the video. I knew exactly what those girls were doing. The sound on the footage had been terrible, but I could have recited by heart the words they were chanting.

Time and again these past few days I had told myself: *Chill out, forget it, there's absolutely no proof.* Well, now that fantasy had been totally shattered. Because it was absolutely, terrifyingly clear that there was.

*

Half an hour later, after getting lost twice, I finally made it back to the hotel. In the elevator up to Mae's floor, I stared at myself in the dim, bronze mirror: damp, dishevelled, exhausted, guilty.

If you watch this video to the end, you will die.

I'd assumed – because Mae had told me – that the footage had been destroyed. A lie. Clearly Alex had kept it, like a memento, but how could a dead man post something online?

Alex had been gone for five years – his body smashed to pieces when his car hit a tree twenty yards from the road. His parents insisted he'd lost control of the vehicle, somehow hitting the accelerator instead of the brake. But Alex had always been an excellent driver and the accident report said there were no skid marks, no other vehicles involved, nothing. No explanation for why he'd careened at sixty miles an hour off a wide, straight road he'd driven a hundred times before . . .

But Alex was dead; no doubt about that, and that meant someone else had got hold of his footage. They'd posted it online and now thousands, maybe millions of people would see it. Most of them would watch it and think nothing of it. But there were a handful of people, maybe more, who would know what exactly it meant and if they saw it, they would go straight to the police.

Shit, shit *shit*!

The elevator doors opened and I stumbled out into the plush corridor. The floor was silent with no sign of any other guests. I knocked on the door to Mae's suite. I was still her guest after all and after glimpsing Emile heading to her room last night, I didn't know what I'd find if I just went barging in there.

No response.

I knocked again, louder this time. Still no answer.

I pressed my ear to the door but of course the wood was inches thick; there was no way I would be able to hear anything. I knocked again, harder, and called out as loudly as I dared: 'Mae? It's Victor. Can I come in?'

I leaned against the door again in another futile attempt to listen – and it clicked open. The door wasn't locked.

I swallowed my heart down from my throat, pushed the door wider and stepped inside.

At first, there was nothing to see. Just the same rumpled opulence of the living area, a dirty towel thrown over the couch and two empty champagne glasses adorning the coffee table.

'Mae?'

The bed was empty. Clothes strewn across it – clothes I had worn. A blazer I'd liked the look of, the crimson shirt. Shit. *Shit.*

I heard sobbing in rough, heaving gulps. 'Mae?'

The door into the bathroom was standing open. Now I saw.

There was smashed glass on the tiled floor – green, the remnants of a Champagne bottle. And blood, a smeared trail of it.

Mae was hunched up in the claw-foot bathtub, crying.

I moved across the room and crouched down beside her, brushing away the shards of glass as best I could.

'What happened? What happened?' I said, gripping her shoulders, fingers digging in, fear trumping compassion.

She gulped. 'He came back early!'

'Who?'

But a split second later, I realized who she meant: the man who was currently paying for all this, who was out of town on business, whose clothes I had worn, and whose money we had spent. Her 'friend' – boyfriend, sugar daddy, whatever.

'He came back early,' she whimpered, 'when Emile was just leaving. He was so mad; he threw the bottle at us, and it smashed on the wall and went everywhere. I tried to run in here and trod on the glass.'

It was only then that I noticed her foot was bleeding; she had wrapped a towel ineffectively around it.

'He's demanding that I leave. He's furious with me for cheating on him. He's coming back again in two hours and he says I have to be gone by then.'

'It's fine,' I heard myself telling her. Though it absolutely wasn't. 'We'll pack up your things; we can go to another hotel. We'll figure it out. But we definitely can't stay here.'

She was rocking herself in the tub, the heels of her hands pressed against her eyes. 'No, I don't want to! What's wrong with me, Victor? Why do men always turn on me like this?'

I wanted to slap her. What a coward I had been for letting her convince me to *do nothing*, letting me curl up in the queasiness of my withdrawals. Mae had always dealt with things that way, breezily moving on from them, and somehow things had always gone her way. Or so I'd thought. I'd thought by staying with her I'd be immune from consequences too, but it now looked like we had both been kidding ourselves.

I grabbed her again, finally giving her the shake she needed. 'We have to go, Mae. We are going to get out of here and track Carrie down. You have no idea what I've just discovered. We've been idiots, Mae, thinking she'd just send an email. She's gone way further; she has seriously fucked us.'

Mae just went on crying, ignoring me, her words mangled by her sobs. 'I don't want to go anywhere. I want to cry; I want to get drunk! He was so mean to me, Victor. So mean!'

What the fuck did I care? I grabbed her by the shoulder, forcing her to turn round and sit upright, and held out my phone to her. I'd already found a dozen TikTok accounts that had shared the video.

'Mae,' I said. 'Get a grip on yourself. You think all that is bad? There's *proof* out there, all over the Internet. Don't believe me? Take a fucking look at this.'

CHAPTER 25

Carrie

2003

It wasn't funny anymore. If this was still a joke, then nobody was laughing.

By now we couldn't get through half a week without one of the seven girls fainting. As obedient pupils of St Michael's, we were supposed to trust that, despite the increasing tensions among the teachers and growing disquiet among the students, the senior staff had everything in hand. So far, only the parents of the affected girls had been (confidentially) informed, and other than Dr Sanderson and the psychologist, no other outside parties had been called in. It was clear the school was trying to keep a tight lid on things, but if they didn't get a handle on it – whatever *it* was – and make it stop soon, it would only be a matter of time before they had an out-and-out scandal – or catastrophe – on their hands.

The psychologist had started her work, but so far it didn't seem to be doing any good. Bryony and Ava were still the worst, and the whole thing felt more disturbed and sinister by the day. I'd reassured myself over and over with the idea that they were faking, but after the incident with Bryony and Ms Myers, I could no longer convince myself of that.

We were in the dining hall again (though at least Bryony wasn't carrying a tray of beans this time). This was late November and we were all attuned to the warning signs by now; most of us had seen at least one of them faint.

They would go stock-still, limbs rigid, eyes glazed. They seemed to lose all sense of where they were; they seemed to disappear inside themselves. You knew then what was going to happen . . . after two seconds or ten . . .

Bang.

Except this time, Ms Myers stepped in. Just as Bryony's legs buckled, Ms Myers grabbed her. 'No! No, you don't!'

She hauled Bryony upwards, refusing to let her sink to the floor. She looked furious. We were all sick of it. We'd all wanted to shake and slap those girls, and Ms Myers almost looked like she was going to.

'Bryony, stop it. Stop it!'

Ms Myers kept hold of her, grappling with her, refusing to let her peel away and hit the floor. Bryony jerked in her grasp, limbs apparently not so weak after all.

'I said, stop it, Bryony. Just *stand up.*'

Everyone's eyes were glued to what was happening.

For a moment, it seemed to work. Stupid Bryony. She'd been faking all along. And now we would see that. Ms Myers was calling her bluff.

Miraculously, Bryony's feet found purchase. Her chin rose and she straightened her spine. I held my breath, heart pounding. This was it, wasn't it? *This* was how you stopped it. Forget about protocol and just *get hands on them*. Surely none of the others would try it now – now that Bryony had been so conclusively caught out. Held in Ms Myers' grip, Bryony didn't collapse; she didn't *rise up out of her body and into the light*.

She didn't faint; she didn't have a fit. She didn't keel over as if she was dying and end up sprawled all over the floor.

Instead, she vomited.

Violently, helplessly, soaking Ms Myers and soaking herself.

And I felt a deep, cold shiver run right through me, because you could fake standing still, looking glazed, falling over. But there was no way on earth she could be faking *that*.

*

Shortly after the incident with Ms Myers, Mae brought up a brand-new suggestion.

My stomach somersaulted when she said it; my cheeks burned. 'You want to invite Alex and Victor?' I echoed.

Mae looked at me in the wide, smudgy mirror. The three of us were in the dormitory bathroom, trying out a new make-up technique we'd got from *Glamour* magazine. 'Sure. They're your friends, aren't they? Don't you want them to join in the fun?'

My face went crimson, my neck blotchy. I could see it all in the mirror. 'I mean . . . I only hang out with them sometimes. Just when you and Serena both have stuff on over lunch.'

'You think we don't know that? I've been waiting for weeks for you to mention it.' Her tone was light, but there was a barb right under it and her smile was more like a smirk: *caught you*.

The question underneath was obvious: *Why didn't you tell us?*

When neither Serena nor Mae had said anything to me,

despite how gossipy St Michael's was, I'd just assumed that word hadn't got back to them. So I'd continued meeting up with Alex and Victor, but they had known all along and had just been waiting for me to say something. And I hadn't.

I laughed nervously. 'I thought you didn't like them. I mean, neither of you really talk to them or anything.'

'But *you* do.'

I swallowed. 'Sometimes, yes.'

'And so . . . are they nice?'

My cheeks were so red. I shrugged. 'They're all right.'

Mae held my gaze in the mirror, making me splodge my eyeliner. '*So-o-o-o* . . . let's invite them. Then we can all get to know each other.'

I hesitated – but why on earth was I hesitating? This would be good, wouldn't it – all five us hanging out, being friends? But for some reason I felt insecure and possessive. Alex and Victor were *my* friends – I didn't want to share them. I didn't want Alex hanging out with beautiful Mae.

I scratched about for a reasonable reason to say no. 'What if they go blabbing?'

'Don't you trust them?'

The thought sprang into my mind: *I don't trust* you.

'No, it's—'

Mae let out a small, impatient sigh. 'Look, now's the perfect time for them to sneak out. The teachers aren't paying attention to anything but the Fainting Girls.'

'Why though?' Serena cut in, her tone bland, like she was confused rather than anything.

We both shifted our gaze to look at her in the mirror. 'How do you mean?' said Mae.

'Well, why do you want Victor and Alex there?'

Mae shrugged. 'I just think it would be interesting.'

I turned to look at Serena in the mirror, watching her paint her puckered lips blood-red. 'Interesting how?' she persisted.

Exactly. What did Mae mean by saying that?

Mae's smile was lopsided. 'I'd like to see how they'd handle it. Anyway, *you* don't have to come, Carrie, if you're worried about them blabbing. Serena and I can always meet them by ourselves.'

'No! No, I'll come,' I blurted. No way was I going to let Mae and Serena meet them alone. Why was I being so resistant anyway? Why shouldn't this work in my favour? Did I think Mae and Serena would run off with them and screw me over? It could give me more kudos, letting the boys in on what we'd been up to. It could bring me and Alex closer; we'd hang out more if we shared mutual friends. Then who knew what might happen between us, in the dark, getting high, up there in the woods . . .

'I think it *would* be fun,' I blabbered on. '*And* interesting.'

'Great,' said Mae. 'What about you then, Serena?'

The usual look of boredom was drawing down on Serena's face. Her sport mattered more to her than anything. 'Sure,' she agreed. 'Whatever.'

'Fine. We're agreed then. Friday night. I'll get some more pills. Carrie – you ask them.'

So I did.

CHAPTER 26

Carrie

2003

Like with me on my first night, we agreed not to tell them anything till we got there. They knew about the high bank – everyone did – but I had never spoken with Victor or Alex about what we did up there. I simply told them to meet us at the back of the gym at midnight.

Plainly, they were just chuffed to be invited to meet up after curfew with us. We told them to keep absolutely silent and ask no questions, and they did what we said.

The little hollow behind the rise was exactly as we'd left it; even the cardigan Serena had forgotten last time was still there.

With the boys there, though, it already felt different. It was the same setting, same time of night, same logs and dank earth and trees. But the whole thing took on another layer.

'This is where you guys come?' said Alex. 'Up here?'

'Yeah,' said Mae. 'It's pretty private. No one's going to see or hear us from down there.'

The boys glanced at each other and I could see the scepticism in their expressions. 'Right . . .' said Victor. 'So, what exactly do you do?'

Mae shrugged. 'Oh, you know. Pillow fights, talk about our periods.'

In the gloom I saw Alex roll his eyes.

'Kidding,' I said quickly. 'Go on, Mae.'

She cocked her head, narrowing her eyes at the boys. 'How do we know if we can trust you? How do we know you won't dob us in?'

Victor crossed his arms. 'Dob you in for what? Hanging about in the woods? Big deal. Anyway, you're the ones who invited us in the first place.'

'If you do tell . . .' said Mae, 'we'll say you assaulted us. Broke into our dorm.' She snaked a hand around her own neck, gripping so as to easily cause the skin to blotch – even bruise.

I saw Alex swallow nervously. 'You wouldn't.'

Serena stepped forward, in line with Mae. 'We would.'

I jumped in. 'They get it, Mae. They won't blab. It's fine. Just show them.'

'I'm just joking.' Mae smirked. She dropped her hand and reached into her pocket to pull out one of Luke's white pills. She held it up, the little disc glowing in the moonlight.

'What's that?' said Alex.

'It's the best feeling,' said Serena. 'You drift right out of yourself – it's a total rush.'

Alex reached forwards. 'Let me see that.'

Mae handed the tiny pill to him.

'Don't drop it,' I said quickly.

We only ever used the same kind of pills: the ones Luke had chosen for us from the start. In the end, from what I'd read, they weren't really like Ecstasy. People took Ecstasy at raves and clubs; it made you feel energetic and like everyone was your best friend. These pills . . . it wasn't like that. They made me feel amazing, totally blissful, but at the same time, it was more like everything just felt apart. Space, time, everything around you just crumbled away. It was like you became nothing, in the best way possible. You didn't need to move, or speak; you had no needs, no impulses. Nothing could frighten or harm you. It was like the world stopped and there was nothing there at all.

Alex turned the tablet over in his palm. 'Looks fake,' he said.

Mae shrugged again and took the pill back off him. 'You don't have to take it if you don't want. You can go back to the dorms and the rest of us will get high without you.'

He shook his head uncertainly. 'I dunno. How am I supposed to know what's in that?'

Mae held his eye through the gloom. 'Aren't you curious? Don't you trust us? Or—' she cut her eyes towards me '—do you always play things so safe?'

'Fine. Give it here. I'll try it.' He smiled at me and I felt myself flush.

Mae held the pill out then drew it back again.

'Wait,' she said. 'We have to do this properly. Here.' She pointed to the muddy ground. 'Sit down.'

'There?'

'Just sit down,' Mae said again, and this time Alex obeyed her. We girls joined him on the ground too, forming a ragged circle.

Mae glanced up. 'Victor? Aren't you joining us?'

He hesitated, then uncrossed his arms. 'Fine.' He lowered himself awkwardly onto the ground beside us, still cowardly but playing it cool. 'Whatever. This better not be some stupid prank.'

Now all five of us made up the ring: a circle and five points of a star. Alex was directly opposite me; I could look directly into his eyes.

Mae passed one white pill each to me and Serena; mine sat sticky in my sweaty fist.

'Now,' she told the boys, 'we have a little ritual.'

It had started out as a silly joke, a pretend spell to ward off bad spirits, but now superstitiously we couldn't seem to take the drugs without it. The three of us hooded our eyes and chanted the words we'd come to know off by heart: an old poem that Serena had found in some dusty English lit book.

'Sexy,' Victor muttered sarcastically. 'Very cool.'

We ignored him and carried on with our chanting. This was *our* ritual. *Our* initiation, *our* rules.

When the words were finished, we opened our eyes again, and Mae passed me a fourth tablet. 'For Victor,' she said. 'Carrie, you do the honours.'

We hadn't rehearsed or planned this bit, so I didn't know exactly what she wanted. *Just make it up,* I imagined Serena saying. Victor was sitting next to me and I turned to him, and as I did I remembered that very first time we'd interacted, that strange moment in chemistry class and the impulse of protectiveness that had come over me then.

I cleared my throat. 'Hold out your hand,' I said imperiously. He did, and I circled my cold fingers round his wrist, pressing my thumb deep into his pulse point. I set the pill in the middle of his palm, then curled each of his fingers around it. I cupped his fist in my hands then released it with a flourish.

That would do. 'There,' I said. 'You're ready.'

When I looked around again, I saw Mae place a fifth white tablet on her tongue. She leaned towards Alex sitting next to her, mouth open, eyes shining. My eyes stung and I pushed down the stab of jealousy as the little tablet passed from her mouth to his. Trust Mae to come up with something like that. Trust Mae always to take things that one step further. Already these last few days I'd been trying to push down my feelings for Alex. I'd heard he'd been back in touch with a girl from his old school. One he used to date and still fancied. And now I had to deal with him and Mae touching tongues . . .

'Go on, then,' Mae said, finishing and sitting up straight again. I looked round.

Victor had already slid his pill into his mouth and Serena was likewise tipping her head back. Eyes still smarting, I swallowed my own.

Mae smiled at us all. 'Good.'

Victor smirked back. 'Happy?'

'Trust me,' she said. 'You're going to feel great.'

And she was right.

That first time with the boys felt amazing. We'd each taken a whole pill, not a half this time, and the effects were more intense than ever.

When it hit, I swooned backwards – we all did – and lay looking up into the sky, aware of Victor's hand somehow in mine, and later of Alex lying warm beside me. I remembered laughing a long peal of laughter, and at one point taking Mae's beautiful face in my hands.

At one point, we found ourselves playing *Light As A Feather*, managing to lift Mae right into the air above our heads, but it didn't feel like lifting her, it felt like all of us were floating. Seconds, minutes or hours later, we fell, toppling to the ground in a pile of tangled limbs, but there wasn't an ounce of pain or fright; there was nothing.

Just the five of us, delighted faces shining in the moonlight, giddy, invincible and high as hell.

From: mhairi_1981@gmail.com
To: katefallon@hotmail.com
Sent: 15.27pm, 05/06/2013
Re: Pictures!

Hey Kate,

So sorry I didn't reply before. Hope you're getting on well. The pictures you sent are lovely – all those palm trees and sun! (It's raining in Cambridge, again.)

The sickness has got a bit worse, which is why I wasn't emailing. I'm seeing the doctor again next week if it doesn't settle and in the meantime, I've had to take time off work and mostly stay in bed. Finn is a bit manic at the moment – he's done loads of research on what stuff we need for the baby. He's been sleeping on the sofa so he doesn't disturb me, bless him. I've told him it's fine – all I can seem to manage to do is sleep! But he insists on it. I think he's a bit worried about the baby, if I'm honest.

Anyway, it was great to see all the photos of where you're staying, and your colleagues and all the scenery. Keep me posted on how everything goes. So proud of you.

xxx

CHAPTER 27

Carrie

2003

The psychologist was meeting with the Fainting Girls twice a week. She was teaching them something called visualization, as well as muscle relaxation (pretty ironic), and something wishy-washy called 'happy, helpful thinking'. Apparently, in the group sessions, always supervised by a teacher, she also made them write compliments to each other and themselves.

I got these details out of Polly.

Serena, Mae and I laughed about it. But they started getting better.

Anna, Cynthia and Polly had only fainted once since the sessions started. They had gone back to whispering, giggling, and gossiping. Mucking about with each other like they used to. Before long, Stephanie and Faye were back to their normal selves too.

When I asked Polly one night in their dormitory what specifically had made a difference, she said – apparently speaking for all five of them: 'We just feel better now. The psychologist helped.'

'Uh-huh.' I leaned on the doorframe. 'But what does she think was causing you to faint?'

Did she tell you, nicely, that all of you were faking?

Polly's eyes darted away from me. A little liar if I ever saw one. The other girls picked at their fingernails, fiddled with their hair, avoiding eye contact. Eventually Polly lifted her chin and said defiantly. 'The psychologist says we don't have to talk about it if we don't want. You know therapy is about, like, *personal stuff.*'

'Well,' I said, snarkily, 'I'm so glad you're all better.'

I was pretty sure those five were bullshitting. They had seen what happened with Bryony and that had started it. They'd enjoyed the drama and wanted a piece of it, and so they'd perfected that dramatic freeze-and-swoon. At most, they'd subconsciously convinced themselves they felt dizzy, all because at some level they greedily craved the attention. Either way, with her *anxiety management* and *self-esteem work*, the psychologist had sorted them out.

Except Bryony wasn't getting better. Nor was Ava.

For them, it was different. Despite all the *positive thinking* and *relaxation exercises* and compliments, they only seemed to keep getting worse.

*

That week, a local newspaper picked up the story. We saw it displayed in the newsagents during one of our trips into town.

'Huh,' said Serena, when she spotted it. 'Look at this.'

It was on the front page, a big colour picture of our school and a half-page spread of text underneath.

'No way. Go on then, read it.'

She flipped the paper open and I craned over her shoulder. 'Mae,' I called across to where our friend was staring blankly at a row of black marker pens, even though the school provided all the stationery we could want.

The headline itself was fairly restrained. *Unknown illness affects girls at local school.*

'Who do you think leaked this?' said Serena.

'No idea.' I honestly couldn't imagine anyone breaking ranks like that.

'Ms Dunham will be so mad. Especially now it's pretty much all blown over. They were hoping to sweep it all under the rug.'

I tried to scan the article. 'What's it saying?'

'Not much . . . That the girls were seen by both a doctor and psychologist . . . that it's still unclear what has been causing the fits . . . Some stuff about the pressures kids experience these days . . . that privileged kids can have a tough time in private schools, blah, blah.'

'Ugh,' I said. 'That doesn't tell us anything.' And Mae hadn't even bothered coming over. I'd fleetingly hoped the article might have provided some definitive answers – not least because Bryony and Ava were still acting weird – but it was clear this hack journalist knew even less than we did. At the end, we were left with the same old questions. Were Bryony and Ava actually poorly, or was the whole thing a big hoax?

The shopkeeper stuck his head out. 'You going to buy that?'

The article was useless, but I bought the paper anyway. I kind of liked that people would be reading it and talking about St Michael's; it was like being famous – or infamous, anyway. Perhaps on a reread we'd discover something new, and at least it would be fun to show the paper around.

But Mr Witham confiscated it on the minibus back.

*

By now, going over the top of the rise had become a regular thing: Friday and Saturday nights; other nights too, if we could get away with it. It was like a respite from all the daytime tension, everyone still shaken by the saga of the Fainting Girls with Bryony and Ava seemingly more disturbed than ever, working in a separate classroom on their own, and spending even more time in the sick bay.

So it was good to escape. It amazed me that we hadn't got caught out on any of this. That we hadn't got rumbled for sneaking out of the school night after night through that stupid unlocked door at the back of the sports hall; that we hadn't got pulled up for the purple bags under our eyes and non-stop yawning in class; that Mae hadn't got caught for fraternizing with someone from town who dealt drugs.

But the school had been so preoccupied that anything else had slipped under the radar. They had been so busy checking up on Bryony and Ava that no one thought of checking up on us.

Most of the time, the five of us just mucked about up there. Alex managed to procure bottles of vodka from a guy in the year below who had a stash. Back in Illinois, at most my friends and I had only ever snuck beer. We stuck our torches upright in the mud so we were illuminated from beneath, and took it in turns to tell ghost stories. Mae's were the best; Serena's were the worst.

Alex and Victor would challenge each other in strength competitions: holding on to a tree branch and seeing how many chin-ups they could do, their shirts riding up, exposing their abs. Victor was usually the winner. Till the branch they were using snapped off.

One time we tried to make a fire and Alex filmed it, because he said he had to practise getting good shots in all kinds of tricky lighting. Alex was always videoing something and what we did, night after night, up there on the hill was such a big part of our lives, it didn't seem that weird – or stupid – that Alex brought his camera up there too.

He filmed us while we piled up twigs and dried leaves, and set it going with Mae's plastic lighter, but the flame kept smouldering and wouldn't take – not until Victor sloshed an arc of vodka onto it. Then the whole thing went up with a whoosh, blazing outwards and sparking the low-hanging, dead leaves above. Clumsily, we stamped down the flames, ruining our trainers and boots in the process, chasing the scattering sparks down, praying that the branches above wouldn't take. Eventually – thankfully – the embers died out, but it had been a stupid thing to do. Later on, when Alex played back what he'd captured, I couldn't help but think about how incriminating that footage would be if we'd burnt down the woods.

A couple of times, we played truth or dare; in one round, Mae dared Alex to tongue-kiss me, and he did, but that was as far as anything ever went. One time, Victor produced a pack of tarot cards and had us pissing ourselves, telling our fortunes. Alex was going to be the next Steven Spielberg; Mae was going to marry an obscenely rich count. Serena was going to win gold at the Olympics and Victor was going to be a millionaire CEO.

Most of the time, we just drank or smoked weed. But every now and then Mae would produce that little plastic packet. We had moved on to even higher doses now, needing more to feel the same effects.

And those nights always felt different from any of the rest. *Those* nights were the ones I lived for.

CHAPTER 28

Finn

2019

At York, I was glad of the chance to stretch our legs. We lugged our bags off the train and found a station café where we could grab another cup of coffee to keep us going.

I agreed to keep an eye on our coats and bags while Mhairi went off to use the facilities. While she was gone, I scrolled through my phone, doing one of my habitual Google searches for St Michael's. Nothing new ever cropped up – only the same links and articles I'd already read.

Except this time, there *was* something.

The link took me to a website. A pigeon scuffled about by my chair, looking for crumbs, one of its feet hobbled. The 4G service in the station was patchy and the page took a long time to load.

When it did, there was a video. I clicked play.

The footage was old and grainy. Kids in a wood. One of them lying on his back on the ground.

I paused it; checked the description.

Spooky goings-on at weird Scottish boarding school! If
you watch this all the way to the end you will die!

Hairs rose up on the back of my neck. What was this?
I scrolled through the comments, eventually finding the words
that had brought me here.

I've done some digging about the location. The boarding
school is St Michael's, I'm pretty sure. See here:

A link back to the Wikipedia article I was so familiar with.
I felt like a fly, caught in some elaborate, sticky web: Kate, her
client, a pupil at St Michael's. I scanned the concourse, but
there was no sign of Mhairi.

If you watch this all the way to the end you will die!

Stupid. Clickbait. I clicked play.

There were five kids in the video, three girls and two boys.
I paused the video again, heart thudding.

Above me, an announcement came over the Tannoy: *The
next train to depart from Platform 9 will be the* . . .

On my phone, I flicked back to the article I'd screenshotted
before: *Five Firm Friends and their Fantastic Results!*

Three girls. Two boys.

'What are you looking at?' Mhairi had appeared in front of
me. I jumped in my seat.

She sat down and I shook my head. 'I don't know. This—'

I held my phone out to her. She took it off me and watched
the video.

'What is this?'

'A video from St Michael's apparently.' The three girls cluster
around a blond boy on the ground. The tall, dark boy in the
background suddenly darts forward.

'What?' Mhairi said.

'Do you recognize them? These five kids?'

On the footage, the girls scramble to their feet.

'Yes. Shit . . . I think so.' She was quick; I didn't have to tell her. 'Carrie and her friends, from that newspaper article.' She hit pause and looked up at me. 'It says, *If you watch to the end you'll die.*'

'Yes.'

'So it's some stupid joke, right?'

'I—'

The announcement came again: *The next train to depart from Platform 9 . . .*

'That's ours,' Mhairi said. 'Platform nine. We need to go.' We scrambled to our feet with our bags. 'But, Finn, what *is* it? What are they all doing?'

'I don't know.' I hurried with her towards our platform.

'Tell me again – what were their names? The pupils in the article.'

I reeled them off as we scanned the length of the train for our carriage. 'Margaret Forsythe, Serena Whittingham, Victor Dupont, Alexander Fontaine. And Carrie.'

In the queue outside the doors to coach C, I flicked to the screenshot for her – and suddenly kicked myself. Why hadn't I googled all these other people before? Each one of them had clearly known Carrie; each of them had also attended St Michael's. There could be all kinds of details about them online for the taking, but I hadn't put their names into a search engine even once. If I had, I might have discovered all kinds of information we needed. Instead, here we were with overnight bags packed, taking a four-hour train journey to some complete stranger's house.

'This has to mean something,' Mhairi was saying, flicking between the video and the school article. 'This can't be a coincidence. I'm right, Finn. *We're* right. This person – Carrie. She and St Michael's are at the centre of this whole thing.'

She was already stepping up into the train, other passengers shoving us from behind. I apologized, clambering up after her. 'Mhairi – we should google their names. The other pupils.'

'Wait,' she said, turning in the packed vestibule towards me. 'The other pupils – on the video, that's Margaret, Serena, Victor, Carrie. But it's not Alexander.'

'What?'

As we crammed into the vestibule, she passed my phone back to me. 'Watch.' She pointed. 'The blond one – when he turns to face the camera.' Just before the end of the footage, the blond boy's face is illuminated. 'In the newspaper, Alexander hasn't got a mole on his cheek like that boy in the video does. And at the end, when the camera jolts sideways. It's handheld. There's a sixth person. Someone else there, behind the lens.'

The train doors slammed shut behind us. *Six people, not five. Someone else, not Alexander.* I thought I might faint. My head was ringing. Forget what I said about googling those names.

I looked again, like forcing myself to look back at a horror film.

She was right. Blond hair. A mole on his cheek, distinguishing him.

I had never met this sixth person – this other boy – but I recognized him.

'Oh fuck, Mhairi,' I said. 'Oh fuck.'

Text from: Kate
Sent to: Mhairi
13.19pm, 06/06/2013

Hey Mhairi,

Really sorry you've been feeling so poorly. Hope it gets much better soon.

I just rang your house and Finn picked up. The line from Florida wasn't great, but he sounded a bit strange.

Can you call or message when you get this?

Lots of love.

xxx

Text from: Kate
Sent to: Mhairi
13.45pm, 06/06/2013

Did you get my last text? Can you call me?

Text from: Mhairi
Sent to: Kate
19.01pm, 06/06/2013

Hey sorry I was sleeping again. It's evening here. What's up?

Text from: Kate
Sent to: Mhairi
14.02pm, 06/06/2013

Did you see my other text?

Text from: Mhairi
Sent to: Kate
19.02pm, 06/06/2013

Sorry – just read it. How do you mean, sounded
strange?
xx

Text from: Kate
Sent to: Mhairi
14.03pm, 06/06/2013

He was talking about not wanting anything to harm
the baby?

Text from: Mhairi
Sent to: Kate
19.03pm, 06/06/2013

What's that supposed to mean?

Text from: Kate
Sent to: Mhairi
14.03pm, 06/06/2013

I don't know. He was talking about there being so many unknown dangers and that he needed to protect the baby? Has he said anything like that to you?

Text from: Mhairi
Sent to: Kate
19.04pm, 06/06/2013

I know he called the company we bought the cot from about safety testing but I think he was just checking something. He's gone a bit mad baby proofing the house ☺ Is that what he meant?

Text from: Kate
Sent to: Mhairi
14.04pm, 06/06/2013

IDK. When did you last speak to him?
A proper conversation about how he's doing?

Text from: Mhairi
Sent to: Kate
19.04pm, 06/06/2013

I don't know. I've mostly been sleeping – and puking. I know he's been reading these wacky parenting blogs about additives and air pollution and chemical toxins, and you know how he can overthink things.

>**Text from:** Kate
>**Sent to:** Mhairi
>*14.05pm, 06/06/2013*
>
>Where is he now?

Text from: Mhairi
Sent to: Kate
19.05pm, 06/06/2013

At the shops.

>**Text from:** Kate
>**Sent to:** Mhairi
>*14.06pm, 06/06/2013*
>
>When you get a chance, talk to him and get more of a sense of what he meant. Message me again once you've spoken.
>   I'm sure it's fine. Maybe he was just tired, if he's been up late and busy getting the house ready for

the baby. He might have just been a bit confused or something.

Text from: Mhairi
Sent to: Kate
19.06pm, 06/06/2013

Okay. I will. He was probably just venting. He's on the phone to those companies all the time. I'll message you again once we've spoken. We miss you, Kate. Speak soon.

CHAPTER 29

Carrie

2003

One afternoon, I had to nip up to the dorm to fetch a forgotten textbook; I swung open the door and found Mae in there.

I stopped short; she was supposed to be in class.

'What are you doing here? Don't you have English?' Me, Mae and Serena knew each other's timetables back to front.

'I'm not feeling well.' She said that, but she was sitting up with pen and paper at her desk.

I stepped into the room, letting the door swing shut behind me. 'You're not going to start fainting and vomiting like Bryony, are you?' It was a joke but when I looked at Mae to see her reaction, her expression was tight.

I swallowed and sat down on my bed. 'Mae? What's up?'

She was doodling randomly on the blank piece of paper in front of her. 'What do you think is really going on with them?' she said eventually.

'Who?'

'Bryony. And Ava.'

'I don't know.'

'You think they're sick? Or are you thinking they're just faking it? The psychologist should have helped them, shouldn't she? She helped the others.'

I had been thinking about this. Really thinking about it. 'I think the others were just . . . copying. Or, like, caught up in it all. But maybe with Bryony and Ava, there *is* something wrong.'

Once I said it out loud, it didn't sound so crazy. I hesitated again, then pushed on. 'There was this one time . . . with Ava. I was right there when it happened. Her skirt rode up and I saw she had . . . marks on her legs. On her thighs.'

Mae seemed to stiffen. 'What kind of marks?'

'Sort of like . . . bruises. I wondered if maybe some of the boys in her year . . .' I swallowed, the remaining words thick and sticky in my throat.

Mae said nothing. I regretted even mentioning it now. It was horrible, wild, wasn't it, to go suggesting that boys were molesting girls at St Michael's? I hurried to correct myself. 'But the doctor checked them all, didn't he? He would have picked it up if there'd been anything like that?'

Mae didn't reply.

'Wouldn't he?' I repeated.

Mae's voice was stiff too. 'I guess so.'

'So I'm sure it's nothing,' I said, straightening up. 'Ava probably hurt herself when she fell over the last time. And like I say, I think it was probably just attention-seeking. Maybe now Bryony and Ava are sort of stuck in competition? You know – about who gives it up first.'

I was rambling.

'Yeah.' Mae went back to scribbling a biro across the blank page in front of her. *Scratch scratch.* I waited.

'Mae?' I checked my watch. 'Mae . . . sorry, I have to get back—'

'We should give them even higher doses,' she said out of nowhere.

I went still. 'What? Who?'

'Alex and Victor.'

My throat went dry. 'Why?'

She shrugged. 'I dunno. See what happens.'

I didn't get it. And I didn't like it at all, either. The psychologist had gone from the school now, but if she were still here, I might have run to her and asked, *Do you have any idea why my friend is saying this?*

I shook my head and stood up from the bed. 'You told us Luke said we should never take more than two. Giving Victor or Alex more would be . . . shitty.' I wanted to say *dangerous*, because that's what I meant, but I was anxious and giddy at speaking up so firmly; normally it was Mae who called all the shots. But she was being weird and I really didn't like it.

She went on jabbing with her pen at the paper, like she wanted to stab something right through. 'Whatever. Forget it. Forget I even said it.'

I went on standing there – like I once did with Mr Witham – waiting for her to say something else. Something reasonable that would go some way to explain her suggestion.

But she didn't.

'Well . . . Okay then, Mae. Get well soon.'

*

It was a Friday night in early December and the five of us were scrambling to the top of the rise when Mae tossed the words casually over her shoulder.

'I've invited someone else tonight.'

I stopped, out of breath from the muddy, slippery slope. Serena and Alex and Victor stopped too. It had rained persistently over the last couple of days: a fine drizzle that had attached itself to everything, sinking in layers-deep. I'd had to grab at clumps of grass and low tree branches to haul my way up. The wet made it cold too, and I had a pounding headache. I had actually been thinking about turning round and going home. I could probably have persuaded Alex or Victor to come with me. They wouldn't have left me to go back through the dark on my own.

'You what?' said Serena.

Mae was a few feet up ahead, towering over us, while I was bent over, holding on to a tree root.

'I invited someone else along. I thought it was time to mix things up again.'

'Who?' I said, my thoughts spinning.

'It's a surprise.' Mae started climbing upwards again, her boots sending a wet landslide of mud down onto me, trickling over my cold hands. 'Well? Are you coming? Or are you guys going to be boring . . .'

She must have known that would get to us.

'Fine,' Serena said, resuming her scramble up the slope. 'Whatever.'

A second later, the rest of us were following her. Silently, except for our ragged panting, we carried on up and over the bank.

*

He didn't look like I'd expected. For one thing, he looked younger – Mae had said he was nineteen, twenty, something like that, but in the blur of our torchlights, at first glance he didn't look much older than us. I'd also pictured someone scruffy, mean and shifty-looking, but he looked just like a normal guy. Maybe even . . . kind of cute.

'And this is . . . ?' Alex asked rudely.

'I'm Luke,' the guy said. He was confident, bordering on cocky.

'He's the one who's been getting us the stuff.' Mae rested a hand on her hip as she did the introductions. Playing it so cool. 'This is Carrie, Victor, Alex and Serena.'

As soon as he started speaking, I had to revise my first impression. He did look young, but his voice was deep – a man's voice, not a boy's – and he didn't seem to have a problem with inserting himself into our group. He took a draw on his cigarette, carelessly flicked the ash. When he turned his head, I saw the dark mole on his cheek.

'I hear you've been having a good time up here,' he said, his Scottish accent brash and thick. 'I thought you St Michael's poshos weren't allowed to have fun.'

Heart thumping, I looked through the gloom at Mae, trying to take a cue from her, but I couldn't read her expression in the dark.

'We're not poshos,' I said. 'We don't do everything our teachers tell us. Like, we'd be expelled if they knew we brought alcohol up here.'

'Wow . . .' said Luke. 'Sounds wild.'

Mae slapped him playfully on the arm. 'Shut up, Luke. They're cool.'

He looked round the circle at all of us. I felt very young all of a sudden, with our silly games of truth or dare and weird rituals, for some reason thinking we were so rebellious and cool. With Luke standing there, sizing us all up, the whole thing suddenly felt babyish and immature. Even if he went away now, I thought, it wouldn't be the same from now on. Something felt different. I felt different.

Mae, what the fuck?

I was also worried about what Mae wanted us to do with him. It was always Mae who set the dares, and thought of new ways for us to push the boundaries. She naturally took charge, even with Victor and Alex there, and sometimes it felt we were little more than her puppets. I still hadn't figured out quite how to say no.

Luke looked past us, taking in the rocks and the woods, the low branches dripping quietly. 'Can't see that you'd have much of a party up here. Bit grim, isn't it. I mean, except for getting high, what do you guys even do up here?'

'Our own kind of thing,' Mae replied. 'We'll show you if you want.'

Her voice had shifted, sounding low and serious, the way she would speak to the younger girls when she wanted to command attention. Suddenly, I imagined her talking to the two who kept fainting, drawing them aside, looking into their eyes, holding them firmly by the shoulders so they couldn't wriggle away. Getting them to spit out the truth.

Or vomit.

We were all sombre now. This is how it was when we were

about to take the drugs. We stopped pissing about. We might have been having fun, but we were serious then. Respectful.

'Yeah?' Luke's tone was still half-laughing.

Mae looked at him, her eyes steady, and so damn black in the gloom. 'If you want.'

He reached into the pocket of his jeans and pulled out a packet. 'Here you go, then.' He tossed it to her, and despite the darkness, shadows wheeling in the beams of our torches, she caught it deftly, then dug in her coat pocket to hand over our pooled money. It felt grubby doing it directly like this. A proper *drug deal*.

'Lie down, then,' she said.

'What?'

'Here, on the ground,' Mae repeated. 'Lie down.'

By now, we'd learned that was the best way: lying supine, tightly held by the others. Held like that, shoulders, arms, legs grasped tightly, the feeling of dissolving was so much more intense.

There was still a smirk on Luke's face, but my heart accelerated. The power was back in our hands again: back with me, Mae and Serena – the original three – but I was still afraid of what Mae might to do with it. I was afraid of what she was going to do with *him*.

Now Serena voice's piped up. A put-on tone: girlish and saccharine-sweet. 'It's fine,' she said. 'You'll like it.'

Luke reached up and scratched the back of his neck. He laughed again, flattered by the attention maybe. 'All right. Whatever. I won't say no when a pretty girl tells me that.'

He stubbed out his cigarette. He'd seemingly only lit it up a minute or so ago, but he crushed the remainder of it into the muddy ground.

I had a strange taste in my mouth. Metallic, and I wondered if I had bitten my cheek. I watched as Luke lowered himself to the ground. Despite everything, it looked strangely familiar: he was just about the same size and colouring as Alex.

Beyond me, Alex and Victor were shapes lost in the shadows; just the beams of their torches shining down on us. Like they were the lamp bearers or something.

'With your arms,' Serena told Luke. 'Do this . . .'

She got him to cross his hands over his chest, the way you might if you were sky-diving – or being packed into a coffin.

'That's it,' said Mae. 'Good. Now close your eyes.'

They encircled him, putting their hands on his hips and shoulders,

'Carrie?' Mae said. 'Are you joining us?'

I'd somehow ended up on the very edge of the group.

I wanted to stop her and tell Luke to get back up. I wanted to warn the others that there was something going on here that was more than a game. But the boy – the man – Luke was looking at me now and it was like he was challenging me or testing me.

Come on, Carrie, I'm a big boy, I imagined him saying. *You think I'm scared of taking a tablet? Don't you want us to have a little fun?*

Like an automaton, I crouched down beside him, placing my hands on his hard shoulders and biceps. This way at least, I told myself, I'd be able to supervise – not that someone like Luke should need that. He probably took all kinds of drugs all the time. But ever since we'd tried to light that fire and after what Mae had said to me that afternoon in the dorm room, I'd had a stupid paranoia about things getting out of hand.

'Close your eyes,' Mae told Luke. 'And don't mind if we touch you.'

Luke laughed again. I wished he'd stop laughing. I really wished he'd pay attention to what was going on.

'Fine. Just you girls though,' he said, opening one eye again. 'Not the boys. I'm not into anything like that.'

'Be quiet,' said Mae, and the words lifted the hairs on the back of my neck. It was as forceful as if she'd pressed a hand to his mouth and hissed, *Shut the fuck up.*

Luke went stone quiet. *Finally,* I thought, with a plunge of my stomach, *he feels it.* It's registering with him. This command that Mae has. That we *all* have.

'Close your eyes,' Mae repeated, and this time Luke obeyed her.

Carefully, I moved my hands to his forehead, half restraining, half checking. Serena snaked her hands around his feet. We'd learned, through our experiments, that having someone hold you like this enhanced the experience. When everything crumbled and dissolved inside and around you, it literally felt like the world burst apart.

'Keep your eyes closed, but open your mouth now.'

I watched like a hawk as, with her thumb, Mae slipped a tablet onto his tongue.

A single white pill.

In a shaky rush, I felt the fear flush out of me. Just one. One tablet – we'd done that a million times. I could feel Mae grinning at me, laughing at me through the gloom.

What did you think I was going to do – kill him?

Mae pressed his jaw closed and I pressed my own hands down firmly now on Luke's forehead and chest. Serena let out a tiny wisp of laughter, and I didn't blame her. The sheer intensity of it all made me feel mildly hysterical.

Now that I wasn't freaking out anymore, it honestly felt like something extraordinary might happen. Maybe Luke would levitate. Maybe rubies and snakes would rain from the sky. Perhaps the trees around us would burst into flames. I pressed my hands harder to Luke's forehead and clavicles. All three of us leaned our weight on him, pressing him against the earth. I could feel his taut muscles resisting us, fighting back, even though he barely moved.

We leaned harder, like we were trying to crush him. We weren't. Honestly, we just wanted him to feel.

Under our hands, we could feel him softening, and it honestly seemed like *we* were doing it to him, not the drugs. It happened slowly, then it went quickly. His legs went loose; then his body, his arms. Right then, there was nothing in his power he could have done to stop us.

We watched him drop, slip. It felt good, overseeing him like that. Like we were in charge of everything that was happening. Like he was passing all the control into our hands. Maybe, I realized, this was what Mae had been after all along.

Gently – so gently – we stretched out his limbs, letting him experience the full weight of dissolving. We sat with him: cradled him, stroked him, moved our hands over him, like those three Macbeth witches, weaving our spells.

The boys came closer, half concerned, half mesmerized. The three of us girls smiled at each other, the exhilaration blooming inside me reflected in their eyes.

Luke went loose, limp; he unravelled. His eyes rolled; he

groaned. I felt the pleasure course through my own body, vicariously.

We stretched him out, and let him enjoy the ride.

*

I hadn't noticed that Alex had brought his camera that night. Despite him turning the lens on almost everything else, we had never filmed the drug-taking before. Part of me had wanted him to do so: I'd wanted to see what we looked like. Whether it looked as beautiful and romantic as it felt . . .

But you know what it's like: observation changes everything.

As soon as we noticed him filming, it felt weird. Voyeuristic and creepy. Like we'd been performing as we recited our poem. Like we were making a porno or something. Moments later, Luke started laughing. He was trying to hold it in, but his shoulders shook.

'Shut *up*!' Serena admonished him, but it was too late, we all knew it. The spell was broken.

Victor came striding forwards as if to break up a dogfight. Luke shook us off and we clambered, giggling, to our feet. Alex groaned in disappointment and let the camera drop.

He ended up with barely a minute of footage. So short and stupid, we nearly forgot all about it. Until it became impossible to forget.

CHAPTER 30

Victor

2019

We left the hotel room in its state of chaos: broken glass and blood on the floor. Let Mae's sugar daddy deal with it. Let the hotel staff ask questions of him.

There was no way now we could keep prevaricating. Not with that footage plastered all over the Internet.

It was surely no coincidence that the email and video had appeared at the same time: just as the planning permission had been granted for the land. Each of those problems on their own was one thing, but both of them together – if we didn't get a handle on at least one of these things, we were fucked. There was little we could do about the video and basically nothing we could do about the land, but we could find Carrie before she did something even more stupid.

'She's not at home,' I told Mae, reeling off each of my attempts. 'I managed to track down the flatmate she lives with in that flat in Islington. I DM-ed her on Insta and established that much before I got blocked. Carrie's not answering her phone; she's not reading messages on any of her social media accounts. I've sent her an email – actually three emails, one to every address I've got for her – saying we need to talk *right away*, but of course she hasn't answered. Do you have *any* idea how to get hold of her?'

Mae sniffed back her last few tears and wiped at the smudged mascara round her eyes. It hadn't taken either of us very long to pack. Despite the extravagance and opulence of the hotel room, in the end, all Mae's belongings fitted into one Louis Vuitton suitcase. And all of mine fitted into the battered travel bag I'd arrived with from Madrid.

'It's been a long time,' she said, 'but I know where she could be. Remember her stepmum? In uni holidays, or when she was between flats, she often used to hole up there.'

'Okay. Fine. Let's go there, then.' It was a needle in a haystack, but to be honest, what other options did we have?

At the airport, Mae paid for both our flights on one of her numerous credit cards. A stopover in London, then on to Edinburgh.

I was seriously jittery by then, craving a hit for the first time in days, seeing shapes and shadows from the corners of my eyes. Under the sickly lights of the airport duty-free, there was a moment when I was even sure I'd glimpsed Alex, his blond hair flaring in my periphery, and my stomach rolled, my heart skipping a beat – a whole bar. But when I rubbed my eyes with the heel of my hand, the apparition had gone, nothing more than a product of my fevered mind.

I was so out of it that it didn't fully hit me until we were on the flight to Edinburgh, that we were going back *there*. The same rugged world: Scotland. I hadn't set foot there since we graduated from St Michael's; instead I'd tried to get as far away as I could. I leaned back in my seat and closed my eyes, listening to the sound of the plane's engines humming as memories dribbled through my exhausted mind. The smell of the cleaning products they used on the school desks, the cold of the tiles in the dormitory showers, the jarring shock of a tackle on the rugby field when the ground was still hard as concrete with frost.

Memories of when we were teenagers. Me and Alex. Then us and the girls.

As the plane began to shudder into its descent, Mae turned to look at me, those jewel-like eyes still shining despite all her crying back at the hotel. When she reached over and took my hand, I knew that she was remembering too. Everything that happened. Everything that, once upon a time, we had done. That *Carrie* had done.

I wrenched my gaze away and looked out of the porthole window at the land rushing up from below to meet us. Mae slipped her small, hot hand back out of mine.

*

As the plane hit the runway, new thoughts started to flip through my head. If Carrie planned to go to the police and tell them everything, why had she not done that by now? Why do all of this in such a clandestine way, sending us details of the land purchase, with a cryptic one-liner: *time to speak up* . . .

In other words, what the hell was she playing at?

'Mae,' I said as we taxied to our destination. 'On second thoughts, we don't have to do this. What if this is all just some fucked-up game Carrie's playing? What if we're walking into a trap?'

Mae was looking at me, glassy-eyed, as she unbuckled her seatbelt. 'No, you were right. You *are* right. We have to talk to her,' she said.

She stood up to retrieve her bag from the locker, hip jutting into my face. I followed her, fumbling with my own bag, clambering out of the plane seat, clipping my head on the luggage rack above. The pain was unnecessarily, shockingly sharp, and I had to grit my teeth not to let out a roar. Mae was already moving down the aisle but the large couple who had been sitting across from us pushed in front of me and I had to wait by my seat, allowing the infuriating pair to lumber past.

Finally, there was a gap and I hurried after her. 'Jesus, Mae, slow down.' It was anxiety as much as anything making me out of breath. 'I know we're both freaked out by this stupid Internet stuff, but slow down a minute. Let's think this through.'

'You don't get it,' said Mae.

'Get what?' We were crossing the airport tarmac now, in shitty Scottish weather, and the shift from the warmth of the cabin bruised my bones. 'All I know is that Carrie has no reason to take this to the police. Why would she? She'd literally be sending herself to jail.'

Mae turned to me. 'And what – you don't think the rest of us are culpable?'

I felt my stomach clench. 'We were just kids, Mae, like you said. It was Carrie's fault.'

She looked at me again. We were inside arrivals now, wet shoes squeaking on the shiny floor tiles. Bright yellow welcome signs loomed overhead.

'What?' I said again. 'It was!'

She was digging in her pocket now for her ticket to get us through arrivals. Suddenly, I had no idea where mine was.

'Stop,' I told her, flustered and panicky. 'Would you slow down for one second while I sort myself out?'

My anxiety was tipping over into frustration and anger. It was this feeling of helplessness, loss of control. I dropped my bag to the floor, kicked it, tore open each pocket. Here it was. My crumpled ticket.

'Right. Found it.' I kicked my bag again, just for the sake of it. But I couldn't just keep moving forwards. People swarmed around us, frowning, tutting, but I didn't care. Screw it if I was blocking their path; this was important.

'Honestly, Mae, what are we doing?' I grabbed her arm. She was so thin, like a doll. Little matchstick arms I could snap. 'You were right: let's just ignore her. If none of the rest of us get involved, it's her word against ours. All right, so the video footage proves that we knew him, that we hung out with him one time. But beyond that, who's to say we were all there *that night*? Who's to say she didn't mess the whole thing up alone?'

I was shaking now; I wondered whether Mae could feel it. She didn't even try to pull out of my grip. It was as if she was too numb even to feel how tightly I was holding her.

Her eyes were hollow divots when they met mine. 'You don't get it, do you, Victor? You think you know everything. But you weren't there the night after, were you?'

The night after. Like she'd said on the night of the yacht party. I let go of her, a wave of cold rushing up through me. I hadn't asked what she meant then and part of me didn't want to know now.

'What are you saying?'

'I'm saying, *you* were right. We need to shut her up, Victor. Trust me. If she's doing all this, it's not because she's playing a game or is trying to mess with us. Carrie's not smart enough for that. The only reason she sent us those emails, giving us a heads up that she plans to confess is—'

I stared at her. 'What?'

Mae looked sick. 'Is because she doesn't fucking *know*.'

CHAPTER 31

Finn

2019

'We should go back,' I said. 'Get off the train.'

'What?' said Mhairi. 'Why?'

'Because—' My hands were shaking. I fumbled with my phone again to find the other article, the Internet connection worse than ever. 'Let me pull it up.'

'Wait. We need to find our seats.'

But the carriage was rammed. An announcement came over the loudspeaker. *We apologize for the overcrowding on this service . . . Seating reservations no longer valid . . . cancelled train to Doncaster . . . passengers transferred . . .*

'Forget the seats,' I said. 'They'll already be taken. Here. Look.'

I showed her the article about the missing local. Aged nineteen. Blond hair, five foot nine. Distinguishing marks: a distinctive mole on his cheek.

Her breathing was fast and tight as she read it. She shook her head. 'I don't understand.'

'This man – this boy – is the one in that video with Carrie.'

'You can't be sure—'

'Can't I?' I showed her the photo in the missing poster again. 'Look at the picture. It's Luke Menzies. It's him.'

A woman with two toddlers was trying to squeeze past. The two of us were crushed up against each other. 'We need to get off and contact the police,' I whispered.

'The *police*?' She wasn't whispering and the woman at my shoulder side-eyed us. I kept my own voice as low as I could, but we were packed in so tightly, I feared everyone would hear.

'This is evidence.'

'Of what?'

'Evidence of whatever happened to this man! You still think we should just rock up at Carrie's stepmum's house to "have a chat", when Carrie might be involved in something like this?'

The doors were closed but the train hadn't left the station yet. There was still time to push our way off. I was hot, sweating; the vestibule was claustrophobic.

'We can't go to the police,' Mhairi muttered. We were both trying to keep our voices down.

'Why not?'

'Because . . .'

'Because *what*?'

Other people were turning to look at us now. I knew what we looked like: a married couple having a fight.

I shoved my phone back into my pocket and hitched up my bag. 'We're getting off,' I said, trying to figure out the best way through the scrum.

'No.' Mhairi grabbed my arm. 'I don't want to. I want to speak to Carrie before we do anything like that. What if Kate was involved in all this?'

'Exactly! We need to take what we know to the authorities.' We both understood now what that tape showed: that figure on the ground, the one with blond hair – that was not Alexander, but a boy called Luke. A nineteen-year-old who, in 2003, had gone missing. Kate's death had something to do with *this*.

Another announcement. *We apologize for the delay . . . awaiting our driver . . . Moving shortly . . . apologies once again*. A baby in the carriage started shrieking.

'Screw you, Finn, you never want what's best for me.'

I twisted back round in shock, fighting with myself not to shout my response. 'What the fuck, Mhairi?' I hissed. 'What's that supposed to mean?'

'You said it. Back then. You said you didn't want her.'

A flood of nausea washed through me. The crowd around us squeezed again as someone else shoved past.

'Mhairi, I was ill back then. I had no idea what I was saying.'

'But you *said* it.'

I wanted to slap her. 'I was *ill*.'

Her face twisted. 'Well, you got what you wanted, didn't you? It all worked out. You got better after that.'

I needed to get off this train. I couldn't stand the words she was saying. 'Excuse me,' I said, shouldering my way through. 'Excuse me, *please*—'

With a jolt, the train moved.

She yanked at my arm. 'You can't get off now, Finn, we're moving.'

I turned back to her. 'Then are you going to take back what you said?'

Her mouth was a stony red line as she looked up at me, her eyes dark pools: so different compared to when we were married. So different even to at Kate's funeral, when she had taken my hand.

The train jerked, heaving us towards and away from each other. This time my voice was more like pleading. '. . . Mhairi?'

'I can't, Finn, I'm sorry. *This* is why I never wanted to talk about it. Because this is how I feel. I always have.'

CHAPTER 32

Carrie

2003

In mid-December, Bryony was sent home – or rather, taken home. Her parents had seen the coverage in the newspaper and were insisting on taking matters into their own hands. The school didn't put up much of a fight; it was obvious to everyone they'd exhausted all their efforts to handle her. Serena, Mae and I watched from our dormitory window as Bryony climbed into her nanny's car and was driven away.

'Maybe that'll be the end of it,' Serena said.

Not long after that – just a day or so maybe – I came across Mae sitting outside Ms Dunham's office.

'Hey,' I said. 'What's up?' I assumed she was there for some kind of head girl business. Either that, or she'd been sent to the head for some misdemeanour, which I highly doubted. Despite all of the school rules we'd been breaking for weeks, Mae was far too smart to let herself get caught.

'I've got a meeting,' she said. 'At one o'clock.'

I plonked myself down beside her in the row of chairs that lined the wall outside. 'Head girl stuff?'

But Mae was chewing on her thumbnail again. I laughed. 'You're not in trouble, are you?'

She went on chewing. 'Of course not.'

But despite what I'd just told myself, I suddenly felt scared. 'They haven't found out anything, have they?' I whispered. I thought we'd been smarter – or luckier – than that. But we had been getting reckless lately. Sloppy. Suddenly I felt stupid. All it would have taken was for one of the other pupils to look out of their window in the middle of the night and see our figures scurrying up the hill.

'No,' said Mae. 'I asked for the meeting.'

What did *that* mean? 'What for?'

Mae was breathing in and out through her nose, hard. She looked up at the plastic clock in the hallway. Five minutes to one. 'It doesn't matter.'

'Why?' I said, trying to sound playful. 'Is it a secret or something?'

'No.'

'Then what are you here for?' I knew I was pushing her, but I was getting edgy. With everything we'd been up to of late, it freaked me out to think there was something Mae wasn't telling me. What if she was planning to say something that dumped us all in the shit?

She went on gnawing at that nail, her leg jiggling now as well. She was a ball of tension.

'Mae—?'

'Forget it.' She leaned down and pulled her bag from under the chair.

I stumbled to my feet as she got to hers. 'Where are you going?'

Her cheeks were two burning spots of red. 'I told you, forget it.'

She set off up the corridor, me trotting behind her. 'Sorry, Mae. What is it? Can I help?'

I followed her as she pushed her way out of the doors that led outside, letting them swing back and almost clip me in the face. I hurried after her, calling stupidly, 'What about your meeting?'

She stopped and turned round to face me. It was freezing out here and there was a horrible, biting wind.

'You know what, Carrie? Sometimes you don't see things, do you? You think you're so observant and clever. You aren't though, are you?' She let out a bark of a laugh. 'School shooting, my arse. Did you think we believed you? Do you think I'm not capable of using Google, checking dates? You were too young to have been at Kelviston High when that happened.'

Angrily she pushed her tangled hair out of her eyes. I had no idea what to say. I was burning with embarrassment and shock.

'I'm sorry,' I said pathetically. 'I should never have said that. But . . .' I took a breath. 'If there are things going on, Mae, you should tell me. We're all in this together, right?'

Her face was twisted in a strange grimace, so many different emotions fighting within her. Her mouth bent into an ironic smile.

'You know what, Carrie? Fine, I'll tell you. I'll tell you *things*. I'll tell you about this guy you might know. About how, whenever I have to meet him, we end up fooling around. How he likes to touch me and do things to me, and how he always wants me to do things to him. How he wants me to set him up with *you* next. How he's kind of bored of me, but kind of interested in *my friend*.'

I couldn't comprehend what she was saying. Shock and disgust went reeling around in my head. And – if I was brutally honest – pathetically, horribly, a tiny flicker of vanity too.

'Who are you talking about?' I croaked. 'You mean Luke?'

Mae didn't bother to answer me. She just looked at me like, *Are you such an idiot, Carrie? Don't you know?*

I thought about how easy it was for her to get the drugs from him. How they never seemed to cost us that much. But – Luke? Really? I hadn't seen any sign of it. And if he was like that, why did she keep on inviting him to join in?

Because maybe she doesn't want to be stuck on her own with him. Because she's just told you, he'd like to get to know you next.

'Then we need to . . .' I trailed off. Needed to what? Stop talking to Luke, stop seeing him? Stop getting the drugs? My stomach clenched at that. I'd thought getting this far away would stop me thinking about my parents – especially since according to my dad they were 'getting on fine now' – but in the night memories of their fights were dogging me worse than ever and sometimes the drugs were the only thing that helped. 'I'll say something to him,' I said, defiantly. 'I'll tell him that isn't going to be how this works.'

But suddenly Mae looked completely deflated. She pressed the heels of her hands to her eyes and shook her head. 'Don't, Carrie,' she said. 'Please, just forget it. I never should have said anything about it to you.'

*

Right away, I told Serena. I had to. She needed to know what we were dealing with, with Luke.

For once I had no homework to do. Mae was still at prep. In our dormitory, Serena was pulling off a sticky wetsuit following her kayaking session, so I had a few minutes to talk to her alone.

I relayed everything Mae had told me – everything, that is, except what Luke had said about me.

To my surprise, Serena just shook her head. 'I dunno, Carrie. Sometimes Mae . . . says stuff.'

I stared at her. 'What are you talking about? Didn't you hear what I just said? She says he's—'

Was what? I wasn't even sure of the right word. Manipulating? Exploiting? *Abusing?*

Serena yanked her dark-blonde hair out of its ponytail, dragging every strand at the roots. 'I know. I heard you. But I *also* know Mae is quite capable at getting what she wants.'

'Meaning what?'

'Meaning . . .' Serena faced me, her muscled body still half encased in black. 'Meaning, Mae isn't stupid. Meaning, Mae doesn't say yes to things she doesn't want.'

My voice shrivelled in my throat. *You can't say that about our friend!* I yelled inside. 'Doesn't she?' I croaked instead.

I was *trying* to make a stand. I was trying to speak up and do right by my friend, but I felt like I was standing on a knife edge, Mae's words and Serena's words clashing in my brain. Mae had been planning to go to Ms Dunham. Why would she do that if there wasn't something wrong? At the same time . . . why *would* she do that – turn herself in, and risk being expelled?

'I don't know . . .' I said. 'How Mae said it . . . I don't think it was like that.'

'Well.' Serena turned away again, headed towards the bathroom. 'You don't know everything, Carrie.' She paused. 'And anyway, are you sure she meant Luke?'

CHAPTER 33

Carrie

2003

Still, despite everything, we couldn't keep away. Like moths to a flame. Like my parents relentlessly drawn back to each other despite the chaos that always eventually ensued.

Maybe we were needing the drugs more than ever. Ava and Bryony had gone from the school now, but news about them still sometimes trickled back in. Last week, we'd learned that Bryony had slashed up her arms – and her face – and got sectioned. A girl who'd once been best friends with Bryony had told us *her* mother had called *Bryony's* mother to find out how she was doing, and Bryony's mum had confided in her, and that was how we all came to know.

And then what Mae had said about Luke – and I was sure it *was* Luke she'd been talking about, because all this time I'd been watching Alex and Victor like a hawk – had unnerved me to my core. So I felt sick when two nights later, we went up the hill and found him there again, in our hollow.

I grabbed Mae. 'Did you invite him?' I muttered.

She shrugged me off and carried on walking forwards. 'No.' But by now he knew we were up there every Friday and Saturday night.

Serena glanced sideways at me, in her torchlight. 'By now, Carrie, I don't think he needs an invitation.'

Well, that's fucking arrogant! I wanted to say. It made me more mad with him than ever.

Victor and Alex were ahead of me, already greeting him, like we were all the best of friends and they were delighted to have another guy in the gang. Mae's words spun in my mind. *He likes to touch me . . . he wants me to do things to him.* And Serena's words. *Mae doesn't say yes to things she doesn't want.* Then Mae's words again. *He's kind of bored of me, but kind of interested in* my friend.

Right at that moment, Luke looked up at me. 'Carrie – good to see you.' His words slurred, and I caught him tucking a half-empty vodka bottle back into his thick coat.

My heart stumbled a beat. *Be cool, Carrie. Be cool.*

Fine, I thought, if Mae doesn't mind him being here, why should I? Why couldn't I still have fun with my friends?

Part of me felt that Mae was an idiot. If even half of the things she had told me were true, then Luke was a dickhead at the very least. And I was quite prepared to treat him as that.

'Hi, Luke,' I called back, my voice smooth. 'Great to see you too.'

*

We let him be the one to go in the centre. It always felt best when you lay flat out and the others circled around, put their hands on you and held you like that.

'My treat.' Luke grinned.

He's not stupid, I told myself. *He's come here willingly.* He was the one putting himself in our hands.

Mae hadn't said anything. Neither had Serena. I slipped off my coat, the long, thick one that was like a duvet, and laid it on the ground for him. 'Here you go,' I heard myself saying.

'Thanks, darlin',' he said, and practically gave me a wink. I smiled back at him, all sweetness and light.

He lay down and, standing there, for a moment, it was like I was looking down from above on the whole group of us. Three boys, and the original three girls. A shiver ran through me. But it was a shudder of anticipation and excitement now, not fear.

Luke opened one eye, impatiently. 'Come on then.'

I took my own pill; just a half this time, I wanted to stay clear-headed, and I was aware of the others swallowing theirs too.

Easy as yawning, the three of us knelt down beside him. Surrounding him like that: it made my blood sing.

Like we'd done so many times before, Serena settled herself cross-legged at his head, hands cupping his temples. Mae placed her hands on his shoulders. A little way outside our circle, Alex and Victor drowsily held the torches, anticipating a buzz of their own. I knelt down beside Luke, the cold damp of the ground pressing through the knees of my jeans.

Serena started up the chanting, those funny words we had co-opted as our own.

. . . I see a lily on thy brow, With anguish moist and fever-dew, And on thy cheeks a fading rose, Fast withereth too . . .

The first time, the words had made Luke laugh, and now I saw him open an eye and frown, squirming under our hands. We went on holding him tight.

I placed the other bitter tablets on my tongue. One, two . . . and then a third. Mae leaned in, her hands sliding over Luke's chest.

I took a deep breath in through my nose and leaned down, catching the scent of alcohol on his breath. Butterfly-like, my lips made contact with his, a burst of warm in the cold of the woods. His mouth opened up to mine and I felt the weak flutter of breath from his nose.

Now it's you he's interested in, Carrie.

I passed the pills over to him with my tongue, thinking of when Mae had done this with Alex, and of the silly game we'd played with Victor's tarot cards, passing The Fool from one mouth to the other, securing it with your breath, your pressed lips, your breath . . .

When I sat back up, even I felt a little swirly. The pills always dissolved a tiny bit on your tongue; I could feel the layer of grit. Serena went on stroking Luke's forehead, his cheeks; his head was now cradled in her lap. Mae curled herself up on the cold ground beside him, arm across his stomach, holding him tight.

I positioned myself at his feet, waiting until the rush came and he went limp. Under cover of darkness, I slid my hands along the flesh of his legs, twisting it, pinching it, while he lay helpless, too out of it to defend himself. I took out all my anger and fear and aggression on his body, itching almost to sink my teeth in and tear at him, feeling the endorphins course through my veins.

*

The following Sunday, I was locking up the sports pavilion after our afternoon hockey game and was just making my way back to the school entrance, last one to trail in, desperate for toast in the dorm, when I heard a car crunch on the gravel behind me.

The headlights swung across me and I stepped to the side, fearing that they'd run me over.

I had no idea who the driver might be.

The car pulled up ahead of me, still a little way from the school steps. I stood motionless, heart thudding. The engine was still running, red tail-lights glowing in the gloom.

I approached slowly – I was going to have to walk past to get back to the school but I had visions of the window rolling down and the car door opening, and someone grabbing me, abducting me and speeding me away.

But when the window buzzed down, it wasn't a stranger at all.

It was the psychologist.

'What are you doing here?' I asked. It was a bit rude, but these last two days I'd been ridiculously on edge.

'Oh. Hi.' She squinted up at me. 'Carrie, isn't it?'

It jarred that she even knew my name, but she'd done her best to familiarize herself with the whole student body.

'I just came by to see how the girls were doing since my last visit,' she went on. 'I've finished my training placement. I'll be moving on now, but I wanted to . . . see how they're doing before I go.'

'Is Ms Dunham or someone expecting you?' My voice was stiff, the question rote.

'Oh. No. I came on the off chance.'

I could feel the heat escaping from her car. I could see my breath in the air, like big thought bubbles that could give me away. *Calm down, calm down. She's just come to check on the younger girls.* 'I could take you up to her office,' I managed. 'See if we can find her.'

'Oh . . . I don't know. It's probably not appropriate without an appointment. I just wanted to know how they were getting on.'

I let out a whoosh of air and wrapped my arms around myself. She was right: I doubted Ms Dunham would have time to see her. 'Well, Stephanie and that lot,' I said in a rush, 'they're all fine now. Whatever you did with them really helped.'

The psychologist's face brightened. It was true. A national paper had recently picked up the story, but *that* article had included a statement from our headmistress: *Happily, the affected girls are all recovered now and/or receiving further appropriate support.*

'That's . . . good. And . . . what about Ava and Bryony?'

I hesitated. 'Ava's moved schools. I think she's doing better. Bryony recently got sent home.'

'Oh. Right. And so how's *she* doing?'

My throat tightened. We'd all heard the rumours: rumours that were almost definitely true. But I wasn't sure the psychologist would want to hear them.

I pushed the words out of my mouth; like wet cement,

hardening fast. 'Actually, I heard that Bryony got admitted to a psychiatric place. Like – sectioned? She was . . . cutting herself. I think it got quite bad.'

The psychologist's face fell like I'd stabbed her in the ribcage. 'Oh. Oh no. I'm so sorry to hear that. That's terrible. I should have . . .' She rubbed at her face.

Suddenly, I didn't want to talk to her anymore. I realised I should never have talked to her in the first place.

'I don't know if that's true,' I said quickly. 'It's just what I heard. For all I know, she's perfectly okay.'

But she didn't seem to be listening. 'I wanted to keep working with them,' she said. 'Give them sessions of individual support. But my placement supervisor . . . and then there were only so many appointments we could allocate. But I would have done more, and I always meant to speak with your friend.'

I flinched. 'My friend? You mean . . . Bryony?'

'No – no, not Bryony. Margaret, isn't it? I think you call her Mae.'

A sharp chill ran through me. 'What does Mae have to do with this?'

She shook her head. 'Never mind. I'm sorry. Listen, I probably shouldn't have come here. Thank you though, Carrie. I appreciate you talking to me.' She put the car in gear and released the handbrake. 'If you're in touch with them, let them know I was asking after them? Ava and Bryony. And Mae? And if you ever need—'

I stepped away from her, away from the car and its heat. My voice was stiff. 'Yes. Of course. I'll do that, Dr Fallon.'

She smiled: a sad, painful, haunted kind of smile. 'Thank you, Carrie. And you know, you can always call me Kate.'

Text from: Mhairi
Sent to: Kate
19.37pm, 06/06/2013

I spoke to Finn.
I don't know what's happening but he's really not okay.
Kate, what do I do?

    Text from: Kate
    Sent to: Mhairi
    14.39pm, 06/06/2013

    Oh Mhairi. Tell me what he said specifically.

Text from: Mhairi
Sent to: Kate
19.39pm, 06/06/2013

He's hung weird charms all over the nursery. He says he
has to stop it.
    He says he just wants all this to stop.
    He's scaring me. I don't know what's wrong.

    Text from: Kate
    Sent to: Mhairi
    14.40pm, 06/06/2013

    I'm calling you right now.

Text from: Kate
Sent to: Mhairi
14.59pm, 06/06/2013

It's okay, Mhairi. I'm so glad the phone connected. You've explained everything perfectly.

Here are the crisis contacts. Call the top number first, and tell the team what I said to you.

They can arrange an urgent assessment for Finn. They'll take good care of him. They'll know what to do.

I'm booking my flight now.

I'm coming straight home.

Text from: Mhairi
Sent to: Kate
20.02pm, 06/06/2013

I'm calling them now.

Text from: Kate
Sent to: Mhairi
09.06am, 07/06/2013

I've landed at Heathrow. I'll be with you as soon as I can.

Xxx Kate

Text from: Mhairi
Sent to: Kate
10.01am, 07/06/2013

An ambulance came with the police. They admitted him
last night.

CHAPTER 34

Finn

2019

It was seven p.m. and raining when we reached Edinburgh.

I was still stunned from the words we'd hurled at each other on the train – the culmination of everything that had been bubbling up between us since Kate's death: the funeral that had thrown me and Mhairi back together, all the conversations and phone calls we'd had to have, all the anger and guilt that had been ruthlessly dredged up. We'd been on borrowed time before everything cracked open. Now our wounds were split and seeping, bloodying everything.

As we pulled into Waverley Station, the light was low, smudged by rain and clouds. Smells hit me as soon as we climbed the steps out of the train station: cold stone, wet pavement, the tang of urine.

A whipping wind and a crush of pedestrians on the pavements slowed our progress, bags and umbrellas catching us as we tried to push through. Above the noisy, rain-spattered Princes Street, the skyline was jagged: the needle of Scott Monument, the ragged ridge of rock that raised up Edinburgh Castle.

'Morningside,' said Mhairi. 'That's where we need to go.' It was as though we were both operating on autopilot now, unable to do anything but run the original programme: *find Carrie, get to Valerie Greaves's house.*

I stepped into the wide road scored with steel tramlines to flag down a passing black cab. The taxi pulled up, splashing us, the cabin filling up with condensation as we clambered inside and I read the address out on my phone to the driver. 'It's not far, is it?' I asked.

'Not at all, mate.'

Mhairi beside me, I slammed shut the heavy door of the taxi, blocking out the worst of the outside noise and chill. The driver pulled away jerkily from the kerb, heading up Princes Street, shops on the right, the Gardens on the left, blue and white flags wrestling in the wind. He drove aggressively, starting and stopping violently at each intersection as questions clawed their way through my head: what are we doing here? How can Mhairi and I do this when we can barely look at each other? What did these kids have to do with Luke Menzies – a missing person? Shouldn't I turn tail, escape Mhairi and go straight to the police?

We turned off the main street, heading south, climbing upwards past a church, a theatre, spaces of green. The driver jarred the brakes again and I lurched forwards.

'That's it,' he said, pointing at a row of grey stone town-houses with grey slate roofs and tall bay windows.

'Here?' I said, just as I spotted it: number 53. 'Yes, sorry, you're right.' I fumbled in my wallet for cash, only able to hand over an English ten-pound note. 'Thank you. Keep the change.'

Then Mhairi and I were on the rain-swept street, staring up at the house in front of us. A neat front garden with a low stone wall and gravel path to a front door painted primrose yellow.

'We don't have to do this,' I said desperately. 'We can still turn back.'

Mhairi shook her head, her lips tight where she was controlling her emotions – her rage? 'We're here now. If Carrie's willing to speak to us, we'll get some answers. If she's not here or if—' She broke off. 'Then we'll contact the police.'

I pressed the doorbell, hearing it ring with a sharp trill inside.

No response.

'Again,' said Mhairi.

The trill of the bell stuttered this time, as though its battery was low or dying. When I pressed it again to make sure, it made no sound at all.

'It's not working,' I said, clutching at the relief, ready to step back, get away.

Mhairi reached up past me, taking hold of the heavy knocker in the centre of the door. Three sharp raps. Undoubtedly loud enough for someone to hear.

But as she did so, the door clicked open. The hall beyond was wood-panelled. I made out cream-coloured walls, the sleek edge of a banister.

'Hello?' called Mhairi, her voice raw.

No one was there. No one had opened the door to greet us. It had swung open under the force of Mhairi's hand.

We stood frozen on the doorstep, too surprised to step back or go forwards.

Until we heard faint voices from inside.

Followed by a scream.

CHAPTER 35

Carrie

2019

I chose Kate for a reason. Not just because she looked kind and intelligent in the photo on her website. Not just because of the impressive qualifications listed there. I didn't even live that near her. I chose her because, once upon a time, she had come to our school.

According to her CV, St Michael's was one of her first training placements. She was probably only in her mid twenties back then. Despite how young she was, she had helped Polly, Cynthia and Anna, Stephanie and Faye. *If you ever need . . .* she had even said to me.

Because of that, and because of what she already knew, I trusted her before we even met for my assessment.

I thought that would help.

Like hell it did.

*

I felt quite crazy when I booked that first appointment. Not totally gone, but increasingly disturbed, paranoid. I couldn't shake the idea that I was *cursed*, because of what had happened back then. Because of what we – *I* – had done. Bad things had kept happening to the people I knew. A girl from uni was killed in a freak accident. A colleague's child was savaged by a dog. A family was murdered two streets over from my flat.

For a time, I told myself not to be stupid. It was bad, but bad stuff happened in the world all the time. You only had to watch the news or go on Facebook.

But then there was my mum with her alcohol relapses. And my dad, now on the brink of his third divorce. *Before* what happened, their lives had seemed to be getting better. *Afterwards*, their lives only seemed to get worse.

Then came what happened to Alex. His car veering and plummeting off the road.

I grew more irrational than ever after that. It no longer felt like statistics or accidents or coincidences, but a pattern. People in my orbit suffered or relapsed or died. The haunted feeling wouldn't leave me alone.

It got so that I was scared to be around people, scared to even go out. My GP diagnosed social anxiety and agoraphobia, but I knew it was much more complicated than that.

If I was *cursed*, then there had to be some way to lift it. That was how I saw it, but I wasn't going to go looking for an exorcist or a medium or anything like that. I thought there was a more straightforward way to make it stop. I still had a toe-hold in reality at that point. I knew at some level that it was irrational thinking.

I told myself I needed to speak up and tell someone.

And the person I chose was Dr Fallon. Kate.

My plan all the way along was to tell her what had happened. I thought she would guide me and tell me what to do. She admitted that she remembered me from St Michael's, but she didn't say anything about it other than that. So boundaried, never letting her own stuff intrude. Or so I thought.

So much tumbled out of me in that very first session, like a polluted reservoir bursting its banks. In that ninety-minute assessment appointment I vomited everything out – or, almost everything. My parents' divorce, my abrupt move to the States. My mother's drinking, my parents' enmeshment. Changing schools yet again to arrive at St Michael's, my desperation to fit in, our nights up on the ridge. My friendships with Serena and Mae and Victor and Alex, and how, not so many years later, Alex killed himself.

And the Fainting Girls – I couldn't seem to stop talking about them. I talked to Kate about how messed up it had all been, and how I'd heard Bryony was still in and out of psych wards to this day.

I think I was so aware of my own madness hovering, desperately trying to tell her, *Please, Kate, I don't want to end up like that.*

I talked about the confusion and chaos and lack of safety I felt back then, because that loss of control seemed to have been the spark for everything, and also because it delayed me from ever getting to the worst part: the thing I'd really come here to discuss.

With every piece of myself that I shared and she listened to, I felt lighter. I felt my sanity knitting back together. I felt safer than I had in a long, long time.

By the end of that first session, I had brought myself right to the cusp of it, ready to tell her everything. I said I wanted to come back for another session; we booked another appointment for two weeks' time. The next time we met, I was going to confess everything. It had been sixteen years; I couldn't do it anymore.

A fortnight later, it was all balanced and waiting on the tip of my tongue. Instead—

*

Instead came the phone call from Dr Sebastian Hart. I was asleep when he rang, in the stultifying fug of a sickly afternoon nap. For some reason, the ringer on my phone was on the highest setting so my phone literally screamed at me. My whole body prickled with raw adrenaline as I fumbled to swipe at the screen and answer.

I didn't recognize his voice. I had no idea who he was.

When he introduced himself as Kate's supervisor, my first thought was: *This is it. You've been found out. It's over.*

I thought that somehow Kate had figured it out, even though I still hadn't told her the whole truth at that point. I was almost relieved. After all, wasn't this what I had wanted all along – to confess?

But that was followed by a flicker of concern, because why was this Sebastian Hart calling me and not Kate? It was Kate I had felt safe enough to entrust my secrets to. It was Kate who I wanted to be by my side for whatever came next.

I pushed my sticky, sweaty hair back from my forehead, and sat up in my rumpled bed.

'Yes,' I said. 'This is Caroline.'

When he told me what had happened, I dropped the phone as if it had burnt me. My whole body went ice cold.

All I could think was: *it's happening again. It's happening again. This curse.*

I felt sick. In fact, I was sick, stumbling out of bed and rushing to the bin in the corner of my cramped room in the flat-share.

Faintly, I could hear Dr Hart's voice on the line, still speaking. I didn't go near my phone again. I didn't touch it. I suppose I feared that if I did, if I let myself speak to him too, he would be the next one to drop down dead.

Instead I just sat hunched in the corner, my arms wrapped around my shins, forehead pressed to the bones of my knees.

Eventually Dr Hart gave up. My phone rang again, three or four times. I didn't answer. Then it chirruped with alerts for a voicemail and a text. I never listened to or read any of them.

Kate was dead, and that hard, black thing was still lodged inside me: my confession, my guilt.

I couldn't bear it.

Back then, we had each made a pact and a promise to one another. A desperate, violent promise. We'd each of us held our hands to the flame of Mae's lighter, holding it there until the skin blistered, promising to take this secret to our graves.

But now I needed to break that scorched pact. I needed them to release me from the promises I'd made.

In desperation, I created an email address – still not brave enough to send this from my own. From backwoods03@protonmail.com I sent matching messages, attaching an article that I hoped would force their hands, appealing collectively to their sense of fear and guilt, in the hopes I could convince them to let me finally speak up.

I sent them to the only other three people who knew.

*

After that, I'm not sure exactly how long I stayed there in the corner of my room. I seemed to have developed a raging fever. Something in my mind had broken, and it had made me physically ill.

At some point, my flatmate knocked on my door. It was dark outside my window by then. My whole body ached. I must have been sitting there for hours.

I managed to call in a croaky voice through the closed door, 'I'm fine. Just hungover. I'm going to stay in bed.' I crawled back under the sheets.

She put her head round the door again some hours later, but I pretended to be asleep, head buried under a pillow. I felt terrible, like the worst flu you could ever have, the highest fever. And my whole body was awash with fear at the same time.

I had my answer now. I had my proof. All these people – my uni friend, my work colleague, the neighbourhood murder and the ones that hurt the most: my mum, my dad, Alex – their tragedies were my fault. And now Kate, too.

I remember lying in that stinking bed, aching, shivering, starving and dehydrated, too weak to move, almost too weak to think. Eventually I must have fallen asleep from sheer exhaustion, because the next thing I knew, my phone was ringing again, but it wasn't Dr Hart this time, or any of my old friends or my flatmate.

It was Valerie. One of the few people in my life who'd never seen me as a problem, who'd always taken an interest without ever looking for something for themselves. She had divorced my dad in 2006 so now wasn't even technically related, but she had been more of a parent to me than anyone in my whole life.

As soon as I heard her voice, I burst into tears.

*

The journey to Valerie's was a blur.

Somehow, I packed a bag and scribbled a note for my flatmate. *Gone to stay with family for a bit.* Somehow I must have got myself on a bus, then a train north, then a taxi to her door.

I was so weak and in pain the whole time. When the taxi dropped me off on Valerie's doorstep, I hardly had the strength to reach up and ring the bell, and when she opened the door, I practically fell into the hallway.

I was swimming in and out of consciousness as Valerie helped me upstairs and into the spare bedroom, which was plain white and blessedly cool. She helped me out of my crumpled clothes, easing me into the clean bed sheets, holding a glass of water to my lips and a cool palm to my cheek.

I fell into a deep, dark sleep then. Dark as the woods behind the school. I dreamed of awful things. Monsters, ghouls, somebody shrieking, screaming, even though that never happened. I must have cried out, because I remember Valerie shushing me, comforting me, and that made me burst into tears all over again.

Each time she left the room, I rolled over, pulling the

blankets up over my face, shivers running through me again, but from fear this time, not fever.

When Valerie came in on the third day, bearing chicken soup, I managed to sit up in the soft white bed and eat some.

When she asked me if I was feeling any better, I nodded, even though it was a lie.

'You were really sick,' she said. 'I called NHS 111 and they said to take you to see a doctor tomorrow if you weren't any better.' She stuck a thermometer under my tongue, the slippery plastic of it feeling familiar. She must have been checking my temperature at regular intervals since I got here.

'Thirty-seven point three,' she announced. 'It's getting pretty much back to normal.'

She went quiet then, setting the thermometer down on the bedside table and letting her empty hands rest in her lap (she was sitting on the side of the bed, trapping my thighs under the blanket). I thought about how Dad had been a fool to divorce her and how she could have been so good for him if he hadn't acted like such an ass.

'So,' she said now. 'Want to talk about it?'

I didn't answer. The chicken soup was thick in my throat, like mud.

'Whatever it is,' she went on, 'we can deal with it.'

But how could I tell her? It had been enough of a risk just coming to her house, inflicting myself on her like that with this thing that I was still carrying around with me, infecting everyone and everything I touched.

Tears spilled from my eyes again, and Valerie put her arm round me. I leaned against her, just letting the sobs come. She was probably thinking I'd been through something like a rape or an abortion, something terrible like that. She would have no inkling of what I'd really done. At school and all the years after, I'd done my best to hide my guilt and horror from everyone, passing my Highers and Advanced Highers, completing a university degree, securing a job, never letting anyone see how I was falling apart. Like that photo of the five of us in the local paper, celebrating our exam results.

Five Firm Friends with their Fantastic Results!

Looking at us, you'd never have guessed what we were each holding inside. Now I couldn't seem to hold anything together anymore.

Valerie held me close, rocking me. 'I'm sorry,' was all I managed to spit out, tears smearing her shoulder. 'I'm sorry!'

At one point, Valerie asked whether she should call my mum or my dad or my flatmate. I just shook my head. I couldn't bear to speak to anyone else. Instead, Valerie said I could stay with her for as long as I needed. *For the rest of my life?* I wanted to ask. Because I had no idea what to do with myself beyond this.

*

Eventually, I felt well enough to get up out of bed. I had eaten almost nothing in the last week, and hadn't been looking after myself particularly well before that. My legs were shaky as a new-born calf's.

Still, I made it downstairs, where I sat on Valerie's soft sofa. She told me she needed to get back to work, and then I realized that she must have taken this whole last week off. She had dropped all her commitments just to look after me. The very fact of it made my eyes well up again.

I wiped the tears away and nodded. 'Thank you for everything. I'm feeling better. I am.' I had managed to have breakfast and get showered and wash my hair that morning.

'It's no problem. And you can still stay here while I'm out. There's food in the kitchen and painkillers in the bathroom. Help yourself to whatever you need.'

After she left, the heavy door slamming shut behind her, her heels clicking away on the pavement outside, I pulled up the blanket, wrapping it around me like a shield, and switched on my phone. Valerie had turned it off days ago, wanting me to rest and sleep, and I hadn't turned it back on since.

Now I scrabbled at the switch, heart thudding as it beeped into life.

There were all the missed calls and a voicemail from Dr Hart: something about Kate and the coroner's office; I deleted those straight away. There were other missed calls from numbers I didn't recognize.

But in my emails was the message I'd been waiting for. Hoping for, dreading, and now here it was.

Got your email. You're absolutely right. We need to talk, immediately.

There was also a day and a time and a place for us to meet. Somewhere I could fairly easily get to, and suddenly my heart was a mess of terror. When the doorbell rang, the jolt of adrenaline seemed to dislocate my bones.

I got up, muscles shaky, head still fuzzy, and dragged myself along the hallway in my blanket, stupidly thinking it was Valerie popping back for something she'd forgotten. It didn't register that Valerie wouldn't have needed to ring her own bell. I caught sight of myself in the hallway mirror, hair damp from my shower, sticking up in tangled tufts round my head.

You look like a mental patient, I thought.

I turned the doorknob and the front door swung open.

It took me a split second to recognize them, but when I did, it felt like the manifestation of all my wrongdoings was standing right there on the step. Stupidly, I tried to slam the door closed again, suddenly terrified to face the realities of my guilt, but my fumbling efforts were ineffective and weak and it only took her hand on the door to prevent me.

Her voice was so smooth and reasonable when she said, 'Hi, Carrie. Don't you think we'd better come in?'

Text from: Mhairi
Sent to: Kate
13.04pm, 14/06/2013

It was awful, seeing him there.

> **Text from:** Kate
> **Sent to:** Mhairi
> *13.04pm, 14/06/2013*
>
> They'll help him. You did the right thing.

Text from: Mhairi
Sent to: Kate
13.04pm, 14/06/2013

I want to run away.

> **Text from:** Kate
> **Sent to:** Mhairi
> *13.06pm, 14/06/2013*
>
> I know it's hard but you have to keep visiting him.
> Finn needs you right now. You can't abandon him.

Text from: Mhairi
Sent to: Kate
13.13pm, 14/06/2013

But I can't bear what he said. It was awful. And when I
visited him last week, he seemed nothing like Finn.

Text from: Kate
Sent to: Mhairi
13.14pm, 14/06/2013

But it IS Finn. It's your husband. He was so ill when
he said that. He didn't mean it. He was so relieved to
see me when I was there yesterday. He's asking for
you.
You have to go and see him again.

Text from: Kate
Sent to: Mhairi
13.17pm, 14/06/2013

You there?

Text from: Mhairi
Sent to: Kate
13.22pm, 14/06/2013

Okay. I will. I'll go.

CHAPTER 36

Victor

2019

The last thing I'd expected was for Carrie to actually answer the door.

The second last thing I expected was for her to look like she did.

Haunted. That was the word that crashed through my mind.

For a moment or two I just stared at her while all kinds of images and memories went reeling through my head. She cannot have expected to see us – two ghosts from her past arriving completely unannounced on her stepmum's doorstep.

'Victor. Mae.' Carrie's voice was little better than a croak. 'What are you doing here?'

She was wrapped in a tatty patchwork blanket and looked as if she was running a fever; her eyes glistened and her cheekbones were flushed red, as if she had been pinching herself. Her dark hair was plastered against her forehead.

For a moment, I thought she was going to slam the door

in our faces, but Mae was too quick for her, reaching out a hand to keep the door open.

'Carrie. Good to see you. Do you think maybe we could come in?'

*

She hardly put up any resistance after that. She obviously had no strength to resist much of anything. We followed her into the house, her stepmother's house, all charming wood floorboards and muted colours, and soft lighting to welcome you in. I followed the grubby tail of her blanket as it dragged over the floor, Mae's boots clicking like little claws behind me.

'Do you want something to drink?' Carrie said as we entered the kitchen. Her voice was a little clearer now, though still pretty weak. She coughed, clearing her throat further. 'Tea or coffee? Or – something stronger?' When she finally shrugged off the blanket revealing the baggy T-shirt and blue leggings she was wearing underneath I saw how skinny she was. Unhealthy skinny, bad skinny. What the hell had been going on with her?

None of us had hugged each other. Three old school friends reunited like this, but for reasons that would be obvious to all of us, none of us had any pleasure at seeing each other.

'Coffee. Black,' said Mae.

Carrie's eyes slid over to me. 'What about you, Victor?'

I shook my head. She looked too unwell to be serving anyone anything. 'No, thanks. Not for me.'

She turned away, lifting the kettle to fill it from the sink. The tendons in her arm strained like ribbons as she braced against the weight, and I grimaced and looked away.

Carrie set the filled kettle back on its base and turned to face us again while it boiled.

'So. Really. What are you doing here?'

Mae smiled, like a wolf. 'We thought you'd be pleased to see us. Haven't you been trying to get in touch?'

Carrie's eyes slipped to me, and I pictured the email she had sent me a week ago – was it really just a week? Seeing her, I was absolutely sure now that it was her who had sent it.

'I didn't think you'd turn up here,' she said.

'Really? When you weren't answering your email or phone or DMs?'

'Yeah,' said Mae. 'Why is that?'

The kettle roared to a boil and clicked off. Carrie leaned her skinny arms on the worktop, her head hanging. 'Well,' she said. 'You're here now. Are you ready to talk about it?'

'Talk about what, exactly?' Mae said.

Carrie still didn't raise her head. When I looked closer, I realized her arms were quivering. I wondered whether she might actually faint.

'About what happened.'

'Oh, Carrie. Why did you post it online?' Mae asked. Her voice was uncannily soft all of a sudden. 'Everything was fine without that. They didn't have any *proof*.'

Now Carrie looked up. 'Post what?'

'The footage. Alex's footage.'

Carrie's head jerked. Her thin lips looked bloodless. 'What? I didn't—'

'Come on, Carrie.' Mae stepped towards her, coming round the side of the kitchen worktop. 'Really?'

These girls. I'd seen glimpses of this side of Mae before:

274

smooth and deadly as a rattlesnake. I had always been wary of her, despite all the things I had allowed her to do to me back then.

Mae was right beside Carrie now; the muscles up and down my back stiffened. 'Carrie, I'm sure you didn't realize what you were doing. But you can't go around messing with this stuff.' I winced as Mae reached out and smoothed Carrie's damp hair away from her temple, the way you'd hold a friend's hair back when they were ill from too much drink.

'I don't know what you're talking about,' said Carrie.

I stepped forwards and set my phone face up on the counter. 'This, Carrie. Forget the land sale and all of that crap. That wouldn't have been enough to connect us. You fucked all of us over with *this*.'

I hit play, watching her face like a hawk as the footage began spooling, crackly sound and all. Our teenage selves were right there in the room with us: the three girls, me, and Alex behind the handheld camera, as always. And lying on the ground, like a victim: Luke.

Carrie's face seemed to register genuine shock as she snatched up my phone. 'I didn't do this. I've never even seen this . . .'

Mae's hands – both of them now – went on twining in Carrie's hair. I couldn't help thinking about how close they were to Carrie's neck. I found myself moving closer to the two of them.

'Then who did?' I said. 'Who's the one trying to expose us all? Alex, who's dead? Serena, who would be sabotaging her whole career? Me or Mae, who've come here to make you stop? We all made that promise back then, didn't we? We did that for *you*, Carrie. We all agreed. And now . . .'

Carrie's chest was rising and falling in rapid pants.

I took a breath. 'And now you want to blow all of that apart?'

'I can't . . . It isn't . . .' Carrie was back to gasping again.

Mae stepped closer than ever, leaning in to speak right into our friend's ear. 'We need you to make that promise again, Carrie. We all need to remake it. Before you make a terrible mistake.'

'I can't . . . Please, Mae, I can't go on like this . . . I have to tell someone.' Carrie was shaking her head again.

'Shh,' Mae hushed her. 'Shh. Silence has served us fine all these years, hasn't it? You're not well right now; you're panicking and not thinking rationally. I know you feel bad – we can all relate to that – but think how much worse it will be if you speak up. Think about how awful it would be for your parents . . . For Valerie. For me and Victor. You never meant what you did, Carrie; we know that. You have to keep telling yourself that and be strong. Think how strong we were when we first made that promise. We need to promise each other again, the three of us, here and now.'

Only three of us, I thought. Well sure, Alex is dead, but what about Serena? Where the hell is she in all this?

That thought – and the unexpected shrill of the doorbell – were enough to distract me a moment from what Mae was doing and where her hands were. A burst of alarm went through me when I realized.

'No! Jesus – stop!' I lunged forward.

But I was too late. Right on the heels of my shout came Carrie's scream.

CHAPTER 37

Victor

2019

One moment Mae was stroking Carrie, hushing her and soothing her, and the next, her arm was around Carrie's neck and her other hand was twisting Carrie's arm behind her back.

I grabbed for her.

'Nobody finds out about this,' Mae was saying. 'Nobody. You get that? It's done, Carrie, it's buried, and it stays that way.'

I tried to grab hold of Mae, one arm round her waist, one hand in her hair. Still she clung on like a limpet; Carrie's eyes were wide with shock. She was pulling at the arm Mae held against her neck, skinny fingers clawing for freedom, her other hand wrenched behind her back, her shoulder jutting like it was about to pop out.

'Jesus, Mae. Stop it!' I shouted. Last time it had been a lighter flame; this time an armlock.

'Say it. Say that you won't betray us,' Mae was saying – hissing into Carrie's ear.

I yanked again, feeling strands of Mae's hair come loose in my fist. 'For heaven's sake, Mae, get off her!'

A wheeze escaped Carrie, a sound I couldn't interpret. Was she choking out a reply? I dragged Mae backwards by her hair and her ribcage, finally ripping her away like a gluey band-aid.

Then I realized.

Carrie had screamed before but now she was laughing, and believe me that sound was more disturbing than anything that had come before.

'Wait. *Wait*,' she gasped, her skinny body shaking. 'That footage? Alex's footage? I've just worked it out! "*If you watch to the end, you will die.*" Oh, it's perfect! He knew what he was doing, Mae, he really did.'

Mae's face was bright red, furious as she went on writhing in my arms. 'What? What are you talking about?'

'It's too late,' Carrie rasped. 'You and Victor might want to keep this buried, but there were always five of us. *Five* of us, Mae.' She laughed again. 'Alex loved that stuff, didn't he? His whole film school application essay was on amateur footage and those crazy online forums. He set this up before he died, Mae; it's obvious. You came here thinking you would win because it's two against one, but it doesn't take a genius to realize he scheduled the upload. Uh-uh. Break my arm, strangle me if you want to, it won't make any difference. You can stop *me*, but Alex already fucked you, Mae, even though he's dead.'

CHAPTER 38

Finn

2019

We walked in and found them in the kitchen. There were three of them.

Two girls and a boy, but grown up now. Adults.

They stood shoulder to shoulder, skin touching skin: a pale, dark-haired woman; a stunning, suntanned, blonde-haired one; and a tall, slender, black-haired man.

All three of them were as familiar to me, real and alive, as if I'd met them before in a dream – or a nightmare. I had studied that newspaper article so closely. Years older now, but still the same: Carrie, Margaret and Victor. Three of the five – or the six.

The small, pale one – Carrie, or a depleted-looking version of her – had her hand at her throat where a red flush blossomed. She was breathing fast and hard, as though she'd just run a race, despite looking too skinny and pale to be running anywhere.

'Uh – *hello*?' the suntanned blonde one said. Margaret. 'Can we help you?'

'Sorry,' I said, gesturing backward. 'The door was open. We heard – some noise.'

None of them responded. They were a closed circle, a wall, closing ranks against these strangers who had come barging unannounced into this home. But then what had we interrupted? What had it been – that shout, that scream?

'You just walked right in here?' said Margaret, as though she was their leader and spokesperson.

'We came here,' I managed, 'to speak to Caroline. Carrie.'

The boy – the man – stepped forwards. 'Excuse me. But who the fuck are you?'

Before I could say anything else – before I could apologize again and find some possible way to explain – Mhairi spoke up.

'I'm Mhairi and this is Finn. We're friends of Kate. Dr Kate Fallon, Carrie's therapist.'

At the mention of Kate's name, immediately the atmosphere shifted. The blonde-haired woman, Margaret, stared at Carrie.

'Dr Fallon? You're seeing *Dr Fallon* for therapy? That useless psychologist who came to our school?'

'I did . . .' Carrie stuttered. 'I told her. . . She wasn't *useless*.'

I was knocked for six all over again. 'I'm sorry – you're saying Kate Fallon worked *at St Michael's*?'

I couldn't believe this; we'd had no idea. On the countertop a phone lay face up grainy footage playing on its screen. My heart jolted. Coincidence after coincidence. It was that same footage that had first made me realize we'd stumbled into something so much bigger, so much worse. An awful connection – and now this?

Margaret turned her cool eyes onto me. 'Yes, Dr Fallon

did some work at our school. Why . . .' she drawled. 'What do you know about it?'

'Dr Fallon – our friend Kate,' Mhairi stumbled on the words, her face chalk white. 'She died a few weeks ago.'

The blonde woman flinched and dragged her hands through her hair. 'This is insane. This is fucking crazy, Carrie. You went blabbing to her – and now she's dead?'

'I didn't blab—'

'Please. We're here to try and understand what happened,' said Mhairi.

'What *happened*,' said Margaret, stepping forwards, as though trying to create a barrier between them, 'is that Carrie here has been losing her marbles. We're terribly sorry for whatever happened to your friend, but we – *Carrie* – has nothing to do with it.'

Mhairi stepped forwards, and I wanted to reach out and drag her back and out of the door. We were far too close to something here. Kate's death, this footage, a missing person, that scream . . . The revelation that Kate had once worked at St Michael's.

'Carrie—' Mhairi was reaching out to her the way you would a skittish animal. One that could lash out and bite you.

'Mhairi,' I said. 'Stop.' This was all in danger of spinning out of control. We needed to get out of here and actually go to the police.

She shook me off. 'I just want to talk to her!'

'Shut up!' Carrie burst out. 'I'm not doing this. I can't talk to you. *Any* of you. I need to go.' She spun round to Victor and Margaret. 'I've told you what I want, what I'm doing. And if you won't support me, I know someone who will. Mhairi,

Finn—' She was already slipping away from us. 'I'm so sorry about your friend. It's my fault, all my fault, I know it. But I have a plan. I'm going back. I'm going to put all of it right.'

And before any of us could move or stop her, she'd swept up a set of car keys from the counter, bolted away past me and Mhairi, and a moment later, we heard a car take off outside.

CHAPTER 39

Victor

2019

Well, now we were truly fucked.

Carrie had run off, and to make matters even more insane we had Mulder and Scully on our tail, like two ghouls next to me and Mae, as we stood outside Valerie's house, staring at the gap in the row of cars on the street.

'Call her,' said Mae. 'Find out where she's going.'

'She's not going to answer, Mae,' I bit back.

'Just *try*.'

I did as she asked, but of course it didn't work.

'What was she on about?' Mae ranted. '*I know who'll support me?*'

'How am I supposed to know?'

Mae pulled out her own phone, calling Carrie herself. No answer. She gave a cry of frustration through gritted teeth. 'Well?' she said, to the two of them standing there. It was getting dark; it was nearly eight o'clock. 'Aren't you going to help?'

Both of them stared back at her like idiots. 'We don't

know where she might have gone,' the guy said. 'We came all this way to talk to her too. We didn't know our friend Kate worked at your school. We had no idea she was involved in . . . in all of—'

He broke off. His voice was shaking.

Jesus, I thought suddenly. *Just how much does he know?*

We needed to get away from them. Mae narrowed her eyes and gave a bark of a laugh. 'I have no idea what the two of you are doing here. If Carrie wanted to talk to you, don't you think she would have said?'

'Exactly,' I said, scrambling back onto the offensive. 'Does Carrie even know you?'

'We need to talk to her,' the woman said stubbornly. The guy had his hand on her arm, like he was holding her back, and I felt again that there was a whole load of shit they weren't telling us.

'Our friend Kate killed herself,' the woman – Mhairi – said. 'Carrie was her patient. Three days before she died, she wrote Carrie a note.'

'A *note*?' Mae's eyes were wide. 'Saying what?'

My mouth flapped like a goldfish's. 'Killed herself?'

'We couldn't make it out,' the guy, Finn, said, 'but it seemed she was trying to apologize for something.'

Mae sat down on the wet kerb in the dark as if her legs just gave out on her. 'This is insane. Fucking insane.'

I crouched down in front of her, trying to block the other two out. The woman had turned away, speaking to someone rapidly on her phone. 'If Carrie's gone to the police, Mae,' I whispered, 'we fucking deny everything.'

'You've no fucking clue.' She dropped her head into her

hands. '*Carrie's* got no fucking clue either. We were all there that night.' She jerked her head back up to look at me. 'But what about the next night, Victor – when it was only me and Serena and Alex who went back?'

'Well?' I hissed. 'What about it?'

She curled her lip. When she hunched her shoulders, I thought I heard a bone in her shoulder pop. 'The point is, Victor, you *don't know*! Because all these years you never cared enough to *ask*.'

I had no idea what the hell she was on about, and before I could say anything else anyway, a smartly dressed woman came up the pavement towards us. As soon as I saw her, I got to my feet. It had been almost ten years since I had last seen her and she definitely looked older, but I still recognized her.

'Valerie,' I stuttered. 'Ms Greaves.'

She squinted at me. 'Victor?' She looked down at my feet. 'Mae?'

Mae looked up at her, like a bedraggled orphan. 'Valerie . . . Hi . . . Look, do you know where Carrie is?'

Valerie's gaze swept the weird group of us. 'What do you mean? She's inside; she's been staying with me. But what are *you* doing here?'

Mae got to her feet, arms wrapped round herself. 'We came to see her. We're worried about her. And she *was* here until a few minutes ago. She let us in, and we were talking. Then she went crazy and drove off.'

I added helpfully, 'In your car.'

Valerie glanced at the gap in the cars on the street, then hurried to her property, where the door was still ajar.

'Carrie,' she called inside. 'Carrie?'

We waited on the street until she came back out again. The woman – Mhairi – was still yabbering away on her phone.

'She's not here. Did she say where she was going?' Valerie asked.

Mae shrugged. 'No. We don't know. We hoped you would.'

Valerie looked back and forth between us. Yeah. I wouldn't trust a single one of us either.

'Please, Ms Greaves,' Mae said. 'We just want to talk to her. And these two people—' she gestured to Mhairi and Finn '—are friends of Dr Kate Fallon, Carrie's therapist. They've been trying to get hold of Carrie too. You must know – you must have seen – Carrie's not herself right now. We're all worried about her. She's not thinking straight. She'd taken your car . . . We're worried she might hurt herself. If you have any idea where she is, please say.'

She was really laying it on thick.

Valerie ran a hand through her hair in distress. 'She never – Carrie didn't tell me anything. She's been ill. She had a terrible fever . . . But in her sleep, she kept mumbling about your old school. St Michael's. I've no idea why St Michael's would be on her mind now but do you think . . . is it possible she might have gone there?'

I wanted to laugh. Where else? Where fucking else?

'Thank you, Valerie,' said Mae. 'Honestly, thank you.'

'But how are we going to get there?' I said.

Now the woman, Mhairi, stepped forwards, finally off her phone call. 'You can come with me,' she said. 'I've just hired a car.'

*

No, I did *not* want to be stuck in a car with those two all the way to St Michael's – but what other choice did we have? If we tried to rent our own car from somewhere, that would take even more time, and the two of them would get to the school before us. We needed to get to Carrie, and we needed to get there before Finn and Mhairi, and if we were all travelling together, we had some control over the two of them at least. Keep your friends close, but your enemies closer.

'Fine.' Mae threw up her hands in surrender. 'Fine! Valerie, give me your number – we'll call you. You stay here in case Carrie comes back.'

We collected the pre-booked car from a rental off Dundas Street and it still took nearly an hour to get to that point, Carrie speeding further away from us all the time.

Mhairi insisted on driving, and I'd only met the woman two hours ago but by now it was obvious she was like a dog with a bone. Never mind that Carrie had literally *run away* from her, whatever mission she and her sidekick had come here on, she wasn't going to leave without the answers she wanted.

But she could fuck off if she thought we were going to give them to her.

'You said Kate once worked at your school,' she was asking us, eyeing us in the car's rear-view mirror instead of keeping her eyes on the road. 'Why? What was she there for?'

'What does it matter?' said Mae. 'It was sixteen years ago.'

'It matters to *me*,' she said. 'My best friend is dead because of that school!'

'And you think we had something to do with that?' I barked back.

'We know *Carrie* did. Or that Carrie knows something,'

said the guy, Finn. 'She chose Kate as her therapist knowing that she once worked at your school.'

Mae glared out of the window. We were swinging across the Queensferry Crossing, its white lights reflected on the river in the dark, the bridge tarmac thundering under our wheels. 'It was nothing,' she muttered. 'A stupid group of girls were having anxiety attacks.'

Stop talking, I wanted to yell at her. *Everything you say is handing over another clue.* I had no idea what Finn and Mhairi already knew, but if we went on like this, they could soon come to know everything. Mae needed to shut up and let this Mhairi drive us to St Michael's, and once we got there we needed to ditch them, find Carrie and stop her from speaking to anyone else.

'And the note Kate wrote? What was she apologizing to Carrie for?'

I saw Finn put a hand on her arm again, shaking his head, like, *Please, Mhairi, stop.* What was he afraid we might do – attack them?

Well, if we have to, I thought, then maybe we will.

'Look,' I said, leaning forwards, seatbelt yanking tight across my neck. 'We have no idea why your friend killed herself, and I doubt very much that Carrie does either. What right do you have to talk to her anyway? Isn't there such a thing as therapist-patient confidentiality? You heard what Valerie said. Carrie's ill. She needs her friends around her. Me and Mae. Not two strangers interrogating her about the past.'

That seemed to shut Mhairi up – for the time being anyway. I jerked back against my seat, screwed my eyes shut and pressed my head into the headrest, that mantra pounding in my brain:

get to Carrie, shut her up, get to Carrie, shut her up, and all the while the road north spilled out in front of us, like a tidal wave carrying us on.

*

It took us five and a half hours in total to get there. Three and a half hours trapped in the car together, plus another two hours standing in a drizzle trying to fix the tyre that had been busted by one of the million potholes on these roads.

Now, finally we were turning onto the familiar route to the school. My chest grew tight. I hadn't set foot in this place since I'd left at eighteen, ignoring every invitation I'd received to come back: lavish alumni reunions, careers fair they wanted me to speak at, all their prestigious fundraising events. All I'd wanted when our final term ended was to get the hell out of Dodge and never look back.

But here I was. Fuck. I gripped the handle of the door as Mhairi drove onwards, the sun starting to come up, a fire-orange ball shining right in our eyes. It was dazzling as we turned up the long sweep of the final road, casting the scenery in a sickly orange glow. A thousand pictures of the place crowded into my brain: the windows, the turrets, the woods, the playing fields. The visceral feel of the place, the smell of it.

But when we finally rounded the last corner, I felt as if I'd been socked in the gut. All the air I'd been holding in rushed out of me.

I knew about the land sale and the development, and I was an idiot not to expect changes, but not *this*. My teenage self had not been expecting this.

'Pull over,' I heard Finn say to Mhairi. We were still some way away, ragged lawns stretching out in front of us. 'We can't drive onto a building site.' Mhairi tugged the wheel, swerving the car onto the grass verge. She hit the brakes and we jerked to a halt.

Our once proud school was covered in ugly orange netting, propped up by scaffolding, from ground to roof. And the land around it was churned up, as if some great beast had torn the landscape up with its claws.

Fuck. Fuck. *Fuck*.

I unsnapped my seatbelt, following Mae who was already up and out of the car.

The two of us set off almost running towards the school, desperate to shake Mhairi and Finn from our tail. We had to get to Carrie first and stop her talking. We had to stop her from letting all our secrets flood out.

There were diggers ahead of us, scooping up chunks of the earth. There were a score of workmen, flashes of orange and yellow: hard hats and vests alongside the hulking shapes of the machines.

They had felled so many trees from the rise behind the school that almost half of the woodland was gone. The hill looked brutalized and bare without its natural covering, and I felt my legs grow weak. Stop it, I kept telling myself, stop it. Just get to Carrie. Convince her there's nothing to be gained by coming clean. Find a way to get her back to Valerie's – or anywhere – with all the promises we made back then still intact.

'Where the hell is she?' Mae asked.

Good question. Now we were here, the whole thing felt surreal. If Carrie was even here, where exactly would she have gone? The place was a building site, not a hotel. She wasn't just going to be hanging out watching TV in the student common room. Had we expected to find her strolling the grounds?

Mae halted, out of breath from how fast we'd been walking. Seemed she wasn't a lot fitter than I was. Glancing over my shoulder, I could see Mhairi and Finn behind us, and the sight of their determined expressions sent a wave of panic through me all over again. If they found Carrie first and started asking their questions, judging by the state of our friend, the whole lot would come pouring out of her mouth straight away.

The workers on the site still hadn't spotted us, too preoccupied with their work. I turned back to the school just as the slicing sun dimmed, a cloud rushing over.

And fuck me.

I couldn't believe it.

I gave a small jerk of my head, whispering to Mae. 'Did you see that?'

She shaded her eyes and scanned the school's frontage then stopped. She had spotted it too.

Two floors up, in a window of St Michael's was a silhouette.

'Is that her?' Mae exclaimed. 'Is Carrie actually *inside*?'

Before I could reply, I heard men shouting. The yells emanated from a group of them on the low slope of the hillside.

'Are they yelling at us?' said Mae. 'Are we trespassing?'

'How the hell am I supposed to know?'

A stocky man came barrelling down from the bottom of the slope. His speed surprised me: he was almost falling over himself as he rushed headlong.

I grabbed Mae's arm and we both took a step backwards, but he wasn't even looking at us.

His hard hat fell off and went tumbling on the rutted ground, exposing his bright-red face underneath. As he reached the front of the school – twenty, fifteen yards now from where Mae and I stood – another man began to stride up to meet him, the leader of the crew, the foreman. They were close enough for us to catch their shouted exchange.

'We need the police and an ambulance!'

Oh Jesus Christ.

'What is it?' barked the foreman. 'Calm down.'

'There's a fucking . . . ! It's sticking out of the ground!'

Mae dragged at my arm. 'Oh fuck, Victor. Oh *fuck*.'

I couldn't speak properly; I could barely get my jaw to work. 'Don't do anything. Don't move.'

The workman leaned forwards, hands on knees, as if he was about to be sick. 'Danny found it. He hit something with his spade.'

'Found what?' said the foreman.

A wave of nausea washed over me. This was it. Everything I'd feared ever since Carrie's email: the one Mae had wanted us to ignore because 'no one would ever find anything'.

'A fucking *leg*, man! There's a fucking *body* down there in the trench!'

CHAPTER 40

Victor

2019

The whole thing had lain buried for sixteen years, and the moment we step foot back on this land, the game was up. You couldn't make this stuff up.

'Jesus Christ,' Mae was panting. 'Jesus Christ.'

'We need to get inside,' I said. 'We need to get up there, to Carrie. We need to get her and get the fuck away.'

To where? Not back to Madrid or to London and my father. Into hiding then? Disguising ourselves and living on funds Mae got from pimping herself to men?

And even that would be pointless if Carrie had already gone to the police. Surely it was too much of a coincidence that everything had come to the surface *now*? My stomach roiled. Has she told them that there was a body to dig up?

In which case, no matter what we did, we were truly, royally fucked.

But maybe, just maybe, she hadn't opened her mouth yet and we still had time to stop her.

'This way,' said Mae, heading for the back of the school. Behind us, I could see Mhairi and Finn approaching the foreman. *Oh God,* I prayed, *please let them not really know anything. Please let them only know that Carrie was a patient of Dr Fallon, and maybe about the Fainting Girls at most. Please let them think that's all there is to it. Please please please don't let them know about Luke.*

Mae had set off running and I sprinted after her. The ground was cracked and uneven, prime terrain for breaking an ankle or your neck. At any moment I expected someone to shout at us, rugby-tackle us, tell us we couldn't go anywhere near the school, pin us to the ground then handcuff us and cart us straight to the cells. But then the rational part of my brain kicked in – how would they know who we were? And they were all too busy dealing with what they'd found. I tried my best not to let myself picture it. *Luke's body.*

'Here,' said Mae.

Incredibly, the door at the back of the gym still offered us entry. Mae got there first and tugged the door open. Inside, I stood for a moment, chest wheezing.

'Is it safe?' I gasped. I pictured groaning timbers, splintered ceilings. If we went inside, would the whole place collapse on our heads?

'Carrie's already up there,' she said. '*She* made it.'

She darted towards the door that led to the main hall.

The school was abandoned, gritty, dilapidated, but I felt as if I'd been hurled back through time, all the details ambushing me in sharp relief: coloured lines painted on the gym floor, green flooring in the corridor. I could have walked this familiar labyrinth blindfolded.

At the dining room, Mae turned right instead of left and I followed her up the stairs that led to the girls' dormitories: an area that had always been out of bounds to us boys. Now the school was gutted and empty we were free to go anywhere we liked.

I fumbled for my phone and turned on the torch; the staircases were dark, and when we reached the corridor at the top, all the doors were closed, the only light coming from a grimy window at the far end.

No, wait – not quite. A shudder ran up my spine as I saw that one of the doors along the corridor stood ajar. I pictured the window framing the pale face that we'd seen earlier. The window two levels up from the ground and three in from the right.

Their room, I realized. *Their* dorm. Serena, Carrie and Mae's.

We stepped along the hallway, towards that open door.

'Carrie?' Mae whispered, and immediately I wanted to clamp a hand over her mouth, as if her voice might summon some wild beast.

There was a scuffling noise, like something – someone – scrambling to hide or get away. '*Carrie?*' Mae called again. 'It's okay. It's only Mae and Victor.'

Six more steps took us to right outside the dorm room. I switched off my phone torch, plunging the two of us back into the corridor's gloom.

Mae took hold of the handle and pushed the door open.

*

When Mae stepped inside, I was hot on her heels but I quickly stopped still in shock.

'Oh my God. What the hell?' The shock propelled the words from my mouth.

She was huddled in a corner of the room. The space had been stripped of all its furniture: the beds and desks as well as the carpets and even the wallpaper. The ceiling was blighted with water stains. Inexplicably, a set of curtains still hung in the window, patterned with the repeating crest of St Michael's, tattered now and speckled with mould. The window was open and the curtains flapped in the breeze.

The word fell from Mae's mouth: totally inane and useless now. '. . . Carrie?'

Her head swivelled as she looked at us, lipstick shining like a bright red gash. Her expensive jeans and windbreaker were smeared with mud – her fingers too.

She took in me first, then her eyes slid to Mae. Her smile was more like a grimace. 'Fancy meeting you guys here.'

CHAPTER 41

Carrie

2019

The first chance I got, I had grabbed the car keys and bolted, yanked open the door of Valerie's car, threw myself inside and started driving.

I had an appointment. I had somewhere to be. I had someone who was still on my side.

I drove for hours, sending Valerie a text at one point so she'd know where I was. Telling her not to worry, I was fine, I was safe. I didn't know if she had texted me back – I was out of reception range by then.

It was the depths of night by the time I got there. Cold. Dark. Just like that night sixteen years ago.

The place looked so different, but I did my best to ignore all that. I wasn't here to pine for what I'd lost. I was here to tell the truth and dissolve the curse that hung over me. Still I couldn't help but shudder and feel sick. *He* was here, somewhere. Close to me now, haunting me. I could almost hear his voice in my ear, feel the sensation of his cool skin under my hands. I had to push those ghosts away; focus on how I could make things right in the present.

My legs were shaky, burning even before I started up the steep rise. For years, I'd had dreams about this place. Nightmares. Now, the trees had been cut down, leaving the rocks where we had gathered on those secret nights sticking up like ugly, grey teeth. Maybe on some tree stump I'd find one of the initials we'd carved. Maybe if I dug in the right place, I'd find the butts from all those joints we'd smoked.

And what else? my mind hollered. *What else would you find?*

I checked my watch. I was hours early. We'd arranged to meet at six a.m.; I hadn't had much choice. The email had been absolutely specific about the time and place for our meeting, and it was me who wanted this; I wasn't in a position to call any more of the shots.

It was three a.m. now. The witching hour. From up here, in the faint star- and moonlight, I saw how far away this spot was from the school. Even if they cut down all the trees, when it came to the housing developments they were planning – would they ever actually need to dig up here?

Maybe there was nothing to be scared of after all. Maybe if I did nothing, it would all go away again, sinking back into the ground. Maybe even the footage Alex had so cleverly uploaded before his death, with that perfect clickbait headline, could somehow all still be explained away. I could turn around and go home. Get on with rebuilding my life, and trust that whatever charm had kept things hidden for this long would go on protecting us.

Except then I would never get this weight off my soul.

Maybe I was leaning on him harder than I should have been. Maybe that was because I was still mad at him for what he'd done.

Maybe I was still angry with Mae as well.

I didn't know at that point that she'd lied.

Maybe – because of what Victor brought up – we weren't properly paying attention.

Maybe we'd attributed more strength and power to him than he ever had.

We were gripping Luke in his comatose haze, and it only seemed to register from far away when Victor murmured. 'You know Mr Witham's leaving St Michael's, right?'

Mae's head jerked up. My own jerked up too.

'You what?' said Serena.

'Didn't you hear?' Victor mumbled. 'He's off to some girls' day school in Sheffield. Ms Myers said he'll be gone after this week.'

Mae raised a hand to gnaw at her fingernails, that horrible nervous habit.

'What?' I said, staring at her. 'What's the matter?'

'Next week?' said Alex, lazily. 'He isn't working out his notice?'

'Maybe he got sacked,' I said, so fucking naïve.

'Oh yeah, Carrie. You *think*?' Mae said, turning to me.

'What *is* it?' I looked right at her.

Serena smirked. 'Honestly, Carrie, you're so clueless sometimes.'

'Don't be a cow, Serena.' Victor sloppily pushed himself up on his elbow. 'Look, Mae – what are you getting at?'

'Like you would ever have a clue,' she snorted. 'You *boys*.'

Now I did lash out. 'Shut up, Mae. Victor and Alex are our friends.'

Mae turned on me. 'No, Carrie. They're *your* friends. I just let them come so we could fuck with them a bit.'

I sat up sharply, lifting my weight off Luke's chest to face her. 'What's wrong with you, Mae? Why are you being such a bitch?'

'Oh, *I'm* a bitch? *I'm* the one in the wrong here?'

'You are when you're speaking to everyone like that!'

'Luke . . . ?' said Serena, giving his arm a shake. 'Luke?'

'Stop that,' Mae said, pulling her hand back. 'Leave him alone, he's enjoying it.'

'You mean, *you're* enjoying it,' I said. 'That's the kick you get out of all this, isn't it? You love making your playthings as helpless as that.'

I didn't even really know what I was saying or where the words were coming from. I just knew I was hurt by her. I didn't know what Mae's problem was or why she was acting like this.

'Fuck off, Carrie.'

'Look,' said Serena.

'*What?*' Mae snapped.

Serena raised her grey eyes to hers. 'Look at Luke.' She giggled at the rhyme. She shook him again and he rolled floppily.

'What about him?' Victor and Alex slouched over. The pool of torchlight widened, spilling light onto the scene.

'His chest isn't moving,' said Serena.

'What?' A granite ball formed in my stomach as I stared at him. 'Yes it is.' In the wavering torchlight, it was hard to tell.

'It *isn't*,' Serena insisted.

She leaned down and slapped him. His head rocked sideways. I waited for him to sit up and yell at us, but he didn't. No wonder he hadn't reacted to my pinches before.

'Shit,' said Alex. 'Are you sure he's not breathing?'

'Wait.' Mae fumbled at his wrist, his neck, her fingers searching for a pulse. 'I can't feel it here. Shouldn't I be able to feel it in his neck?'

'Let me try.' But Victor was as clumsy as her.

'Pinch his earlobe,' said Alex.

No one moved, so I leaned down and did it myself, digging my nails deep into the fleshy pad. Nothing. His skin was cold to the touch, but it was freezing that night, so that could have meant anything.

'Shit,' said Mae. 'Shit!'

'Give him CPR,' Victor said. 'You know . . . breathe into his mouth . . . press his chest?'

'Yes,' said Mae. 'Victor, go on.'

'No way.'

'Serena, you then.' Mae's voice was getting panicky.

I pushed forwards. 'I'll do it.' I had already kissed him anyway. And I was the one who had slid three tablets onto his tongue. Three. Not two or one or a half. Three – more than any of us had ever taken in one go.

I knelt down on the ground again and pulled him towards me, limbs dragging on the ground, a dead weight. He was facing upwards, but his legs were still sideways, his body corkscrewed.

'Tilt his head back,' said Alex. 'You have to lift his chin.'

Mae scrambled to position herself and take hold of his skull, levering it so that his chin rose and his neck strained. It looked so uncomfortable.

'Hold his nose,' said Victor.

I squeezed his nostrils. Something wet and sticky dribbled out onto my hand, and I couldn't help myself – I let go with a jerk.

'Hold his nose!'

'Fuck off, Victor!'

I wiped my hand on my jeans and tried again. All of his skin was clammy, sticky. I shuddered, feeling sick. Doing this with him was the last thing I'd imagined.

I sucked in a breath and pressed my lips to his. The air went in. It went somewhere. I pulled back up, wiping the wet from my mouth.

'Do it again,' said Mae.

'We have to do chest compressions too, don't we?' said Alex. 'Like, thirty?'

'Put him on his back properly, then. And Victor. You do it. Push on his chest.'

Victor handed his torch to Alex, the light wavering and swinging around us. I grabbed Luke's nose again and breathed another lungful of air into his mouth. I felt most of it leaking out of the gaps between our lips.

Victor pulled at Luke's legs, trying to straighten out his body. I felt hysterical laughter bubbling up in me. The whole thing was so ridiculous, so slapstick. It was like some stupid joke, such a mess. I still thought Luke would sit up at any moment and laugh at us all, call us a bunch of idiots, berate us for being so useless, so dumb.

'You have to press on the middle,' Serena was pointing. 'His – what do you call it – sternum.'

Victor clasped his hands and set them on Luke's ribcage.

'Are you *sure* he isn't breathing?' I said.

'Yes! Shut up,' said Mae. 'Now push down.'

Victor thrust his hands into Luke's chest; Luke's body jerked, and we all jumped back.

Then he was still again. 'Do it again,' said Mae. 'Just keep going.'

'Oh God.' Victor thrust again, Luke's body jerked again. 'Oh God.'

It hit me then that none of us had called 999. How long had it been now? Four minutes, five? And how long had he lain there not breathing before that, while we were arguing about stupid Mr Witham? One of us should have run back to the school right away and called an ambulance. We were fucking this up. We were completely fucking this up. And it was my fault, wasn't it? I was the one who'd given Luke the three tablets, on top of the fug of alcohol I'd smelled on his breath. Three was an amount Luke himself said could be dangerous. *Shitty.* An amount *I* had warned *Mae* would be too much.

'It's my fault,' I said.

'Carrie!' said Alex. 'Stop talking, just breathe for him.'

'But it *is*.' I was desperately trying to get the guilt off my chest. 'I gave him three tablets.'

'*Three tablets?*' Mae said. 'Why the fuck did you do that?'

'Because of what *you* said. He was fucking with you, Mae!' My voice sounded pathetic: childish and shrill.

'Carrie,' she half-screamed. 'You're a fucking *idiot*.'

'Shut up,' said Serena. 'Shut up! Do want someone to hear us on top of everything else?'

'I fucked up,' I whisper-cried. 'I'm sorry!'

'I need a rest; someone needs to take over,' said Victor. 'My arms are tired.' He'd only done about fifteen pathetic pumps.

'Here.' Alex almost shoved me aside, no doubt furious with me as well. 'I'll do it.' He wasn't as strong as Victor and his movements were even more ineffectual. Luke jerked about floppily under his hands. 'Is it working?' Alex said, gasping for his own breath. 'Is it helping?'

'You just have to keep doing it,' said Mae. 'Just keep on pumping his heart.'

Even though it could be ten minutes now since he stopped breathing. No one survived a delay like that, surely. Alex went on for maybe thirty seconds before Serena grabbed at him, pulling him off.

'Stop,' she said. 'That's enough. We don't know what we're doing. He's dead. It's grotesque to keep pounding on his body like that.'

*

Once Serena told us to stop, we did. And then the real panic set in.

To this day, I can't recall who said it first. I just remember the words.

We have to hide this.

As soon as they were said, we all knew it was true. There was nothing else for it. We had killed him – *I* had killed him – and now we had to cover it up.

'We'll dig a hole.' I think maybe Alex said that, but I don't really know. At that point, it felt like we were all moving as one, like a colony of ants, with one purpose.

Alex and Victor lifted his body out of the circle of logs. They were strong, but not strong enough to lift him properly so his body scraped along the rough earth.

They set him down again just beyond the trees. Then the five of us began digging.

The earth was freezing cold and hard. I felt one of my fingernails break off.

'We should have called an ambulance,' I said. My teeth were chattering and the words began flooding out of me. 'We should have done it straight away instead of trying to save him ourselves.'

I pushed my fingers harder into the ground, desperately trying to wrench another chunk of earth free.

'One of us should have run back to the school. I should have—'

'But you didn't.' Through the darkness, Mae was glaring at me. 'They would have called the police, Carrie. And then where would you be? This is all your fault – you just said that. You gave him three tablets, when you know we never, never go above two.'

My eyes were brimming with tears. There was nothing I could do but keep digging.

Victor stood up. 'This isn't working.'

I ignored him and went on scrabbling at the earth.

He yanked at my shoulder. 'Forget it, Carrie – I said, it isn't working! The ground is too hard. We can't dig anything just with our hands.'

He was right. Of course he was. Despite the efforts of all five of us, we'd barely dug down more than a few inches. Wasn't a grave supposed to be at least six foot deep?

'Then what are we going to do?' said Serena.

'We need proper equipment. Spades. And it's raining now. That will soften the ground after a while.'

He was right. The rain was coming down in fat, freezing drops; I was so numbed I had barely felt them. I looked over at Luke's body beside us, hunched up where Alex and Victor had dropped him.

'Then we'll go back to the school now,' I said. 'Fetch them.'

'No,' said Mae. 'We can't tonight.' She tilted her muddy wrist to look at her watch. I caught a glimpse of the hands: twenty to five. 'The porters will be up in half an hour. We can't go rifling about the place now for spades.'

'What then?' I asked. 'You said before, we can't just leave him!'

'We'll have to come back tomorrow,' said Victor. 'As soon as we can after lights out.'

'And until then?'

'We'll just have to cover him with something. Branches, leaves, whatever. Just do the best we can.'

I tried not to let the reality of it hit me as we arranged him in the shallow hollow we had scraped out and covered him in a lattice of branches. I tried to pretend it was some innocuous task, one of those character-building outdoor activities that got us things like Duke of Edinburgh awards.

We had all stopped talking. There was nothing to hear but the scrape of branches, and the crash of the wind and the rain. The occasional groan or grunt and the ragged pant of breathing.

This was my fault. I knew all of my friends thought that. Now they were implicated too, having to step in to cover up my deeds. Now we were all guilty, because of what I'd done.

Stop. Stop thinking. I went on dragging more branches over, laying them on top of Luke's body, trying not to notice the way the twigs and barbs tore at his skin. Alex hefted a thick branch onto the pile, the thick end of it crushing down on Luke's ribs. I jerked my head away, imagining I had heard one of them crack.

We placed a few leafier branches on top and finally you could no longer see him. It was raining heavily now, the ground under our feet growing slippery with mud. The temperature must have been close to zero.

'We need to go,' said Mae, always our leader. 'Get back now before anyone wakes up.'

I wiped the dirt and mud from my hands on my jeans.

She was right. We had done what we could. We just had to leave him and hope no one found him before tomorrow night.

So that's what we did.

*

We made it back to our dorm rooms at five minutes to five. It was a miracle no one saw us. We washed the mud from our bodies in the bathroom, stripping our clothes and rinsing them as best we could.

When I finally got into bed, it felt like my brain shut down, like pulling out the wall plug on a computer.

In the morning though, I remembered everything with a sickening jolt. I sat up in bed, pressed a hand to my mouth, then ran into the dormitory bathroom to be sick.

At lunchtime, Alex and Victor told us they had found spades. I wasn't sure where they got them from; I didn't need to know.

We decided that Serena, Mae and Alex would do it. I was in too much of a state to go with them, and Victor chivalrously said he'd stay with me. I snuck him into our dorm room where he flopped himself out on Serena's bed and I tried to stifle my sobs. For the next two hours, we waited.

*

Serena and Mae crept back into our dorm room close to two a.m. Alex was with them. Victor and I both sat bolt upright, wide awake.

'Did you manage it?' asked Victor. 'Is it done?'

I was glad he'd asked the question. I couldn't find the words to say anything.

I'm sorry.

Thank you.

What have we done?

Mae sat herself down carefully on the bed. Nobody switched a light on. We spoke at barely more than whispers. Imagine if the five of us got caught like this now.

'Come here,' Mae murmured to all of us.

I shuffled over to sit next to her on her bed. Serena lowered herself on the other side of her, and Victor and Alex stood alongside, looking down.

Mae dug in her jeans pocket and pulled out a lighter.

'Hold out your hand,' she said to Serena: her ally, her follower.

'What for?' Serena muttered.

'We need to seal this. We're going make a pact.'

'Come on, Mae . . .' said Victor.

'Shut up, Victor.' Then to Serena: 'Just do it.'

Serena placed her hand in Mae's. Mae lifted it and turned it palm down. When she flicked the lighter wheel, the flame scorched my retinas; the flame licked up towards Serena's fingers.

She tried to yank her hand away but despite all Serena's training, in that moment, Mae was stronger.

'Swear on the pain that you'll never say anything. If the police come asking questions, you'll say we don't know him, never met him in our lives.'

'Ow, Mae,' growled Serena. 'Fuck!'

'Promise!' The flame was so bright.

'I promise!'

Mae released her. Temporarily, she let the flame go out.

'Victor next,' she said.

'Fuck off.'

'No, fuck *you*, Victor! You're the one who brought up Mr Witham, distracting us so we didn't notice Luke!'

Victor scoffed. 'Really? You're saying this is *my* fault?'

'It doesn't matter whose fault it is,' said Serena, scorched hand pressed to her mouth. 'We were all there. We all have to promise.'

'Coward, Victor?' Mae said. 'Going to tell on us?'

'Fuck you,' he repeated, but he held out his hand.

The lighter sparked.

'Swear on the pain that you'll never say anything. We never went up there; we never did drugs.'

Victor's breath was high and quick from the pain. 'Yes! Fuck, Mae, yes – I promise.'

She kept him there for another two seconds. He wrenched his hand away and she finally let go.

'Alex now.'

He stuck his hand out. 'Hurry up, then. Get it over with.'

She eyed him for a moment. 'Ready?'

'Yes. Jesus Christ . . .'

'Fine . . . Swear on the pain that you'll never say anything. You'll delete every scrap of film footage of him – and that place – that you have.'

Alex's voice was a croak in his throat. 'I promise.'

When it came to my turn, Mae didn't say the words. I didn't need her to, and I didn't need her to hold my hand either. When I balanced my palm over the flame, the pain was agonizing, but I welcomed it, embraced it, punished myself with it. I wanted to hold my hand there until the skin melted and turned black, but in the end Mae clicked the flame off.

Next moment, I felt something thick and black settle on me like a weight. I wanted to get Mae to do it to me again: to my other hand, the soles of my feet, my face.

Instead, she handed the lighter over.

'My turn,' she said, pressing it into my grasp.

Alex, Victor and Serena held her arm and wrist for her. Like a sleepwalker, I struck the flint, passing the violent flame

310

under her palm. She kept her hand there longer than anyone else had, and she kept her eyes locked on mine the whole time.

Swear on the pain that you'll never say anything.

I promise.

In that moment, I honestly never thought that I would ever break my word.

CHAPTER 42

Carrie

2019

A slit of light was just glimmering over the horizon when she arrived. I must have fallen asleep, because one moment there was nothing but me and the cold and the scarred hillside and the dark, and the next moment, a figure was leaning down over me.

I scrambled to my feet. 'You made it!'

She was wearing jeans and a slick green cagoule, a matching baseball hat pulled down over her hair.

'Jesus, Carrie. What's going on?'

She stepped forwards and embraced me in a hug, the muscles in her arms and torso almost crushing me.

I wanted to burst into tears. The two of us had never quite figured out our friendship at St Michael's, always needing Mae to make up the three. But now she felt like my best friend in the whole world. My biggest ally. My teammate. My saviour.

I sank back down to sit on one of the cold rocks, my head in my hands. She lowered herself carefully down beside me.

'You came. You actually came, Serena, thank you. I feel like I'm going mad. It's a nightmare.'

A silence. 'What is?'

'You know.' Hunched in the gloom, I started to rock. 'Everything that happened back then. I've kept it to myself all this time, but I don't think I can do it anymore. I kept telling myself: the more years that go by, the easier it will get. But it didn't get easier, it only got worse.'

In a jumble, I told her about the deaths and disasters that had punctuated my life. The growing sense that I was the one responsible.

'I began seeing a therapist,' I said. I let out a hiccup of a laugh. 'You'll never guess who?'

'Who?' Her voice was still neutral. Unfazed. Serena was always so calm; it's why I'd found it so difficult to read her when we were at school.

I scraped my straggling hair back from my forehead. The dew had come down now, and it might as well have rained on me; I was soaked.

'Remember the psychologist who came to help with Bryony and the other girls? I went to see her. I thought: she'll understand. She was kind to me once. And she knew St Michael's. I thought she'd understand what it was like, being at school here. Why we did all the crazy things we did.'

Serena's voice was sharp. 'You're telling me you went to see *Kate Fallon*?'

'Yes. Yes. I had an assessment with her. I was trying to explain everything. It felt so good, Serena, you've no idea. To *talk* about it. To finally *tell* someone.'

'Oh, Carrie . . .' Serena's eyes were wide.

'I was going to do it. I told her all about the Fainting Girls, and what it did to us. How it made us feel, how Mae started behaving, and how that was the start of us using the other drugs. The very next session, I was going to tell her everything.'

Now it was Serena's turn to drop her head into her hands. 'I don't believe it,' I heard her whisper. 'You did *what*?'

'But I *didn't* tell her, Serena! That's the whole point. I was just about to and then she . . . died!'

Just saying the words made the hair on my neck stand up all over again.

'She what?'

'She killed herself. Because I showed up! I think I'm . . . cursed.'

Serena stared at me. I could almost see her hectic mind whirring away behind those grey eyes.

'The Fainting Girls,' she said. 'What exactly did you say about them?'

'I . . . I don't know. I told her about how Mae reacted to it. Then . . . about Bryony still being in and out of hospital. Maybe I mentioned Ava's drug problems too? I can't remember! She knew the rest of it, Serena; she was *there*.'

'Right.' I could almost hear her brain working.

My throat ached. My whole body ached. I was exhausted, cold. I wanted my mum. My real mum. 'I was desperate, Serena. I can't go on living like this.'

'. . . But you didn't tell her about Luke?'

'No! But she still died!' I cried. I wanted to burst into tears again, through sheer suffering this time. I wanted to throw up. 'Because that's what *happens*, Serena. Because

I have this horrible secret inside me that means anybody who gets near me dies.'

Even I cringed at how crazy the words sounded.

For a few seconds, Serena said nothing. Then a choking sound burst from her, her shoulders heaving. It took me a moment to realize she was laughing. 'Oh my God,' she gasped. 'Oh my God, Carrie. You idiot.'

I was mute, in shock at her reaction.

'Why are you laughing?!'

'Jesus, Carrie, were you always like this? I guess you were. You and your Point Horror stories. Always ready to believe anything about demons and spooks.'

'Serena, please. That isn't helping.'

She drew a big breath, like making a huge effort to compose herself. She angled herself round on the rock so she was looking straight at me.

'Okay . . . let's go through everything. You spoke to her about the Fainting Girls, right?'

I nodded, my muscles aching from anxiety and the cold.

'About Mae, the way she started behaving?'

'Yes.'

'And about Bryony and Ava still being fucked up.'

'*Yes.*'

Serena spread her palms. 'Well then.'

'Well then, *what*?' I wanted to shake her in return. Hammer my fist right into her head.

'Oh my God, you really don't know, do you? You really have no idea what was going on back then.' She made a move to get to her feet and I grabbed at her arm – the way I'd done that first night in the dorm, when I'd caught her and

Mae sneaking out. *Let me in on the secret. Don't leave me in the dark.*

'What? *What?!*'

'I bet you a million pounds that *she* knew. Dr Fallon. I reckon she had it figured out from day one. Maybe she never figured out *who* it was exactly. But she wasn't fooled by stories about "stress" and "attention-seekers". I reckon she sniffed out what he had being doing to Bryony and Ava from the start.'

'Stop. Please stop. I'm not following.' My mind flashed back to that conversation I'd once had with Kate, that dim afternoon by her car. I shook my head like that would make all the pieces come together.

'When you pitched up in her clinic, I bet she thought he'd done it to you too.'

'Done what? Who? I'm talking about Luke!'

Serena laughed again, cracking up at my ignorance. 'Of course *you* are. But what do you think *Kate* thought you were talking about?'

'I don't *know*!' I sounded so childish. I really had no idea.

'Oh my God, Carrie. *Mr Witham.*'

The name blindsided me. For a second, it hooked onto nothing, and then a confetti of memories descended on me.

A hand on Mae's knee.

Crashing into him in the corridor. His charming smile.

'Mr *Witham*? What are you on about?'

'Don't you remember,' said Serena, her voice almost coy, 'all those one-to-one English meetings Mae used to have?'

'So what? They were . . .' I stuttered. 'They were . . .'

'They were with Mr Witham. They would go to that weird little office round the back.'

Whoops! You've got chalk on your blouse!

My body began to shake as the pieces drew together.

There were hands on me . . . Hands . . . I rose up in the light . . .

I'll tell you about this guy you might know. About how whenever I have to meet him, we fool around . . .

'That office . . . the one with the skylight . . .'

'That's the one. See, you remember after all.'

'Mr Witham was—?' I couldn't bring myself to say the words. I didn't need to. Any woman or girl would know what I meant. This whole new reality came crashing down on me, one I'd literally walked among day after day, totally blind, caught up in myself, my own illusory world.

'Of course he was,' Serena replied. 'And Kate Fallon didn't expose him or stop him. Why do you think he left the school so abruptly? The school, the . . . *system* just covered it up. All that happened was that he got shuffled off to a new school. Think what that must have been like for poor Dr Fallon all these years. And then *you* come crashing back into her life, telling her all about poor Ava and Bryony, and how fucked up they still were, and about to say that you were abused too.'

My breath was tight in my chest. 'She thought I was blaming her.'

'Yeah – no shit.'

'And then she killed herself.' A wave of black sickness threatened to engulf me again.

'Well,' said Serena reasonably. '*That* part wasn't specifically your fault.'

My gums were watery, my mouth filling with saliva. 'Serena?' I said. 'Please, we have to go to the police.'

'Ah, come on, Carrie . . .'

'No – I mean it, even more so now, after what you've just said. We have to . . . to expose Mr Witham. Serena, please, I *have* to tell someone. Honestly. I can't go on living like this.'

'But don't you get it?' Serena grabbed my shoulders, pinching me, like her anger and ridicule were laced with anxiety too. 'You just told me you've been freaking out thinking you were *cursed* or something. I've just explained to you – it was nothing like that.'

'I can't, Serena. I'm so tired. I know it won't get better until I hand myself in. And anyway, how long until they . . .' I swallow, my throat tight as a straw, sweeping my hand over the land around us. 'Until they find *him*.'

'I was willing to take my chances, Carrie. I still am.'

I stared at her. 'Then why did you reply to my email? Why did you ask to meet here?'

'Why do you think?'

Idiot. She was right. I was an idiot. 'You wanted to stop me. You wanted to find out what I was planning and persuade me to stop.'

Because I had always been so persuadable, hadn't I?

She gripped my shoulder again. 'What did you expect, Carrie? You want to go to the police, because of your guilt, your struggles. But we made a pact, Carrie. Remember? We *swore on the pain* that we'd never say anything.'

'I know, I know—' But that was then and I couldn't have imagined how hard that promise would be to keep. I shook my head. 'Listen, Serena, I'll tell them it was just me. I'll tell them I made you. I'll say all of you were just witnesses. Bystanders. Forced into it. I'll make it clear it was all my fault.'

Serena's face was blank.

'No – even better,' I stumbled on. 'I know. I'll say you weren't even there that night. I'll say I went up there and met Luke by myself. I'll say it was me – the whole thing was me. The drugs, the overdose, hiding the body, everything. I'll confess to everything without even mentioning your names.'

She turned to look at me, slowly. 'You still don't understand, Carrie, do you?'

'Understand *what*? Listen, please, just give me your permission. Let me do this. Please just let me out of the pact.' In those moments, I was terrified that breaking my promise without her blessing would only unleash some other hellish curse.

'You'll tell them it was only you there that night?'

'Yes! Yes, Serena – exactly!'

'But what about the next night, Carrie? The one when you *weren't* there?'

My mind flickered. 'What about it . . . ?' I didn't get what she was talking about. The night *after*? That night was simply . . . tidying up.

'You go to the police and tell them about Luke, and the first thing they'll do, Carrie, is dig up the body. I know it's been years, Carrie – almost two decades – but you think they won't still try to find out how he died?'

'The drugs,' I stuttered. 'An overdose. He'd been drinking too, Serena, don't you remember? I'll tell them all of that. I'll tell them the whole thing—'

I broke off as she pulled me to her, yanking me so close that her mouth was in my hair. I could smell her breath, catapulting me back to the day I first met her. She pressed her lips right up to my ear.

'Carrie,' she said, 'I'm going to tell you the truth.'

For what felt like hours, weeks, years, I sat there, frozen as her words poured into my ear. My eyes widened in horror until the muscles around them shrieked; my stomach was a hollow pit; my mind a lurid scream.

When she finished and pulled back, I was gasping for breath. She stared at me, her lip curled upwards.

'Now do you see?'

I did, I did, and I felt blinded by it. I stumbled to my feet, wrenching away from her, careening in blind panic without intention or goal, only horror and fear. I hurled myself down the bank to get away from her, away from *there*, a scene of horror so much worse than I'd ever realized. I slithered in the mud, tree roots tripping me, sharp rocks gashing me, plummeting my way to the bottom.

'Carrie!'

I heard Serena's yell, heard her crashing down behind me. Like a panicked animal I tried to move faster, desperate to outrun her, even as I heard the thud of her boots gaining ground. At the bottom, where they'd dug one of many muddy trenches, I glanced back, and there she was: my friend. My one hope.

There she was, in her bright green cagoule, coming down the hill after me, shouting, 'Carrie, please! Wait!'

She was flying down towards me, the way we used to helter-skelter down the hill at the end of each of those illicit nights, and in that instant, a wave of hope caught me up. Maybe, just maybe, she was willing to help me. Maybe together we could find a way forwards because surely there had to be a way to get through this, a way I could unburden myself without letting all the rest of the horror seep through, without breaking my pact.

'Carrie!'

But now her cry was more like an alarm – a warning.

I flinched. I stumbled . . .

My lungs emptied; I couldn't breathe. I threw up; it went black.

There, above me, floated the light.

Text from: Kate
Sent to: Mhairi
15.01pm, 14/06/2013

Mhairi, how did it go? Did you see him?

Text from: Kate
Sent to: Mhairi
16.04pm, 14/06/2013

Mhairi? How was Finn?

Text from: Mhairi
Sent to: Kate
16.07pm, 14/06/2013

I think I'm having

Text from: Kate
Sent to: Mhairi
16.08pm, 14/06/2013

What?

Text from: Kate
Sent to: Mhairi
16.10pm, 14/06/2013
I'm trying to ring you, Mhairi. Can you pick up?

Text from: Kate
Sent to: Mhairi
16.21pm, 14/06/2013

I called the psychiatric ward to see if you were still there. They said you never visited.
 Come on, Mhairi, what are you doing? What is this?

Text from: Mhairi
Sent to: Kate
17.02pm, 14/06/2013

I was on my way to see him. On the bus.
I didn't make it.
 They took me to Addenbrooke's and now they've transferred me to The Rosie.

Text from: Kate
Sent to: Mhairi
17.05pm, 14/06/2013

The Rosie? The maternity hospital? Why, what happened? Are you okay?

Text from: Mhairi
Sent to: Kate
17.21pm, 14/06/2013

I couldn't get to him. I had to go to hospital.

    I'm having a miscarriage.

    I had a miscarriage.

    Finn said he didn't want it. Now I've lost it. I've lost the baby, Kate.

CHAPTER 43

Victor

2019

A wail of sirens spilled into the dormitory from outside. Through the window, I could see the ambulance and police cars arriving.

A fucking leg, man! There's a fucking body in the trench!

They would be pulling him out any moment: what was left of him. What had happened – a mudslide, subsidence? My brain crackled with the image of Luke crawling there by himself, his dead body zombified, reanimated, crawling towards the outline of the school.

We needed to get out of here.

'It's good to see you, Serena,' Mae whispered to the figure in the corner, like she was talking to a tiger who was desperate to bite. Or trying to talk someone suicidal down off a ledge. 'We had no idea you were even in the country.'

'Well.' She grimaced. 'I got Carrie's email.' Her eyes swept us both. 'Didn't you?'

Mae took a step towards her. 'What are you doing *here* then? Where's Carrie?'

Serena turned her head to the side, away from us. 'She wanted to go to the police. I had to stop her . . .'

More shouting outside and the grind of diggers, weaving in with the whirling blue lights. I knew if I looked out of the window right now, I would see them lifting Luke's bones out of the ground. My stomach turned over and over on itself. I kept my eyes on Serena.

'They've found him,' I told her. 'Did you realize that? They've found Luke's body.'

Serena frowned. 'Luke . . . ?'

'Yes,' said Mae. '*Luke!*'

'At the bottom of the hill?' Serena dropped her face into her hands; I thought she was sobbing, but it sounded like laughter. 'Oh God,' she moaned. 'Oh God.'

Mae moved forward and crouched down beside her. 'Carrie was right,' she said. 'Wasn't she? She knew they'd find him when they started digging up the land. Now we need to get to her, and stop her from saying anything. There's still nothing linking us to him. Not if we get out of here. Not if we're smart.'

'Except for the video,' I said pointedly. Had she forgotten that inescapable piece of evidence? 'Alex's video.'

Serena groaned again, rubbing her muddy arms. 'That's *right*. I saw that.'

'It's gone viral,' I said. 'Someone's bound to recognize Luke eventually. Recognize us.'

'Yes.' Serena raised her head, her lipstick smeared. Through the open window I could see that the back of the ambulance was open. I had no idea what the paramedics thought they could do for Luke now.

'I *told* Alex to get rid of that footage,' Mae said. 'That night when we all swore, I told him to destroy it. You were there. We all heard him promise. Afterwards, he told me he'd done it, but guess what? Carrie's right – who else could have uploaded it? Alex promised us, and he lied.'

My breathing was high in my chest. Police were swarming the grounds now, stretching out police tape. That teenage pact we'd made was falling to pieces. We had to get away, try to salvage it. We really needed to get out of this place.

Serena shrugged. That grin. I honestly wanted to throttle her. 'I guess, unlike the rest of us, Alex couldn't live with the guilt.'

I stepped forwards and dragged Serena to her feet. She yelped, but I didn't care if I hurt her.

'We have to go,' I told her. 'We have to get the fuck out of here. They are *digging up Luke's body*.'

Serena's head lolled. She leaned all her weight on me like a Fainting Girl, and I struggled to keep her upright.

'Luke's body?' She almost giggled.

'Shut up, Serena,' Mae said. 'We need to get to Carrie and stop her saying anything. You can at least tell us where she is.'

Serena slid her eyes over to her. 'Don't you know that, earlier, I was thinking exactly the same thing? *We need to stop her talking.*' But instead of moving, Serena turned back to me. 'Mae . . . Victor . . .'

'*What?*' I wanted to slap her.

'Mae,' she slurred. 'You know we buried Luke at the top of the hill. Over the rise.' She waved a hand towards the scene outside the window. 'Now, what would *Luke's* body be doing at the bottom of the hill?'

327

The blood drained out of me. I almost dropped Serena on the torn-up dormitory floor. Instead I shook her so hard I almost heard the teeth rattle in her horrid skull.

'Serena. Where – is – Carrie?' Mae gasped, my mind shrieking with the terrible knowledge too.

CHAPTER 44

Carrie

2019

There was black all around me. Dead silence, except for the frenzied panting of my breath.

I fought myself to breathe slower, conserve oxygen, even as my mind shrieked with the horror of what had just happened, where I was. My body screamed in pain; I feared I'd broken a leg, maybe even my back.

I was hyperventilating, terrified.

The last moments of daylight replayed in front of me.

My heart leaping in a blaze of sudden hope when I heard her shouting, 'Carrie, please! Wait!'

Serena flying down towards me, the way we used to run down the hill at the end of our nights on the rise.

But when she shouted my name again, it sounded all wrong.

I flinched backwards, my foot slipping on the edge of the trench. I fell, plummeting, and the ground at the bottom smacked my head, my back. My lungs emptied. I couldn't breathe.

I was in a black hole, pale sky above me.

I couldn't move. I threw up.

'Serena,' I gasped. 'Serena!'

She appeared, silhouetted against the faint daylight, peering down at me. 'Oh, Carrie . . . !'

'My leg . . . my back. I think it's broken. Please call an ambulance. Oh my God, Serena, be quick.'

'Don't move,' she said. 'Wait there.'

Her figure disappeared, leaving me in a wave of terror. 'Serena! Don't leave me! Oh, please don't go!'

She reappeared at once, craning down over me. 'Shush, Carrie! I'm not going anywhere.'

'Call an ambulance,' I moaned. 'Please hurry.'

I closed my eyes, straining my ears to catch the sound of her phone, her voice. The pain made me throw up again, filling the space with a hideous acrid scent.

I clenched my jaw, kept my eyes closed. I felt something land on me. Cold, wet – was it raining?

I opened my eyes. My twisted body was spattered with dirt.

'Serena!' I croaked. 'The sides are crumbling!'

Her silhouette appeared again. I began to cry, I was so desperate, so frightened. 'The sides are crumbling! It's going to collapse!'

'Don't be silly, Carrie. 'Course it's not.'

But a moment later, more earth came raining down, faster, thicker, and I couldn't move. I could hardly speak. I was help-less.

The dirt, the earth, the mud kept tumbling down as Serena's silhouette weaved and flashed above me.

I closed my eyes, praying to a god I didn't believe in, unable to accept the horror of what was happening. Soil was covering my face, the light fading.

There was an air pocket above my nose and mouth, a space under my raised arms, but every breath I took lost me another lungful of oxygen. If I kicked or screamed, I might set off another landslide, crushing me. My limbs burned with pins and needles. I floated in and out of consciousness. There was scraping, shifting. The ground moved inwards, crushing tighter, crushing me, folding me into itself, down, down, down. I tried to scream but there was no air left; not a drop. Earth filled my ears, my nose, my gullet, my eyes.

My chest caved in.

My world stopped.

CHAPTER 45

Victor

2019

'It's Carrie!' I shouted, shoving Serena away from me. 'What did you do to her?'

Again with that awful rictus grin. 'I hid her. Wouldn't be the first time, would it, Mae?'

I stared at her, frozen. 'We have to get down there.' But I didn't move. Going down there meant handing ourselves in. Going out there meant it was absolutely over. I raked my hands through my hair, tearing at the roots, welcoming the pain.

'Oh fuck, Serena, what have you done!'

'I had to. I've told her everything, see. I thought it would persuade her not to go to the police if she knew the full story. Knowing she'd be incriminating us all. But Carrie was always so emotional and naïve. She went running off instead, like a lunatic. She fell and I – took the opportunity. At least she can't tell anyone now.'

'What do you mean, she fell?' cried Mae. 'What do you mean, you told her?'

'I told her about the second night, Mae. What we did.'

I gaped at them. 'What about the *second night*? What are you two on about?'

Mae spun round to glare at me. 'Oh, that's right. You weren't there either, Victor, were you? You kept yourself out of it. No blood on *your* hands.'

'Listen, Mae. I don't know what the fuck you're on about, but we need to get out of here *right now*. We need to get away from here, and away from Serena, who apparently has just *murdered our friend*.'

I couldn't believe it. Never, ever had I thought it'd come to this. What happened with Luke was an accident, that was all – a stupid accident. We weren't monsters. We weren't *psychopaths*. We were just dumb kids who made a stupid mistake.

'Come on!' I said to Mae. 'Leave Serena – we need to go. If we're seen with her, we're going to have fucking murder on our hands.'

But if the three of us kept our promise, kept our mouths shut, there was still a chance I could get out of this mess. If Serena refused to confess to anything – and surely she'd do anything to protect her career – then Carrie's death could go down as another accident, on a building site, in the dark. I tried not to think about the video online, about Finn and Mhairi, and everything they knew . . .

I reached out and grabbed Mae's hand, yanking her like a toddler across the room. 'Keep your head down,' I barked, even as I gawped out the window myself. There was a stretcher now too, wheeling a white shape into the ambulance.

Carrie.

Oh fuck. Oh fuck.

Outside, someone shouted.

Two words, clear as a crack of thunder.

Two words that turned my stomach to jelly.

CHAPTER 46

Victor

2019

'She's alive!'

The world tipped up on its end once again. What the fuck? What the actual fuck?

After everything, it really felt like the end of the road for us, all our pacts and promises completely unravelling.

No more hiding, no more chances to escape. Everything would come pouring out now. Carrie's confession, Alex's video – one testimony corroborating the other.

In that disorientating moment, I saw Serena silhouetted in the window, arms braced against the rotting frame, and my anger at her all drained away. I had no energy left to be angry with her. It was hopeless now. I barely had enough energy to notice what she was doing.

Everything was falling apart and I couldn't think of any way to save ourselves. The floodgates would open; the truth would pour out.

Coward that I was, the thought never even crossed my

mind. Even when Serena lifted a knee onto the windowsill, I didn't get it.

Even when she levered herself to stand up there, it didn't click.

The open window; two floors up.

When she launched herself, for a moment it was like she was flying. Arms spread, she was like a swallow, an eagle, glorious, triumphant, the way all of us should have been – favoured alumni of St Michael's.

She hung in the air for a moment, the rising sun behind her.

Then gravity took her, and she was gone.

CHAPTER 47

Mae

2019

The police arrested us for trespassing, initially. Despite the chaos with Carrie and Serena, they were onto us as soon as we emerged. I wanted to laugh, thinking of all those times we'd snuck out of St Michael's unscathed and undetected. This time, the police surrounding the school spotted us at once.

I had told Victor everything by then, laying it all out to him as we stumbled back down the dilapidated staircases, knowing that our arrest was inevitable. He'd swanned about all these years not even knowing the half of it. Living like an ostrich until Carrie's stupid email forced his hand. Why shouldn't he have to deal with things properly for once? Why shouldn't he carry the full weight of the truth?

He had to understand what was at stake now, in whatever decision he was going to make in this mess.

I told him all of it in the dark of the stairwell: no flame, no lighter this time, just my voice and his.

2003

He and Alex got hold of the spades – just two of them, but hefty and sharp enough, and by that afternoon, it had become clear there would only be three of us using them anyway.

By that afternoon, Carrie was even worse than when she'd woken up. She was completely falling apart.

She'd got herself in such a state that when I found her crying in the girls' toilets, for a moment I was tempted to fill her in on everything. I wanted to say: look, it was me who started it. I was the one who suggested those drugs; I was the one who asked Luke to join us. I wanted to admit it wasn't entirely her fault, even if she'd been the one to give him the overdose. I was the one who'd made her take things further and further. I was the one who had let her get mad at Luke, when actually he'd never laid a finger on me.

As Carrie pressed yet more soggy toilet paper to her nose, I almost spilled out the whole pathetic tale: *This isn't your fault, Carrie. It's mine. It's my fault for getting involved with him. It's my fault for letting him flatter me and make me think I was special. It's my fault for kissing him when we were alone that time after class. It's my fault for letting him put his fingers inside my bra. Inside of* me, *while I kept my eyes on that grubby ceiling and pretended to escape away through that skylight. It's my fault for saying that I liked it, when I didn't. It's my fault for believing him when he said it was* romantic, *and for protecting myself and protecting* him *when he started on the other girls – Bryony and Ava who were only fourteen and thirteen.*

Carrie was my friend, and I did feel bad for her. But the whole thing with Mr Witham was so ridiculous and shameful, I couldn't do it. Plus, I knew if I told her she'd completely lose her shit.

Instead, I told all her teachers that Carrie had a migraine, and Ms Kennedy told her to go sleep it off. At dinnertime, Victor said he'd stay with her that night to keep an eye on her. Like, to make sure she didn't go running to the head.

Sure, I thought. I bet that suits you, Victor.

Leaving us to do the hard work.

*

So that second night, it was just me and Alex and Serena.

It wasn't raining anymore, but it was bone-chillingly cold and the ground was sticky and thick with the rain from before. Kind of a good cold though – one that stopped me thinking. Like, about what we were heading up there to do.

'No one's going to see us, are they?' Alex kept asking.

'Not if we're quiet,' I kept telling him, 'and quick, and we keep our mouths shut.'

It seemed to take ages to reach the top of the rise, longer than any night before. Finally we were up and over the bank, and a moment later our torches picked out the pile of branches we had dragged together last night. It looked the way we had left it, thank God. I'd had visions of some fox or badger or something getting in there and dragging Luke's body out, tearing it apart, scattering him all over the hill.

'All right.' Serena hefted up one of the two spades and headed a little way down the back slope, to an even more inconspicuous spot. 'Let's start digging.'

The rain had helped soften the ground and the spades had good sharp edges. Serena wielded one spade (all that training had made her ridiculously strong), and Alex and I took turn about.

It was gruelling work; soon my shoulders were screaming, but I ignored it. Every so often scenes flashed through my brain from that film *Shallow Grave*. Gross, macabre, and now here we were doing practically the same thing.

Feel nothing. Think nothing.

Eventually, we had dug down about four feet. I looked at Serena. 'Will that be enough?'

She was standing in the hole, the earth we'd dug out scattered in piles all around. She eyed our work in the torchlight. 'Probably.' She stuck her spade into the mud again. 'Why don't you and Alex start lifting off the branches and I'll dig down a little bit more.'

'Sure,' said Alex. 'Fine.'

I followed him over to the pile of branches, trying not to think about Luke's body lying underneath. We had just taken hold of the first heavy branch and begun to lug it off when I froze. 'What's that?'

'What?'

'That noise!' I killed the torch and we both listened. I could hear Serena's spade still going: *shuck, shuck, shuck*. Then that noise stopped too, and I could hear it for sure now: a thrumming, coming from above. And light too – a spotlight. Instinctively, I hunkered down, crouching on the wet earth.

I dragged Alex down next to me, hoping Serena was hunkered down in the hole as well.

'A helicopter?' Alex hissed. 'What the fuck?'

'Are they looking for Luke?' I said. 'Do they know?'

'It's only been a day. He can't have been reported missing already.'

The thrumming went on, circling above us. I had never been so glad of the thick canopy of trees. It felt as if we squatted there for hours, but it could only have been a couple of minutes at most.

When the noise and light faded, I stood up, pins and needles buzzing in my legs.

'Come on,' I hissed at Alex. 'Hurry up. We need to do this.'

We dragged the rest of the prickly branches off as fast as we could. Serena had got out of the hole now too to help us.

Eventually, we'd uncovered him fully. He lay there, not a doll or a mannequin, but Luke with his skinny arms and that mole on his cheek. I could almost believe he was just unconscious or sleeping if I hadn't witnessed everything that had happened last night.

'We need to pick him up,' said Alex.

'A leg,' I said. 'I'll take a leg.'

Serena joined me and Alex lifted him under the arms. I thought maybe rigor mortis would have kicked in by then, but he still seemed floppy and soft. I remembered how we used to cradle him when he was alive: head and legs.

'Come on,' Alex growled. 'Come *on*.'

But before we'd managed more than ten stumbling steps, the helicopter was back again, drifting over us.

'Down,' growled Serena. We dropped Luke, and crouched

over him, pulling the darkness of our coats over our heads. It was like the way we'd crouched over him barely twenty-four hours earlier, when it had all been a game and Luke had been enjoying himself. Now we were crushed up next to his dead body. I pictured peeling off my skin, scrubbing all the places it had touched.

I counted all the way to a hundred and twenty before finally the helicopter left and we managed to make it another few yards, but then it came back again. The stupid thing wouldn't leave us alone. God knows what it was supposed to be doing – like Alex had said, surely the alarm couldn't have been raised about Luke already – but what if they had spotted something moving about in the trees and now they were hovering to get a closer look? If they spotted three kids dragging a body through the woods, you could bet your ass they'd be on us like a shot. But we couldn't just wait forever for it to leave. It could go on circling around here for hours, and we needed to get this done before anyone at school realized we were gone.

'Why did we dig the hole so far away?' I whispered fiercely as we crouched down over Luke's pale white corpse yet again.

'The ground was softer,' panted Alex. 'And that spot is better hidden.'

He was right, but Jesus, with that thing overhead getting there was such a risk.

At last, the helicopter's thrum faded and we heaved Luke's body up again. Finally we got him to the hole. *Don't think. Don't feel.* I couldn't hear the helicopter at all now. It seemed it had finally left us alone.

I looked away as we tipped Luke in, blocking my mind to

the thud he made when he landed. It was done. He was in there, just the last part to go now – the easiest bit.

Following Alex and Serena's lead, I heaved in a first then a second thick, wet spadeful of earth.

Then it happened.

At first, I thought it was Alex or Serena, messing around.

Then the sound came again – not from their direction.

I went still, icy still, and stared in disbelief. 'Did you hear that?' I whispered.

Silence.

I shone my torch down. Luke's body lay at the bottom of the hole, a broken tangle of limbs. Last night, he'd stopped breathing, didn't start again, even after we'd pounded on his chest for ages; we'd stuffed him under a pile of branches, leaves and logs; we'd left his body out in the rain and the cold all night, then pulled him out and tipped him into a five-foot-deep hole.

In the beam of my torch, the tangle of limbs twitched.

Unbelievable, but there was no denying it.

The moan came again: louder this time.

*

'We have to get him out of there,' I said. Every damn inch of my skin was crawling. 'We have to climb down and get him to a hospital.'

'What are you talking about?' said Alex. He was working a few feet back from the hole, shovelling at the earth that we'd scattered wide.

'Didn't you hear that? Didn't you *see*?' After everything we had done to him, Luke was *not dead*.

Alex shook his head. 'See what? What is it?'

Serena though – she was right on the edge of the grave, next to me.

'Serena? You heard him, right? You saw it?'

She let the shovelful of earth she was holding fall into the hole. 'I didn't hear anything,' she said.

'He *moaned*,' I said. 'He *moved*.'

Serena hefted up another mound of earth. 'Don't be ridiculous. He couldn't have.' She threw that cascade of earth over him too.

This was ludicrous. This could not be happening.

We should call an ambulance, get him to hospital. We should tell the doctors he needed immediate help, that he'd overdosed and we hadn't realized. That we'd stuffed him under branches and left him exposed for twenty-four hours, then come back and tried to bury him for good. We could tell them all that, and how he'd been hanging out with us for weeks, taking drugs with us while we snuck out from our school. We could tell them . . .

Nothing.

My mind pulled up short.

We could tell them nothing.

Serena was still lifting earth, dropping it. 'Maybe you imagined it,' she said. 'You know how our minds always play tricks up here.'

Yes, I thought. Maybe I imagined it. Maybe there had been nothing going on at all. You could do that, couldn't you, up here in the woods. You could wipe away everything you wanted rid of. You could turn it all into nothingness. A blank slate.

Wouldn't it be nice to black out like that whenever you wanted? Just go away and step out of everything.

'You're right,' I said, forcing myself to laugh. 'Just my mind playing tricks on me. Losing it, just like Carrie. What am I like? *Come on, Mae, get a grip!*'

I switched off the torch again. Alex stepped up to the hole, his shovel weighted. 'It's fine. I didn't hear anything either,' he said.

*

2019

Oh yeah, I buried it deep that night. Those five feet might as well have been five hundred. I buried what I'd heard and what I'd seen. Along with it, I buried everything that had happened with Mr Witham.

It felt good to bury it all in there that night.

Later, the pact we made in the dorm room was like sealing the gravesite. I buried the very thought of what we'd done. None of us would talk of this, ever again.

I really thought you could do that. Bury your secrets and the shit that happened to you, and I really thought it would stay buried and dead.

Of course, it doesn't work like that, does it? Memories are like zombies. They keep fucking coming back.

And after all, it was a pretty shallow grave.

CHAPTER 48

Finn

2019

Serena fell, the police swarmed everywhere and it was absolute chaos. In the aftermath of the ambulances and the medical teams' procedures, of course the police wanted to talk to us. They wanted to talk to everybody on the scene. Mhairi and I stood there in the strobing blue lights and told them everything. Everything we knew, at least.

We told them about Kate's death, and the links to Carrie, to St Michael's and to Luke.

We showed them the online video we'd stumbled on.

It was that footage, I think, that led them to Luke's body. Kate's suicide had led us all the way to that.

*

When we finally tracked Carrie down again, she was in a hospital bed with her leg in traction, breathing through an oxygen mask. Honestly, it was outrageous for us even to be there, but even after everything, Mhairi wasn't going to return home without trying to speak with her just once.

And to our amazement, Carrie agreed to have us as visitors; it was almost as if she wanted to talk.

We sat in that room that smelled of antiseptic and dead flowers, and in response to Mhairi's questions, Carrie told us about the teacher, Mr Witham, and what happened to her friend Mae and the younger girls at the school.

'It obviously never left her,' she mumbled. 'All Dr Fallon's life, she felt it was her fault. And when I pitched up in her clinic room, it must have felt like a reckoning . . .'

Then Carrie's lawyer came barrelling in, telling her to immediately stop talking. What the hell was she doing, completely jeopardizing her case?

He practically shoved us out of Carrie's hospital room, so abruptly that we bumped into the suited police officer approaching outside. He was tall and broad, and he entered Carrie's room and banged the door shut behind him. He was a detective, I realized, not just an officer. A detective investigating Luke Menzies's death. Perhaps he'd just been speaking to Serena down the hallway, Serena who'd survived her fall – or jump.

Through the glass, I saw the detective approach Carrie's bedside. She looked so tiny next to his domineering bulk. I stepped closer to watch as he pulled out a notebook. In the white bed, I saw Carrie cross her thin, pale arms.

There was a tap on my shoulder. 'Come on, now, time you two were leaving.' A ward sister was trying to hustle us away.

'Yes. Of course,' but I didn't move, not quite yet; I went on watching, for as long as I could.

The detective's head twitched as he asked his questions; Carrie's lawyer hovered anxiously at her side, eyes darting.

Even at this remove, it wasn't hard to read Carrie's lips as she answered. Two words, three syllables. I made out the words as Mhairi tugged me away.

No comment.

*

We drove the hire car back to Edinburgh and took the East Coast train back home the next morning. It was like travelling in a dream, returning from a nightmare, my mind scrambling to come to terms with everything that had happened since we'd pitched up at Valerie's, everything that had come crashing together at St Michael's, and everything our conversation with Carrie had revealed.

We finally had answers, but now we had to deal with the truths we'd unearthed. About Carrie. About the disappearance of Luke. About Kate.

And the narrative underneath all of that: about us.

Since that terrible argument on the train up here, Mhairi and I had barely communicated. Not properly, not about what had been said, about ourselves. There had been far, far too much else happening: coming face to face with Mae and Victor at Valerie's house, Carrie's flight away from there, the crazy drive to St Michael's, Carrie's awful accident, Serena's terrifying fall . . .

But we were travelling away from all that now, and it was just the two of us again, in an almost-empty carriage. No witnesses anymore. We had given our written statements to the police; it was up to them to follow things up.

We had an answer to what had happened to Kate.

The police would discover what had happened to Luke.

There was only one gaping wound left.

We'd passed York before either of us initiated anything. We might have made it all the way home without a word.

'Finn?' Mhairi's voice was tentative. I swung my eyes to look at her on the opposite side of the plastic table. My face felt haggard. All of me felt grey.

I forced my voice to work. 'Yes?'

'Never mind – I'm sorry. Nothing.'

I let out a sigh filled with weariness. 'Say it, Mhairi. Whatever it is, just say it. We're going home now, it's almost all over. Who knows how much we'll speak after this? You'll go back to your life and I'll go back to mine. We managed to say nothing to each other for years. So if you want to get something off your chest, now's the time.'

I rested my head in my palm against the window, watching the overcast scenery slide by. I was exhausted, wrung out; I just wanted to sleep.

A member of the train crew rattled past with the trolley.

'Refreshments?'

I shook my head and Mhairi mumbled, 'No thanks.'

I wasn't going to push her anymore, or fight for this. I had fought with Mhairi uselessly for such a long time.

I closed my eyes again.

Waited.

She only spoke up again after Newark. 'What I said before . . .' Four small words, but the start of something – maybe. 'I can't take it back.'

Or maybe not.

Painfully, I pushed myself upright and shrugged one shoulder. How did she expect me to reply to that?

'But . . .' She was twisting her fingers.

I rubbed my eye. 'Go on.'

'But I *do* want to move forwards. Properly this time.'

The flattened scenery went on tumbling past alongside us. 'Okay,' I said, eventually. 'So how do we do that?'

'What I said to you on the train at York – I had to. I had to let you know how much your words hurt me back then. How devastated I was that I . . . we . . . lost her. Baby Kate.'

'And you think I didn't—' Already I was rising to my own defence.

'Wait – listen. All of that anger, it sat inside me for years. I was blinded by it. I couldn't move on.'

'Well,' I said. 'You didn't exactly try.'

She was quiet. 'You're right. I didn't.'

I was glad she was admitting this; I'd needed to hear it. All the same, everything felt hollow in my chest.

'The anger wasn't everything, though, Finn, do you get that? It was just easiest. Easier than feeling bad for you, or forgiving you. A million times easier than accepting what we'd lost.'

'Easier just to start over with Tom.'

She hesitated. 'Yes.'

I steepled my hands over my nose, like an oxygen mask. 'It wasn't just baby Kate, Mhairi. It was our lives together. Our whole future. *Us.*'

'I know that, Finn. And you know the worst of it?' Our eyes caught for a moment before she looked away. There were tears in hers. 'The worst of it, is that as soon as I said those words to you, all crushed up in that stupid train vestibule, all of that

349

anger – it just went away.' The tears were leaking now. 'I'd held on to it for years, because I just wouldn't tell you. I wouldn't say aloud the bloody words: *I blame you for her death.*'

I didn't move or say anything. It would do no good to lash out and punish her for giving me her truth.

Because it *was* true. It fitted. Because the truth – *my* truth – was that in the immediate hours and days after hearing that Mhairi had lost the baby, I'd felt such a searing, overwhelming relief.

The pain stopped. The terror stopped, and after hours, days, weeks I could breathe again. I'd cried, sobbing in my sparse bedroom on the ward. One of the nurses came and put his arm round me, thinking I was crying with grief.

But it wasn't that – not then. It was nothing but uncontrollable relief.

I lifted my head now so that I could look at my ex-wife, the would-have-been mother of my child – and she could look at me if she wanted to.

'You're right, you know,' I said. 'What you said to me on the train up to Edinburgh: after the miscarriage . . . after we lost her, I *did* get better. I wasn't afraid anymore. I wasn't losing my mind because I couldn't protect her. It sounds awful, I know, but it's true and you're right. It was the sheer terror of what could happen to her that tipped me into that psychosis. After she was . . . gone . . .' My heart was agony in my chest. 'After she died, I didn't have to be terrified of that anymore.'

Those were the horrible, devastating facts of it: two weeks later, I was well enough to be discharged, and Mhairi didn't want me home, so I went to stay with Kate. She put me up in her house, cooked for me, looked after me. Said I could stay for as long as I wished. Meanwhile, Mhairi said she wanted to separate; she wanted a divorce.

'Finn, I . . .'

And in those days after discharge, the sickening reality crowded in.

'That relief?' I interrupted. 'It only lasted a few days. A week at most. You and I weren't speaking, even though Kate was doing her best. I'd lost you; I'd lost my child, my home, my whole future. Anyway . . .' I wiped my tired eyes. 'The point is, I know it sounds awful, but that's where my mind was, before I went into hospital. That's why I said what I said, when I was ill.'

'Thank you . . .' Mhairi said. 'Thank you for explaining.'

'Ditto,' I said. She'd always loved that film, *Ghost*.

She was silent after that. We both sat there, all our words seemingly run out. Well, I guessed at last we had reached our ground zero.

Was that it then? Full decks on the table, every stone turned over and the truth laid bare? No more hiding. I only wondered if there was any way back up.

We weren't too far from Peterborough now. Soon we'd be getting off and going our separate ways. I pulled myself together to smile at Mhairi, an attempted gesture of reassurance. *It's okay.* I stood up to pull my coat down from the rack, getting ready, off kilter with the carriage's movement, heavy with fatigue. I wondered if I'd make it back to work next week like I'd hoped to, whether I was possibly in a fit state for that. But mostly, all I could think about was reaching home and laying my head on a pillow, praying to sleep without the nightmares of the damned.

A staff member came down the aisle, plucking the used reservations from the seat backs. She smiled at me as she passed and murmured, 'Nearly there.'

I nodded back at her. 'Yes. Not long now.'

I recognized the warehouses just outside of Peterborough. The voice was so soft; I thought I'd imagined it.

I looked down. Mhairi was looking straight up at me.

She repeated her words. 'I know you never meant it, Finn. Kate always said that. *It's not his fault. He was ill.*' She shook her head. 'I've always known that; I was just never able to say it – not till now. Now that you've explained it, and let me be angry.'

I sat down again, in the seat right next to her this time.

'Now it's like the cork's out of the bottle,' she continued. 'Now I can say, it was my fault, too. I was sick when I was pregnant, and you were doing so much for me and I never thought to ask how you were. I always thought – after what you'd dealt with in your childhood – that you were stronger than me. More resilient. So I leaned on you and assumed you'd be fine.'

I let out a shaky sigh. 'How could you have known any different? I didn't tell you.'

'Maybe. But you know what, Finn?' She looked at me with eyes full of regret and sorrow. 'I should have learned, after everything that happened. Instead, I treated Kate in exactly the same way.'

I didn't say anything. I just slipped an arm round her, pulling her into my chest. We sat like that, letting the train sway us.

As the train drew into our station I murmured my last words to her.

'We've been on a long journey, Mhairi, and I'm glad of it. I'm glad we did this: went searching for answers about Kate.

I'm glad of what we've finally been able to say to each other. We can move on now, if you want that. I forgive you and I'm sorry for everything I did.'

*

I half expected my new-found peace to disappear once I returned home, to my own empty house, with the same dull furniture and crockery and quiet.

But it didn't.

It stayed with me. Finally, it felt as though something had truly shifted.

I pushed open the front door, stepping over the handful of letters on the mat, and dropped my overnight bag in the hall. I'd unpack and sort everything later. The house felt a little stale and musty, so in the kitchen I opened the window. I thought of Kate, remembering her, processing all we'd learned about what she had been through. The helper who hadn't let anyone help her. Not me, not Mhairi, not even Sebastian. Instead, she had tried to make things right by fixing other people, lightening their burdens and shouldering their loads. The wise one who underneath had carried such guilt.

I made myself a cup of tea and waited quietly while it brewed, then sat down with it on my familiar sofa in the lounge. From habit, I pulled out my phone and checked it. There were a couple of texts from Mhairi, saying she was back home with Tom and that Kitty and Imrie were happy to see her. I tapped out a quick reply:

Me too, love to all of them and speak soon x

To read her messages so casually would have been unthinkable two weeks ago, but it had become so straightforward to talk with Mhairi since then, the air between us finally free and clear.

The tea tasted good: strong and comforting. I had picked up fresh milk on my way home from the station. It was a mixed day outside, crisp but sunny with a buffeting wind. Little ideas fluttered at the edges of my mind: opportunities, possibilities. Unfamiliar thoughts about the future.

Once I'd finished my tea, I picked up my phone again and called a familiar number. It went to voicemail: she was probably out shopping or at tai chi or the beach.

I left a message for her.

'Hi, Mum, it's me. I'm back home now, and not going any-where else for a while. All is good here. Hope you're good, too. Chat soon.'

I hung up and drained the last of my tea.

Then, knees aching a little, I stood up. There was one more task I had to do before dinner. Something small and easy, but immensely symbolic.

I pulled on a pair of old trainers by the back door and let myself out.

The garage door screeched as I levered it open and for a moment I felt a stabbing echo of fear through my chest. But I flicked the light on, took a breath, and it passed. The strip light flickered for a moment, then steadied. Not that I needed it: there was plenty of daylight shining in from outside.

Tomorrow, I would give the space a good sweep and a tidy-up. Sort through the junk: choose what to keep, what to bin, what to sell.

For now, I set my hands on the stepladder, climbing up rung

by rung until I was just a few inches from the ceiling where a small spider scampered over my hand and away.

I reached out and tugged at the canvas strap I'd tied up there. It came undone surprisingly easily. Maybe even if Mhairi hadn't called me right then, and I'd tried to go through with it, it wouldn't have held me anyway. Clearly I hadn't tied it very tight.

Either way, I didn't need it there anymore.

I undid the knots, dismantling the noose.

DRAFT EMAIL [*created: 16.08pm 08/01/2011*]

From: katefallon@hotmail.com
To: mhairi_1981@gmail.com
Subject: Time Travel

Hey Mhairi,

You know you asked me the other day about my New Year's resolution and I mentioned time travel? I wanted to explain what I meant and I'm not even sure how to tell you because I've never talked to anyone about it – ever, but I did this placement at a school called St Michael's, when I was training. There was a group of girls aged thirteen and fourteen who were having these fainting fits. The school doctor thought it was anxiety so I was called in.

I just knew from the start that there was something wrong at this school. The whole place – the atmosphere. It reeked of old-fashioned sexism and misogyny. As an assistant psychologist I'd worked in an adult sexual assault clinic, and I thought two of the schoolgirls referred to me showed signs of abuse.

Withdrawal. Hypervigilance. Dissociation.

One of them had been bed wetting too.

There was an older girl as well, and I suspected others, but I was only there a few weeks.

My supervisor was off sick, I didn't have her to talk to. I tried to speak to the clinical manager of my team, but he said it was a serious allegation I was making, when none of the girls had directly disclosed. He implied that my previous work made me biased, and warned me how dangerous it was for well-meaning therapists to go digging for abuse.

He was our clinical lead and so much more experienced than I was, and I hadn't worked with boarding school teenagers before, so what did I know? So I pushed down my suspicions and did the anxiety management work the school had requested, like a good girl, and actually the girls all got better – except those two.

A month or so later, I heard about a teacher who had moved on from the school. No notice period, no real explanation, nothing. A sudden transfer. And that's when I realized: maybe I'd been right all along.

But I still didn't do anything. The referral had been closed, the girls discharged from our service, and I had moved on to a completely different training placement by then. What did I really know about that teacher's situation? What did I really know about what was going on at that school?

So, I never did anything, Mhairi, and even if I tried to speak up now, who would listen? I don't have any evidence except the memory of my feelings back then. My gut.

But I still lie awake at night, thinking about it.

About the girl who quit that school and the other one who ended up in a psychiatric hospital.

And I keep thinking, what if, Mhairi? What if?

From: mhairi_1981@gmail.com
To: katefallon@hotmail.com
Sent: 15.05pm, 17/05/2019
Subject: The end

Kate,
I know you'll never get this message but I had to write to you anyway. I need you to know that I understand everything now.

You'd lived for years with that guilt inside you. I remember once, I tried to ask you about it – but I didn't push it. A horrible failure on my part. But maybe even if I had, you would still never have opened up.

It was Carrie who broke the walls down, wasn't it? Accidentally – she wasn't to know. You thought she was blaming you, with all her stories about the Fainting Girls. You thought she'd been abused by that same teacher too.

You blamed yourself, Kate. That was your error. You cared so much and thought that somehow, against everything you were up against, somehow you should have been able to fix the whole world.

You were such a good therapist, Kate. Such a good friend. I'll never forget what you did for me and Finn, and how hard you fought for us and our marriage. In the end, you couldn't put us back together either, but that was because of me and *my* failings, Kate – not you.

People do terrible things, Kate, and you tried to help fix them. But when you can't, it doesn't make it your fault.

Anyway, maybe you're looking down on all of this from heaven (or wherever blameless souls go after death), in which case, you'll know all of this already.

But I just wanted to write and tell you myself. I'm not angry anymore, Kate. Just sad and so sorry: I know now what happened, and why you did what you did.

Rest in peace, Kate.

Love, Mhairi

xxx

CHAPTER 49

Mae

2019

Currently, there's only a trespassing charge against me. For now, I've been released on bail, pending further investigation – further investigation that's already well underway. With Carrie's near-miss and Serena's death dive, the police wanted to speak to everyone on the scene. Including those two weirdos, Finn and Mhairi, and you betcha they told the police about that online video of us and Luke.

Within twenty-four hours, they'd found and dug up Luke's body. Finally, his disappearance was solved.

But despite what Serena had feared, after sixteen years there was only a skeleton. No way of reliably determining the cause of death. So all the police will have to go on are our testimonies of what happened that night. I know detectives have already been speaking to Carrie in hospital.

So what is my testimony going to be?

*

These last few days, I've spent hours reading up on trauma and its symptoms. My kind of trauma, especially. It's weird how accurate the descriptions are. The articles I read describe it all: my self-loathing, my 'promiscuousness', my self-destructiveness – it all fits. I can see now that I've spent my whole adult life reliving it. Over and over, through every guy I slept with that was decades older than me, or married, or wanted me to 'meet his friends', and who every time would screw me up more.

Serena, I know, will fight tooth and nail to deny everything – even what she did to poor Carrie. *An accident!* she'll say. *Carrie slipped, the sides must have crumbled!* That's Serena: self-protective to her core. (And yes, of course Serena survived her leap.)

With Carrie, though, I fear it's so much more complicated. Because on the one hand, Carrie told us she couldn't go on without confessing everything to the authorities. She said that to me, to Victor and to Serena.

On the other hand, what would telling the whole truth really mean for her? It would mean betraying all of us: her best, most loyal friends.

I fidget about in this crappy, cramped hotel room (I'm still in Perthshire, not allowed to leave the UK), waiting to see which devil wins out for my friend. I go back and forth and back and forth in my mind about what's most likely: whether Carrie will come through for us and leave us out of it, like she offered Serena. Whether she'll tell a lie to protect her faithful friends – after we kept *her* secret all these years. Whether she'll find a way to unburden herself while still sticking to those perfect teenage promises we made.

Or not.

I sit here, waiting to see what my old friend will do. And all the while, after everything I've gone through these last couple of weeks, a new desire is sparking up in me, like a glowing candle flame, burning brighter all the time. I'm finally starting to see things clearly. Finally, I'm starting to understand myself.

Now that I've read up on it – now that I have a framework, the right words, some insight – I can see that for so long I've been living my life on the run, trying to outpace those memories, that shame. I've been clawing my way from one day, one city, one man to the next, telling myself I was enjoying it, loving it, that I was in control of everything I chose.

Well, that was bollocks.

Now I know that all I was doing was surviving (barely). Margaret (Mae) Forsythe: gorgeous, alluring and seriously fucked up.

Well, I don't want that anymore, I've decided. I've wasted sixteen years in glitzy self-sabotage and I'm sickened now at the thought of falling back in. I want something different for myself going forwards: the chance to make something better of my life. I want to get some half-decent therapy and sort myself out. I want to turn over a new leaf – uproot the whole fucking tree.

I want to get on with the life I should have had, if Mr Witham hadn't done what he did to me.

That's what I want. And I think Carrie owes me that.

After all, I buried Luke for her.

But it's in her hands now: my fate, and what she does with me. Little Carrie, the new girl at St Michael's. It's up to her now.

Who'd have thought.

CHAPTER 50

Carrie

2019

No comment, is all I say to them. *No comment.* Each time the detective – or his friendly female colleague – come to see me, I make sure I have my lawyer there, and I repeat:

No. Comment.

*

I spoke pretty freely to Finn and Mhairi, though – those friends of my therapist. I'd calculated it was safe to share some stuff with them at least. For all kinds of reasons, I felt like I owed them. If they hadn't come looking for me, caring so much for their friend Dr Fallon, where would this have ended? Would I ever have found out the whole truth? And when I saw Mhairi that second time, perched so awkwardly on my hospital bed, I saw how much she was burdened by guilt.

I knew what that felt like. I'd blamed myself for decades. Kate had too.

At least I could help Mhairi stop blaming herself.

*

Now they've gone, and lying here in hospital, I've had lots of time to think. I've been thinking quite calmly (I think the morphine helps).

In between police visits, I count the ceiling tiles and weigh up my options.

It was a terrible thing they did that second night: Serena, Mae and Alex. But they wouldn't have been in that position if it hadn't been for me.

I was the one who gave Luke three tablets, on top of however much vodka he'd drunk. My actions led to his overdose; my friends were only trying to clean up my mess.

In fact, it goes back way further than that, if you really think about it. If you weave all the little threads together, like in a friendship bracelet, you see the patterns that come from all those one-by-one knots.

Luke got to know us because of the drugs we bought. We bought those drugs because of what was going on at the school. The chaos with the Fainting Girls. With Bryony and Ava. Lying in hospital, I've been doing my own research and I've learned about flashbacks, dissociation, and *vasovagal syncope* – fainting caused by acute emotional distress. Even without Dr Kate Fallon, I can join up the dots. Bryony and Ava hadn't been mucking around or faking. They were victims of abuse – just like Mae.

And who was ultimately to blame for all *that*?

He's the knot in the thread that started this. And *he* got off scot-free.

He did die young, I guess – at only forty-one – but his obituary from three years ago said he'd been survived by a wife and two daughters, and was *remembered fondly* by hundreds of pupils and staff.

How is that fair? What's right, then, anyway? How are you supposed to define justice and who's to blame after that?

We never meant any to harm Luke. We didn't. We were stupid, damaged teenagers, playing games to try to cope.

We weren't the first movers: that was Mr Witham.

We were the victims. Not evil. Just reckless, at most.

I guess what I'm saying is, I forgive them. All of them – even Serena and what she did. I get why she tried to trap me in that trench. She couldn't have me running to the police; she was terrified I was going to completely ruin her career – her whole life.

So, after all my thinking, I've decided what to tell them – that bullying detective, and his pretty, friendly teammate.

I lie on my back in the hospital bed and feel tears dribble from my eyes onto the pillow, my breaths through the oxygen mask coming in gulps.

It began as a throwaway remark to Serena, when I was panicking up there on the ridge, and throwing out all kinds of ideas. But now I realize it's exactly the right plan.

I'm going to say that it was only me there that night. I'm going to say it was a secret meeting: just the two of us. I'll say Luke overdosed and, all by myself, I buried him.

I'm going to say my friends had nothing to do with it. They didn't even *know* about it, I'll say.

The tears tickle in my hair. I'm remembering those first few days at St Michael's, when Mae and Serena took me under their wing. I'm remembering the first night they let me come with them up the high bank, shared a joint with me, and took me with them every night after that.

In the starched hospital bed, I run my fingers round the macramé friendship bracelet on my wrist – the one I still wear after all these years. They didn't make it for me, Mae and Serena, but it reminds me of them – it always did.

The tears come faster as I remember the night after Luke died, when Mae made us each hold our hands to the flame.

What's that, if not loyalty? What's that if not friendship – the only thing I ever wanted? They did that for me, all of them. And they kept their promises. Even Alex – mostly – by giving me a whole sixteen years to come clean.

Swear on the pain you'll never say anything.

I close my eyes and press my thumb into the scar on my palm that still shows there.

I know what I'm going to do; I'm decided.

I made them a promise, and I'll keep it. I'll keep it tomorrow when I hand myself in, and I'll keep it all the way to my grave.

A wave of relief sweeps through me as I make the decision. Maybe it's nothing but another timed dose of morphine, but I really do think I feel that blackened curse lift.

EPILOGUE

Victor

2019

I laid out the whole truth to my lawyer, and it wasn't really breaking that old pact, since attorney-client privilege is a thing.

To begin with, I planned to say I wasn't there the night Luke died. Technically true – and also it would fit with what I knew Carrie was going to claim. I'd managed to talk to her two days after her 'accident' – even though she wasn't meant to talk to anyone – and she had promised that was absolutely what she'd say. She was going give a statement that she met Luke alone that night, gave him the drugs alone, buried him by herself. She was going to keep our names completely out of it. She was going to keep her promise that way.

And I thought: *fucking great*.

Okay. So I'd thought attorneys just had to do what you wanted, but as it turned out, it doesn't quite work like that.

My attorney had advice of his own.

On the basis of everything I'd told him, he counselled me not to rely on anyone else's testimony. Sure Carrie was my friend, he said, and sure you trust her. But she's going to be up in a court of law, liable for perjury if she doesn't tell the truth.

Far better for you, my lawyer maintained, to unequivocally stick to the facts.

After all, he went on to explain to me, all you did was hide Luke under some branches and – because of a legal oddity – you might not be charged with anything for that. Luke had been alive when we hid him, so they couldn't charge me with *concealing a body* – he wasn't dead.

He really is good, my lawyer. And his argument makes sense: tell the truth, don't rely on Carrie; look, there's a chance you could get off scot-free. With the full weight of the justice system bearing down on her, he repeats, do you really trust her not to incriminate you? If not now, he ruminates, then in another sixteen years – or six months.

Far better to tell the truth now – the whole truth and nothing but the truth, up front. You'll get a suspended sentence, he tells me, at most. Tell the truth and be done with it, he counsels me. Free yourself up to get on with your life.

*

I've only got the weekend to think about it; I've been summoned for a formal police interview first thing next week.

For now, I'm at my parents' place in Edinburgh. Both of them have flown up here to be with me, and whenever we speak, my father insists I take my lawyer's advice (he's paying for it, after all). And he insisted on knowing everything too, because how can he help me if he doesn't know what's what?

All of Sunday, I lie in the bed I slept in during school holidays, staring up at the Kaiser Chiefs poster on the wall, going round and round in my head with the decision. Should I trust Carrie to keep her promise to protect us – keep myself completely out of it and let her take the full fall? Or should I get in there and protect myself, before she inevitably throws us all to the wolves?

I wish I could speak to Carrie again to check with her, but unsurprisingly she's no longer answering my calls. I wish I could get her and Mae and Serena in a room again, with a Bunsen burner, a blowtorch, to make another pact.

But that's impossible; I know it. We're each on our own now. As my lawyer likes to say: *sauve qui peut*. But saving myself means betraying my friends, and maybe I'm tired of being the kind of guy who does that.

On the other hand . . .

The hours tick by and honestly it's just so hard to come to a decision. So instead, I take a bump of the coke I've managed to procure, and curl on my side in the familiar bed, close my eyes and imagine the five of us: me, Alex, Carrie, Mae and Serena. I like to picture us in America somewhere, a little fantasy to escape into – Louisiana maybe, or Tennessee. Out on Highway 61. We've got a car, a vintage XJS Jag convertible; we've got the soft-top down. Alex is driving and I'm beside him, hair slicked back, sunglasses on – like in that song. The girls – Serena, Carrie and Mae – are a tangle of smiles and fly-away hair in the back. It's hot and the breeze is rushing over our faces. We're totally free, five special graduates of St Michael's.

Yeah. That's what I like to think about. *That's* what I picture. The five of us full of dreams and potential. It's a nice image. A happy one; I like it.

It makes it easier to accept what I reckon I'm inevitably going to choose.

ACKNOWLEDGEMENTS

Publishing my fourth novel has been a surreal experience. The chances of publishing even one book are tiny; the likelihood of publishing more than three is vanishingly small. And yet, somehow – here I am! It's terrifying, exhilarating and disorientating all at once.

I couldn't have done it without the help and support of some amazing people. First, my incredible editor, Cicely Aspinall. My books owe such a lot to her astute and brilliant input (as you'll see if you read my #AmEditing threads on Twitter). She helps me realise exactly the book I'm trying to write, the best and sharpest version of my story.

Thanks to editorial assistant Seema Mitra, copy editor Helena Newton, marketing assistant Hanako Peace, press officer Natasha Gill, cover designer Anna Sikorska, and the whole amazing team at HQ/HarperCollins. They have all worked so hard turning my manuscript for *A Guilty Secret* into a real live book, and I am immensely grateful.

Huge thanks to my steadfast agent Sarah Hornsley, who always believes in me and my writing, and pushes me to achieve my very best. Five years in, and she remains the best cheerleader I could have.

I am also hugely grateful to PFD's Kate Evans for being such a helpful and steady cover agent.

Thank you to Victoria Dowd for guidance on some legal points (all the errors are mine). I'm also really grateful to Philip Abraham for acting as such a helpful authenticity reader.

Thank you to the best collection of people in the word: booksellers, book bloggers, book reviewers and festival organisers. I totally owe you for all you have done for me and my books over the years.

Big, big thank yous to each and every reader (yes, you!) who has spent time with my stories: library-borrowed, charity shop-nabbed, snuck from your mate or bought full-price – I don't care. Thank you, thank you, thank you for reading my words.

Thank you to my family and friends who encourage my writing, buy my books and lend them to their friends. Thank you to my fellow authors, both in person and online, who loyally commiserate and celebrate with me through all of publishing's ups and downs. Thanks especially to my dear friends in CoT. Lastly but never leastly, thank you to my spouse Ellie for always, always believing in me and for yelling 'good luck!' every time I head to my writing room. Hang in there, Ellie: one day I'll get those millions for us.

Discover more gripping psychological suspense from Philippa East...

She only looked away for a second...

Anne White only looked away for a second, but that's all it took to lose sight of her young daughter.

But seven years later, Abigail is found.

And as Anne struggles to connect with her teenage daughter, she begins to question how much Abigail remembers about the day she disappeared...

Out now in paperback, ebook and audio.

Home can be the most dangerous place...

In a small London bedsit, a radio is playing. A small dining table is set for three, and curled up on the sofa is a body...

Jenn is the one who discovers the woman, along with the bailiffs. All indications suggest that the tenant – Sarah Jones – was pretty, charismatic and full of life.

So how is it possible that her body has lain undiscovered for ten whole months?

Out now in paperback, ebook and audio.

ONE PLACE. MANY STORIES

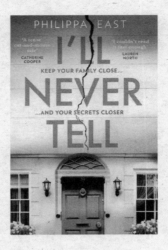

Keep your family close, and your secrets closer...

To the outside world, the Goodlights are perfect.

Julia is a lawyer, Paul a stay-at-home dad who has dedicated his life to helping their daughter Chrissie achieve her dreams as a talented violinist.

But on the night of a prestigious music competition, which has the power to change everything for Chrissie and her family, Chrissie goes missing.

She puts on the performance of a lifetime, then completely disappears. Suddenly every single crack, every single secret that the family is hiding risks being exposed.

Because the Goodlights aren't perfect. Not even close.

Out now in paperback, ebook and audio.

ONE PLACE. MANY STORIES

ONE PLACE. MANY STORIES

Bold, innovative and
empowering publishing.

FOLLOW US ON:

@HQStories